TRAITOR'S BLADE

TRAITOR'S BLADE

SEBASTIEN DE CASTELL

Jo Fletcher

New York • London

Jo Fletcher Books
An imprint of Quercus
New York • London

First published in the United States by Quercus in 2014

ISBN 978-1-62365-400-9

Library of Congress Control Number: 2014931813

Distributed in the United States and Canada by
Hachette Book Group
1290 Avenue of the Americas
New York, NY 10104

Manufactured in the United States

10 9 8 7 6 5 4

www.quercus.com

To my mother, MJ, who once took
me aside as a young boy and said,

"Well, we need to make money and the
easiest way to do that is to write novels."

She never bothered to tell me that
she'd never sold a book in her life.

Avares
DUCHY OF ORISON
DUCHY OF PUTNAM
The Eastern Desert
DUCHY OF HERVOR
PIHAN
THE ARCH
MONASTERY OF GAZIA
Tristia
DUCHY OF DOMARIS
"THE SPEAR"
DUCHY OF RIJOU
"THE BOW"
RIJOU
DUCHY OF PERTINE
ARAMOR "HOME OF KINGS"
SOLAT
DUCHY OF LUTH
CASTLE ARAMOR
DUCHY OF BAERN
CHEVOR

CONTENTS

1
LORD TREMONDI

Pretend, just for a moment, that you have attained your most deep-seated desire. Not the simple, sensible one you tell your friends about, but the dream that's so close to your heart that even as a child you hesitated to speak it out loud. Imagine, for example, that you had always yearned to be a Greatcoat, one of the legendary sword-wielding magistrates who traveled from the lowliest village to the biggest city, ensuring that any man or woman, high or low, had recourse to the King's Laws. A protector to many—maybe even a hero to some. You feel the thick leather coat of office around your shoulders, the deceptively light weight of its internal bone plates that shield you like armor and the dozens of hidden pockets holding your tools and tricks and esoteric pills and potions. You grip the sword at your side, knowing that as a Greatcoat you've been taught to fight when needed, given the training to take on any man in single combat.

Now imagine you have attained this dream—in spite of all the improbabilities laid upon the world by the ill-intentioned actions of Gods and Saints alike. So you have become a Greatcoat—in fact, dream bigger: pretend that you've been made First Cantor of the

Greatcoats, with your two best friends at your side. Now try to envision where you are, what you're seeing, what you're hearing, what wrong you are fighting to right—

"They're fucking again," Brasti said.

I forced my eyes open and took in a bleary view of the inn's hallway, an overly ornate—if dirty—corridor that reminded you that the world was probably a nice place once but had now gone to rot. Kest, Brasti, and I were guarding the hallway from the comfort of decaying chairs taken from the common room downstairs. Opposite us was a large oak door that led to Lord Tremondi's rented room.

"Let it go, Brasti," I said.

He gave me what was intended to be a withering look, though it wasn't very effective: Brasti's a little too handsome for anyone's good, including his own. Strong cheekbones and a wide mouth clothed in a reddish-blond short beard amplify a smile that gets him out of most of the fights he talks his way into. His mastery of the bow gets him through the rest. But when he tries to stare you down, it just looks like he's pouting.

"Let what go, pray tell?" he said. "The fact that you promised me the life of a hero when you tricked me into joining the Greatcoats and instead I find myself impoverished, reviled, and forced to take lowly bodyguard work for traveling merchants? Or is it the fact that we're sitting here listening to our gracious benefactor—and I use the term loosely since he has yet to pay us a measly black copper—but that aside, that we're listening to him screw some woman for—what? The fifth time since supper? How does that fat slob even keep up? I mean—"

"Could be herbs," Kest interrupted, stretching his muscles out again with the casual grace of a dancer.

"Herbs?"

Kest nodded.

"And what would the so-called 'greatest swordsman in the world' know about *herbs*?"

"An apothecary sold me a concoction a few years ago, supposed to keep your sword arm strong even when you're half-dead.

I used it fighting off half a dozen assassins who were trying to kill a witness."

"And did it work?" I asked.

Kest shrugged. "Couldn't really tell. There were only six of them, after all, so it wasn't much of a test. I did have a substantial erection the whole time though."

A pronounced grunt followed by moaning came from behind the door.

"Saints! Can they not just stop and go to sleep?"

As if in response, the groaning grew louder.

"You know what I find odd?" Brasti went on.

"Are you going to stop talking at any point in the near future?" I asked.

Brasti ignored me. "I find it odd that the sound of a nobleman rutting is hardly distinguishable from one being tortured."

"Spent a lot of time torturing noblemen, have you?"

"You know what I mean. It's all moans and grunts and little squeals, isn't it? It's indecent."

Kest raised an eyebrow. "And what does decent rutting sound like?"

Brasti looked up wistfully. "More cries of pleasure from the woman, that's for sure. And more talking. More, 'Oh my, Brasti, that's it, just there! Thou art so stout of heart and of body!'" He rolled his eyes in disgust. "This one sounds like she's knitting a sweater or cutting meat for dinner."

"'Stout of heart and body'? Do women really say that kind of thing in bed?" Kest asked.

"Try taking a break from practicing alone with your sword all day and bed a woman and you'll find out. Come on, Falcio, back me up here."

"It's possible, but it's been so damned long I'm not sure I can remember."

"Yes, of course, Saint Falcio, but surely with your wife—?"

"Leave it," I said.

"I'm not—I mean—"

"Don't make me hit you, Brasti," Kest said quietly.

We sat there in silence for a minute or two as Kest glared at Brasti on my behalf and the noises from the bedroom continued unabated.

"I still can't believe he can keep going like that," Brasti started up again. "I ask you again, Falcio, what are we doing here? Tremondi hasn't even paid us yet."

I held up my hand and wiggled my fingers. "Did you see his rings?"

"Sure," Brasti said, "very big and gaudy. With a stone shaped like a wheel on top."

"That's a Lord Caravaner's ring—which you'd know if you'd paid attention to the world around you. It's what they use to seal their votes when they have their annual concord—one ring, one vote. Not every Lord Caravaner shows up for the concord each year, so they have the option of lending their ring to another to act as their proxy in all the major votes. Now, Brasti, how many Lords Caravaner are there in total?"

"Nobody knows for sure, it's—"

"Twelve," Kest said.

"And how many of his fingers had one of those gaudy rings on them?"

Brasti stared at his own fingers. "I don't know—four . . . five?"

"Seven," Kest said.

"Seven," I repeated.

"So that means he could . . . Falcio, what is it exactly that the Concord of Lords Caravaner is going to vote on this year?"

"Lots of things," I said casually. "Rates of exchange, dues, trade policies. Oh, and security."

"Security?"

"Since the Dukes killed the King, the roads have fallen into disrepair. The Dukes won't spend money or men, not even to defend the trade routes, and the Lords Caravaner are losing a fortune on private security for every single trip they take."

"And we care about this why?"

I smiled. "Because Tremondi's going to propose that the Greatcoats become the Wardens of the Road, giving us authority, respect, and a decent life in exchange for keeping their precious cargoes out of the hands of the bandits."

Brasti looked wary. "They'd let us reassemble the Greatcoats again? So instead of spending my life being branded a traitor and hounded from every overcrowded city or Gods-forsaken village the length and breadth of the country, I'd get to run around the trade routes beating up bandits—*and* I'd actually get paid for it?"

I grinned. "And from there, we have a much better chance of fulfilling the King's—"

Brasti waved a hand. "Please, Falcio. He's been dead for five years. If you haven't found these damned 'King's Charoites' by now—and *still* no one knows what they are, by the way—"

"A charoite is a gemstone," Kest said calmly.

"Whatever. My point is: finding these gemstones with no clue whatsoever as to where they might be is about as likely as Kest here killing the Saint of Swords."

"But I *will* kill the Saint of Swords, Brasti," Kest said.

Brasti sighed. "You're hopeless, both of you. Anyway, even if we do find the Charoites, what exactly are we supposed to do with them?"

"I don't know," I answered, "but since the alternative is that the Dukes hunt down the Greatcoats one by one until we're all dead, I'd say Tremondi's offer works for me."

"Well then," Brasti said, lifting an imaginary glass in the air, "good on you, Lord Tremondi. Keep up the good work in there!"

More moaning came from the room as if in response to his toast.

"You know, I think Brasti may be right," Kest said, standing up and reaching for one of the swords at his side.

"What do you mean?" I asked.

"At first it sounded like lovemaking, but I am beginning to think I really can't tell the difference between these noises and those of a man being tortured."

I rose carefully, but my battered chair creaked loudly as I leaned toward the door, trying to listen. "They've stopped now, I think," I murmured.

Kest's sword let out only the barest whisper as he pulled it from its scabbard.

Brasti put his ear to the door and shook his head. "No, he's stopped, but she's still going. He must be asleep. But why would she keep going if—?"

"Brasti, move away from the door," I said, and threw my shoulder into it. The first try failed, but at the second, the lock gave way. At first I couldn't see anything amiss in the gaudily appointed room, decorated in what the proprietor fondly believed to be the style of a Duke's bedroom. Clothes and discarded books were strewn across what had once been expensive rugs but now were moth-eaten and likely homes for vermin. The bed had dusty velvet curtains hanging from an oaken frame.

I had just begun to move slowly into the room when a woman stepped out from behind those curtains. Her bare skin was smeared with blood and, though I couldn't see her features through the diaphanous black mask that covered her face, I knew she was smiling. In her right hand she held a pair of large scissors—the kind butchers use to cut meat. She extended her left hand toward me, fist closed tight, palm to the ceiling. Then she brought it close to her mouth and it looked as if she might blow us a kiss. Instead, she exhaled, and blue powder billowed into the air.

"Don't breathe in," I shouted to Kest and Brasti—but it was too late; whatever magic was in the powder didn't require us to inhale to do its work. The world suddenly slowed to a halt and I felt as if I were trapped between the stuttering ticks of an old clock. I knew Brasti was behind me, but I couldn't turn my head to see him. Kest was just in my sight, in the corner of my right eye, but I could barely make him out as he struggled like a demon to break free.

The woman tilted her head as she looked at me for a moment. "Lovely," she said softly, and walked casually, even languidly toward us, the scissors in her hand making a rhythmic *snip-snip* sound.

I felt her hand on the side of my face; then she ran her fingers down the length of my greatcoat, pushing at the leather until she could sneak her hand inside. She placed her palm on my chest for a moment, caressing it softly before sliding it down my stomach and below my belt.

Snip-snip.

She stretched up on her toes and leaned her masked face close to my ear, pushing her naked body against mine as if we were about to embrace. *Snip-snip* went the scissors. "The dust is called aeltheca," she whispered. "It's very, very expensive. I needed only a pinch of it for the Lord Caravaner, but now you've made me use my entire supply." Her voice was neither angry nor sad, just as if she were merely making a dispassionate observation.

Snip-snip.

"I'd cut your throats out, my tatter-cloaks, but I've some use for you now, and the aeltheca will keep you from remembering anything about me."

She stepped back and twirled theatrically.

"Oh, you'll remember a naked woman in a mask—but my height, my voice, the curves of my body, these will all slip away from you."

She leaned forward, placed the scissors in my left hand, and closed my fingers around them. I struggled to let them go, but my fingers wouldn't move. I tried as hard as I could to memorize the shape of her body, her height, the features of her face through the mask, anything that would help me know her if I saw her again, but the images faded even as I watched her. I tried turning the words to describe her into rhymes that I might remember, but those too left me instantly. I could stare right at her, but each time I blinked my eyes, the memory was gone. The aeltheca was certainly effective.

I hate magic.

The woman went back to the curtained bed briefly, then returned with a small pool of blood held carefully in the palm of her hand. She went to the wall opposite us, dipped her finger in the blood, and wrote a single word upon the wall. The dripping word was "Greatcoats."

She came back to me once more and I felt a kiss on my cheek through the gauzy fabric of her mask.

"It's almost sad," she said lightly, "to see the King's own Greatcoats, his legendary traveling magistrates, brought so low; to watch you bowing and scraping to a fat Lord Caravaner barely one step up from a common street merchant . . . Tell me, tatter-cloak, when you sleep, do you imagine yourself still riding across the land, sword in hand and a song on your lips as you bring justice to the poor, wretched people trapped under the heels of capricious Dukes?"

I tried to reply, but despite the effort, I could manage barely a tremor to my lower lip.

The woman brought her finger up and smeared blood on the cheek she had kissed a moment ago. "Good-bye, my lovely tatter-cloak. In a few minutes, I'll just be a hazy memory. But don't worry, I'll remember *you* very well indeed."

She turned and walked casually to the wardrobe and picked up her clothes. Then she opened the window and, without even dressing, slipped out into the early morning air.

We stood there like tree stumps for a minute or so more before Brasti, who had been farthest away from the powder, was able to move his mouth enough to say, "Shit."

Kest came out of it next, and I was last. As soon as I could move, I raced to the window, but of course the woman was long gone.

I went to the bed to examine the blood-soaked body of Lord Tremondi. She had gone after him like a surgeon and had managed to keep him alive for a long time, somehow—perhaps another property of the aeltheca. The passage of her scissors had forever imprinted a map of atrocity across the surface of his body.

This wasn't just a murder; it was a message.

"Falcio, look," Kest said, pointing at Tremondi's hands. Three fingers remained on his right hand; the rest were bloody stumps. The Caravaner rings were gone, and with them, our hopes for the future.

I heard the sounds of men coming up the stairs, the steady *thump-thump* of their footsteps marking them as city guards.

"Brasti, bar the door."

"It's not going to hold for long, Falcio. You kind of broke it when we came in."

"Just do it."

Brasti pushed the door back into place and Kest helped him shove the dresser in front of it before turning to help as I searched for anything that would link to the woman who'd killed Tremondi.

"Do you think we'll find her?" Kest asked me as we looked down at Tremondi's butchered remains.

"Not a chance in any of the hells we're headed for," I replied.

Kest put a hand on my shoulder. "Through the window?"

I sighed. "The window."

Fists were banging on the door. "Good night, Lord Tremondi," I said. "You weren't an especially good employer. You lied a lot, and never paid us when you promised. But I guess that's all right, since we turned out to be pretty useless bodyguards."

Kest was already climbing out as the constables were beginning to force the door of our room.

"Hang on," Brasti said. "Shouldn't we—you know . . ."

"What?"

"You know, take his money?"

Even Kest looked back and raised an eyebrow at that one.

"No, we do *not* take his money," I said.

"Why not? It's not like he needs it."

I sighed again. "Because we're not thieves, Brasti, we're Greatcoats. And that has to mean something."

He started making his way out of the window. "Yeah, it means something: it means people hate us. It means they're going to blame us for Tremondi's death. It means we're going to hang from the noose while the mob throws rotten fruit at our corpses shouting, 'Tatter-cloak, tatter-cloak!' And—oh yes—it means we also don't have any money. But at least we still have our coats."

He disappeared out of the window and I climbed out after him. The constables had just broken down the door, and when their leader saw me there with the wooden sill digging into my chest as I eased myself out of the window, there was the hint of a smile on his face. I knew instantly what that smile meant: he had more men waiting for us below, and now he could rain bolts down on us while they held us at bay with pikes.

My name is Falcio val Mond, First Cantor of the Greatcoats, and this was only the first of a great many bad days to come.

2
CHILDHOOD MEMORIES

The Duchy where I was born is called Pertine. It is a small and simple place, largely ignored by the rest of Tristia. The word "pertine" has a number of different meanings, but they all come from the flower that grows on the leeward slopes of the mountain ranges that ring the region. It is an odd sort of bluish color, and you would call it bright at first, but then as you looked on it further, you'd find yourself adding words and phrases like "oily" and "runny looking" and finally "sort of disturbing." The pertine has no known medicinal properties, it makes you sick if you eat it, and it smells horrible once plucked from the ground. Needless to say, you'd have to be pretty stupid to make it the one thing people remember about your region. However, somewhere in the distant past, some warlord decided to pick one of these flowers, put it on his cloak, and name this land of my birth Pertine. I imagine he was born without a sense of smell.

But the folly continues. The guardsmen who watch over the town and comprise our troops in times of war wear tabards of the same color and general consistency as the flowers that grace our homeland, which inevitably means they are dubbed "the Pertines"—because they are, after all, blue, oily, runny looking, and ultimately quite stinky.

I was born to this rich heritage; my father had chosen not only to live in Pertine but also to serve in the Pertine Guard. He wasn't a very good father to me, nor husband to my mother, and I think he realized that, for he fired himself when I was seven years old. I always assumed he got himself a new job as husband and father somewhere else, but I never bothered to find out.

I paid the fate-scribe at the Monastery of Saint Anlas-who-remembers-the-world a good deal of money to write this, though I will never see it myself. How they can transcribe the events of a man's life from afar, I do not know. Some say they read the threads of fate, or they bond with a man's mind and capture his thoughts to put down on paper. Others say they just make this shit up, since by the time anyone gets to read it the person it's about is almost certainly dead. Whichever it is, I hope they at least get this next part right, because there are two stories separated by twenty-five years and I think they're both important, so try to pay attention.

The first is this: I was eight years old and living with my mother on the outskirts of a town that bordered the outskirts of the next town. My mother often sent me on errands that, in retrospect, now seem a bit suspicious. "Falcio, run into town and fetch me a single carrot. Make it a good one, mind you." Or, "Falcio, run into town and ask the messenger to confirm how much it will cost us to send a letter to your grandfather in Fraletta."

Now, I don't know how it is where you live, but the cost of sending a letter along the main roads hasn't changed in Pertine for fifty years, and I'm still not sure what one can make with a single carrot. But me being away pleased my mother well enough, and it gave me time to go to the tavern and listen to Bal Armidor. Bal was a young traveling storyteller who spent a great deal of time in our town. He brought middle-aged men of means news of what was happening outside of Pertine and regaled old men with crooked backs with righteous stories of the Saints. He sang young girls sweet songs of romance that made them blush and their admirers boil . . . and he told me stories of the Greatcoats.

"I'll tell you a secret, Falcio," he said to me one afternoon. The tavern was almost empty and he was tuning his guitar and preparing for the evening's entertainment. The bartender, washing last night's mugs, rolled his eyes at us.

"I promise not to tell anyone, Bal, *ever*," I said, as if taking a solemn vow. My voice was kind of creaky, so it didn't actually sound much like a real vow to me.

Bal chuckled. "No need for that, my trusty friend."

Good thing too, I suppose, since I'm about to break the oath.

"What's the secret, Bal?"

He glanced up from his guitar and looked around the room before motioning for me to come closer. He spoke in that whisper of his that sounded like it could travel on the wind and reach you from a hundred miles away.

"You know how I told you about King Ugrid?"

"The evil King who disbanded the Greatcoats and swore they would never again use cloak and sword to help the people of the land?"

"Now, remember, Falcio," Bal said, "the Greatcoats weren't just a bunch of swordsmen running around fighting monsters and evildoers, were they? They were the traveling Magisters. They heard the complaints of the people who lived outside the reach of the King's Constabulary, and they meted out justice in his name."

"But Ugrid hated them," I said, hating the embarrassing whine in my voice.

"King Ugrid was very close to the Dukes," Bal said evenly, "and they believed it was their right to administer and set the laws on their own lands. Not all Kings agreed with that idea, but Ugrid believed that as long as the Dukes paid their taxes and levies, then what they did on their own lands was their business."

"But everyone knows the Dukes are tyrants," I started.

Bal's hand came out of nowhere and slapped me hard across the face. When he spoke, his voice was deadly cold. "Don't you ever say such a thing again, Falcio. Do you understand me?"

I tried to speak, but couldn't. Bal had never taken a hand to me before and the shock of his betrayal stayed my tongue. After a moment, he set his guitar down and put his hands on my shoulders. I flinched.

"Falcio," he sighed, "do you know what would happen to you if one of the Duke's men heard you use the word 'tyrant' when speaking of their Lord? Do you know what would happen to me? There are two words you must be very careful about ever saying aloud: 'tyrant,' and 'traitor'—because they often go together, and usually with terrible results."

I tried to ignore him, but when he removed his hands, I couldn't help myself. "So what is it?"

"What is what?"

"The secret. You promised to tell me a secret, but then you hit me instead."

Bal ignored the jibe. Resuming his whisper and conspiratorial manner, he leaned closer, as if nothing had happened. "Well, when King Ugrid decreed that the Greatcoats would never ride again, he said it would be for all time, right?"

I nodded.

"King Ugrid had a counselor named Caeolo—Caeolo the Mystery, they called him—and some people believed he was a wizard of great skill and wisdom."

"I've never heard of Caeolo," I said, excitement overwhelming sore cheek and wounded pride.

"Very few have," Bal said. "Caeolo vanished mysteriously before Ugrid died, and he never appeared again."

"Maybe he killed Ugrid . . . Maybe he—"

Bal interrupted me. "Now don't start that mind of yours tumbling all over itself, Falcio. Once it starts, it won't stop until you pass out from exhaustion." The storyteller looked around the room again, though there was no one else there except for the tavern master cleaning cups at the other end of the room. I don't know if he could hear us, but he had good ears on him.

"Well, as the story goes, after the decree was read aloud in the court, Caeolo took his King aside and said, 'My King, though you are Lord of all things and I but your humble counselor, know that the words of a King, no matter how powerful, outlive him by no more than a hundred years.' Ugrid looked at him, shocked at the impertinence, and cried, 'What do you think you're saying to me, Caeolo?' Unperturbed, Caeolo answered, 'Only this, my King, that in a hundred years the Greatcoats will ride again, and your mighty words will fade from memory.'"

Bal looked down at me with what, at the time, I thought was a sparkle in his eyes, although now, looking back, I think it might well have been a tear.

"And do you know how long ago King Ugrid died?" Bal asked me. When I shook my head, he leaned in close and spoke directly into my ear. "Almost a hundred years."

My heart leapt straight up out of my chest. It was like my blood had been replaced with lightning. I could—

"Damn you, Bal," the tavern master shouted from across the room. "Don't you go filling that boy's head with your horseshit."

"What do you mean?" I asked. My voice sounded strange to me for a moment.

The tavern master stepped out from behind the bar. "There never were no damned Greatcoats. It's just a story people tell when they ain't happy with the way things are. Traveling Magisters going about armored in leather cloaks and fighting with swords and hearing complaints from damned peasants and servants? It's shit folktales, boy. It never happened."

Something about the way he dismissed the Greatcoats so easily—so *completely*—made the world feel small and empty to me—as small and empty as a house filled with nothing but the idle fancies of a small boy and the sad longings of a lonely woman who still stared outside on cold winter evenings, waiting for her long-gone husband to return.

Bal started to protest the tavern master's comments, but I interrupted, "You're wrong—you're *wrong*! There were too Greatcoats, and they did do all those things. Stupid rotten King Ugrid banned them, but Caeolo knew! He said they're going to come back one day and they are too going to come back!"

I ran for the door before someone else could hit me—but then I stopped and turned around and I put my fist up on my heart. "And

I'm going to be one of them," I swore. And this time it really did sound like a vow.

The second story I need to tell you took place two years ago, in Cheveran, one of the larger trade cities in the south of Tristia, and it began with a woman's scream.

"Monster! Give me my daughter!" The woman was close to my age, perhaps thirty years old, with black hair and blue eyes like those of the little girl I was carrying in my arms. I imagined she was quite pretty when she wasn't screaming.

"Mommy, what's wrong?" the girl asked.

I had seen the child fall when her foot had got caught on the table leg of a fruit seller's stand next to the alley that had apparently been her destination. Her eyes full of terror, she'd told me a man in Knight's armor was pursuing her but when I looked for him he was gone. I'd carried the girl the entire way to her home, which wouldn't have been very far except that she kept getting confused about the right way back.

"Her ankle is sprained," I said, trying to shake the water from my hair to keep it from dripping into my eyes. It's always raining in Cheveran.

The woman ran back inside her house—I'd assumed it was to get towels, but when she returned she was in fact brandishing a long kitchen knife. "Give me my daughter, Trattari," she cried.

"Mommy!" the girl screamed into my ear.

There's a great deal of screaming in this story. Best get used to it now.

"I told you, her ankle is sprained," I said. "Now kindly let me in so I can put her down. You can try and stab me afterward."

If the woman thought I was in the least bit clever, she covered it up by yelling for help. "Trattari! Oh, help me! A tatter-cloak has my daughter!"

"Oh, Saint Zaghev-who-sings-for-tears, just let me put the girl down!"

With no apparent help coming, the woman eyed me warily and then backed away into the house, the knife still between us. I wasn't worried for myself—my coat would blunt any impact from being stabbed—but there was a decent chance the woman would end up hitting her own daughter in the process.

In the central room of the house there was a small settee. I placed the girl on her side, but she immediately sat up, then winced when her foot touched the ground.

The woman ran to her daughter, wrapping her arms around her and squeezing her before pulling back to look at every inch of her. "What have you done to her?"

"Other than help her when she fell, carry her here, and listen to you scream at me? Nothing."

The girl looked up at us. "It's true, Mommy; I was being chased by a Knight and then this man helped me."

The mother kept an eye on me and her knife between us. "Oh, sweet Beatta, silly child, no Knight would ever harm you. He was probably trying to protect you."

Beatta made a face. "That's silly. I was just trying to buy an apple from the fruitman."

At that moment, two men and a boy of about twelve ran into the house. "Saints, Merna, what's the matter?" the taller of the two men asked. All three were of a set: sandy brown hair and square-jawed, dressed in the brown overalls of laborers. The two men were carrying hammers and the boy held a rock in his fist.

"This Trattari had my daughter!" Merna said.

I held up both my hands in a gesture of—well, please-don't-attack-me. "There's a misunderstanding, I—"

"There's a misunderstanding, all right," one of the men said, taking a step forward. "You seem to think a tatter-cloak is welcome to come here and attack our women."

"Aye," said the other. "Servants of the dead tyrant aren't welcome here, Trattari."

Despite my desire to calm the situation, I found that my rapier was in my right hand, its point close to the man's neck. "Call the King that again, friend, and we'll have a problem that your hammer won't solve."

Merna was doing her best to cover up Beatta with her body, but the child poked her head out. "Why do you call him that? What's a Trattari?"

"A Trattari is a tatter-cloak," Merna said, spitting the words. "One of damned King Paelis's so-called magistrates."

"Assassins, more like," the taller man said. "We should hold him and send Ty to fetch the constables."

"Look," I said, "I came here because the girl was hurt and scared—she believed herself in danger. She's safe with you now, so just let me be on my way."

The sight of my rapier made that suggestion sound sensible enough to the workmen, who began moving aside to let me pass.

"Wait," the girl said.

"What is it, Beatta?" the woman asked.

"I said I'd give him some of my supper. He dropped his apple when he came to help me and I said he could share my dinner."

"Don't worry about it," I said. "I'm not—"

To my surprise, the girl's mother rose from the settee. "Wait here," she said.

The two men and the boy did a remarkable job of looking like they were keeping me at bay despite the fact that nothing was actually happening.

"Why do you call him Trattari?" Beatta repeated, this time addressing the two men.

It was the boy who replied. "It means tatter-cloak," he said. "They called themselves the Greatcoats, and their coats were supposed to never show wear so long as their honor held."

"But of course they had no honor," the shorter of the two men said.

"Because they served the tyrant, Paelis?" Beatta asked.

"Oh, aye, they were bastards for interfering with the lawful rule of the Dukes. But no, child, the reason they're called tatter-cloaks is because when the Dukes came with their armies to put a stop to the tyrant's ways, these so-called Greatcoats stood aside and abandoned their King just to save their own skins."

"But if the King was bad, then wasn't it good that they stepped aside?" the girl asked.

Her mother returned from the kitchen carrying an apple and a piece of cheese, which she hastily stuffed into a small sack. "No, dear. You see, the Knights teach us that any man has honor, so long as he serves his Lord faithfully. But these traitors failed to do even that much. So we call them Trattari now—tatter-cloaks—because their coats are as torn as their honor."

"Keep the food," I said. "I've lost my appetite."

"No." The woman stood her ground between me and the entryway, holding the sack out to me. "I want my daughter to learn right from wrong. She promised you food, and food you shall have. I'll have no presumed debts to a traitor."

I looked at her, and at the men. "What about the man?"

"What man?"

"The Knight. The one she said was chasing her. What if he seeks her out again?"

Merna laughed. It was a remarkably unpleasant sound. "As if one of the Ducal Knights would ever harm a child! If there was a Knight there, more than likely he saw you eyeing her and thought he needed to protect her." The mother looked at her child. "Beatta's a silly girl. She was probably just confused."

The situation bothered me. I didn't think it likely that a child would confuse whether or not a Knight was chasing her. I couldn't for the life of me think of a reason why Beatta might be pursued, but I didn't want to take a chance. I turned to her. "Beatta, are you still afraid of this Knight? Do you want me to stand guard outside tonight in case the man comes here?"

One of the men started to speak, but Merna held up her hand. "Beatta, dear, tell the Trattari we don't want his help."

Beatta looked at her mother, then at me. With the innocent cruelty of a child she said, "Go away, dirty tatter-cloak. We don't want you here. Evil King Paelis was a stupid pig and he's dead and I hope you die too."

The child had probably never seen King Paelis when he was alive. The Dukes had won, and history was already bearing the marks of their victory. Even if someone was after the girl, what could I do about it? The Greatcoats were disgraced and disbanded and it felt as if most people would rather see their child dead at the hand of a Knight than saved by that of a Trattari.

I reached out and took the small sack of food from the girl's mother, if only because it was the fastest way to make her step out of the way. I walked out the door and away from their home.

A few days later, on my way out of the city, in the quiet of night I walked past Beatta's house again. I knew there'd be Gods to pay if I was seen, but I felt a strange compulsion. The lights were out and there was red paint on one of the windows in the form of a bird, the sign used in Cheveran when a child has been lost.

3
THE CITY OF SOLAT

The fall from the second-floor window of the inn played against my strengths. Kest was inhumanly coordinated; he could probably fall from the top of a tower without hurting himself. Brasti was unbelievably lucky and managed to hit a wide awning above the rear entrance. He slid down to the cobblestoned courtyard. I was neither agile nor lucky, so I just kind of fell. Hard.

As I rose to my feet I saw eight men arrayed in front of us, all armed with pikes. I hate pikes almost as much as I hate magic. Twelve feet long with a sturdy wooden shaft and a wicked iron spearhead, a properly grounded pike had enough stopping power to take down a Knight charging in on an armored warhorse. At the same time, it was a simple enough weapon that even an amateur could wield it effectively in battle. And the more men you had with pikes, the easier it was to take out a group of swordsmen, regardless of their skill.

But that wasn't what was bothering me. What was bothering me was that I hadn't heard any bells. When the city constables of Solat patrol the streets, they go in pairs, and that way, if they discover a crime and it looks like trouble, one of them can go and ring one of the huge bells placed throughout the city to call for more men. There's a code, with each district allocated a specific number of chimes, so that reinforcements know where to go. But I hadn't heard any bells ringing, so I was beginning to suspect that these men were specifically looking for us.

"Eight men here with pikes and two above with crossbows, Falcio," Kest said, slipping his sword from its sheath. "I believe this might just be a trap."

"Do try to keep the enthusiasm out of your voice, Kest," Brasti said as he looked longingly toward the edge of the courtyard, where his bows were strapped to the saddle of his horse.

"You'll never make it," the constable opposite him said, smiling so wide it made his helmet tilt.

Brasti grumbled and reluctantly drew his sword.

A voice above us shouted, "The pike or the crossbow, Trattari: which would you prefer?"

I looked up at the man leaning out of the window of Tremondi's bedroom. The collar of his leather armor displayed a single gold circle, marking him as a senior constable. "If you put down your swords, I can promise you a relatively painless death," he said. "That's more consideration than you gave Lord Tremondi."

"You can't seriously believe we killed Tremondi, can you?" I shouted back.

"Of course I can. It says 'Greatcoats' right here, and in the Lord Caravaner's own blood."

"Saint Felsan-who-weighs-the-world," I swore. "Why in all the hells would we kill our own employer?"

The senior constable shrugged. "Who knows with your kind? Aren't you Trattari fond of seeking revenge for the death of King Paelis? Perhaps Tremondi supported the Dukes when they removed your King? Or maybe it's simpler than that: he caught you stealing his money and you killed him to keep him from revealing how the so-called Greatcoats have become nothing better than brigands and thieves."

"Except his money's still sitting there right beside him," Brasti shouted back, giving me a dirty look.

"Hmm? I don't know what you're talking about, Trattari," the senior constable said, smiling. "There's no money here—none at all."

The men in front of us laughed. Evidently thievery was only a problem in Solat when it was someone other than the constables doing it.

"You're doing it again, Falcio," Kest said quietly.

"What's that?"

"Talking when you should be fighting."

I pulled my rapier from its sheath and raised the collar of my greatcoat, hoping the bone plates sewn inside would protect my neck. Kest was right; there wasn't anything we could say now that was likely to get us out of this mess.

"How would you rate our chances?" I asked him.

"We'll win," he replied, "but I'll get wounded, probably in the back. You'll get hit by one of the crossbow bolts and likely die. Brasti will almost certainly be killed by one of the pikemen, once they get past the weak defense he puts up with his sword."

"You've been a real joy to work with, Kest, you know that?" Brasti said, shifting his guard.

Kest rolled his right shoulder, preparing for the first attack. "Blame them—they're the ones planning to kill you."

Brasti gave me a look that indicated it wasn't the constables he blamed. "I don't suppose you have a better plan than just dying?" he asked as he brought his sword in line with the belly of the guard closest to him.

"Sure," I said. "We teach them the first rule of the sword."

One of the guards, the one closest to Kest, tightened his grip on his pike in preparation for the attack and said jeeringly, "And what's that supposed to be, tatter-cloak? Lie down and die, like the traitors you are?"

He was a big man, well muscled, his broad shoulders perfectly suited to using a pike.

"No," Kest said. "The first rule of the sword is—"

His words were cut off as the guard jabbed his pike with the speed of a metal ball flying from the end of a pistol.

"—put the pointy end into the other man," Kest finished.

No one else moved or spoke. The exchange had been so fast that only the final result was visible. The back of Kest's left hand was now pressed against the haft of the pike, and the point was deflected safely behind him. His body was extended in a tight forward lunge and the point of his sword was six inches deep into the constable's stomach.

With a gentleness that belied the nature of the encounter, Kest slid his blade from the guard's belly and watched as he slumped to the ground.

For a moment—just a moment—the constables in front of us looked so shocked that I thought they might actually back away. But then I heard the metallic twang of a crossbow firing and felt the impact against my back. As the sting spread throughout my body I thanked Saint Zaghev-who-sings-for-tears that the bone plates had kept the bolt from piercing my body. It still hurt like the red death, though.

"Damned coats," I heard the senior constable mutter from the second-floor window.

"Under the awning," I shouted, and the three of us took up positions beneath the wide cloth awning above the back door of the tavern.

"This won't stop crossbow bolts," Brasti pointed out.

"I know, but it'll make it harder for them to aim."

The two constables nearest me started jabbing at me with their pikes. The one on the left, the smaller of the two, had a face like an angry ferret. The one on the right was taller and stocky, reminding me more of a bear than a man. I parried the point of Ferret's pike and grabbed the shaft with my free hand as I swung my blade back to block Big Bear's weapon half a second later. Ferret tried to pull his pike back, but I grounded myself and used my greater weight to prevent him from recovering it. The frustration on his face would have been rewarding if another crossbow bolt hadn't shot past my ear, landing just between us. I used the momentary confusion to knock the shaft of Big Bear's pike downward with the hilt of my rapier, then stepped on the shaft, driving the point to the ground. When Ferret tried pulling again I leapt toward them both, using the momentum of Ferret's efforts to help me bridge the gap between the tip of my sword and Big Bear's throat. As the big man fell to the ground, detaching himself from my blade, I drove the point into Ferret's shoulder and he too fell to the ground, but with considerably more screaming.

Another bolt forced me back under the dubious protection of the awning, and I took the opportunity to see what else was waiting for me. Fortunately, the other guards closest to me were a little warier now, so I took advantage of their hesitation to see how Brasti was doing. I never bother checking on Kest—watching him fight just makes me feel like an awkward teenager fumbling his first kiss.

Brasti was trying to edge away from the constables, but there wasn't much room to move without leaving the cover of the awning and becoming a target for the crossbows.

"Damn it, Falcio, this is all your fault," he grumbled.

"If we die now, Brasti, I'm going to order Kest to tell everyone you went to your death poor, hated, and rated a lousy lover by women everywhere."

"You know I can't fight pikes with this damned thing," Brasti shouted back as he swung his sword in an awkward arc in front of him. He was a good enough swordsman, considering he almost never practiced, but fighting two or three men with pikes is hard for anyone. Of course, if he'd had his bow, it would have been a different matter entirely . . .

"Kest!" I shouted. "Help Brasti get clear."

Kest glanced at me as he parried a frantic attack from the constable in front of him, and I knew he'd understood. But, "*Crossbows*, Falcio," he reminded me as he slipped under the attack of the man in front of him to join Brasti.

Damn it, I thought, *he's right*. If Brasti made a run for the horses, the men on the second floor would aim straight for him. They needed a more attractive target.

"Fine. Do it—*now*!" And with that, I pulled a throwing knife from the bracer inside my coat, stepped out from the awning, and threw it straight at the senior constable on the second floor. The blade jammed into the windowsill not six inches from his face and I cursed whichever Saint was supposed to be helping my aim.

The senior constable was an experienced man; he ignored the knife and took aim. I jumped to my left just as the bolt hit the ground between my feet. Without hesitating, he put down the crossbow and took the loaded one from the guard next to him, but something in the middle of the courtyard caught his attention—it must have been Brasti—and I saw him reposition his weapon. I threw another knife at him, making it clear that I was the more pressing threat, and this knife did a better job than the first and hit him in the shoulder. Unfortunately for me, he stumbled and let loose the bolt. I had my coat open so I could reach my knives, and with the luck afforded me by Gods and Saints alike, the wayward bolt stuck into my exposed thigh.

"Got you, Trattari bastard," the senior constable cried as he fell backward into Tremondi's room.

There was a yell behind me and I turned, cursing at the pain shooting through my leg, to find that one of the remaining constables had his pike aimed squarely at my chest and was ready to strike. I swung my sword arm toward the pike, knowing it wouldn't be fast enough, only to see the shaft of an arrow appear through the man's neck. He fell to the ground in front of me and I looked around to see where the next attack would come from—but there was no next attack. There were two other bodies on the ground with arrows in them next to the two I had slain, and the three remaining men were lying dead or wounded by Kest's blade.

"The crossbows have stopped," he said, stepping out from under the awning.

"That means they're coming back down. Time to go."

"That was a good idea, Falcio, covering Brasti so he could get to his bow. I hadn't thought of that."

I leaned my hand on his shoulder, taking some of the weight off my wounded leg. "Kest, next time you think the most optimistic outcome possible is everyone but you dying, try to think harder, okay?"

We joined Brasti and the horses at the other end of the courtyard and I thanked Saint Shiulla-who-bathes-with-beasts that the horses hadn't been hit during the fight. While Brasti went to recover his arrows, I wondered out loud who had set this up.

"Gods, Kest, when did it become so easy to believe the worst in us?"

"Times have changed, Falcio," he said, pointing behind me.

I turned to see Brasti, reclaimed arrows in one hand, searching the bodies of the fallen men with the other.

"Brasti, stop stealing from the constables," I shouted.

He looked sullen, but nonetheless ran to his horse. "Fine," he grumbled. "Wouldn't want to take anything from the nice men who were just doing their jobs trying to kill us." He hopped up on his brown mare. "I mean, that wouldn't just be dishonorable. It would be—oh my Gods and Saints—*impolite*."

"Interesting," Kest said, taking the reins and pulling his horse around.

"What?" Brasti asked.

Kest pointed at me. "I've just realized: he talks too much before a fight and you talk too much after. I wonder what it means?"

He kicked his horse and took off down the street, Brasti following behind. I looked back at the dead men on the ground and wondered how long the Greatcoats could last before we became what people said we were: Trattari.

The second-worst feeling in the world happens when your body discovers that yet again it's about to get into a fight for its life. Muscles start to clench, you start to sweat, you start to smell (luckily, nobody ever notices that at the time), and your stomach sinks down to your nether regions.

But the first-worst feeling in the world is when your body realizes the fight is over. Your muscles start to give out, your head throbs, you keep sweating, and—oh yes, you notice the smell. Last but not least, you realize there's a crossbow bolt sticking out of your thigh. It was the crossbow bolt that finally forced me to stop.

"It's going to have to come out," Brasti said sagely, looking down from the rooftop where he was scouting for the constables.

I could have killed him, but that would require asking my body to repeat the whole cycle again and, frankly, I smelled bad enough as it was. We had found ourselves a decent alleyway with two exits to hole up in for a breather. The horses didn't like trying to race around corners on cobbled streets, and we needed to deal with my leg.

Kest looked at me. "Punch-pull-slap?"

I sighed. It hurt. "I don't suppose we have time to find a doctor, do we?"

Brasti climbed back down from the roof of the building. "They're doing a house-to-house. The men don't look all that eager to find us, but the head guy—the senior constable, the one who shot you—is pushing them hard. It's only going to be a matter of minutes before they get to this alley."

Damn. "Punch-pull-slap," I said, already dreading it. "But make it hard this time, Brasti."

Kest poured water on the wound, making me whistle through my teeth.

"Just don't scream this time," Brasti said. "We're trying to avoid being caught."

While I prayed to Saint Zaghev-who-sings-for-tears to come down just this one time and meet my good friend Brasti, Kest got a firm grip on the shaft and then nodded at Brasti.

The three of us invented "punch-pull-slap" some time ago. One of the things you discover after you've been wounded enough times is that the body really only keeps track of one source of pain at a time. So, for example, if your tooth hurts and someone pokes you in the stomach, your body momentarily forgets about the tooth.

So the way this is supposed to work is like this: Brasti punches me in the face, Kest pulls the bolt out of my leg, and then Brasti slaps me so hard my brain never has time to register the bolt and therefore I don't scream at the top of my lungs.

I screamed at the top of my lungs.

"*Shhh*! You need to keep quiet, Falcio," Brasti said, leaning in and wagging a finger at me. "They might hear that. You need to toughen up."

"I told you to hit me hard!" I said, watching the stars form in my vision.

"I hit you as hard as I could from that angle. Kest was in the way."

"You hit like a girl."

Kest stopped bandaging my leg and said, "Almost a third of King Paelis's Greatcoats were women. You trained most of them. Didn't they hit hard enough?"

It was a fair point, but I wasn't in the mood for semantics. "They hit like angry damn Saints. Brasti hits like a girl," I grumbled, holding on to the end of the bandage while Kest padded the wound.

"So I suppose we're off to Baern, then?" Brasti asked.

I pushed myself up. The leg felt a lot better with the bandage on tight: a throbbing pain instead of a burning one. "It's that or stay here and try to teach you how to not hit like a girl."

"Falcio, if you say that again, I'll punch you myself," Kest said.

"It's just a phrase, 'you hit like a girl.' Everyone says it. It's funny."

He handed me back my rapier. "No," he said, "it just sounds absurd."

"It's funny *because* it's absurd," I replied.

Brasti slapped me on the back. "Don't pay him any mind, Falcio. He lost his sense of humor the day he learned to swing a sword."

Oddly, since Brasti had no way of knowing it, he was absolutely right.

4
THE CARAVAN MARKET

I mentioned that my mother and I lived on the outskirts of our town, which bordered another town named Luth. There was a wooden marker between the two, and Kest and I met there as boys when we were both around eight years old. I was very poor, with no father and no prospects, other than a possible future as the village idiot. Kest Murrowson was the child of a wonderful mother who worked as a healer and a father who was the town smith. Kest told jokes all the time—thereby putting me to shame even for the role of village idiot—but he never made fun of me for being poor or not having a father, and that instantly qualified him to be my best friend. He was a gentle boy who didn't like to hunt or fish and never wanted to play with swords. I, on the other hand, was going to be a Greatcoat one day, just like in Bal's stories.

Kest's father made some of the best swords in the region, and he had learned fighting ways in the wars with Avares, the country to the west that is populated by barbarians who occasionally gang up and make their way across the mountains and try to raid us the way they do their own people. They lose every time because our troops can fight war-style, in units, while theirs just sort of run at you shouting and pissing on themselves as they try to cleave your skull with whatever is handy.

Anyway, Murrow, Kest's father, was a fine swordsman, and since Kest showed no interest, he thought he could induce him to jealousy by teaching me. He showed me how to fight with the broadsword, often called the war-sword these days because duels are now fought with lighter weapons. But the sword I most fell in love with was the rapier: straight, sharp point, lightweight—at least in comparison to a war-sword—and with an elegant style that felt like dancing with Death. I was a good student, and I loved spending time with the family. But strangely, Kest was never swayed by the jealousy his father had sought to create. He watched me, complimented me periodically, but never showed any interest in taking up the sword himself.

When I was ten years old, Murrow took me aside after practice one day and said, "Falcio, my boy, you're going to be a fine swordsman one day. A fine one. I've never seen anyone take to it so quickly."

A ball of warm fire lit itself in my chest. He had never called me "my boy" before, and it made me feel something, just for a moment, that I hadn't felt in a long time. I resented Kest, not for having a father, or even for not caring, because he did, but rather because he didn't try half so hard to please his father as I had done to please mine. But I didn't really hold a grudge with Kest over his disinterest. He was smart, he told jokes; everyone liked him. He was good at plenty of things. I was happy he had left the sword to me.

Years passed but I hardly took notice and before long we were turning twelve. My birthday had just passed and Kest's was coming up. I won't ever forget the day he came over to my mother's cottage to tell me—

Well, here's how it played: He knocked on the door. I came out with a half-eaten piece of bread in my hand and he said, "Falcio, I need to ask you something. Well, to be truthful, I need to tell you something."

I placed the piece of bread down on the step and put my hands together in front of me, a nervous habit I had in those days. "What is it?" I asked.

"Well . . ." He hesitated for a second, but then he took a breath and said, "I'm going to take up the sword, Falcio."

I let out my own breath all at once. "Damn, Kest, you scared the Saints out of me."

"I'm serious, Falcio. I'm going to take up the sword. I'm going to start today. I don't want you to be upset or offended—it's not because of anything to do with you. I just have to do this. I have to take up the sword."

I looked at him. I wanted to ask why, but somehow I knew he would never tell me. "Does this mean we can't be friends?" I asked, confused and a little hurt.

"No—of course we'll always be friends. That's why I'm telling you this now, so you won't think it's something bad between us."

I thought about that for a second. "Well, okay then. That's good. We can practice together. We can be the two best sword fighters in the town. People will come from all around to watch us. We can go see your father and start today!" I figured I was being nice, since Kest was almost twelve and would never be able to catch up to me.

Kest grinned, and we went to his house. When Murrow saw Kest, somehow he knew something had changed, and he pulled down another sword from his shelf without anyone saying a word.

When Kest first picked up the sword, I thought it would be hard for him—sure, he had watched me train and he probably had a good idea about how the parries and strikes should go, but he was bound to be awkward, and he hadn't built up his muscles the way I had from years of practice. And, for the first hour or so, he was, missing the parries and falling all over himself whenever he tried a cut. But he just kept at it, going back and repeating move after move, stroke after stroke.

By the end of the morning, he could beat me every time. By the end of that evening, he had beaten his father, and by the time Kest's thirteenth birthday passed, there was no one on this earth who could best him with a sword. He never told me why he changed his mind about fighting, but he was the greatest swordsman in the world, and he didn't tell jokes anymore.

"Let it be, Brasti," Kest said, but Brasti shook his head and climbed down from his horse.

"Right, of course, why bother complaining about it when we're good and buggered no matter which way we go?"

All the main exits from town were sealed except for caravan traffic.

"Hide, fight, or flee?" Kest asked me.

I started to think about it for a second, but Brasti didn't wait. "I already told you, we can't get out of here. They aren't letting anyone but the Saints-damned caravans through, and we can't fight them all. We have to hide out until things die down."

"Things won't die down until we do, or until we find the assassin," Kest said. He folded his arms and went back to waiting for me to say something intelligent.

Whoever had killed Lord Caravaner Tremondi had worked out their plan perfectly. Everybody knew he was rich and everyone knew his bodyguards were Greatcoats. It wasn't hard to believe that three Trattari would kill their employer to take his money. If we were caught, no one was likely to believe us, and if we escaped—well, that just proved our guilt, didn't it? Either way, the murderer was completely free of suspicion. She was probably walking around the city right now, enjoying the rest of her day.

"There's no way we're going to be able to track down the killer," I said. "We can't possibly say we were right there in the room with her but can't describe what she looked like. In a few hours the whole city of Solat is going to be looking for us."

Brasti threw his hands up in the air. "So we run. Again. Like cowards."

"We've got fairly skilled at it," Kest pointed out.

"You can get good at anything if you practice every day."

"We go to the caravan market," I said. "The constables are still searching for us in the city—they know we'll try to hide out, so they'll want to catch us before we go underground. But they won't have alerted anyone in the caravan market yet."

"Brilliant," Brasti said, clapping his hands. "The caravan market—and I thought I was supposed to be the dumb one."

"Don't worry," Kest said evenly, "you still are."

"I thought you didn't tell jokes."

"I don't."

I let the two of them bicker while I considered our situation. Our best chance at getting out of the city and getting hold of some money was to be hired as guards or duelists at the caravan market. A warrior who could fight military-style or solo was a great asset on the roads these days. But other than Lord Tremondi, few caravaners were willing to hire Trattari, so that meant we'd have to take what we could get—and take it quickly—before the constables decided to search the market. I suspected it was the last place they would want to find us, though; word that a Lord Caravaner had been murdered in the city would spread quickly, and that wouldn't do much for trade. Better for the city constables if they could keep it quiet for a while. Better for us, too.

"We stick to the plan," I said at last. "We were heading out with Lord Tremondi because he was taking the southern trade routes and we needed passage to Baern, right? We don't have any money, and even if we could sneak our way past the civilian gates, we won't get far without coin. So I say we make for the caravan market, get ourselves hired with another caravan, and follow them right out of the Market Gate. The constables don't control that one anyway, so we're less likely to get caught."

"What about Tremondi's plan? What about the Greatcoats becoming the wardens of the trade routes?" Brasti asked.

"That's likely as dead as Tremondi himself now," Kest replied.

I had to agree. "Even if someone does bring it up for a vote, they'll never take a chance on us now."

"Well then, Falcio," Brasti said, his voice thick with anger and frustration, "let me be the first to thank you for ensuring that the three of us die in pursuit of a fruitless quest for your personal redemption!"

"We still have a chance, Brasti—even Tremondi had heard rumors of the King's jewels in Baern."

"Sure," he said, "just like there were rumors about Cheveran and even damned Rijou. 'Look to the lowest of the noble families.' What in all the hells is that supposed to mean? None of them wants anything to do with us—"

"If we can find—"

He turned away from me.

I didn't need to, but I said it anyway: "It's my *geas*, Brasti. It's the last thing the King asked me to do."

The week before the Ducal Army took the castle, the King met with each of his one hundred and forty-four Greatcoats individually, and he gave every single one of us a mission. He called it a *geas*—something he'd read in one of his old books, no doubt. Some of us he swore to secrecy, others he did not. My mission was to find the King's Charoites. I'd never heard of any such thing before, but it wasn't the first time the King had commanded me to do something without bothering to fill me in on the details.

Brasti threw his hands up in the air. "He gave all of us *geasa*, you idiot—you, me, Kest, and all the others too. But the King is *dead*, Falcio. They killed him, and we stood by and let the Dukes take the castle. And when they were done with him, they stuck his head on a pole in the courtyard, and we stood by while they did it. *At your orders*."

"You shouldn't start this again," Kest warned, but Brasti was on a roll now.

"And *you*, you damn great ass—what was the fastest sword in the world doing while they took the King? Resting in its damned sheath, wasn't it?"

"I didn't see any arrows flying, either," Kest replied calmly.

"No, you didn't, because I was a good little Magister, just like you were. But where does that leave us? We gave up our lives for a stupid dream, and now it's dead, and we're the only Gods-damned fools who haven't figured it out yet."

"If it's all such a joke, then why is it you've never told us what your *geas* is, Brasti?" I asked. "It's because he told you to keep it a secret, isn't it?"

Brasti turned away, but I grabbed him by the shoulder and spun him back around. "If everything he cared about died with him, then why do you still keep his secret? I'll tell you why, Brasti, it's because you know the dream doesn't have to be dead if we keep believing in it." But even as I said the words, I realized I had made a mistake.

"Damned Saints, Falcio, you're the worst," Brasti shouted, and I couldn't stop myself flinching. "You bought into all those ideas about justice and freedom just as much as Paelis did." He swung his arms wide. "Look around you, Falcio. People hate us—no, they *despise* us. They curse our very names. When a man does something so heinous that they can't find a word bad enough for it, they call him Trattari. That's not how I wanted to spend my life."

"You think life is easier on peasants? Or for that matter on anyone else living under the Dukes, the self-styled Princes? These men who rule their Duchies like Gods were only ever kept in check by the King and by us."

"Don't start 'The Song of the Peasants' with me, Falcio. I was born just as poor as you were and I saddled up and rode out there as much as you did. I risked my life plenty of times, and I was willing to die a hero's death, too. But I won't die a traitor's death. It's not right, it's not—"

"Fair?" Kest asked.

Brasti stopped for moment, and I could see the pain inked across his face. When I first met him, he was one of the most contented people you could imagine. He wore the world like a gold cloak on his shoulders, and he walked about in the utter certainty that all was well with Brasti and all was well with the world. And in five minutes' time, he'd put that mask on again and you'd never know the difference.

But that's all it was now: a mask. Underneath he was so bitter, betrayed by everything and everyone, and probably me most of all.

I wondered how long it would be before he stopped listening to me when I told him not to steal. I wondered how many of us had already turned to thievery or banditry just to survive. We had been heroes for a little while and now we were just traitors with useless pardons, no allies and no purpose. Maybe we really were tatter-cloaks now.

Kest said something else to Brasti and he answered back, but I didn't really hear it. For five years I had been following the only clue the King had given me: I'd sought out his allies amongst the lesser noble families. Many were dead now, of course, slaughtered by the Dukes' Knights on a variety of trumped-up charges, and the few who remained refused to deal with any Greatcoats. The one exception came in the form of a hastily scrawled note, handed to me by the servant of Lady Laffariste, once a confidante of the King's; it said, simply, "Not now. They need more time." It was faint hope, and not nearly enough for Brasti, no matter how loyal he was underneath it all. The argument over the King's last command was an old one between us, and one neither of us would win. Either the King's Charoites were out there somewhere and we would find them, or we would end our days at the end of a noose.

I got back up on my horse and started down the cobbled streets toward the market. I assumed Kest and Brasti would follow eventually, but at that precise moment, I didn't really care either way.

It took us an hour to make our way from the center of the city to the caravan market without being discovered. I still reckoned our best chance was to head south for Baern, where Lord Tremondi's rumors placed one of the King's Charoites—supposedly "wandering around" the coast near the city of Cheveran. Despite Brasti's reasonable objection that we still had no idea what the King's Charoites were, even he didn't have a better destination in mind. We had to get out of Solat, and they hated us in the north from Rijou to Orison. Mind you, we weren't particularly liked anywhere.

"We don't hire damned tatter-cloaks here," the caravan captain told me, pushing my chest with a callused hand, "so just be off. Go try and screw someone else out of their money." The old man was a veteran; you could see it in his stance and wiry muscles. There were seven carts in his caravan, and the lead carriage was an ornate monstrosity that presumably housed the caravan owner. I looked it over critically. It would make a remarkably good target for brigands.

"Look," I said as amiably as I could manage, "you're short several men, and you're not going to be able to find anyone as capable as the three of us, especially not for what you're paying."

"I'm not paying horse droppings to you, Trattari."

Even for an old man, he filled out his leather jerkin well enough to make a man hesitate before getting into a fight with him. I'm a cautious person by nature, so I turned to leave, preparing myself to try again with one of the other caravans, but a second later, he called out to me, "Why don't you go and mount that King Paelis of yours one more time, eh? I reckon he'd be willing, and his body's probably still lying where they left it. Of course, you'd have trouble finding the pole they put his tyrant head on!"

Now that was strange. Somehow my sword was in my hand and I was facing the caravan captain and I felt good. *Really* good. I was completely relaxed. I was going to follow the first rule and put the sharp end of my weapon through his mouth, and that was going to feel really, really good because, for the rest of my short life, I would always know there was one person less in this world spewing filth about my King.

Five of his men drew swords on me, and I spotted another behind the lead carriage with a pistol. Damn, that was going to require some fast work on my part. Once you get hit with the ball from a pistol, you really only have a few seconds to get the pointy bit into someone's mouth before you fall down and die.

"Now boys," Brasti said, drawing back his bowstring, "if I see your friend with the pistol so much as hold his breath I'll end him. And trust me, the five of you against the three of us makes for very bad odds for you."

The captain was about to give the signal to attack when a voice called from inside the carriage, "How about five against one, then?"

The voice was female, and it had a mocking quality buried under what would have normally been a seductive tone.

"My lady—" the captain began.

"Peace, Feltock. You may be captain, but I own this caravan."

"Your lady mother does, anyway," he muttered as a young woman in a blue handmaiden's dress exited the carriage and walked timidly toward the captain.

She had dark hair and delicate features, and she paused to collect herself before looking up at us shyly. "My lady commands that if the Trattari—forgive me, sir, the *Greatcoat*—can best five of our men, then she will employ you and your fellows at the full caravan guard rate."

"Trin, get back in the carriage with your mistress," Feltock growled. "It's not safe here."

Trin, her eyes lowered, ignored the command. Brasti favored her with a sly smile and a wink before calling out to the carriage, "My lady, I thank you for your kind intervention in this matter, but we were just about to leave. Unless perhaps I could kiss the hand and gaze upon the face from which this beautiful voice issues?"

The captain was grumbling to the man next to him.

"Five bested by one—what did you mean, exactly?" Kest asked, and suddenly I had a terrible feeling. The only thing that really interested Kest these days was the opportunity to get into some awful odds and see if he could get me killed while trying out his latest sword technique.

"I mean what I say," the voice from the carriage said. "Your leader against five of my men. If he wins and none of them are dead, I will hire the three of you. But for every one of my men he injures beyond use, you will provide me with one of your men at no cost."

These kinds of market challenges were common enough—after all, how else could you assess the abilities of the men you hired? But five against one wasn't a challenge; it was a beating—and even if I could take on all five of these road-tanned buggers, there was no way I could do it without injuring them. And if I injured three of them, we'd be working for free.

"Forget—"

"Agreed," Kest shouted back.

I turned to him, trusting Brasti to keep an eye on the caravan captain and his men. "Are you out of your mind?" I murmured. "I can't take on five men and not injure them—no one can."

"It can be done; trust me."

"You've never done it," Brasti said, still watching the caravan guards, "and you've never been bested."

"That's not true," Kest said. "Falcio beat me in a duel."

Brasti's eyes went wide.

"It's true," Kest said.

Well, it was technically true. The Greatcoats weren't just wandering Magisters. We were trained to be the best duelists in the world. It sort of went with the job, since sometimes the only way to enforce the King's Laws was to challenge the Duke himself and face his champion. If you won, the Duke would usually capitulate. If not, they sent home your remains wrapped in your coat. So our training involved competing with each other—and no wooden swords, either. A Greatcoat should be able to wound a single opponent enough to stop him without killing him. That's how good we were—or how good we were *supposed* to be, as it didn't always turn out that way.

So when the King held a tournament, the winner to become First Cantor of the Greatcoats, I *really* wanted to win—more than that, I decided I *would* win. I believed in what we were doing more than anyone else did, and I wanted to lead them more than anyone else.

And I fought through the rounds one after another until it was just Kest and me vying for the prize.

I suppose I had hoped he might slip up before it got to that point, or that he would have lost interest—that happens with Kest, when someone doesn't meet his standard or the fight is too easy, he'll sometimes just walk away from it. But this time he didn't, so we fought and I won, and I'll never tell another soul how I did it. Even Kest doesn't know—which is probably why he likes to put my life in danger now.

"Hells, Kest, you yanked a bolt from my leg just a few hours ago and now you want to send me off to fight five men—why don't you go and duel bloody-faced Saint Caveil-whose-blade-cuts-water?"

"When the opportunity presents itself, I'll do just that," Kest replied, looking strangely upset.

"You'd fight the Saint of Swords? You really are completely insane, aren't you?"

"A Saint is just a little God, Falcio. If I meet him, rest assured, I'll fight him."

"Oh Gods, you're serious, aren't you?" I said, turning away. If Kest ever becomes a Saint, the transcendent expression of an ideal, he's going to be Saint Kest-who-never-fucking-learns. Unfortunately, my need to live up to his expectations of me has always been slightly stronger than my desire to punch him in the face.

"Fine," I said to the caravan captain. "Clear a damned space and let's get it over with." I figured that if I could just put up a good showing, the caravan owner might still take us on.

The captain chuckled and moved some of the horses out of the way. He pointed out five of his men and they stripped to the waist and took up arms: two war-swords, a spear, double-knives, and an ax. Damn, I hate fighting against axes. You spend so much time hoping they're not going to hit your blade and shatter it that you forget to watch out for your skull. I had one advantage, though: these were all strapping young fellows, and they obviously wanted to show off their fine muscled chests for the ladies in the crowd that was starting to form. I, on the other hand, had no intention of taking off my coat, and that would give me some protection against these bastards.

I pulled out my rapier and drew the second, which was sheathed in front of my saddle.

"Falcio?" It was Kest.

"What now?" I asked.

He almost looked sheepish, which is an awkward expression for Kest.

"Well, it's just that they aren't fighting in armor, so really—"

"Just you shut your Gods-damned mouth right now, Kest, or I swear I'll stick a sword through my own belly just to embarrass you." I turned on the five men in front of me. "Any of you want to wear armor, you go right ahead," I said.

They smirked at me.

Keep smirking, boys. At least a couple of you are going to have fine scars to show off to your children. Unless I cut off your balls first.

Brasti thankfully pulled Kest away, and I focused on my opponents and my two problems. Problem number one: how not to get killed; problem number two: how not to kill any of them. I chose to leave problem number two aside for a moment and concentrate on not getting killed. I was a good thinker when I set my mind to it. Being a Magister wasn't just memorizing the King's Laws. You had to sift through the evidence or work out how to enforce the law, or figure out the best way to break out of some Lord's jail.

I decided I'd rather fight one battle at a time than five at once. I wasn't likely to get them all to agree to that, but my mouth has got me into enough trouble over the years that I'm pretty good at building up enthusiasm over who gets to punch it first.

"Hang on," I said as the men started to circle. "We said five men. This isn't fair."

The caravan captain looked at his men, then at me. "There's the five of them there—what's your complaint?"

"What, are you blind? We said five men. *Men*." I pointed with my left rapier at the smallest of the group, the one carrying the spear who looked a lot like the one with the double-knives. "That one's barely a boy. His mother will weep, and I don't need to have his drunken, cow-born half-piece whore of a mother muttering curses in my name at night. I have enough trouble sleeping without that on my conscience."

The spearman swore at me. "Call me 'boy'? You damned tattercloak, I'll show you who's the boy here." He barreled at me with his spear, not realizing that the point of my left sword was already in line with his chest. I used my right blade to knock aside the tip of his spear as it came toward my belly and he stopped with the point of my sword six inches from his chest. He tried to pull back, but I used the same trick on him as I had with the constable earlier: I stepped on his spear. But he was a lot stronger, this one, so he kept a grip on it. Stronger, and dumber. I did a little stunt Kest and I used to practice as boys and ran right up the length of his spear, forcing him to drop it to the ground and letting me get within a foot of him; then I shifted my hands around so the points of my rapiers were aiming away from him and struck him on both temples with the pommels. I didn't have to do it that way, but I had a plan—one that required that I really embarrass him.

Spear-boy dropped like night in winter and I started talking to his unconscious body. "Now don't you go telling your whore mommy that you got beat up at the caravan today."

I heard a yell from my right side and turned to see Double-knife coming at me. So I was right about that, at least, and now big brother was going to come and save the family honor. If there was one thing I'd learned in life, it was that honor just gets you into trouble.

Double-knife had good technique, though. He had the look of a rigger, the one who keeps the wagons repaired. A lot of riggers tended to be former sailors who for whatever reason couldn't get work on a ship anymore.

He kept in close so I couldn't make use of the reach of my rapiers. If you've ever seen a sailor really go at someone with knives, you know the idea of parrying is preposterous. The knives are moving too fast and by the time you've parried one thrust, you've grown four other holes in your belly. You have to thrust into the attack and take a few cuts to the arm. The only problem there is that you can't do that up close with something as long as a rapier—thrusting becomes impossible. But I've been fighting double-rapier since I was eight, and I have a few of my own tricks. If you've got limber wrists and you're willing to grow a couple of scars, you can windmill the blades fast enough to give your opponent twice as many cuts as he gets on you.

I'll give the man his due: judging by the white scars all over his forearms he obviously wasn't afraid of being cut. Or maybe he was afraid of being cut, but was also really clumsy. Whatever it was, he soon realized he was getting the worst part of the deal, so he changed his style, binding my right blade back and trying to come in under my left to get at my neck. It almost worked, and I had to take the pain of leaning all the way on my wounded leg. But then I saw my opening and since I was already putting all my weight on my bad leg, I decided to take a chance.

Knife fighters tend to ground themselves hard: they fight with both feet flat on the ground, and only move to step in on you. They never think about protecting themselves against anything but their opponent's blades and the occasional head-butt, so it came as a complete surprise to him when I rammed the heel of my left boot as hard as I could just below his kneecap. I heard a crunching sound, as satisfying as the contented sigh of any lover, as his knee broke, and he tumbled down next to his brother. Bless you, Saint Werta-who-walks-the-waves; your children are as thick as boards.

The captain ran over to his man just as the two men with war-swords started toward me.

"Leg's busted," the captain said. "He won't be much use to us now."

The lady in the carriage laughed. "That's one of yours for mine, Trattari."

"Damn, Falcio. You're losing us money now, you realize that?" Brasti said.

I muttered a curse in his mother's name and tried to shake off the pain in my leg as the swords came at me. Fighting two swords is obviously more than twice as hard as fighting one, but that wasn't what was bothering me; I was more concerned that the man with the ax didn't come with them. I wasn't foolish enough to believe that I could keep baiting them into fighting me one at a time—so why would he not take advantage of the situation and come at me from behind?

I put the questions out of my head and focused on the two men in front of me. One was blond and slim, and the other was black-haired and burly, with a beard reaching halfway down his chest.

I decided to call them Blondie and Blackbeard. Not very original, maybe, but I wasn't planning on knowing them for long. They were both around the same height, which was good for me and bad for them. Fighting men of different heights means having to change your own stance all the time, which I couldn't have done with my injured leg.

"*Ifodor*, Falcio, use *ifodor*," Brasti shouted needlessly. Maybe he thought he was helping.

"Yes, I've heard of it," I shouted back. *Ifodor* is a technique Greatcoats use to fight against two swordsmen; it literally means "enclose the blades." It involves a lot of forearm strength, and you have to be ambidextrous to do it. I would have found the suggestion somewhat less insulting if I hadn't been the one who taught Brasti how to do it.

Imagine two opponents, each of whom wants to outflank you, so they try to move apart from each other and circle toward you in an attempt to get either side of you. You, on the other hand, clever fellow that you are, don't want to let them get on either side of you because it means you'll get killed. So you step backward, and occasionally follow the same circle toward one of them, so that the other is slightly out of reach of you, and now you're only fighting one man for a moment and you have a chance to eliminate one enemy. Your opponents, on the other hand, bright fellows that they are, don't want you to do this, so they keep adjusting their footing to keep you at equal distance from them, creating an arrowhead position with you at the point and them at the sides of the triangle. This sounds elegant, but in reality it mostly looks like two men jabbing repeatedly at one man who is trying his best to bat aside their blades with roughly the same amount of grace as a cow trying to step on a mouse.

And then we come to *ifodor, enclosing the blades*. You have to wait for the perfect moment, when both your opponents, through the natural rhythms that gradually bind all men together, suddenly try to thrust low at the same time, and when this happens, if your blades are in an upper guard position you can circle them downward and enclose each of your opponents' blades with one of your own. Now comes the tricky part: you've got both your opponents' points out of line and your own swords on the inside. You flip your points up and step straight forward, keeping your blades in contact with the lower half of their swords—and thrust your points into their bellies.

Ifodor is a hard technique to perfect, but it's devastatingly effective, and I was just about to do it when I heard Kest cough and realized I was about to kill two men and end up either dead myself or working for free. At the last second, I dropped the points lower to hit their legs. I got Blackbeard, but missed Blondie by an inch. Fortunately for me, he tried to sidestep and got his left leg tangled up in my blade. I pulled it hard and fast across his inner thigh and heard a collective gasp from the men in the crowd as I scored a wicked cut just below his nether region. I pulled my right blade out of Blackbeard's leg with a twist that sent him down and got the point of my left rapier just under Blondie's chin.

There was a sweet moment of silence when all I could hear was my own breathing. Then I heard someone clapping. Blondie backed away, and I saw that the applause was coming from the axman. He was smiling. He must have been six and a half feet tall, and he looked about twice as strong as me. I was already tired, and my right leg was ready to give out.

The axman stopped clapping and started putting on armor. I swore a little curse in Kest's name, that he should one day get to see the blood-red face of Saint Caveil. This man knew what he was doing. He had watched my style and he had seen that my right leg was wounded. He could tell I was tired, and he knew that rapiers weren't much good against plate armor. The only way to stop an armored opponent was to get your point up between one of the plates, and even then you would have a tough time getting through the chain-mail undershirt. Rapiers are dueling weapons, not war weapons, and he knew it. And that's why he was smiling. The real question was: why was I smiling?

"Damn," I heard Kest saying to Brasti.

"What is it?" Brasti asked.

"I just wish he hadn't smiled at Falcio like that, that's all."

5

ALINE

In Pertine, we say, "Life is a deal you make with the Gods." If you want to be a soldier, then you swear to fight hard and true your whole life, and you make a deal with War and shed blood in his name. And War, in turn, grants you strong bones and thick blood. If you want to be a merchant, then you swear to travel the lands and cheat only a little, and you make a deal with Coin, and in return Coin grants you safe journeys and gullible customers. I made a deal with Love, and swore my heart to one woman for my whole life. And, in return, Love gave me sweet smiles and warm nights, for a very short time.

Aline was wonderful and beautiful to me, and I won't waste your time describing her to you because you might not agree, at which point, I would have to teach you the first rule of the sword—or worse, you might fall in love with her yourself, and that would bring you only a small piece of the sorrow that fills my life.

We were seventeen when we met and twenty when she died. We married, loved, argued, talked, faced famine, fought neighbors, barely survived a curse placed on our home, and once, almost made a baby together. And in the end, she died for no better purpose than that the Duke who ruled our land wanted to bed her.

I loved King Paelis, but I hated all Kings before him and none more than his father, King Greggor.

I don't know why it was that the King and the Duke and their men came down the road past our cottage. Perhaps they were looking for wild game as they began their trip to Castle Aramor, the King's home in the south. Perhaps one of our neighbors who craved our land had played some trick on us. Perhaps Love, offended by my lack of prayers, decided to break our deal. But however it came about, the King's party rode right past our cottage, and the Duke asked him to stop for refreshment.

It is the Lord's Right that anyone in his Duchy can be called upon to provide sustenance in times of war or civil unrest. The Duke had a loose interpretation of war, and so demanded that we provide what food and drink we had to him and the King. We brought everything we had, even our winter stores. I was as miserly as the next man and twice as belligerent, but I was not stupid and I didn't play games with Kings.

Yered, Duke of Pertine, actually looked pleased with what we brought. King Greggor showed no interest and neither one included their men in the meal, so I counted myself lucky that there might be something left for us after they were done. I was foolishly optimistic.

"You are one of my subjects, are you not?" the Duke asked.

The question wasn't quite as stupid as it sounds; we lived on the border between Pertine and Luth and there was always some dispute with the neighboring Duke, Holm, as to who we should pay our taxes to.

"I am indeed your subject, my Lord, and have paid my taxes every year," I said with humility.

"Indeed? Well, that makes you the exception, my good lad."

He and his men had a good laugh at that, and I started to feel almost safe. I could handle this. I could keep my mouth shut and bow and curtsy and whatever else they wanted if it would get them off my land.

"But who's this now?" asked Yered, and I turned and saw Aline closing the gate that one of the Duke's men had left open in order to keep the goats from wandering out.

"That is my wife, my Lord," I answered.

"Damn fine woman you have there, boy. Come here now, girl, let your Duke have a look at you."

"It's getting late, Yered, and I'm getting hungry for something that wasn't picked up off the floor this morning." King Greggor sounded irritated and bored—a good sign, I prayed.

Yered laughed. "I too am hungry for something different, your Majesty. Pray, give me a moment to ensure my proper rights are observed."

Greggor waved him away. "Please yourself."

Yered stood up before me. He was slightly shorter than I was, so I tried hard to stoop and not let him be offended by my height.

"Now, boy, you tell me you've paid all your taxes?"

"Yes, my Lord."

"All? Are you quite sure?"

"Yes, my Lord. We paid seven pieces last season, and eight this one. I have a note of receipt from the sheriff. I could go find it for you if you—"

"Enough! Don't bray at me like some sheep. Have a spine in you, boy."

The Duke turned to his men. "You see this? This is the stock I have to go to war with. It's a wonder the damned barbarians haven't overrun us yet."

He picked up his wine goblet and handed it to me. "Here, you drink this piss. Perhaps it'll put some grit on your bones, eh?"

I drank it, seeing as it was my wine anyway.

"Now, back to the issue of the taxes. You paid taxes on your land?"

"Yes, Lord, four pieces to the sheriff, Lord."

"Good, good. And now, you also paid taxes on those goats?"

"Yes, Lord, two pieces."

"And on your, ah, chickens?"

"Yes, Lord, two for them."

The Duke counted off on his fingers. "Well now, that's eight pieces, isn't it?"

"Yes, Lord; eight pieces this season, as I said, Lord."

The Duke's men were chuckling. They had heard this joke before.

"Well now, you've paid for your goats and for your chickens, but what about the rest of your livestock?"

I shook my head, pretending not to get the joke. "I'm sorry, Lord? I don't under—"

"Your cow, man!" he said, pointing at Aline. "When are you going to pay the taxes on your cow?"

There was a great roar of laughter—or perhaps just a little laughter, but a great roaring in my ears.

"I'm sorry, my Lord, I didn't realize. I will pay whatever price is due."

Now I noticed several of the men winking at each other. In my effort to placate the man and hide my anger, I had walked right into the meat of his joke.

"Ah, pay the tax you will, boy," the Duke said amiably. "But keep your little silver pieces. In this case, it's the cow that pays the tax!"

Another round of laughter, and now one of the Duke's soldiers who obviously knew how this joke ended came forward and took Aline's arm. That was strange. All of a sudden there was a stick in my hand, and it was pointed at the soldier's eye.

But before even the Duke could act, Aline shook off the soldier's grip and slapped me hard across the face. I dropped the stick in shock. "Stupid boy," she said. "Don't ever stand in the way of my happiness!"

The Duke laughed and waved down his archers and I realized she had just saved my life. "Look there, the little harlot thinks she can be my wife!"

Everyone was laughing, even Aline. The Duke bellowed something about the wine and one of his men began digging through our meager supply. Aline grabbed my head with both hands and spoke into my ear. "Don't you dare, Falcio," she whispered fiercely.

"I know you love me, and I know you would fight for me, but not here, not now. I will do this thing, and I will pay the price for both of us. I will not scratch or claw or scream, but I will instead make this tiny man feel like a giant. It's well known the Duke only beds any woman once. And when he does, he will leave us and go with his filthy men and his filthy King, and you and I will grow old together and laugh at the day these silly birds came to rest in our fields."

She pushed me away and walked toward our cottage, beckoning the Duke to follow her. At the front door she turned back and called to the Duke's men, "Be gentle with him, will you? I hate it when he cries at night."

The Duke's men laughed, and even King Greggor chuckled as he spat out a piece of the lamb we had planned on eating for supper. And I waited and prayed and I hated myself even as I thanked Love for giving me a wife as wise and brave as the one who was even now being raped by a man I would kneel before and thank in a few minutes.

True to her word, she had him grunting and moaning, and in a few minutes, he gave out a great bellow and stopped. For a moment, I feared Aline had put a knife in his genitals, but the chuckling of his soldiers told me this was the Duke's way.

Aline came out first, hair flying free and doing up her blouse. "Gods bless you, my Lord. I am a new woman!"

The Duke came out of the cottage. His clothes were carefully done, but his hair was disheveled, and he was red-faced and still sweating like a pig.

"Saints smile on you, boy. You're a rich man indeed. I should up your taxes next year!"

I swallowed my pride and my honor and whatever other forms of dignity I had left to me and knelt down on one knee and said, "I am grateful to you, Lord, for your generosity and protection."

"And for finally satisfying that woman of yours, eh?" The Duke laughed in the grunting way pigs do right before you cut their throats.

"Yes, my Lord, and for doing what I myself have been quite unable to do."

"Hah!" the Duke shouted. "You're a toad, boy, a rank little toad. But you know your place, and that's the best we can hope for in a peasant. Don't worry; we'll leave, and I'll tell my men not to put your cottage to the torch."

The thought hadn't even occurred to me before then, but I bowed and scraped gratefully regardless. The King and Duke mounted their horses and their men followed suit—all except one, a tall man with a great scar running from his forehead down past his lips. He carried a war-ax on his back. "My Lord Duke," he said, looking straight at me, "should we not bring the woman, in case you happen to be hungry again later on? The fare is unlikely to be so sweet at the inn where we stay tonight."

The Duke barely turned his head. "What's that you're blathering about, Fost? You know very well no woman satisfies the Duke twice."

"Yes, my Lord, but wouldn't you say this one was different? She seems an especially fine cow to be left to a boy who can't properly milk her."

The Duke was about to wave him away, but King Greggor spoke up. "Hells, Yered, just bring the damned girl. Your men have had to listen to you grunt away enough times—perhaps they see something in her that you don't."

As much as I despised the Duke with all my being, I believe he would have left us, had it not been for the King's rebuke. But he was stung by the comment. "I have no further use for her, Majesty—but Fost, since you seem so keen on her, you bring her. She can entertain the men while I'm 'grunting' with finer fare."

Fost never took his eyes from me, and he never stopped smiling, the scar on his face crinkling in response. He motioned to his men and two of them took Aline while two more aimed arrows at my chest. Then he mounted his horse and followed his men down the road while I stood and stared like a peasant. Like a toad. Like a boy who knew his place.

Aline was a good girl, and she was wise too, but even she had the limits the Gods place on our sanity, and so by the time I had walked to the next town and found her on the floor of the tavern, she was two days dead. She had fought, my brave girl, and there were bits of skin under her fingernails and bruises on her arms, and her beautiful face was cleaved in two, as if by a great war-ax.

I felt very strange. I seemed to be in the caravan market of Solat, standing over the axman, who appeared to have gone and died of something. It looked as if what he died from was having swords thrust into both of his eyes and into his neck. I wondered for a moment who would do something like that and then noticed that I was shaking. Kest pulled me away from the man.

Feltock's hand was on his weapon and the girl Trin was crying into his shoulder.

"Damn, Falcio," Brasti said, looking at the corpse. "You were only supposed to wound him."

"Shut up, Brasti," Kest said. I thought that was very funny, and so I laughed out loud, but for some reason no one else thought it was funny. I also noticed that my face was wet. Oddly, that only made me laugh more.

"All right, so he had to kill him, but why did he have to draw that scar down the man's face after he was already dead?"

"Speak again, and I'll put you down," Kest said. Kest was a very scary man when he said things like that, and it made even me stop laughing. He was rubbing my arms, which was pleasant but seemed somewhat inappropriate.

"Do you remember Aline?" I asked him. My voice sounded strange—creaky, like when I was a boy. "I don't know why, but I just started thinking about her."

Kest put his hand on my face, just for a moment. Then he motioned for Brasti to come and watch over me and stood in front of the carriage. The caravan captain stepped in his way and put a warning hand on his chest, but Kest ignored him. "We have our deal. One man dead and one injured. I mark that one and a half men's pay for the work of three."

"My rigger's not going to be good for much with a broken leg, Trattari," the captain said. "Just be off and pray I don't get the constables on—"

"One man dead and one man useless," I heard the woman in the carriage say, her voice cutting through the noise. "I mark you one man paid and three men fed."

Kest looked over at me, but I was still looking at the bloody gash I had put down the axman's face.

"Marked," Kest said. "One man paid and three men fed." Then he turned to the other caravan guards. "And mark you all: any man wants revenge for one of these best remember that it was five men to one, and Falcio was injured at the time."

"Yeah," Brasti said, "and he wasn't even very angry yet."

A couple of the men I'd fought grunted and muttered under their breath, but no one looked us in the eye except for Blondie, who looked to me and said, "Fair fight's a fair fight. Besides, no one ever liked this big bugger anyway."

"Trin, go and file our papers with the market clerk," Feltock said, handing a small leather packet to the handmaiden. Then he kicked the axman's body. "And tell them Kreff lost in a duel, fairly fought. I doubt anyone'll care."

She nodded and left us, and the crew readied the caravan for travel. Minutes later, we were on our horses and headed out the Market Gate. I don't know if the constables were still looking for us or if they knew we were part of a caravan now and didn't want to deal with all the problems of jurisdiction posed by the market laws; either way, we encountered no resistance, and for the first time that day, it looked as if we might be moving in the right direction.

"We're going in the wrong direction," Kest said.

I looked ahead. The caravan captain was leading the wagons toward the bridge. We trotted ahead up the ranks to the lead wagon. "You're going the wrong way," I said. "The bridge takes us up the Spear—to the northern trade route."

Feltock said, "Her Ladyship has her own reasons for wanting people to think we're going to Baern, but this caravan is headed north, for her Saintly mother's home of Hervor."

"But that's almost three hundred miles north—and five hundred miles out of our way!"

"No, it's not, it's right on your way," the captain said. "After all, you marked your deal. You're part of this caravan now, and where it goes—well, that's where you go. Unless you three want to break market law and be marked false. I reckon that wouldn't be good for Trattari now, would it?"

Being marked false would be a death sentence for us. Trattari couldn't be prosecuted for prior crimes, but we had no protection under the law, either. Unless we were employed by someone with power and influence, we were targets for anyone who wanted to make a name for himself. And now we were being dragged in the wrong direction in a caravan of people who hated us, in the employ of a woman we knew nothing about and who had reason to hide her travels.

Brasti and Kest gave me sour looks as our horses wandered slowly toward the bridge. "Fine," I said at last. "Go ahead and say it."

Brasti shook his head in disgust, but Kest took me literally. "There's an excellent chance that you've just got us killed, Falcio," he said.

6

THE GAME OF CUFFS

Other than the Lady, who ignored us, and Trin, who was reasonably friendly with us, the emotions we elicited from most of the caravan crew during our first week ranged from outright hatred to whatever it is that's much, much worse than outright hatred. It made the first part of the journey a lot like—well, a lot like everything else we did.

After an awkward first night of repeated references to "the dead tyrant" we had served, the "whore's sons" that formed our order, and the "tattered, stinking rags" that were our greatcoats, we nearly came to knives with our fellow guards, so I decided it would be best if we spent most of our evenings by ourselves, on watch for the caravan and on watch for our own backs.

Trin came by, after the others had eaten, with food—I suppose it was a logical thing to do, since otherwise I'm certain we would have been accused of taking more than our share, but I still thought it was remarkably decent of her. She was pretty, with long dark hair and lightly tanned skin. Her eyes, when you could see them, were the color of stream water. She even sat with us for a while, listening to our stories and asking questions about the old laws, giving her shy smile when one of us threw in a joke here or there.

She told us very little about the Lady she'd served her whole life, other than that she was a noble daughter of a great house. Trin had been first a playmate, when they were children and Trin's mother was the Lady's nanny, then later a companion for her lessons. Now she was the Lady's handmaiden. I wondered what that must have been like, to start as a child, a playmate, and then every passing year become less and less an equal and more and more a servant. Trin appeared to think it was the most natural thing in the world, though, and laughed at Brasti when he suggested she could always steal the Lady's best dress, run away to a southern city, and claim to be a Princess, since she looked just like one.

"Saints of my mother, no," Trin said. "That wouldn't work at all!"

"And why not?" Brasti asked. "You're certainly pretty enough."

Trin looked down and laughed. "With hands like these?" she said, holding up hands that were nicely shaped, but with the telltale calluses of a servant.

"Let me see here," Brasti said, catching her hand and inspecting it closely. "As I suspected, as smooth as lake water and bright as gemstones. Now, as to taste—" Then he leaned in to kiss the back of her hand.

"Brasti?" I said, a placid smile on my face.

"Yes, Falcio?" he asked, turning to give me one of those pouty, angry looks of his.

"I was just thinking how long it's been since we practiced our feather-parries. Shall we get some work in tonight during first watch?"

"Feather-parries? Why in hells would I want to do that?"

A feather-parry uses the back of the hand to deflect a blade. It's sometimes necessary when your blade is already engaged, but it's not pleasant—that's why no one ever really wants to practice feather-parries. You come away with hands that sting for hours.

I kept smiling. "Because it might save your life one day. Perhaps today, even."

Brasti let go of Trin's hand.

"Bowmen don't practice feather-parries. We need our hands to have precision and control."

Trin looked at him quizzically. "But don't swordsmen need the same qualities?"

Brasti scoffed. "Them? Nah, it's all just swinging and poking with swordsmen. Just 'put the pointy end in the other fellow first' or whatever. An archer—now, an archer needs real skill."

I rolled my eyes at Kest. We'd heard this lecture many times before, but Trin hadn't, so she stepped right into it.

"Is it really so hard?" she asked.

"My dear, not one man in a hundred can be a proper archer. And not one in ten thousand can become a master."

"And you are one? A master archer, I mean?"

Brasti smiled and contemplated the nails of his right hand. "One might fairly say so, I believe."

"One says so frequently," I observed.

"But how did you become a master archer? Is it something you're born with? Did you have a teacher?"

"I did." He said the words as if they were full of secrets.

"Well," Trin asked, "what was his name?"

"No idea." Brasti looked solemn. "We never talked about it."

"You never talked about your own names? You studied archery from this man, but he never told you his name?"

"It just never came up. I was poaching rabbits on the Duke's land one day, barely old enough to be away from my mother's skirts, and he just stepped out from behind a tree."

"What did he look like?"

"Tall—very tall. He had long gray hair down to his shoulders in what we call archer fashion."

"Why 'archer fashion'?" she asked, sounding fascinated.

"Down to the shoulders: easy to tie back."

"You mean like yours?"

"Exactly like mine."

"And he taught you the bow, but he never taught you his name."

"Correct. Now that I think about it, I don't think we ever spoke at all."

Trin gave him a suspicious look, probably thinking that he might be making fun of her, but Brasti smiled reassuringly. "My dear, truth be told, it's a story that's legendary in the telling, and these two louts have heard it before. Perhaps tomorrow night I might tell you the story in a more private setting?"

Trin blushed, Brasti grinned, and later that night Kest and I threatened to beat him senseless if he tried to bed the girl while we were with the caravan.

The next day we set out again on the ancient road that caravaners call "the Spear" because it runs the north–south trade route in a fairly straight line. Having a long, straight thoroughfare was a good idea in principle, since you could make good time between trading destinations from Cheveran and Baern in the south all the way to Orison in the north, passing close enough to spit at other major cities like Hellan and even—though Saints keep me from it—Rijou. But if having a long, straight road was good for caravans, for brigands it was like sucking at the tit of Saint Laina. Since we had no King now, we had no proper military presence to protect the trade routes, and no foresters to keep trees and brush from turning both sides of the road into perfect hiding places for anyone with a sword and a hungry belly who planned on turning to banditry. The Dukes had no interest in maintaining the roads since the Lords Caravaner refused to pay tariffs, while the caravans themselves were usually in competition so no one wanted to pay for the bread that someone else would eat. So the clearings gradually began to grow over and the bandits laid ambushes at their leisure. Things got worse if you tried to run for it, as you were stuck in a long, straight tunnel, perfect for men on horseback to outpace the nags pulling your heavy wagons. All in all, it was a good time to be a brigand.

We were attacked twice in that first week. The first time, we nearly lost a man because the others wouldn't stand formation with Kest, Brasti, and me. Fortunately, the brigands' charge lasted only a few minutes and the three of us took them out with no serious damage to our own party. The wound I had taken in town had settled down a bit and I could move reasonably well, so long as I was willing to pay the price later when it ached like the devil at night.

After that fight, the caravan captain threatened the other guards with the lash, and they quickly learned their lesson. When the second attack came, we were ready. Eight men on foot, four with crossbows, tried to ambush us. But Feltock had the wagons circle quickly while we rushed the brigands and Brasti took out the crossbows one at a time. A crossbow is a good weapon if it's loaded and your opponent isn't too far away, but a good bow can outdistance and outshoot a crossbow two to one—and, as I might have mentioned earlier, Brasti never missed.

Eventually the rest of the brigands realized they were likely going to get picked off one by one, so they charged us. I fought side by side with Kest and Blondie—who had a name, but it turned out everyone really did call him Blondie, so I did too. He was solid with the war-sword once you got him away from Kurg, the black-haired man with the long beard. The two had fought together for years and they had fallen into bad habits.

It didn't take long for us to chase off the bandits, but Feltock still wasn't happy with the crew's performance, and he decided it was our job to train the men, ready them for any more attacks we might encounter.

"I'm not paying you to just sit on your horses," he said. "If you're supposed to be such great warriors, then let's see some proof of it."

"We did beat back two groups of brigands already," I pointed out.

"Piss-poor peasants with bad weapons and no discipline—barely covers your supper, if you ask me."

"We could beat up your men some more," Brasti offered helpfully.

"Just you go and try it, tatter-cloak," Kurg shouted. Kurg—Blackbeard—still hadn't quite found it in his heart to forgive me for the beating he'd taken at the caravan market.

"Shut your mouth," Feltock shouted back. "You'll do what you're damned well told. You're the last man should be bragging right about now. Got beat like a girl, you did!"

"See," I said to Kest, "it's not just me."

Kest ignored me. "There's a problem," he said.

I was about to ask what, but Brasti grabbed his longbow and slid off his horse. "I hear it, too," he said.

"What?" Feltock demanded. "What in all the hells are you talking about?"

I couldn't hear it either, but I'd learned to trust Kest and especially Brasti about these things.

"Men," Brasti said. "A dozen at least, and from the sounds of the horses, they've been riding hard."

"Arms up!" Feltock shouted. "Circle the damned wagons around the carriage and guard the Lady!"

"There's no time," I said. I could hear the horses now; they'd be here before we could rearrange the caravan.

"Damn trees," Feltock said. "Can't see far enough to watch for bandits, and the damned Caravan Council ain't got no protection on the roads since—" He realized what he was about to say and let it slide.

I didn't. "Since the Dukes killed our King and the Greatcoats were banned from protecting the trade roads?" I offered.

"Falcio," Kest said, pulling his sword from its sheath as the first of the horses came into view. "You're doing it again."

"Doing what?" I asked, just to annoy him. I drew my rapiers, but then I got a good look at the man in the lead. "Shit," I said.

Feltock and his two injured men had crossbows out, and the rest of the guards had their usual weapons. "What is it? Are there enough of them to take the caravan?" the captain asked, blinking furiously as he tried to squint the hundred yards between us and them. His vision obviously wasn't quite as good as it used to be—maybe that was why someone who had obviously been military was now reduced to guarding caravans.

"I don't think they're after the caravan," Kest said.

"Then what in all the hells are they after?"

The men dropped from their horses and came toward us in tight formation: thirteen men, with one in the lead.

"Drop your weapons, Trattari, and kneel on the ground," the one in front ordered. He was the only one of the group wearing armor—proper armor, mind you, not the kind of patchwork greaves and mismatched plates you might find on a jumped-up sergeant. This man was a Ducal Knight, probably a Knight-captain.

Now, you might be wondering what the differences are between a Knight and a Greatcoat, since we both apparently have at least some connection to the law and fighting. Well, there's the obvious part: they wear armor, and we wear our coats. They're suited for war, and we're suited for duels. Then there's the fact that they swear their oaths to a Duke or Duchess, while we swear ours to the King's Law—not the King himself, mind you. The Knights consider an oath to an idea to be no oath at all, and furthermore, the fact that we bow before no one in the course of our duty is, to them, an abomination. There are other differences, of course, but the most important one is that Knights are absolutely honorable and prize their honor above all things. Greatcoats, on the other hand, value justice, and tend to have a difficult time understanding how theft, rape, and murder all suddenly become honorable pursuits just because a man you swore an oath to asks you to commit them.

But being a Knight meant that this man knew how to fight, knew how to lead, and given how much he was probably looking for any excuse to rid the world of us, was someone we'd do well to deal with diplomatically.

"Fuck you, metal man," Brasti said casually, and let the aim of his bow slide casually toward the Knight's chest. The Knight's men pulled swords and three of them aimed crossbows right back at us. Those crossbows would make the odds a lot worse if we had to fight our way out. The Knight just smiled, which made him look more familiar to me somehow.

"Feltock, what's going on?" the Lady called out. "Why haven't you killed these bandits so that we can move on? I don't want to lose the light."

"Lady Caravaner," the Knight-captain began, keeping wonderful composure—Knights are very good at that, much like trained cats—"my name is Captain Lynniac. My men and I have been sent by Isault, Duke of Aramor, to arrest and prosecute these men as the murderers of your fellow Lord Caravaner, Lord Tremondi, and to retrieve the monies they stole from him."

"Prosecute" meant "kill on the spot without a trial," in case you're wondering. I thought Captain Lynniac looked a lot more interested in retrieving whatever money we were supposed to have stolen than in avenging Tremondi's murder.

"Well, he'll just have to wait. I need these men to help guard my caravan," she said lightly. "After we reach Hervor, I'll be sure to send them back, and you can prosecute them then."

The captain didn't appreciate her tone. "The Duke is sovereign in these lands, my Lady, and his orders are that these men lay down their weapons and come with us."

"No law makes a Duke sovereign of the roads," I said casually. It was one of those phrases I'd heard the Lords Caravaner use periodically, so I thought it might light a spark. "Furthermore, the likelihood that the Duke would pursue a crime perpetrated against Lord Tremondi—who, I should tell you, despised the Duke immensely—is about as low as the chance that you plan to let the caravan go along its merry way after you take us. What, pray tell, is the Duke's interest in this caravan?"

"Shut your mouth, tatter-cloak," the captain said, his voice tight with self-righteous fury. "My Lady," he began again, "it would ill suit your purposes, whatever they might be, to make an enemy of Duke Isault."

There was a pause. I had to admit that was a very good point, and a solid counter to my legal argument that they didn't actually have any jurisdiction over the caravan routes.

"Very well," the Lady said from her carriage. "Trattari, you are hereby ordered to lay down your weapons."

Well, now this was a bind. Brasti and Kest looked at me for instruction, but I wasn't sure what the right move would be.

Technically, we were the Lady's employees. If she told us to drop our weapons, we had to drop our weapons. Also, we were trapped between the men the Duke had sent to arrest us and the caravan guards, who hated us.

Captain Lynniac smiled. "Wise choice, my—"

"However," she continued, "Trattari, if you go with these men and abandon this caravan, I will consider you to have breached our contract and will ensure that the Caravan Council knows of your failure to fulfill your contract."

Brasti turned and stared at the closed carriage. "What? You're saying we have to lay down our weapons but not get arrested? What are we supposed to do—fight them bare-handed?"

"My Lady is wise and just," Captain Lynniac said.

"Of course, any of my men who wish to assist my tatter-cloaks are welcome to do so," she said, as if in passing.

Captain Lynniac's eyes darted to the rest of the caravan guards, but not one of them made a move. That just made him smile more. He really did look familiar when he did that. Where had I seen that smile?

"Well, boy," Feltock whispered in my ear, "there's a lesson in here somewhere. Can't tell you what it is, but I'm sure you'll figure it out eventually."

The captain's men laughed. Brasti looked confused. I tried desperately to think of a way out of this, and Kest just smiled, which only made things worse.

"Kest," I said slowly, "considering we are the very definition of damned if we do and damned if we don't, would you mind telling me why in the name of Saint Felsan-who-weighs-the-world you're smiling?"

"Because," he said, dropping his sword to the ground and unrolling the bottom of his coat sleeves, "now we get to play cuffs."

You have to understand how the sleeves of a greatcoat are constructed. The leather of the sleeve is itself quite formidable and can save you from a lot of damage. Oh, you could pierce it with an arrow if you get enough force behind it, but even a fairly sharp blade won't cut into it. But the cuffs at the end of the sleeve, those are something different. They contain two carefully carved bone pieces sewn into the leather itself. They can take a hit from just about anything—Kest believes that they could even block the ball from a pistol, but we haven't yet had occasion to test his theory.

There are occasions in the course of a traveling Magister's duties where he or she might not be able to draw a weapon, either because the physical space is too tight or because, for one reason or another, you don't actually want to carve up the person who is attacking you. For these situations, the King demanded that we be able to defend ourselves even if we were weaponless. So you unfold the cuffs of your coat and loop the leather strap attached to them to your two middle fingers. You now have a way of parrying swords, maces, or other weapons that might otherwise do you harm. That is, of course, if you move really, *really* fast and don't miss any of your blocks.

When we practiced fighting like this, which, thank Saint Gan-who-laughs-with-dice, we did a lot in the old days, we called it "playing cuffs."

"This isn't going to work, you know," I said to Kest as I flipped my cuffs over and pushed my fingers through the leather loops. "They're going to get smart and use those crossbows to pick us off at a distance."

"You'll figure something out," he replied.

"Figure it out soon," Brasti said. He was probably the best bowman in the civilized world, but he rarely won at cuffs. I was pretty good at it. Using rapiers as your primary weapon, you have to learn precision, and I was never much good with a shield, so cuffs wasn't a bad alternative.

But being good at cuffs wasn't a strategy. The first part would be easy enough—get them to fight us up close so that their friends with the crossbows couldn't get a clear shot. Even if we could hold them off, though, this Knight and his men would soon get tired of being made to look bad. If they couldn't get us with swords, eventually they'd just pull back and let the crossbowmen do the job. If only our "comrades" in the caravan guard had been better disposed toward us and kept their own crossbows on our opponents, we'd have stood a better chance. Unfortunately, just then they were rooting for the other guys.

"Is there a plan?" Brasti asked, looking at me. "Because if there's a plan, then I'd love to know what it is, and if there's not and I get killed going hand to sword with a bunch of Duke's men, then I may start to lose respect for you, Falcio."

I did have a plan. It might have sounded like a terrible plan at first hearing, but it really was not as bad as all that . . .

"Sir Knight, before we begin, may I say something?" I called out.

"Last words? Remarkably prescient for a dog."

"I just wanted to say that all Dukes are traitors, all Knights are liars, and the road belongs to no one but the caravans."

Captain Lynniac growled, and he and his men charged us.

Brasti said, "Please tell me that wasn't the entire plan?"

"Stop talking," I said, beating the first blade out of the way as they came upon us like a thunderstorm, "and start singing."

I took Lynniac's blade on my right cuff, using a tight circle to beat it out of the way as I sidestepped to my left. The secret to playing cuffs is that you have to pair every parry or sweep with a complementary movement of the feet; otherwise you're likely to end up with broken hands and wrists from the force of the blows.

The first man behind Lynniac tried a thrust to my midsection while the Knight himself tried to get his blade back in the air for a downstroke. I slid back to the right and let the thrust go right by me and kicked Lynniac in the chest before he could ready the blow. In my periphery, Brasti was using both hands in a downward block to counter a thrust from a war-sword. I could already hear Kest in my mind chastising Brasti for poor technique: you never want to use both hands to block a single weapon, as it leaves you vulnerable to the next man. I didn't bother checking on Kest because—well, he's Kest and that would just depress me. Instead I started the song, which, after all, was the core of my plan.

"A King can make all the laws he wants,

A Duke can rule all the land he wants,
A woman can rule my heart if she wants,
. . . but no man rules my caravan!"

The last line coincided nicely with my backhanding one of the soldiers in the jaw as his mace missed my shoulder in a failed downstroke. Unfortunately, no one joined me on the chorus.

"The Army can tax the cow in my barn,
The Duchy can tax the rest of my farm,
The landlord taxes my own left arm,
. . . but no man taxes my caravan!"

Kest and Brasti picked up the second verse with me. All Greatcoats learn to sing. In smaller towns and villages you often had to pass judgment by singing the verdict so that it would be easier for the townsfolk to remember. Brasti's voice was a classic baritone, well suited to songs like this one. Kest's voice would surprise you if you heard it—it was smooth and sweet and completely out of character. But their voices weren't the ones I needed.

One of the men with the crossbows tried to get a shot in, but I'd been waiting for just such an occasion. I was pushing off one man while another was trying to brain me with his mace, but that gave him a heavy-footed stance and by sidestepping the blow, I got on the other side of him in time for the crossbow bolt to take him square in the chest. I was starting to get a little winded, so I was glad that Kest and Brasti were holding up their end of the singing now.

"Beat me in a fight, well, I bet you can,
Cheat me at cards and I'll fall for your plan,
Take my own life if you think that you can—"

I let the dying man who'd been my shield slide down to the ground, only to see another soldier with a crossbow raising it toward me. I took a step to the right and raised my arms up to cover my face.

"—but you'll die long afore you touch my caravan!"

The crossbow bolt narrowly missed me, but fortunately, it didn't miss the man who had worked his way behind me. I suspected that

Captain Lynniac would be having a severe talk with his bowmen after this fight. Even better was the fact that I thought I might have heard someone from the caravan sing that last line with us.

But our time was running out. We'd taken out half of them, but that just left more openings for the crossbows. Brasti had some blood on his temple where he'd taken a glancing blow. Kest was doing all right holding off two men, but he was getting dangerously open, and if one of the men with crossbows saw the chance . . . To make things worse, the ground beneath our feet was turning into mud and muck and it wouldn't be long before one of us slipped or tripped over another man's body. And worst of all, we were running out of verses to the damned song.

"My Lord is the one what owns my land—"

I took down the man in front of me with a kick to his knee, followed by a strike to the side of his head. I saw that Kest had taken both his men down, but Brasti was struggling, swinging wildly to block the blows of the swordsman in front of him. He wasn't singing anymore.

"My Saint is the one what guides my hand—"

Captain Lynniac was stepping back from the fray and shouting to his men. Two of the men with crossbows were reloading, but the third was taking aim.

"My God knows I am his to command—"

At his shout the rest of the Knight's men pulled back and I saw Brasti looking around frantically for an opponent and not seeing the crossbow aimed squarely at his chest not twenty feet away. I tried to push past my own last men in a futile effort to get there in time. I could see Kest, not moving, his overly practical nature telling him there was no point. Brasti's head turned and saw the crossbow too late. His hands started to move reflexively to guard his face when a bolt appeared in the throat of the Knight's bowman.

There was a second of dead silence, and no one moved. Then I turned my head and looked behind me at a man in one of our wagons holding an empty crossbow. It was Blondie. "But my brother is the man who guards my caravan," he sang softly.

And that, I thought, is the old saying: "The song is swifter than the sword."

I turned back to the fight. Most of the captain's men were on the ground now. Two were still standing, but they were wary, and edging back. Lynniac himself was looking straight at me as he raised his right arm up in line with my gut. He had taken the cocked crossbow from his dead man. Knights don't normally use bows—they consider them coward's weapons. And knives are good enough for a soldier's need, perhaps, but not good enough for a Knight's honor. In my entire life I'd never seen a Knight who would even touch a crossbow. But Lynniac had lost a fight, and a Knight's sense of honor could not forgive that. He had watched his men beaten by outlaws he considered less than dogs, and without weapons. And apparently he had no more use for honor and he was going to put a bolt into me out of pure spite. He gave me something that was a cross between a snarl and a smile, and again that sense of familiarity flared.

Then he started to laugh, and suddenly made himself known to me.

I remembered that laugh. At first it was just the soft touch of a sour memory, but it quickly filled up my world until I couldn't really see Captain Lynniac, and I didn't see if the sword, which I had just grabbed off the ground and thrown at him like an amateur, had hit him or missed entirely, because all I could see were the five hundred Knights who'd come to Castle Aramor to depose King Paelis and outlaw the Greatcoats. I couldn't tell if the bolt that he had loosed had lightly grazed the side of my neck or if it was jammed in my throat, because all I could feel was the heat emanating from the burned wreckage of the King's library—the hundred ashen corpses of the texts that had meant so much to him. I couldn't tell if Kest's and Brasti's shouts were encouragement or a warning that someone else was behind me, because all I could hear was the laughter of the Ducal Knights as my King's head was jammed onto a pole and hoisted up atop Castle Aramor's parapet. *That laugh.* As impossible as it seemed,

Captain Lynniac's laugh was how I remembered him, and it was both the reason and the means for me to put him out of this world.

I can't explain what happened to me except to say that my anger gave way to a recklessness that felt like a soft, gray place of infinite indifference. The first time it had happened to me had been years ago, before I'd met the King, but there had been other incidents since then, and they came closer together now. Coming out of it was getting harder and harder too. That was why I was grateful, in a distant and uninterested way, when Kest struck me down with the pommel of one of the fallen Knight's swords.

7

BERSERKERS

I came to a little while later sitting at the base of a tree and staring at the bodies of Captain Lynniac and his men. How had they caught up with us so quickly? And more importantly, why had they bothered? Word of Tremondi's death couldn't have reached the market until after we'd already left—and even if it had, since when did Knights give a Saint's testicle about whether a Lord Caravaner lived or died? The only explanation was money: someone had told Captain Lynniac that we'd killed Tremondi and taken off with his money. It wasn't exactly a noble motive, but these weren't noble times and, no matter what the old songs say, Knights aren't noble people.

Blondie and the others were searching the corpses for coin and finding spare weapons where they could. I noticed that none of them tried to pocket what they found but set it out on a blanket that Feltock had laid out in the dirt. There was a fair amount of money there; the men had been well provisioned, probably from waylaying other caravans earlier in the week.

Feltock put the extra weapons in one of the wagons and divided the coin between his men. He came up to me and handed me a pouch. "Market rules. You fought, you feed, same as everyone else. I don't like Trattari much, but you did your jobs."

I waved him off. "Thanks, but I can't take it. We only take what we earn as pay. Give it to your rigger. He isn't healing well, and he's not being paid for this trip."

Trin overheard us and came forward. "Her Ladyship insists," she said. "You risk offending her if you refuse."

"In that case," I said, "we'll definitely pass."

Feltock shook his head and laughed. "Are you serious, man? I never took you for no monks."

Brasti grumbled from somewhere behind me, "Me neither."

"That's the way it goes," I said.

The captain must have taken some small liking to me, because he put a hand on my shoulder. "Listen, boy, you earned this and you take it. I've seen lots of Trattari in my time. Trust me, there's them that take what they can find and count themselves lucky for it. There are even some that have taken to robbing caravans."

"You're wrong," I said. "Greatcoats don't steal, not unless the King's Laws have been broken and the fine has to be collected, and then it's only from those who broke the law."

"Believe that if you want to," the captain said, "but you're lying to yourself if you do." He wandered off and I thought that was that, but a few moments later, he came back with three wineskins. "Here," he said, handing them to me. "It's just wine. I reckon you're still allowed to drink, right?"

I nodded gratefully. A good night of drinking would get the three of us back to right again, or as close to it as we got those days.

Feltock held up a finger. "Just promise me you won't be singing that damned song all night. Half the men are still humming that damned tune. Is that why they call you a Cantor of the Greatcoats?"

I grinned. "Go to any small village and try getting people to remember the details of how a particular law was applied in a particular case, and they won't remember it past the next night of drinking. In fact, the average person probably can't name a tenth of the laws that govern them. But give it to them in a song, and they'll remember it their whole lives. The drinking only helps."

"Well, that's as may be," Feltock said, scratching his head. "Seems to have worked on my men, anyway."

He tossed me a pair of coins. "It's this week's pay. And I'll give your share of the rest to Cheek—he's my spearman, the one you embarrassed at the market. It'll keep him from wanting to kill you in your sleep."

Comforting thought. I took the coins and wineskins over to Kest and Brasti and we set up camp for the night. The two of them were in an odd mood, so we didn't speak much at all.

I took first watch and drank a little of the wine to keep me warm. I was surprised when Feltock again sought me out, which was unusual; he didn't take a watch at night, as he had to be sharp all day.

"Seen anything?" he asked.

I shook my head and offered him a wineskin. He accepted it and took a swig, dribbling a bit down his chin. He looked as if he'd had some wine already.

"Lad," he began, "I need to talk to you about something. Now, I'm an old soldier, and I know how men fight. I know what they can do, and I don't bandy with false words. So I'll say it straight out. You're good fighters. Your man there with the bow is a devil, and the tall one is as fast with a blade as I've ever seen."

"And?" I asked.

"And you're the one what scares me," he said. He waved his hand before I could speak. "No, let me say it plain. You're a good man with the sword, and some Saint made you a damned good tactician. You kept the boys together in that first trouble even when they were acting fools, and you saved us a good deal of grief from this so-called Knight and his men." He motioned for the wineskin and took another swig before handing it back to me.

"I thought you said you were going to speak plainly," I said.

"I'm getting to it, just give me a chance." He sighed. "You're a good fighter, but I won't have no berserkers in my guard. I put up with a lot, Saints know I do, but I won't have that."

"Berserker? Me? Name your Saints and I'll swear by them: I'm no berserker."

He looked me straight in the eye. "I saw what you did to that great lout with the ax. I never wanted that bugger in my caravan, but her Ladyship overruled me then, just like she did with you. Truth be told, I never even got his name. But the way you went after him, boy, I never wanted to see that again."

I hadn't thought about the incident at the market since we'd left—I didn't really want to. The man was trying to kill me and he was wearing armor and I had no choice.

"Now don't go fooling yourself, lad," Feltock said. "I can see by the look on your face you're trying to write a story in your head, and I'm telling you it's false. You say you aren't a berserker, fine. Your friends swear up and down you aren't. But tell the truth now: you were growling and shouting nonsense at that man, and you sounded more than a little crazy in that market."

I thought about that for a moment, then I said, "No, Captain, trust me, that wasn't crazy. I've been crazy before, and that's not what it sounds like."

Feltock's mouth was open. "Saint Birgid-who-weeps-rivers, boy, what does it sound like then?"

"Quiet," I said. "Mostly very quiet."

He took another drink from the wineskin. "And that Knight, Lynniac? You ran straight for him like a madman—any man what knew how to hold a crossbow proper would've skewered you. Was that you being your own sane self?"

"No," I said, "that was my answer."

"Your answer for what?"

I looked out at the night sky and the stars that winked at us as if they were all in on some great joke. "Five years ago, after the Ducal Army took Castle Aramor, they killed our King and hauled his corpse up to the top of the castle. They mounted his head on a pike. Some men cheered, some men looked away." I took another swig of my wine. "And some men just laughed."

"So Lynniac was there, was he?"

"Lynniac was there," I said. "Commander of a division of Knights. I didn't recognize him at first, but when he was pointing that crossbow at me and he started laughing . . ."

Feltock bit the inside of his cheek. Then he said, "And you think you remember everyone who was there that day?"

I thought about it for a moment. "Not everyone," I replied. Feltock was looking at me intently, trying to see if I knew, if I did remember. *More trouble than it will be worth*, I thought, but I was a little drunk and a little tired so I said, "But since you're asking, yes, General Feltock, I remember you."

Feltock's eyes went wide for a moment, but then he gave a bitter laugh. "Not 'General,'" he said. "Not for a few years now."

We drank some more in silence.

"So," he said, uncrossing his legs with a crack. "Are you gonna come for me next, boy?"

I sighed. "No."

"Why not? I was there, wasn't I? I was one of those what took down your King, wasn't I? So what's the difference between me and Lynniac?"

"You didn't laugh."

He just looked at me for a while and then said, "Huh." Then he stood up and started walking back to the wagons.

"Why 'Captain' Feltock?" I asked when he was a few paces away. "Why aren't you a general anymore?"

Feltock turned and gave me a sour grin. He tossed the rest of his wineskin back to me. "Because, boy, when they put the King's head on that pole, I forgot to laugh."

8

TO MURDER A KING

I can't say for certain what happened after I found Aline in that tavern. I remember some of it—fragments, pieces of eggshell that I put together in my mind. But the shapes they form are never quite right. I know I stood there for a long time. I think I may have buried her out back, though I can't be sure.

There was a tavern master there and, though I don't remember him talking to me, oddly, I can remember things he said. He told me he tried to stop them, and I had no reason not to believe him except that he was still alive. He told me his own daughter had been killed too, when she started screaming too loud. But I didn't see his daughter's body anywhere around. I'm not sure if I killed the tavern master or not. It's hard to say. There were so many people to kill, after all. I think I asked him where Castle Aramor was, and he told me it was four days' ride south. But I didn't have a horse, so there was no easy way for me to get there. But I wasn't thinking about horses or travel. I wasn't thinking about anything except that it was very important to me to go to Castle Aramor and kill the King. I would have to kill the Duke, too, obviously, and all his men, and definitely Fost with the ax. But the King had to come first and, after all, I wasn't likely to forget the rest of them.

I remember it was night when I left the tavern. Having no horse or money, I just started walking south. I don't think I was going all that fast, but I did just keep going. I walked and walked, and when I couldn't walk anymore, I would just fall by the side of the road and sleep. Then I would walk again. I must have eaten at some point, because four days' ride is at least twenty by foot, but I don't remember that. I think I was attacked once or twice, but I couldn't afford the delay so I killed them and moved on. It had to have been twenty days, but I only ever remember the nights.

Sometimes Aline would talk to me. She would tell me to stop and rest. She would say that if she just spread her legs for the Duke and his men one more time, they would leave us in peace and we would grow old together and laugh about it. I think history has proved her wrong on that point, but when she said it I laughed anyway, just to see what it would feel like. Sometimes Aline would tell me I had just killed someone and it wasn't going to bring her back to life, and I would ask her if, now that he was dead, she was going to bed him in the Afterlife. That wasn't a very nice thing to say, but I wasn't thinking very clearly and I was just imagining her anyway.

So I kept walking. I must have encountered the Duke somewhere on the road because I was carrying a sack with me and his head was in it. I wondered how I had got past his men, but perhaps I had found him in an inn somewhere and killed him while they slept. I seemed to be pretty cunning then.

At one point there was an old lady who gave me something to eat. I didn't have anything to give her in return, and when I offered her the Duke's head, she told me to put it back in the bag, and we went outside together and buried it in her garden. She gave me more to eat then, and we put some food in a bag that I took with me.

Sometimes I wonder if some of the things I remember really happened at all. It seems unlikely that I would have run into the Duke on the South Road, and even less likely that I would have managed to cut off his head without anyone noticing. And the truth is, I don't kill people very often, even when I'm angry. And Aline—she's never talked to me since, so either I imagined that part or else I said something very bad and she's still mad at me.

So I walked on, southward, to Castle Aramor, where the King lived—at least for a little while longer. Sometimes it rained and sometimes it didn't. The distinction didn't feel very important anymore. I didn't really talk to anyone I encountered, except for the old woman, but she did most of the talking anyway. So I suppose that's why, by the time I reached Castle Aramor and started my long, slow climb up the tunnel that carried away human waste and animal carcasses, I hadn't heard that the King was already dead. It wouldn't have mattered much if I had: there would always be a new King, and that one would need to be killed too.

The first thing I noticed was that he wasn't as big as I'd remembered. In fact, he was just about the scrawniest individual I'd ever seen. And his hair was all wrong. King Greggor had short gray hair in a military cut. This man had long, stringy brown hair beneath a slight, ill-fitting crown. And he smelled bad, which is saying something, since I had spent the better part of a day clawing my way up a narrow stone tunnel that carried refuse and human waste from Castle Aramor down to the gully that might once have been part of an effort to dig a moat.

No, this man was all wrong. But he was kneeling before me and I did have my sword resting on his neck and in a moment his head would go flying across the room and hit the wall with a pleasant *thunk*. I was looking forward to that *thunk*. I had dreamed about it through the endless miles and rain that had brought me here, on foot and half-dead.

The man was about to say something, but then a small coughing fit overtook him and I felt it polite to wait a moment, since he looked rather undernourished and no doubt had a nasty cold. I also didn't want any noise when I took his head off.

A moment later, the coughing stopped. "Before you kill me, would it be inappropriate to ask a question?" His voice was thin and wheezy, and to my ears sounded half-calm and half-crazy, but I was a poor judge, being completely crazy myself at the time.

"You want to know why I'm going to kill you?" I asked.

"No, I already know that," he said. "I was just wondering why you brought me here in the first place."

I was confused by the question, and I really didn't have much time for confusion, since soon enough someone would decide to follow the trail of filth I had left behind me to the King's chamber. So I decided to cut off his head and bring it with me and we could discuss the situation on my way home.

"What I mean is," he said, interrupting my train of thought, "if my father had wanted me dead so that Dergot could become King, why go through all the trouble of having me brought here?"

"You're stupid," I said. "I have to kill King Greggor. You're in his room and you're wearing a crown. And I have this sword with me and the bag that the old woman gave me with food but the food's all gone so now I need to put something in the bag and—"

"You have reason to hate King Greggor?"

"I do," I said. And then, if only because I had rehearsed it in my mind and it felt wrong not to tell someone, I recited the entire speech I had planned for the King, about what he had done to Aline and my life, and how the Duke, though he definitely deserved to die, would probably have let us alone if not for the King, and how I was going to kill him now and no God would embrace him or speak his name, and how I would make sure that his reign wouldn't be remembered for anything but the fact that one night a filthy peasant had sneaked into his room and murdered him.

I had worked it out on the road, and it was short and not too badly composed, I thought, but then I kept going, and I talked about the walking and the rain and the men who had tried to kill me and the Duke's head, which was now buried in an old woman's garden. I talked about what it felt like to not be a human being anymore, not really, and to finally climb up a river of shit to kill a man who needed killing more than any other man who had ever lived, only to find that he'd been replaced by a scrawny man who said stupid things.

I told him all that and he just sat there on his knees and listened. And when I was done he asked, "Are you still going to kill me?"

I thought about it for a moment. "It's really all I can think of doing right now."

"Can I tell you who I am first?" he asked.

"If I listen will you promise to stop talking so I can hear the *thunk* when your head hits the wall?"

The scrawny man thought about that for a moment. "Marked," he said.

"What's your name?" I asked.

"Paelis," he said. "Paelis the Pathetic, twenty-two years of age, son and greatest disappointment of King Greggor and Queen Yesa. Deemed lacking in physical and moral fortitude and therefore removed by royal decree as first heir to the throne in favor of his three-year-old brother, Dergot, who, as it turns out, fell out of a window when no one was watching him, some two hours after the King died yesterday."

The scrawny man started coughing again and I wondered if his head would still cough once it was separated from his body. After a moment, he stopped coughing and went on, "Since the day, three years ago, my father finally managed to pull another son out of my stepmother's womb, he has kept me locked in a tower with no warmth, little food, and only as much water as leaked through the roof to drink. He waited for me to waste away and die, for no other reason than that my words displeased him. He didn't want the Saints' curse for spilling royal blood.

"You are not the first man whose life was destroyed by King Greggor. You say your grief is worse than mine, and I accept that. You say you want to see his reign forgotten for all time? I say, I am your man. I have spent every day of my life dreaming—no, more than dreaming, *planning*—a way to rid this world of my father's benighted touch. You want his kingdom destroyed? Then I say again: I am your man."

"I am your man." It was the first time in my life that anyone had ever sought to put themselves beneath me, and it had come from a

King. I thought about what he'd said and about what I would do next and I said something, but I don't remember what it was because that was when the crossbow bolt hit me in the back.

I awoke to the sound of what I thought was my mother's sewing. She liked to use a stiff, strong needle and thick thread when she worked, and the soft pop of the needle through the fabric was inevitably followed by the snaking sound of the thread being pulled. I tried to stay in that moment as long as I could, but even hazy as I was I remembered that my mother was several years dead, that I was a twenty-year-old man, and that I had tried to murder a King.

"You may as well open your eyes," a woman's voice said, and when I did as she asked I saw an old woman sitting on a chair near my bed, sewing blue fabric with gold thread.

"I've seen you before," I said.

She nodded, but kept on sewing.

"In the cottage by the South Road. We—did we bury a head in your garden?" I asked.

She snorted. "Probably best not to talk about that now, I'd say."

I looked around the room. It looked like the same room where I'd tried to kill the King. In fact, I was almost certain it was.

"I'm in his room," I said to her.

"The maids tell me he wouldn't let them move you. Figured you wouldn't survive it, what with your wounds and all."

"I heard someone fire a crossbow. I think they hit me in the back," I said stupidly.

"The bolt? Sweet ugly Saints, boy, you were bleeding from a dozen festering wounds by the time they found you. I think they only kept you alive to figure out which God made that deal with you."

Death. Love abandoned me and so I made my deal with Death.

"Are you a seamstress?" I asked.

She wrinkled her nose. "Seamstress is what you call the person who fixes your dress, boy. I'm a tailor. The last real tailor, in fact."

I had the feeling that it would be impolite to inform her that every city in the world had a dozen tailors. "Fine, a tailor then. What are you doing here?" I asked.

She didn't bother looking up this time. "Well, a good tailor knows which way the threads are moving. After you left, I thought about it for a while and reckoned they might have need of my skills here."

"The King doesn't have his own tailors?" I asked.

She looked at me as if I was an idiot. Which is fair, I suppose. "I told you, boy, there ain't any other tailors left. Besides, there ain't no one else knows how to sew what I'm making."

"Which is?"

Someone knocked at the door and I thought the woman would say something, but she just kept sewing. After a moment the knocking repeated.

"It's your damned bedroom," the woman called out. "Whose damned permission are you waiting for?"

The door opened and the man from the night before—the King, I guess—entered the room. "Now if only I could get all my loyal subjects to treat me with such respect," he said jovially. "Most of the ones I encounter just want to kill me."

He had changed his clothes and bathed and looked a lot more kingly to my eyes. He looked like he'd eaten better, too. That thought woke me up. "How long have I been unconscious?" I asked.

"You've been mostly dead for twelve days," the King said.

"*Twelve days?* How is that possible?"

He coughed a bit and then walked over and sat on the edge of the bed, which struck me as rude, but then I remembered it was technically his bed.

"You were in Death's embrace, remember? You hadn't slept for Saints know how long and you probably hadn't eaten for a week."

I was feeling irritated now, which told me I still wasn't quite right in the head. "So how come I didn't die of hunger if I've been unconscious for the past twelve days?"

The Tailor warned me off. "Best not to ask. It wasn't very pretty. Involved a cloth tube and some sticks."

The King ignored her. "Don't worry, my strange friend. You had the best of care." The Tailor snorted but the King went on, "I took care of you myself, with the help of the royal doctors."

I found that hard to believe. "You took care of me *yourself*? Washed my wounds and changed my sheets?"

"And wiped your ass," the Tailor chimed in happily.

"Well," the King said, "it was only fair. It was my man who shot you in the back, so I thought it a fair trade. The world should be fair, you know."

The world should be fair. For some reason that started me laughing and I thought about all the things that had happened and I just kept laughing over and over, and then suddenly the laughter turned to something else and I heard great wracking sobs pouring from my mouth and my eyes were bleeding tears and I swear I thought I would drown in them because for some reason I just couldn't stop.

The King whispered in the Tailor's ear and she got up and left, and then he did something very strange. He reached over and took my head in both his hands, just the way Aline sometimes did when she needed me to listen, the way she had done that day at the cottage. And the King said this: "A wise man would tell you she's gone, friend, and that you must let her go because nothing will ever bring her back. But I'm not a wise man—not yet, anyway. So I promise you this: I will bring her to you. I swear to you, friend, that someday, somehow, through whatever influence a King may have on Gods and Saints, I will bring her back to you. They say everyone faces Death alone, but I will break that law if that's what it takes." He let go of my head and his hands dropped to his sides.

He coughed and wiped something from his mouth. "But not today. Today, I need your help. I need to change the world, because the world won't last the way it is much longer. I can do this—I know in my heart and in my mind that I can do this, but I need someone like you. I need someone who can walk for twenty days and nights and fight through every hell on earth to get justice—but not just justice for himself, justice for others." He let the words hang there for just a moment before he said, "I will bring you to your wife one day, but today I need you to bring justice to my people."

He sat back and his shoulders hunched and he was the weak, skinny man I'd almost killed once again. I had stopped crying, though I knew I would start again soon. This little King was mad, as mad as I was, but there was nothing else left. I knew what he said was true. Even the Gods, as feckless and fickle as they were, would not long suffer a world of King Greggors and Duke Yereds to survive.

"I'm not ready," I said.

"You have to be. It has to start now."

I choked on my own spit for a second. When they take the last good thing from your life, how do you answer?

"How does it begin?" I asked.

The King got this little smile on his face, small, almost unnoticeable. I would learn this was one of his most defining characteristics. "What's your name?" he asked.

"Falcio," I said. "Falcio val Mond."

"Falcio," he began, "when you were a boy, did anyone ever tell you stories about the Greatcoats?"

9

THE GATES OF RIJOU

"And I swear to you, your Ladyship, you don't want any part of Rijou," I shouted back. "They don't call it the City of Strife for nothing."

The voice in the carriage was even, but I could hear an edge of anger as she said, "And I have told you, my tatter-cloak, that we have business with Jillard, Duke of Rijou, and we will enter the city tonight."

"My Lady . . . he's not completely wrong about this." Even Feltock was with me on this one, and he *never* contradicted the Lady. Rijou was a city with nineteen noble houses, all of which fought with each other in endless cycles of intrigues, assassinations, and occasionally outright war. The Duke of Rijou did nothing to stop the violence and everything to encourage it, not least because the murders kept those vying for his position in check and the wars kept their private armies small and manageable.

But, for everyone else, Rijou was an awful place. From a distance it gleamed. I don't mean it shimmered, nor did it shine; it gleamed, the gleam of oily skin on a corpse, or the gleam in the eye of a man who fancies he can kill you without consequence. The city might be rich and opulent, but it was treacherous for anyone without a sheriff in their pocket and an army at their back. In Rijou there was nothing to stop a landlord from changing the terms of a lease anytime he wanted, so long as he could get authorization from the sheriff. The King had sent Brasti and me there once to hear a jeweler's dispute with his noble landlord. In this case the landlord had changed the terms to allow himself to set the jeweler's prices. We heard the case and passed judgment in the jeweler's favor, only to find him dead the next morning. The Duke paid the fine without question, and the smile on his face told us we were welcome back any time we wanted to see someone else killed. I had sworn then that one day I would come back and bring justice to this shithole. But I had failed in that, as I had in so many things since. How much justice could I hope to bring to an entire city if I couldn't even keep one old man alive?

"My Lady," I tried one last time, "no one can promise to protect you once we are inside the city gates."

"Nonsense," she said. "We have ten good men with us and you've done an admirable job so far of fighting off brigands."

"But you see, we can't take the whole caravan into the city. The Duke's men won't allow it. And if you try to enter with more than two or three men-at-arms, someone will think you're starting a house war and you'll be killed."

I waited as she considered this behind her curtains. Finally she said, "Very well then. Feltock, take this tatter-cloak and two others and follow my carriage into town so that I may conduct my business with the Duke."

It was my turn to pause as I tried to find the right words. "My Lady, it's unlikely the Duke will agree to see you. I have no doubt that in your home of Orison you are a person of great consequence, but in Rijou you will be nothing more than another target."

"Nothing more?" she said from behind the curtains of the carriage. The tone of her voice didn't bode well for me. "Feltock?" she asked after a moment. "Tell your pistolman to put a steel ball in that man's head if he does not immediately mount his horse and lead us down into the city."

Feltock didn't hesitate to signal the little man who carried the pistol. He turned to see what I would do. He liked me better these days, and he probably agreed with me about Rijou, but he was a military man and he followed the orders he was given.

Kest was standing by my left shoulder. I couldn't see Brasti, so I assumed that he had hidden himself, his bow at the ready, behind one of the trees that lined the road into the city.

"I think I might be able to stop the ball from the pistol," Kest said matter-of-factly. "Using the angle of the barrel, I should be able to figure out roughly where the ball should hit."

"Roughly?" I asked.

"It's never been done before. You've got to take a few chances with this kind of thing."

"For what it's worth, my advice is let's not die right now and save that idea for another day," I said, and mounted up on my horse.

I looked around and saw Brasti resting on top of some blankets on one of the open wagons.

"That's some fine cover you were giving me there, Brasti."

He yawned and patted the bow that rested against his leg. He had ten arrows arrayed in front of him, so I suppose I should have been grateful for that.

"I have every confidence in your diplomatic skills," he said, "especially when it involves following orders. But you're crazy if you think going back into Rijou is better than trying to parry pistols. Don't worry. I'll stay here and guard the caravan."

"Get off your ass, boy, you're comin' with us," Feltock growled. "Since you all appear to know so much about it, I'm sure you'll do a fine job of guarding the Lady's dignity along with your own skins."

"The three of us could always kill you and leave once we're away from the rest of the caravan, you realize," Kest said.

"True," Feltock said. Then he started laughing. "But then you'd still have no money and no employer and, from what little I've heard, Duke Jillard don't waste a lot of sentiment on tatter-cloaks now, does he?"

"I may just kill you on principle if you keep calling us that," I said, but Kest, Brasti, Feltock, and I led the carriage along the wide, tree-lined avenue that leads from the caravan route, past the first gates, and into the city proper. Rijou isn't exactly a fortress town, but it does have three sets of iron gates. The first we passed through looked unguarded, but the trees that grew alongside the road provided excellent hiding places for the half a dozen guards with crossbows. If you don't look suspicious enough to be shot on sight and no one has paid the guards to kill you, you can carry on to the second gates, where the men are armored and the gates run on a sliding track between stone pillars. When the lever is pulled, the gates can come down in a second, instantly impaling anything caught in their way. The guards of the second gate have this great joke: you don't need to ask permission to enter Rijou; you just walk under the gate. If they decide to drop it on your head, that means admission is denied and you should come back tomorrow and try again. Well, it makes them laugh . . .

Feltock didn't favor that approach. Instead, he handed one of the guards the packet of credentials he carried on the Lady's behalf. The guard looked them over and then passed them on to another man, who scrutinized them more closely. The first guard walked up to us and stared me up and down. He was a younger man, with dark hair and a short, sparse beard that didn't favor him. But he carried himself confidently, and looked like he must be solid under his plate armor.

"You're one of them tatter-cloaks, is that right?" His accent was thicker than I had expected. It reminded me that the three weeks we had been on the road had taken us far from the caravan market, and even farther from Baern, where we should have been by now.

"We don't use the term, but yes, that's right."

The guard stared at my coat and then reached out casually and pulled at a piece of it, examining it closely. A few of his buddies were gathering around us. "Is it true then that you sleep in them coats?" He turned to his fellow guards. "Sure smells like it!"

Now the fact is, the greatcoat is the single most valuable thing a traveling Magister owns. It's made of leather, but the thin, very light plates made from some kind of bone and sewn into different panels can ward off the occasional blow—if you're lucky, even a knife thrust in the back from some disgruntled plaintiff. And it can keep you alive if you're stranded on the road in the cold.

"And is it true," the guard went on, "that you hide a hundred weapons in those coats?"

According to the stories, there were more hidden pockets in my coat than even I had ever been able to find. No one is entirely sure how they're made, because there was only ever one Tailor of the Greatcoats and no one knows what happened to her after the King died.

"No," I answered, "but I do keep a hundred chickens in my coat."

Brasti spoke up. "I keep a hundred fish in mine. I don't eat chicken."

The other guards laughed at that, but we had stepped on the first one's effort at a joke.

"Well, maybe I should take me both of them coats, then. I like chicken and fish."

"Only one problem with that, friend," I said calmly.

He looked at his fellow guards and then at me. "Yeah? What's that?"

"Well, if you had my coat, you'd have to wear it."

The rest of the guards broke out laughing again and the first one decided he'd had enough. "Damned right. But if I did want it, you'd hand it over quick enough, that's for sure."

It was an idle threat—not because everyone knew there were more than a few weapons hidden inside our coats, but because no one has ever stolen a Magister's greatcoat. In the old days, when we were admired, everyone knew that a man or woman who managed to take one from a Magister would be hunted down to the ends of the earth. Nowadays, no one wanted to be seen dead with one. So fame and infamy really weren't that different after all.

Eventually his commander let us through and we wound our way to the third gate. There are no armored guards at the third gate, no crossbows, arrows, pikes, or swords, just a small man with a quill and journal who sits at a small desk at the end of a thirty-foot-long tunnel. The ceiling is about twelve feet high, and both walls and ceiling are peppered with dozens of small holes and slots. The whole thing might look like it's made from gray cheese, but everyone knows that if you irritate the little man at the desk, you will very quickly discover that there are a remarkable number of deadly things that can be shot, dropped, or poured out of small holes in the stone.

Feltock handed over the same credentials he had shown at the second gate. The little man barely looked at them before he said, "Denied."

Feltock stepped down from his seat at the front of the carriage and looked at me with raised eyebrows. Neither one of us knew what to do. We both knew for certain that arguing with the little man would be a grave mistake.

"With respect, your Lordship," Feltock began.

"Not a Lord. I'm a clerk," said the man behind the desk.

"With respect, your—ah, clerkship, they . . . Well, they accepted our credentials at the second gate."

The clerk looked up at us. "Of course they did, you idiot, otherwise you wouldn't be here. You'd have steel bars going through your skulls. If it makes you feel better, you can go back and I'll pass a message down for them to drop the gate on you."

Brasti smiled at me. "I like him. He reminds me of you."

The look Feltock shot us was half-threatening and half-pleading.

"Right Honorable Clerk of the Gate," I began, using his formal title, "although there is no requirement of you to tell us, might we inquire the reason for your very reasonable decision to bar us from the city? Can I assume that we are 'of person but not purpose'?"

The clerk snorted. "Hah! Trattari, eh? You can always count on a Greatcoat to parrot the laws back to you. Yes, you are indeed 'of person but not purpose.' So you can turn yourself around or we can see what this lever does." He motioned to a stout piece of wood inset into the stone wall by his desk. I already had a suspicion as to what the lever did, and I had no intention of being there to see what exactly would drop on my head from the ceiling if he pulled it.

"Feltock," the Lady's voice called from the carriage, "what is the reason for our delay in this dank little cavern?"

Feltock looked at me. "You better tell her," he whispered. "I don't know what all this business of 'persons' and 'purposes' is about."

I walked back to the carriage. "My Lady, the clerk informs us that your credentials of person, that is, *who* you are, are fine for entering the city. It is the credentials of purpose, the reason *why* you are asking to enter, that are being disputed."

"*Disputed?* I'm coming to see the Duke! Who is this little worm who questions me?"

I prayed that the clerk couldn't hear us.

"I heard that," he shouted back. Then he hopped off his chair and half-waddled toward us. He came to a stop in front of the curtains. "You go home now," he said in a tone suggesting she was a half-witted child. "Crazy Lady no see Duke today. Duke important man. Has important things to do. Hump Crazy Lady some other day."

Then the clerk smiled and looked up at me. "I like you, Trattari. You know the law and that makes me happy. But either you turn her around, or in about ten seconds you're going to discover which hurts worse—burning oil on your head or a dozen crossbow bolts in your chest."

"It's the oil," Kest said.

"Enough!" her Ladyship shouted from the carriage. I had never heard her shout before. She sounded almost childish. "You will admit me to the city this instant. You will signal ahead for an escort, and you will ensure we have the smoothest of journeys to the Ducal Palace."

The clerk looked like he was about to signal to someone I couldn't see when the curtains of the carriage drew apart and the Lady emerged.

I confess I'd had a small fantasy that the Lady Caravaner was actually Trin in disguise. After all, we saw a lot of Trin going into and out of the carriage, but we never saw the Lady herself. Trin, though she lacked the demeanor, certainly had the looks and grace for the daughter of a noble house. More importantly, it would have been nice to think that the woman in charge of this emerging disaster was actually capable of being sweet, even if only as part of some kind of elaborate game.

The woman who exited the carriage wore several different shades of purple. Her silk blouse was fashionably low and her silk pants were cut for travel. Her head was uncovered, but she wore a necklace and bracelets of cut gems, and rings sparkled from the middle fingers of each hand. Her hair was a rich shade of dark brown and almost as silky as her clothes, which surprised me because even inside a carriage it's hard not to get messy traveling for weeks on end. For a brief moment I thought it might indeed have been Trin, emerging triumphant from her cocoon, but this woman was taller and more assured, and besides, Trin herself came out of the carriage behind her. Oh well, so much for that fantasy.

It occurred to me that the Lady must have been very careful to ensure that her men—or most of them, at least—never saw her. Feltock didn't look especially shocked, so I assume he had, but none of us had seen her even once in all the weeks we had been on the road. We certainly wouldn't have forgotten, for she was a stunning beauty, with bright ocean-colored eyes and delicate features. She saw me staring and smiled, and for some strange reason it hurt me more than she could possibly have intended. I looked at Kest and saw that even he was overtaken for the moment.

The clerk wasn't. "Yes, dear, you're quite pretty, and I imagine you're very rich. But the Duke is pretty too, and probably a lot richer, so you still can't see him."

"And why not, little man?" Her voice sounded the same but now I could hear that it was younger than I had previously thought.

"Well," said the clerk, "because you kind of look like a whore and the Duke is a married man with several important mistresses and we wouldn't want to offend any of them, would we?"

I expected the Lady to launch into a tirade at that point, but instead she calmly held out her hands, clenched into fists, in front of the clerk's face. "Little man, look closely at my rings."

The clerk did so, and then he looked as if he'd seen the end of his life, right there in front of him. "Damn me," he said.

I stepped behind him and got a look at the rings just before she pulled them back and crossed her arms in front of her. The ring on the left was the Ducal ring of Hervor, meaning her mother wasn't the Duchess of Orison, as we had suspected, but was in fact Patriana, Duchess of Hervor.

"Damn hells," Kest said. It was unusual for him to swear, but I echoed the sentiment. Patriana was the worst of the nobles; it was she who had put the spine into the other Dukes and persuaded them to move on King Paelis. I could have slit her daughter's throat right then with less regret than I had for the axman in the market.

"Hervor," I said to Kest, who was shaking his head.

"No, you don't understand. The other ring: it's the Ducal ring for Rijou. She's claiming to be the daughter of Patriana, Duchess of Hervor, *and* Jillard, Duke of Rijou. She's claiming transcendent blood!"

The Lady smiled at us, then back at the clerk. "Do my 'credentials' satisfy you now, little man?"

The clerk sputtered for a moment. "Well, that is—I mean, I cannot verify—that is to say . . . Welcome, welcome to Rijou, your, ah, Ladyship."

"Highness," she said. "The term you are groping so ineffectually for is 'your Highness.' Or if you prefer, your Royal Highness Princess Valiana."

The clerk bent down to one knee. Feltock, who didn't look at all surprised, did the same, as did Trin. Kest, Brasti, and I stayed standing. By King's Law, Greatcoats bowed before no one, not even the King himself. And besides that, I was probably going to kill her.

Despite my prejudice against the place, Rijou is really a very beautiful city at twilight, if you can forget where you are for just a moment.

The Clerk of the Gate had sent word for one of the Duke's advisers, and a man named Shiballe arrived to escort us into the city. Shiballe was overfed and too well dressed for a messenger, but it wasn't really my problem at this point. The worst he could do would be to assassinate Valiana, which might not be such a bad thing.

When Shiballe kissed her hand, the Lady looked at me and smiled as if this were all a grand joke she'd played on me personally, as if I should somehow be stunned senseless by her cleverness. That itself would have been enough to make me dislike her, not to mention the fact that her mother was the bitch who helped kill my King. But for some reason what offended me most was watching Trin humble herself, walking three feet behind her mistress, as docile as a lamb off to be sheared. If we did decide to go back on every vow we'd ever taken and kill Valiana, we'd have to kill Feltock first—that wouldn't be such a hard thing to do; the man was a soldier and he'd made his own bed. Trin would die too, though, before letting anyone touch Valiana, and that was just a shame. When Shiballe kissed Trin's hand, she looked as if a horse had just shat on it, which only served to make me like her more.

The Lady stopped for refreshment with Shiballe. Feltock and Brasti stood guard while Kest and I were sent to scout the rest of the way. I took the opportunity to enjoy the city between sunset and moonrise: twilight in Rijou is quite possibly the only time when, for reasons only the Saints know, the nobles of the city don't feel the same need to murder their fellow citizens. Unfortunately, we weren't fellow citizens.

"We have to do this, Falcio," Kest said for the hundredth time. He rarely repeats himself because he eventually just does whatever it is he thinks needs doing and deals with the consequences later, so I had to assume he wasn't trying to change my mind so much as ease me toward the inevitable conclusion. "You know this is what they've been planning while we've been fumbling around the country," he went on. "To set up a new monarchy—one completely controlled by the Dukes, so they never have to fear the rise of a new King like Paelis."

"The Dukes run everything as it is," I said. "So what's the difference?"

"The difference is that their rule will be entrenched across the entire country, not just in their individual Duchies anymore."

"Look around," I said. "The world has become as corrupt and oppressive as any of us could ever have imagined."

"Yes, and if we let them sit this girl on the throne it will get *much* worse. As bad as they are right now, the Dukes still shy away from actively breaking King's Law. They know it would put them in jeopardy if a strong, decent Duke comes to power or, Saints hope, a new King rises. But if we let them get away with this, then the most self-serving, oppressive rule in our history will become law. King's Law, Falcio."

"If it goes that way then we'll fight, won't we? And we'll win—we always win in the end."

"Don't make Brasti right about you," Kest said. "You know as well as I do that there aren't that many of us left. We were a hundred and forty-four at our peak and now we're fair game for anyone with a blade. I doubt there are still fifty Greatcoats left. And who knows what most of them have turned into? I can beat anyone with a sword, Falcio, but I can't beat ten men with pistols. The old rules won't work for us. We can win the fight, but I don't think we can win fair."

I stopped my horse for a moment. "You want to pass judgment before she's even committed a crime. The King never would have allowed that. It would have destroyed him. It would destroy us."

"What about Tremondi?" he asked.

"Tremondi? What's she got to do with him?"

Kest sighed. "You really haven't figured it out?"

"Pretend I haven't."

Kest pointed at the carriage. "We know Tremondi was having an affair with the woman who killed him. Who fits the old pervert's tastes? Valiana does. Who benefits by his death? She does. Who, when we appeared at the market in Solat, managed to find a way to both keep us on a short leash and to ensure the rest of the caravan guards hated us? It was her, with that challenge she put you up to."

"Which you made me accept," I said.

"Nothing gets by you, Falcio, except for the damned obvious. Almost as soon as we left the caravan, once we were away from the city and anyone who might have believed our story, Lynniac and his Knights show up—and what does she do? She makes us fight them bare-handed."

"She could have just let them take us."

"No—too much chance we might've escaped on the road. This way she'd know for sure we were dead. It's *her*, Falcio. She's the one who killed Tremondi. If it wasn't for the aeltheca she hit us with, we'd be able to identify her. But it's likely that she kept hidden from us as long as necessary to make sure any partial recollection we might have had would be well and truly gone by the time we saw her."

I had nothing to counter with. Everything Kest said made perfect sense. We'd probably convicted men on lesser proof—Saints know the Dukes would have convicted us on less. But we were supposed to be *different*. We were supposed to be *better*.

"It's all right, Falcio," Kest said quietly. "I know you can't do it. I'm not asking you to."

"Do what? Commit murder?"

"Set things right. But I'll do it. I can do this by myself, when the time is right, when we can be sure. But for the sake of our friendship, don't try to stop me when it happens."

I stared at him. "What kind of friendship will we have then?"

"The same kind we had before we became Greatcoats. I know you loved the King, Falcio. I did too. But they killed him. They can't kill his dream, too."

No, I thought as I pushed my horse forward, *they can't. We're doing that ourselves.*

Half an hour later I signaled a stop to the carriage. A group of men in black uniforms were surrounding a large mansion. They had pikes in hand and were blocking the windows and doors with great slabs of stone that were arriving on oxcarts. There was also a wagon filled with casks.

I motioned to Feltock to come forward and asked, "Do you have any idea what's going on?"

"You've seen what a war looks like, haven't you?" said the captain.

I ignored him and dismounted. I walked over to the man driving the wagon with the casks. Two of his fellows stood in front of me with shortswords in hand, but I called out to him, "What's going on here?"

"What do you think is going on, man? Come midnight it'll be the first day of Ganath Kalila, so keep to your own affairs if you don't want to find yourself on the wrong side."

That was strange. It almost sounded as if the man had said "Ganath Kalila." But of course that couldn't be possible, because if it turned out we were here during Ganath Kalila I would simply have to concede that at this very moment a thousand virgin brides were cursing my name . . .

"Sorry," I said to the man, "I think I misunderstood. I thought you might have said—"

The two men with shortswords pushed me back.

Feltock came after me and Kest followed, a hand on the grip of his own sword.

"What'd he say?" Feltock asked.

"Ganath Kalila," I replied. "The Blood Week. We've come here just when the Duke has called the Blood Week."

"What in the five hells for fools is that? Try and remember that I haven't been to this city before, boy, and this'll go faster."

"Ganath Kalila is a tradition in Rijou," I told him. "The Duke's father brought it back with him from his travels among the Kingdoms of the Eastern Desert. They call it the Blood Week because for seven days there are no rules except one: what you can't hold, you don't own."

An old soldier sees a lot of insanity and violence in a long career, but this took Feltock aback. "How is that supposed to work? The man with the biggest army takes what he wants? It'd be mayhem."

"The Duke likes mayhem," I replied.

"Not necessarily," Kest said. "I've read about the politics of this, and it's actually quite complex. A series of alliances and patronages ensure that most people fall under the protection of someone above them, who has protection from someone else above them, who—"

"Eventually has protection from the Duke. So he gets to shake a few more pieces out of his flock, is that right?"

"Only sometimes the Duke makes it known who he *doesn't* plan on protecting, you understand?"

Feltock did. "So hunting season has arrived in Rijou for a few poor buggers."

"These buggers don't look that poor," I said, looking at the mansion. It was elegant in the Rijou style, but it also looked well fortified. They probably had bows and maybe even pistols. But the men surrounding the building wore armor, and they were rolling more and more carts with stone blocks up to the doors and windows.

"I don't understand the point of the blocks," Kest said.

"Fire," Feltock said. "They're going to smoke them out."

"Or burn them alive," I said.

"Or perhaps they're going to build them a nice guesthouse here in the street," a jovial voice called out from behind us. Shiballe eased his way out of the carriage, followed by Valiana. They were taking sips from tiny cups containing some kind of bubbling liquid.

"Feltock," she said, "I don't want to disappoint my Saints-blessed father, the Duke. This reunion must happen tonight."

Kest and I looked at each other. She must be here for her confirmation, legitimizing her lineage: so that meant she was exactly eighteen. If she really was the offspring of two Ducal rulers, then nineteen years ago Jillard, Duke of Rijou, must have been secretly—and briefly—married to Patriana, Duchess of Hervor—and then he must have divorced her almost immediately, because he married his current wife shortly after. It was possible, but an odd thing to do: to sire a child and then immediately go and marry someone else. I suppose it did make a twisted kind of sense if what they really wanted was to raise a royal-blooded Princess in secret—but that conspiracy had to be planned long before Paelis took the throne, during Greggor's reign, and it didn't make sense because the Dukes had never had any complaints with Greggor. He had let them run as wild as they pleased on their own lands.

"Aye, your Highness," Feltock said. "No point in sitting here watching these people shoot at each other all evening."

"Oh, I hardly think there will be much shooting," Shiballe said, smiling amiably.

"Why not?" Kest asked.

"The Tiarren family guard aren't in the city, you see."

"The Tiarren family?" I looked at Kest. "Amongst the lesser nobility, Lord Tiarren was counted one of the King's closest allies."

"Really?" Shiballe said casually. "How interesting. I believe the Duke ordered Lord Tiarren to send his men off to deal with a dispute on the border. His wife has been quite vocal on local politics in Rijou in her husband's absence." The fat little man smiled up at the house. "I do believe someone is about to learn a harsh lesson." He glanced at the darkening sky. "Oh, in about two hours."

"So no one can start fighting until midnight?" Feltock asked.

"That's right, not until Ganath Kalila begins," he said with a sly smile.

Feltock pointed at the men unloading blocks on the sidewalk in front of the house. "Then what are they doing?"

"Silly man. There's no harm in getting ready now, is there? So long as no one fires a shot or strikes a blow."

I looked up at one of the open windows. A woman in her late thirties was looking out, the crossbow in her hand dangling helplessly. She must be Lady Tiarren. Children were arrayed behind her, and I could see them pulling at her robes.

"You're telling me she and her children and her servants have to stay there watching these men begin blocking their exits and readying the fire intended to burn them all alive?" The Tiarrens had been allies of the King. What if they knew the location of the King's Charoites? What if one of the jewels was in the house even now? I stepped toward the men setting the blocks.

"Keep your place, Trattari," Shiballe warned. "That's exactly what I said. But don't worry; Lord Tiarren has a big family. And I'm sure the Duke will allow him to remarry in due course. No doubt this time he will choose someone who will advise him better—and show greater fidelity—than Lady Tiarren did."

I turned to Kest immediately. "Get back outside the city. Get as many of the guards as will come. Make sure to bring Blondie and Kurg; see who else they can convince."

I motioned to Feltock. "Take Lady Valiana to the Duke's home. Kest and I will follow as soon as we can."

Feltock pulled on the lead horse's reins on the carriage to get them ready, but Valiana turned on him. "Stop this instant," she commanded.

"My Lady, it won't be safe," I began.

"It will be safe—perfectly safe," she said, "because you and your men are going to accompany us, right now. You work for me, not for this Tiarren woman. Do you understand?"

I felt heat rise in my chest. "Are you *insane*? They're going to burn them alive! They're going to block the doors and windows and wait until they burn or jump out the windows to their deaths!"

"You do not speak to me in such tones, Trattari," she warned.

"You want to be a Princess?" I shouted. "You want to rule over your subjects? Well, there they are." I jabbed a finger at the woman and her crying children framed in the window. A couple of the older-looking boys held swords in their hands: man enough to carry a sword and boy enough to believe it would do any good. "You want power? Stop thinking about how you're going to get it and start thinking about what the Saints want you to do with it!"

I had overstepped my bounds by miles, but she looked for a brief instant as if she might be swayed. Then I heard a cough and turned.

Shiballe had a pistol in his hand, pointed at my chest. "Don't be so dramatic, my tattered friend," he said. "If the Tiarren woman is not stupid she will drop her family crest from the window and show defeat. And even if she is stupid, she still has several servants in the building, many with military training, and they will force her to surrender for her own good."

"And then what happens?" Kest asked, sizing up Shiballe.

"Then the Tiarren name will be struck from the noble lists and she and her brats will live out their lives as well-fed servants to the victors."

"And who are the victors, in this case?" Feltock asked carefully.

"I don't know," he said. "As you can plainly see, these fine men aren't wearing any crests on their armor."

Kest whispered in my ear, "This is what the whole world will be like, Falcio, if the Dukes get their way."

My head was spinning and I struggled to keep myself under control.

Shiballe was having no difficulty managing the situation, however. "Now, my fine tattered birds, I suggest you do exactly as Princess Valiana has suggested, and do your jobs." He wagged a finger at Kest. "And don't waste your time in idle fantasy, my friend. There are several of my men with crossbows stationed in the building behind us. I never travel without guards during the Blood Week."

I knew we had to comply, but for some reason I couldn't move. My legs were rooted to the ground and my right hand refused to stop its gradual progression across my body toward my rapier.

Valiana stepped in front of me. "Falcio, stop."

It was the first time she had ever used my name. She had always called me Trattari before.

"I am . . . not insensitive to your concern for these people. But Shiballe is right: the woman will surrender before blood is spilled and that will be that."

I tried to speak but it came out in a whisper. "And what then, your Highness? Servitude? Slavery?"

Valiana stared into my eyes. She was a beautiful woman, but beauty had long ago lost its hold on me. "I will speak to my father the Duke on her behalf. I promise you that if you come with me I will secure his guarantee that she will not be enslaved. I *promise*."

I realized she had moved beyond simply placating me. I looked back into her eyes and saw something there I hadn't seen before: not frustration, but fear. She wasn't sure about Shiballe, and she didn't believe herself safe with only his men and Feltock as an escort.

I would have left her to his machinations—but then what? I didn't have enough men to fight off the entire city of Rijou, and if I did try and fight, I might end up making things worse for the Tiarren family. Right now they were headed only for poverty; if they were seen as allies of the Greatcoats, they would fare far worse.

I felt the ground release my feet from its hold and my hand relaxed. "Thank you, your Highness. We will do as you suggest."

Shiballe secreted his pistol somewhere in the folds of his shirt and clapped his hands together. "Excellent!" he said. "So good to see a man who knows his place in these troubled times."

10

THE COMING OF THE GREATCOATS

Those early days were the best, I think. King Paelis and me, sitting and playing ancient war games, talking about strategy and tactics, philosophy and ideology, justice and law. We ate a lot in those first few months—neither one of us had much meat on our frames at that point, so every meal felt like a grand event. My wounds still hurt and he continued to have the occasional coughing fit, which wasn't surprising since the weather was turning, but all in all we were hale and hearty. I taught him how to swing a blade and he showed me sword techniques from books I had never heard of.

"The only luxuries my father granted me in those three years I spent in the tower were books," he told me one afternoon in the practice field outside the barracks. "He would have denied me those, too, but I asked him if he was truly so afraid that I could beat him with books. I thought he'd kill me then, but you know, the old superstition against spilling royal blood was strong in him."

"So what did you read?" I asked.

"Everything," he said. "We had only twenty books in the castle library—fantastic old books on war ways and fighting styles. Falcio, I could show you books from swordmasters from four hundred years ago, great masters, whose techniques are hidden amongst layers and layers of verses. But when I finished with those, my mother, bless her, sent to the monastery in Gaziah for more. I read the works of philosophers and tyrants and clerks and kings, and when I was finished, I turned back to the beginning and read them again."

"You never talk about your mother," I said.

He looked down. "She prefers it that way."

I felt as if I'd embarrassed him somehow. "I read a book once," I said. "It had some dirty parts in it. Those were nice."

Paelis smiled and cuffed me on the back of the head. "You speak to your King that way? Besides, you don't fool me for one second, Falcio. You're a man of words as much as I am. The servants have seen you sneaking books out of the library at night."

I stuttered, "I don't sleep a lot anymore and there's not that much to do with my evenings . . ."

I thought for a second he would make some remark about the ladies of the castle but, if he had intended that, he thought better of it. "Books make good friends sometimes, Falcio." He clapped me on the shoulder. "Take as many as you like from the library."

Kest was the first one to join us. I found him back in Luth, where I'd left him as the days of our childhood friendship had waned and we moved on to other companions.

"Waiting for you," he answered when I asked him what he was doing still forging swords in his father's smithy. Before I could say anything further he put down the blade he was working on and pulled a pack down from the top shelf. "Well, let's go," he said.

"Don't you want to know what we're doing?" I asked. "Or at least tell your parents that you're leaving?"

"My parents have known for some time that I'd be going. I said my good-byes long ago. As for what we're doing, well, I imagine it must be interesting if you came back to find me."

As we left the smithy, Kest finally noticed Paelis.

"Oh, hello," Kest said. "Who are you?"

The smithy was full of smoke and dust and the King coughed for a bit before he answered. "Paelis the First," he said. "Your King."

"Ah. That must be nice. Well, let's go; I can see clouds up ahead."

Kest was a strange man, but I had missed him. And setting out across that field on horseback, the best friend of my youth at my side and the two of us following a young, idealistic King who wanted to bring the Greatcoats back, was truly one of the happiest moments of my life.

The high point of those years happened a few months later. There were twelve of us by then, nine men and three women: Kest, Brasti, Shana, Quillata, Morn, Bellow, Parrick, Dara, Nile, Winnow, Ran, and me—twelve traveling Magisters who knew the King's Law and could judge fair, ride fast, and fight hard. We were a little cocky, perhaps, but we were ready, too.

The first day of spring is a good time to bring change to the world. The King summoned us to the throne room and we assumed this would be some kind of event in our honor, with flowers and a parade maybe. I had purchased a long coat from a local seamstress—I knew I was probably trying to live a fantasy, but I had always dreamed of being a Greatcoat as a child and this was most likely as close as I would get. If nothing else, it gave Brasti a good laugh.

"Gods, Falcio," he said, sniggering, "if you're captured and tortured, I beg you, don't reveal that you're one of us. I don't think I could stand the embarrassment! And please, try not to make a fool of yourself in front of the throngs of adoring women the King promised me."

I let the jibes pass because nothing Brasti could say would make me take my coat off. It was shabby and not very sturdy but I would wear it even if the entire court laughed at me.

When we entered the throne room there was no one there but the King and an old woman.

"Tailor!" I said. I had not seen her since the day I awoke in the King's room to the sound of her sewing.

"Aye, boy, it's me, come to see you off proper."

Brasti snorted. "This is my throng of adoring women?"

"I don't know about adoring," the Tailor said, "but if you really need it I suppose I can give you a tumble." She smiled crooked old teeth at him and made a rude gesture that seven Saints couldn't get me to repeat.

I noticed that the King was sitting on a large crate.

"Traveling gear?" I asked.

"In a manner of speaking," he answered. He opened the crate, and inside there were some kind of rough packing reeds, which he pulled out carefully and set on the floor. When he was done he stepped out of the way and beckoned me to come forward and look inside.

Inside that battered wooden crate I saw the foolish ideals of a young boy made real: greatcoats, twelve of them in all, and each one perfectly tailored to our individual bodies. They were made of the toughest leather you can imagine on the outside, and inside, a fabric softer than fleece and warmer than wool.

"You won't freeze on the road with one of those on your back," the Tailor said. "Nor will a man put a knife in your kidneys by surprise."

She showed us the panels inside that held the strange pliable plates textured like bone. They could stop a knife thrust and maybe even an arrow, she said. She showed us secret pockets that concealed small blades, pieces of tough string, flint, almost everything one might need to survive a long journey in the middle of nowhere.

Each coat had a different but subtle inlay embossed into the leather panels in the front. The King took mine out of the crate and held it up for me. It was nothing at all like I had imagined, and exactly what I had always dreamed it would be: armor, shelter, and badge of office. On the right breast I saw the inlaid pertine in subtle blue crossed with a silver rapier.

"I think we've finally found what the pertine was meant for," the King said.

I couldn't speak, but I took the greatcoat from him and put it on.

I wasn't ashamed of the tears I shed that day, nor were any of the eleven others whose tears washed their faces and their pasts clean.

"Saints, it's a good thing I made these proof against the rain," the Tailor said. "With this bunch they're likely to get good and wet often."

The others laughed, but I stood straighter and taller than I ever had before, and I marked that moment indelibly in my memory, proof against tears and proof against sorrow, because that was the proudest moment of my life.

11
THE DUCAL PALACE

"So how does this work?" Brasti asked as we led the carriage down the wide cobbled Avenue of Remembrance toward the Ducal Palace.

"What do you mean?"

"I mean, how exactly does her Ladyship over there go from uptight bitch to Queen of the world?"

I glanced back at the carriage containing Valiana and the Duke's man to make sure neither they nor the carriage driver was paying attention. "I'm not exactly sure. I think it has to do with the Council of Dukes having the power to select a Realm's Protector . . ."

"No," Kest said, "that's only if there's an heir under the age of thirteen. This is about the Regia Maniferecto De'egro."

"The what now?" Brasti said.

"It's in Auld Tongue: 'Regia' meaning 'rule,' 'Maniferecto' meaning 'governing law,' and 'De'egro' meaning 'of the Gods.'"

"Ah well, that clears it all up then."

"You should have read more and drank less during our training, Brasti."

"We can't all be walking encyclopedias, Kest."

"I imagine it suits a Magister more to have an encyclopedic knowledge of law than it does to have one pertaining only to ales."

Brasti smiled. "Now see, that's where you're wrong. I've solved more cases with beer than you have with your arcane knowledge of laws nobody cares about."

Feltock snorted. "Saint Zaghev-who-sings-for-tears, is this how you Greatcoats solve the world's problems, then? No wonder everything is fucked."

Kest ignored him. "Well, this law is one you'll probably want to learn, and it's easy enough to remember: the Regia Maniferecto De'egro, or Godly Edict of Lawful Rule, is exactly seven lines long. It states that the Gods demand that only a King or Queen may rule, not a council. It further states that the Gods imbue the line of Kings with favored blood and the prosperity of the kingdom is tied to the quality of the blood of the ruler."

"What shit," Brasti said. "Blood is blood, so long as it's red."

"Nevertheless, the Maniferecto—and I suspect the Dukes—disagree."

"So what would the Gods feel about this situation then?" I asked, assuming they thought nothing of it at all. Most of these ancient texts were notoriously light on useful judicial details.

"Surprisingly," Kest said, glancing back at the carriage, "the Maniferecto does indeed address this, in the seventh and final line. Paraphrasing, it states that royal blood never dies but re-manifests itself according to the will of the Gods."

"Well, that's useful," Brasti snorted.

"I wasn't finished. According to the will of the Gods as witnessed by those of 'worthy blood.'"

Shit. "And 'worthy blood' here would mean—"

Kest nodded. "The Dukes."

"Well, isn't this just wonderfully convenient for everybody then?" Brasti said, a little too loudly for my comfort. "The fucking Dukes murder the King and then, according to this arcane damned law written by some in-the-pocket cleric, the same people who killed the King suddenly have the magical power to see where the royal blood lies next. Thank the Saints I became a Greatcoat to fight for such farseeing laws!"

"It's not that simple, though, is it?" Feltock said, rubbing his chin. "I mean, if it were just as easy as that, I reckon the Dukes would have picked one of themselves right quick, wouldn't they?"

"You're right: it's not as easy as that. You were one of the Duke of Pertine's generals. Do you think he'd have sat back while another man no more noble than he took power? Hells, you work for Patriana now—how do you think the Duchess of Hervor would feel?"

Feltock took a swig from the wineskin. "The Duchess isn't always the most sharing of individuals. I suppose you're right. So then why allow my mistress to take power?"

"Because she's an idiot," Brasti said lightly.

Feltock's hand dropped to the knife at his belt. "You'll hold your tongue, boy. I don't expect you to love the Lady, but you speak of her with respect."

Brasti threw his hands up in a gesture of mocking submission. "You're right, you're right," he said obligingly. "Given her parentage, she's practically a fucking Saint."

"This is getting us nowhere," Kest said to me.

"Why?" Feltock threw back. "'Cause I'm just a stupid old army man, too soft in the head for your grand Greatcoat thinking?"

"Feltock," I said, "not to give offense to her Ladyship, but the reality is that she's young, inexperienced, guileless, and completely malleable. If the Duke of Rijou is truly her father, then the other Dukes likely see her as easily controlled. Rijou himself cares nothing for the world outside of his domain, so he's unlikely to seek to use her to expand his own influence, and his region is completely dependent on trade, so he'll want to keep the other Dukes content. Valiana will be as happy as a child with a new puppy, with a lovely throne and pretty clothes, and all the while the Dukes will have free run in their lands."

"Well now, I'm glad you're not intending to give offense."

"If you want to see offense, watch what the Dukes regularly do with the young daughters of the peasants on their land," Kest said.

"Or what happens to families when every strong back is suddenly conscripted to build a Duke's petty temple or statue, or to fight an unnecessary border war so that the Duke can call himself a warrior."

Feltock locked eyes with him. "I'm not stupid. I know what can happen when a bad seed takes the Ducal seat."

"If that's what you think, then you are stupid," Kest said quietly. "A Duke who treats his people with anything less than an iron fist soon finds his fellow Lords coming to call with Knights at their backs, the length and breadth of their honor defined by how quickly they split a peasant's head open when their own Duke commands it."

"So then what now?" Brasti interrupted. "We go to a ceremony and that's the end of it?"

"No, but it's certainly the beginning," Kest replied. "She needs Patents of Lineage, which must be signed by all the Dukes or else there could be questions of legitimacy later on. Nobody, not even the Dukes, want a civil war."

"They'll bring a mage in to test her with a Heart's Trial too, I'd guess," I added.

"Test what now?" Feltock asked. I could see him tensing up. "They'll not put irons nor spells against my Lady."

"It's not what you think," I said. "It's just a ritual by which the mage can apparently test the content of her heart. Is she telling the truth about being the daughter of Jillard and Patriana? Does she hold any ill will toward the Dukes? Does she have evil in her heart? Does she plan anything nefarious—?"

"My Lady may be difficult at times, but there's nothing evil nor conniving in her."

Kest looked at him wearily. "Exactly—and that's why the Dukes will accept her, and why she'll make a perfect tool for the Dukes to use to ruin this country forever."

Then Kest looked back at me. I didn't need any Heart's Trial to know exactly what he was thinking.

* * *

The Ducal Palace was like everything else in Rijou, built on three levels of increasing decay. The foundation had been formed hundreds of years ago when the men and women of Rijou had fought like iron bears against aggressors from the north, south, and east. They had carved and carried indomitable eidenstone from quarries miles away in order to build a foundation and walls that would never be shattered by enemy forces. The foundation itself continued outside the palace, forming a promenade on which all major civic ceremonies took place. The promenade was known as the Rock of Rijou—the summoning place where the city would gather if ever they had to fight again to protect their homes.

Above this noble foundation sat hundreds of years of corruption. Seven Ducal families had taken their turns tearing down and rebuilding the overblown palace ballrooms and chambers, filling the palace with secret passageways and hidden alcoves, dungeon cells and rooms specially designed for torturing enemies: it was a harsh scab marring the hard-tanned skin of an otherwise great people.

But like any whore, Rijou's Ducal Palace disliked revealing the lines and scars of its history, and so the current Duke squandered city monies to gild the vast chambers and hallways with precious metals and swathe it in rich fabric. Like many forms of lunacy it was somewhat ingenious in its manifestation. The Ducal Ballroom was built in several tiers. The Gemstone Tier at the top held the Duke's table, the Golden Tier seated favored nobles, and the Silver was for those nobles who pleased the Duke too little. The military, tradesmen, and musicians were to be found on the Oaken Tier, along with the dance floor, and below that the Iron Tier housed the kitchens and other utilitarian rooms behind great doors.

The ballroom and lighting were elegantly designed so that, while everyone could see the levels above them, giving impetus to elevate themselves in the Duke's good graces, none could see the levels below, and thus could only imagine what might await them there should they fail to please their Lord. The Duke and his special guests shone like gemstones, to be admired by those beneath, but they needed never see the lower orders beneath them—and the Duke no doubt considered this stunningly idiotic arrangement a show of confidence that none would dare attack him.

"I could kill him in seventeen steps," Kest remarked as he broke off a crust of bread.

"Reckon I could kill him in one with my bow," Brasti said as we watched men in elaborate gold livery serve the main course on the levels above.

Feltock whispered angrily, "Reckon you'll get us killed in no steps at all if you don't shut your traps, fools."

I looked around at the other peons on the Iron Tier. For the most part, everyone consigned to this level was working: fetching food and drink, moving empty dishes into the cleaning rooms, bringing brushes and pans to sweep up broken dishes. The only people eating with us were other bodyguards or nobles' attendants not deemed well groomed enough to sit behind their masters. The fact that all the horribly uncomfortable tables and chairs on our tier were made entirely out of rough iron rods—despite the huge cost—told me everything I needed to know about the Duke.

"It's starting," Kest noted.

The Duke rose from his gilded seat. His dark red velvet robes didn't conceal his strong physique. Golden bands encircled his waist and arms, and on his head he wore a simple crown, not much more than a flattened loop of gold, really, but embedded at the front was the largest diamond I'd ever seen.

"Must tip forward a great deal," Brasti observed.

"*Shh . . .*"

"My Lords and Ladies," the Duke's voice boomed out.

"Good acoustics, too," Kest said.

"Would you stop encouraging him?"

"My friends!" the Duke continued, a smile across his face, then, "No, not just *friends*: my *family*. As we assemble here on the eve of Ganath Kalila, our most blessed celebration, in which we rebind the ties that make Rijou a true family, my heart is full!"

A great deal of cheering ensued. Unsurprisingly, the cheers were more muted the farther down the tiers I looked.

"My heart is full and my soul soars, not only because today my beautiful daughter is brought into my life—" And here he revealed Valiana, dazzling in deep purple, with softly colored lilac gemstones woven into her hair, as she rose to the *oohs* and *ahhs* of the assembled crowd.

"I say, my joy is not only that I am rejoined by a daughter, but that she has been so well protected by both Ducal guardsmen and brave Trattari, who have risked their lives to bring her to us safely."

There was a gasp from the crowd. That may have been the first nice thing said about us by a noble in—well, possibly forever.

"Well, that was nice, really," said Brasti.

"Yes, but why?" I wondered.

"And this, the love and devotion of such disparate moral characters for my daughter, shows all of us . . ."

"Ah," I said. "There it is."

". . . further, shows to *all* of us, men, Saints, and Gods alike, that Valiana is and will be the glory that unifies all our peoples. From the noblest family to the basest criminal . . ."

"See, now I'm not sure if he really likes us at all," Brasti said.

"Shut up now. This is where it happens."

". . . all of our people will come to love, to admire, and above all else, to *need* Valiana to lead us into the future. She has passed her Heart's Trial and, with no stain or malice in her soul, she will bring us together: one people, united and free, under the benevolent rule of the Princess Valiana!"

A roaring cheer emanated from the Golden Tier; no doubt these favored nobles had already been well briefed about their imminent enthusiasm. From the Silver Tier there were some muted sounds, and I thought I could distinguish some cries of shock, even anger. From the Oaken Tier there was confusion, followed by rampant cheering and clapping, not because they understood what was going on, but because they understood that they had better start expressing their pleasure at the announcement. I doubt anyone cared what sounds came from the Iron Tier.

"I can take her out before the guardsmen get in the way," Kest said. Then he turned to Brasti. "But I can't get the Duke as well. They'll have me by then. Can you get there and kill him before they catch you?"

Brasti looked at him, then at the stairs that joined the levels.

"I—"

Feltock had his dinner knife in his hand and was ready to launch himself at Kest.

"Saints, all of you, shut up and sit down," I said.

"This is it, Falcio," Kest said to me urgently. "This is how they're going to destroy everything the King worked for. Tell me why not—give me one reason, one *good* reason, why I shouldn't stop this storm before it begins?"

I grabbed him by the back of the neck and pulled him hard so that his nose was an inch from mine. I locked eyes with him. "Because. We're. Not. Fucking. Assassins."

"I should have the lot of you killed, you damnable treachers!" Feltock growled.

"Now, now; the Duke's all for unity—he said so," Brasti said. "Let's not spoil the party."

"On your fucking honor—whatever that's worth. On your fucking honor you swear to me you won't hurt that girl, or I vow, Greatcoats or not, I'll take the lot of you down seven hells with me."

I turned to Feltock. "I am Falcio val Mond. I am the First Cantor of the Greatcoats. I swear neither I nor any of mine shall lay arms against Valiana, be she a Princess, a Queen, or simply the foolish, half-witted girl I've grown accustomed to."

Kest's eyes never left mine.

"I want to hear it from him," Feltock said, pointing his knife at Kest.

"It is as he says," Kest spoke softly. "For so long as Falcio is alive and First Cantor of the Greatcoats, I will not raise arms against your mistress."

Feltock put his knife down.

"Well then, I suppose that's as settled as things are likely to get," Brasti said cheerfully. "Oh, and look, they're about to start the dancing." With that he bounded off and up the stairs to the Oaken Tier. Having no desire to sit in the company of Kest and Feltock, I joined him.

All might come to enjoy the musicians and the dancing on the grand oval-shaped floor, from the highest to the lowest tiers. The first few dances were lovely reels, interspersed with one formal dance and the occasional slower dance for couples. Only a few of the nobles joined in, but the Duke himself, accompanied by who I imagine were several of his favored families, took a turn on the floor. Brasti was brazen as always, dancing with any woman who would tolerate him. He came close to dancing with a young noblewoman, until her father cast an angry eye in her direction and she hurriedly pulled away.

Me, I was more interested in watching the musicians. There were a full dozen of them, on a low stage to the right of the dance floor. They were young, for the most part, but led by an older man who seemed ill-suited to the task. His gray hair was cut in the long troubadour fashion, falling just above the shoulders, and his clothes were elegant enough, dyed in the Duke's colors of dark red and gold. His face was weathered and lined, but he would have been handsome once. And he was blind. It took me a moment to understand that, because he appeared to have shining blue eyes. Then I realized they never moved nor blinked: he had gemstones in the sockets where his eyes should have been. As I gazed at him further, I noticed something else: there was something wrong with his feet. He wore a troubadour's thigh-high leather traveling boots, but his feet didn't move, even when the rest of his body was swaying along with the music. It's true that not every musician taps a foot when they play, but I couldn't recall ever seeing one whose feet stayed so firmly planted in the ground. *The man must have no feet*, I thought, *and his legs must be splinted to wooden stumps of some kind in his boots.* I hadn't seen him come in, but there was a boy, no more than ten, standing next to him and accompanying him on the pipes. I could see he was keeping hold of two black canes. Every once in a while, the man would put his hand on the boy's arm and tap some complicated sequence on his arm, and the boy in turn would pass him water, or switch out his guitar, or whisper the next song to the other musicians.

Even though I'd been staring at him for ages, it was only when he began to play the slow, soft dancing song called "The Lovers' Twilight," his guitar sounding out the rapid melody that seemed so simple but that I knew was gruelingly complex to perform, that I recognized him. Bal Armidor: the man who had come to my village and sung such songs and stories that they had shaken my soul. Bal Armidor: the man who sang of Greatcoats.

Bal's hands were moving swiftly upon the strings and the rest of the musicians intertwined their own instruments in and around his melody. The boy opened on the pipes, but after the first verse he put them down and sang a beautiful treble that well suited the song. But I had ceased paying attention to the music, for confusion swirled in my head. How had Bal Armidor come to be here, in the Duke's palace? I had thought him long gone across the Eastern Desert to the Sun Tribes, where he'd sworn he would be the first Western troubadour to master the music of the East.

As the song ended, I started moving toward the stage, but they immediately launched into another piece, this one a little faster but still for couples.

"Will you dance with me, Falcio of the Greatcloaks?" a voice came from behind me. I looked over at Bal, wanting to signal him somehow, but his head made the slightest movement left and right. *Not now*, he seemed to say.

I turned back to see who had spoken to me. Valiana was resplendent in her lovely gown, her hair straying a little from the perfection of earlier after much dancing, but still bedecked with gems and gleaming. Trin was a few yards away, dressed in a simple purple gown no doubt designed to complement Valiana's own. She was in her own way as beautiful as any Princess, and yet there she stood, forever in the background—alone. She caught me looking at her and dropped her eyes.

"Greatcoats," I said absently, my eyes refocusing on Valiana.

"What?"

"Greatcoats. Not 'Greatcloaks.' Great*coats*."

"Ah, well of course, that makes sense, doesn't it?" She laughed lightly. "Shall we dance then, Falcio of the Greatcoats?"

I looked around and saw several nobles trying very hard to light me on fire with their cold stares. I saw the Duke, smiling.

I shook my head. "No, my Lady, I—"

"Your Highness," she corrected.

"What?"

"Soon the whole country will know me as their Princess, Falcio, so as long as we're being formal, I should prefer 'your Highness.'"

I bowed. "Your Highness, I thank you for the honor, but I'm afraid I'm ill-suited to dancing."

Her smile faded. "Ill-suited to dancing, or just ill-suited to dancing with me?"

"I simply fear that I might tread on your royal toes while my mind struggles to keep track of my own feet and I try to understand what game you're playing just now."

She glanced briefly back at the Duke, then at me.

"Then I will make it equally simple: my father feels it would be a show of great humility and unity for me to dance with a Greatcoat. If it makes it easier for you, then consider it an order from your employer."

I shrugged casually but spoke loudly. "As your employee, Highness, of course I accept." I took a deep bow, my right hand extended behind me while my left reached toward her, palm up. It was the customary invitation from a romantic suitor, and entirely inappropriate for this situation.

I was surprised when she accepted my hand and stepped lightly into my embrace for the opening of the dance.

"How clever you are, Falcio of the Greatcoats," she whispered to me as we turned. "How much more wise and canny you are than the foolish girl before you. I asked for something that would cost you nothing, but you didn't like my phrasing and so now you have humiliated me."

"Perhaps you should have asked one of the others," I replied.

She laughed. "Which one? The one who wants to murder me or the one who wants to murder my father?"

Feltock must have told her what happened.

"I am curious about one thing, my Lady. How did—?"

"Your Highness, you mean," Valiana said.

"Yes, well, about that: how exactly did you manage to pass the Heart's Trial? I'm told the spell is very difficult to fool."

"And you think that I must have cheated somehow? That I lied about who I am or what I intend? You do realize that in the days before King Paelis, it was considered treason to question the honor of the throne?"

"I'm surprised, your Highness, that I am not therefore in irons."

She ignored the question. "Why do you despise me so, First Cantor of the Greatcoats?"

"I do not despise you, your Highness. I am afraid of you."

"What cause have I given you to fear me so?"

I looked into her eyes, searching for mockery but finding only an honest question. "Little to none, your Highness," I sighed, "but you have shown no wisdom either, and I believe you are being elevated as part of a conspiracy to bring false credibility to a new line of Kings and Queens, once again ruled wholly by the Dukes. I doubt you are evil—you might even be a nice person. But the Dukes will use you like a well-schooled animal and you will be like unto a monster for this world. And I am in the business of stopping monsters, your Highness."

She stopped and I almost tripped over her, but she held me tight. "Why not kill me, then? Or at the very least, let your man, who is so eager to do so, do it for you?"

I held her eyes in mine. "Because my King would disapprove."

For a moment she didn't move at all; then she gave a very slight nod and we stepped back into the rhythm of the dance.

"Then why treat me so foully? If I am such a fool and you so clever, why not ingratiate yourself with me, manipulate me for the benefit of your Greatcoats, just as you claim my father and the others will do?"

"Because, your Highness, I am not like them, and my King would not approve of that either."

"Then why—?"

"Highness," I asked softly, "what is it that you want?"

"I—" She leaned in closely and whispered in my ear, so quietly that I almost missed it when she said, "I am afraid."

I leaned back from her. "Has someone threatened you?"

"It's not like that, nothing so overt—it's just, when I'm with them, I sense what you say, that they do not listen to *me*; rather, they listen only to ensure I say what they have told me to say. My mother—"

"Your Highness, forgive me, but your mother is the Duchess Patriana. If we speak of her, I cannot guarantee your safety."

Valiana looked around. "From whom? I do not see Kest or Brasti."

"From me, your Highness. From *me*."

"Ah. You blame her for the death of the King."

"I do."

"Do you take no responsibility at all? Does it not matter to you that the King broke ancient laws, dismissed pacts and agreements of long standing held by his ancestors and the Dukes?"

"I know little of that, your Highness. I know only that this country is weak and decaying, and it is breaking apart, thanks to the injustice heaped on it by the nobility. I know only that my King tried to bring a measure of fairness and mercy to the people of this land. I know only that your mother and the other Dukes had him killed for it."

"If you truly want a more just rule, Falcio, a more compassionate rule, then *help* me. Be one of my advisers. I would—I would even consider reuniting the Greatcoats, with some compromises. I need someone I can trust, someone who isn't simply seeking more power for their family or house. Feltock says he believes in you, despite what conventional wisdom tells him. Be loyal to me, and I swear to you we can help the very same people you claim to want to save."

The dance was coming to a close. "My Lady—your Highness, this afternoon you said you would intervene for the family whose home is under siege as the Blood Week begins."

"I have not forgotten."

"Save them," I said in her ear. "Save one family."

The last note hung in the air for a moment as we separated and she looked at me. I bowed, properly this time, not as a suitor, and waited for her sign that I should leave.

She curtsied back. Before the musicians could start again, she raised a hand in the air, and everything stopped.

"My Lord Duke of Rijou," she said in a clear, commanding tone.

Her father was standing a few feet away, at the edge of the dance floor. His eyes were cold when he said, "Daughter?"

"I have a boon to ask of you."

"This hardly seems the time, sweetling."

"There is a family here in Rijou; their fate is in dire jeopardy."

He laughed, "It is Ganath Kalila, daughter. I should say their fate is well in their hands, as has always been the case amongst the strong people of Rijou."

"Still, I would ask that you put them into your care."

The room grew cold. This was a dangerous first test of her stature.

The Duke smiled, then walked over to her, taking her in his arms. The gesture looked innocent, even loving, but I could see him holding her too hard, too close. His pelvis was pushing into hers.

"My dear Lords and Ladies, forgive my daughter, for she is still young and knows little of the world outside her home. But we shall teach her, shall we not?"

Laughter and applause. *The sound of a hundred hyenas smelling blood.*

Valiana pushed away from the Duke. "Dearest Father, you are correct. I have much to learn." She knelt down in front of him, her hands by her side in a gesture of submission.

"Of course, my dear, this is quite understandable when one—"

"Nevertheless," she said.

The room went quiet again.

"Nevertheless, I must insist that the Tiarren family be protected. They are under siege in a manner most foul by bandits in black cloth, and the city guards do not defend them."

"Daughter, it is the Blood Week."

"It was not the Blood Week when they began to barricade them in their home. The city guards should have intervened. Your man, Shiballe, should have intervened. He did not. In fact, he prevented my men from lending assistance."

The Duke's eyes were embers burning angrily in the shadows that had descended over his face.

"*Shiballe*," he said, and in an instant the soft, obsequious man was by his side.

"My Lord?"

"See to this. My daughter has made a request, in front of me, in front of all these people, that the lives of the Tiarren household be my responsibility."

Then he raised his voice to the assembled nobles. "Lords and Ladies, be most assuredly aware: the fate of House Tiarren is of great interest to my daughter, and now to me. I hold their lives dearly, as I do all my subjects, and their future has been set in my royal hands and no others. I will see that my will is done in this matter. Have you heard me, Lords and Ladies?"

Sounds of assent rung out and Valiana rose, smiling. "Thank you, Father, you rise even further in my heart with this compassion."

The Duke smiled at her, this time genuinely. I found it unsettling.

Someone tugged at my arm: the young singer.

"He would converse with you now," he said.

The boy led me to a table near the musicians' stage. The others continued to play, but Bal sat at the table with a mug in one hand. I sat opposite him, and the boy stood by his side.

"Bal—it's me! Falcio—"

He didn't reply, but put his hand on the boy's arm and tapped something with his fingers, as I had seen him do earlier.

"He recognizes you," the boy said.

"Why does he not speak?"

Bal opened his mouth wide and I saw the ruin of his tongue.

"*Saints!*" Bal Armidor had had a voice that could sneak honey from bees and had snuck many a woman from the arms of her husband in his day. "What happened to him?" I whispered, aghast. "Was it the barbarians?"

He began tapping again on the boy's arm.

"He says his tongue was the last thing to go."

"What does that mean?"

More tapping.

"He came here years ago, on his way east. He stopped to play for the Duke, hoping to earn enough coin for his journey."

"What happened?"

"The Duke was fond of his playing, and generous in praise and reward. He offered Bal the position of Chief Troubadour. Bal said he was grateful, but like all troubadours, his feet itched for the road."

Bal used both his hands to lift one of his legs out of its boot. Below the shin the flesh and bone had been replaced with a wooden leg inlaid with gold.

"The Duke generously resolved the issue for him."

Bal placed his leg back in the boot and took the boy's arm again.

"Then Bal found favor in the eye of one of the ladies of the court, and she found favor in him. The Duke suggested they cease their affair, as he had his own interest in the woman. He offered Bal one of his mistresses instead and when Bal said he had eyes only for Senina, the Duke was thoughtful enough to have his eyes put out, to be offered to Senina as a gift. In his infinite generosity, he replaced the gift he'd taken."

The gemstones in his eye sockets. *Saints, I should have let Brasti murder him.*

"The Duke's son, Tommer, took a liking to Bal, and asked that Bal be made his tutor in music and history. Being a fool—"

Bal gripped the boy's arm hard, then tapped again.

"Bal agreed and taught the boy. He taught him music and voice and history. He taught him about the Kings and—"

"The Greatcoats. He taught him about the Greatcoats, didn't he?"

"The Duke was furious and commanded him to stop," the boy said. "But Tommer was only seven years old and he didn't understand why he couldn't have what he wanted. Bal loved the boy and relented, but would only tell him more stories of the Greatcoats in secret. One of Shiballe's men overheard him one evening, and the Duke had Bal's tongue pulled the next day."

I reached out and grabbed Bal's other hand. "I'm so sorry, my friend. I thought . . . I thought you'd gone east and stayed there."

Bal removed his hand and shook his head.

"He says he needs no pity. He says you must leave this place, tonight if you can. There is nothing here for you but pain and death. He says to go back to the Lord Caravaner, and accept Tremondi's proposal."

"Tremondi's dead," I said.

Both Bal and the boy were silent for a moment. Finally, Bal tapped something very short.

"Then," the boy said slowly, "there is nothing for you anywhere but pain and death. Either way, you must go."

"But there's more I need to know, so much Bal can tell me about—"

Bal slammed the table with one fist before tapping furiously on the boy's arm again.

"He says he cannot speak to you now, nor ever. He has two things left in this world, fingers to make music and ears to hear it. He says you must not take those away from him."

I sat back in the chair, suddenly conscious of all the people who could see us, every one of whom could whisper into the Duke's ear and take away all that remained of Bal's humanity.

I rose. "I'll go." I started to turn but then stopped. "Only . . . who are you? Are you related to Bal in some way?"

The boy shook his head. "No. I am simply commanded by the Duke to serve Bal whenever he performs. I must go now. I see my father calls me."

The boy stepped out from the table and walked purposefully toward the stairs. I looked after him and saw the Duke standing there, his eyes on me.

As I walked back down to the Iron Tier I found Kest and Brasti drinking with Feltock. Apparently they were reconciled.

"Falcio!" Brasti said. "Quite the show up there. I never knew you had it in you. What's next? Will you be dancing with the Duke himself?"

I gripped his shoulder. "Let's get out of here. I want my room and a bed. In the morning we stop at Lady Tiarren's mansion and find out what she knows about the Charoites, and then I want to get out of this Gods-forsaken city as fast as possible."

"You go," Brasti said, raising a cup in the air. "If I can't take the Duke's life then at least I can drink enough of his wine to make him hurt a little."

Kest looked into his own cup, his eyes unfocused. "That would be difficult, Brasti. The Ducal Treasury of Rijou is likely quite vast. You would need to—"

"Shut up and drink more wine," Brasti said. "This could take a while."

I left them there and took the door from the Iron Tier out to the corridor that led past the kitchens toward the servants' quarters. I turned a corner and nearly collided with a woman in a purple dress. It was dark enough in the corridor that for an instant I thought it was Valiana. A moment later I realized it was Trin.

"Falcio," she said. "I'm so sorry, I—"

"It's fine," I said. "Are you all right? Shouldn't you be with Lady Valiana?"

She corrected me. "Princess Valiana."

"As you say. Why are you here?"

"I . . ." She put a hand on my arm, and then took it away again. "It was very brave of you to try and save that family."

"I don't know what you mean," I said. "It's Valiana—*Princess* Valiana—who is taking the risk here."

Trin rolled her eyes just for a moment, before looking back at me. "Her father the Duke and that fat slug of his will know where the idea came from." Trin's hand appeared on my arm again. "They will look for ways to do you harm."

I had to laugh at that. "My dear, the Dukes and their various fat slugs, all of them, have been looking for ways to do me harm since the day I put on this coat. There isn't much I can do to make that any worse."

She leaned into me. "I wish I could be half so brave."

The smell of her hair was intoxicating, as was the feel of the curves of her body against mine. "You?" I said, putting my hands on her arms and gently pushing her away. "Valiana would be lost without you."

Trin's expression was bitter. "Oh, the Princess loves me, much as she did her favorite cat as a young girl. She was positively ruined when that cat died—she cried and cried. For almost a full day. Then she asked for a new cat."

"I'm sure that's not . . ." The words drifted away from me. I was too weary to deceive her, even in the interests of making her feel better.

"Valiana will take the throne," Trin said, "and you and the others will go to find your fortunes elsewhere. Will you forget me, Falcio of the Greatcoats?"

I looked at this young woman, who had shown herself both clever and quiet, beautiful and shy. "I don't think that would be possible."

She smiled as if I'd just given her a prize, and her lips parted, just a little.

"I should go," I said. "It's late and I'd like to spend as few hours conscious in this city as possible."

"The Princess has told me to leave her alone tonight. I've never walked the hallways of this palace, and I would not dare to do so alone, though I am told it is very beautiful. Perhaps you and I could find some reason not to sleep?"

She was lovely and intriguing, and I do not get many offers as sweet as that one, not since Aline, my wife, first sought me out at a market dance and—

"No," I said. "I'm sorry, but I have to go."

I felt sorry for her, being alone and afraid in a nest of snakes. She was right to want to find some beauty in the world, some companionship, wherever it might be. "Perhaps Brasti would—" I instantly, yet far too late, realized my mistake.

Trin's face went as cold and dead as a gravestone in winter. "I thank you, First Cantor, for your thoughtful recommendation. I have taken up too much of your time."

She walked right past me down the corridor.

"Trin, wait . . ."

But she was already gone.

I stood there for a few minutes, torn between trying to find her to apologize and leaving. She had come to me with kind words and generous intent and I had turned her away. There were a hundred things I could have said to refuse her while still showing her compassion. Instead, I'd made her feel like a whore. *Saints*, I thought, heading to the shabby little room they'd given me to share with Kest and Brasti, *get me out of this Gods-damned city before I fail at something else.*

12
A COWARD'S VOW

Staring at the burned wreckage of the mansion that morning was one of the worst moments of my foolish failure of a life. A few bits of wall still stood, but the rest was a husk, slowly breaking into smoldering pieces, supported by the tall stone blocks that had been used to prevent anyone from leaving the house even as the attackers shattered cask after cask of oil onto the building before setting it on fire.

Valiana had been as good as her word. She had asked the Duke, her father, to promise freedom for the Tiarren woman and her children when she surrendered, and he had agreed all too willingly: a welcome gift to his child. But the attackers had picked up the falling crest that signaled surrender and doused it in oil before putting it to the torch with the rest, and then they had watched as everyone inside suffocated and burned.

Kest was with me. Feltock tried to keep the Lady Valiana inside her carriage with Shiballe, but she pushed him aside and joined us at the wreckage, Trin at her side silently shedding tears. Feltock wasn't stupid. He had a pistol with him, ready for the moment when I would try to kill Valiana.

"Leave it," Feltock said. I could hear the fear in the old man's voice. "The Princess has been commanded by her father to take her Patents of Lineage to Hervor. We have a job, you and I. That's all we got, that's all we can do. This isn't a matter for men like you and me."

Valiana said my name, softly, tentatively. "Falcio . . ."

"I am somewhat occupied at this precise moment, your Highness," I said. My voice was calm, natural. I wasn't a fool. I wasn't going to get myself killed just to assuage my guilt over the death of the Tiarren family. It was too late for them now, and all that was left was a proper burial and useless vengeance.

"Say it, Trattari. I know you want to," she said to me.

If this woman thought she knew what I wanted at that precise moment, then she was surely out of her mind.

Feltock called out, "My Lady, please, there are three of them. I can't be sure—"

"You blame me for this, don't you? You think I'm evil—go ahead and say it," she demanded.

Kest had his hand on his sword. He was ready for me to lose my temper and for Feltock to shoot me and, when he did, Kest was going to draw that sword like a bolt of lightning and cut Valiana's throat. And then what? Wait for the next stupid offspring of Dukes to come and become the next tyrant—what would that solve? When would it ever end?

"No," I said softly.

I don't think they knew who I was talking to because they all hesitated at once. "No, Valiana, Duchess, Princess, Empress, whatever you like to be called. I don't blame you."

She looked at me and her eyes widened and her mouth opened a little, but she said nothing. She was waiting, cautiously, for absolution.

But I had none to give. "I believe in evil, my Lady. I've seen it. I've seen it in my home, and I've seen it in the furthest reaches of this country. And yes, I've seen it here in Rijou. I saw it in Shiballe with his false smiles and secret plans, and I saw it in the Duke when you asked him to forbear for the sake of the Tiarren family and his eyes lit up, enjoying his private joke. I've brought justice to men like that. I've even killed them, when I've had to. And one day Shiballe and Duke Jillard will find a Greatcoat's sword in their bellies."

I picked up a small piece of still-smoldering wood and let it burn my hand for a moment before letting it fall.

"But most of the terrible things that happen in this land don't happen because of evil men, not really. They happen because of people who just don't know any better. A tax collector who never wonders if this season's crops might be too small to warrant the silver he has just collected: a family's entire income. A soldier who never questions why he's been told to take casks of oil and condemn a mother and her children to a fiery death. And a woman, barely more than a girl, who thinks only about how fine it will be to have a big castle and a pretty throne, and never wonders why so many great intrigues have been set in play to put her there. So no, Valiana, Lady, Duchess, Princess. I don't think you're evil. I think you're much, much worse."

She looked at me and then stumbled back, and Kest, his reflexes outpacing his intention, caught her before she fell to the ground. Feltock was wise enough to keep his cool and allow Kest to lift her into the carriage.

Shiballe stepped out, a smile on his lips. But then the smile disappeared as he looked past me. Trin, looking in the same direction, went white.

I turned and saw something coming out of the wreckage of the mansion: a girl, young, no more than twelve or thirteen years old. She was covered in soot and she looked disoriented. She stumbled and, as Kest ran to the saddlebags, I ran to the girl. I lifted her out of the carnage that had been her home and laid her down on a bench on the other side of the street, near the carriage. Kest passed me water and bandages. I thought her skin might be charred, but cleaning her arms with water revealed that she wasn't badly burned at all.

"How did she survive?" Kest asked.

"I don't know," I said.

Shiballe called to his guards and began whispering to them.

The girl opened her eyes and coughed. I gave her a little water and she drank it down, but when she tried to speak, wracking coughs overtook her.

I waited until they had passed before giving her a little more water. "Don't try to speak if it hurts," I said.

She shook her head. "I can—I can talk," she said.

"The girl will come with me," Shiballe said, coming toward us.

"Take another step forward," Brasti said, "just one more step forward, you fat little monster—"

"She is a citizen of Rijou and under the Duke's—"

"The Duke hasn't done a very fucking good job then, has he?"

"How did you survive the fire?" I asked the girl.

She coughed again. "The crawl space," she croaked. "When Mother dropped the crest and the men lit it on fire instead of letting us out, she told us to go down to the crawl space. But there wasn't enough room—it's so small—and my brothers wanted to fight, which was stupid because you can't fight fire with swords. And then the little ones ran back up and I couldn't reach them because something fell on top of the hatch. It's all stone down there, so the fire couldn't reach and I had water and towels to put on my face."

She took another sip of water. "I kept trying, but couldn't get out of the crawl space—and then I guess the stuff that fell on the hatch must have burned off . . ."

"Falcio," Kest said.

I looked at him.

"She's the last of the Tiarrens. If someone sees her, she's dead."

"Shiballe's seen her," Brasti said. "I say we kill him now."

"Then we'll be dead too," Feltock said. "I'm afraid we have to move on now, men."

I stared at him. "How can you serve Valiana now, when you've seen the cost?"

The old man's eyes looked sad. "I'm a soldier, boy. I serve one master at a time and I go where I'm told. You'll do the same if you're smart."

"The girl can come," Valiana said to me as she stepped off the carriage. "It is the least we can do."

I said nothing.

"And I am the least of women, aren't I?" she finished. Her tone was bitter, but I couldn't tell if it was aimed at me or at herself.

Kest packed up the bandages. "We need to move out now. It will be dark soon, and the violence will begin again."

"I'm afraid not," Shiballe said, his guards standing behind him.

"By what right do you contradict me, Shiballe?" Valiana asked, a mixture of anxiety and anger in her voice.

"Your Highness, this is still your father the Duke's domain. His orders on this are very clear."

"His orders were for her to be protected."

"No, your Highness. Every noble of Rijou is required to remain in the city during the Ganath Kalila as a demonstration of their courage and fealty. The child will remain in the city, and the Duke will care for her as he sees fit."

"I will not go," the girl said.

"See, the child knows her place is here, with her people."

"You've slaughtered her people," Brasti said.

"And you have some proof of this, do you, tatter-cloak?"

"The girl comes with me," Valiana said firmly.

"Then, your Highness, you will not reach the outer gates alive. You will be slain for conspiring to impede a citizen of Rijou in the performance of her duty to the Duke."

"My father would never—"

"It is treason, your Highness. Your father will be saddened by your loss. But that is all."

Valiana looked at me. I looked back, and whatever was in my eyes was too much for her. "My father swore in front of his nobles that he would protect her family!"

"No, your Highness, he did not. He swore to look into the matter personally, and ensure that his will was followed in the matter, and he did precisely that."

"There must be a way," she said to Shiballe, pleading.

"The girl stays here. She stays until the end of Ganath Kalila. If she is still alive then, on the Morning of Mercy she can go to the Rock of Rijou, where her name will be spoken by the City Sage and her presence recorded."

"How much fucking chance does she have to stay alive with no family?" Brasti demanded.

"It was not I who forced her mother to make such unwise decisions about whom to take to her bed, nor I who advised her husband, Lord Tiarren, to tolerate it."

The girl tried to run at Shiballe, but Kest gently held her back and sat her on the bench again.

"Duke Jillard would kill a woman and her family because adultery so distresses him?" I asked, my voice tight and my hand sliding to the hilt of my rapier.

Shiballe smiled. "No, not that. It was the choice of lover the Duke found distressing."

"Come, girl, come with me. We'll find a way out of this for you," Kest said to her.

"No," she said, very firmly.

He stared at her. "What do you mean, no?"

The girl put her hands on the back of the bench and pushed herself up. "It is true: it is the Blood Week. If I do not attend the Duke's ceremony at the end of the week, my family's name, everything we have, becomes the property of the men who did this. My name—my rights of blood—will be gone forever."

She looked up at me, desperate. "I won't do that," she said. "I won't run away."

"Then you'll be killed," Kest said, as kindly as he could.

"I'm smart," she said, "and I'm pretty small. I'll hide in the city—I'll move around a lot. I just need to last the week and then be there to place my name on the Duke's list."

I couldn't believe what I was hearing. This child, no more than twelve or thirteen, had just lost everything, her entire family, and now, as if that wasn't enough, she was going to be killed by the Duke's men or Shiballe's men or someone else for an offense she'd had no hand in at all. And yet her answer was that she would stay and fight.

"What's your name, girl?" I asked.

"Aline," she said. "Aline Tiarren."

My heart stopped and I felt my eyes darken. Kest put a hand on my shoulder, but I shrugged it off. It was a name, that's all—a very uncommon name, true, but a name nonetheless. A stupid name, given to a little girl who knew no better.

I knelt down in front of her. "Do you know what I am?" I asked.

"You're a Greatcoat," she said. "You're one of the King's Magisters."

"And do you know what we do?"

"Falcio . . . ," Kest warned.

I raised a hand and ignored him. "Do you know what we do?" I asked again.

"You hear cases," she said. "You give verdicts. You fight."

"We hear cases, we give verdicts, and we fight. A crime has been committed, Aline. Do you want me to hear your case? Do you want me to give a verdict?" I paused. "Aline, do you want me to fight?"

The girl looked into my eyes as if measuring my sincerity. Then she said, "I want you to fight."

"Falcio," said Kest, "you can't do this. The Covenant—"

"Fuck the Covenant," I said, rising and pushing him back. "And fuck you if you don't know any better, Kest. What's your solution? What's your answer? Look," I whispered fiercely into his ear, "we don't even know what's going on. What if the Tiarrens were killed so that they couldn't tell us where the King's jewels were? What if this girl knows something about it? Keeping her alive is the only way we can figure out how to stop the Dukes. She's part of it, I'm sure of it.

"My Lady," I said to Valiana in a clear voice, "I feel a cramp in my leg. I am afraid I would delay your journey if I came with you. I beg your pardon to rest my leg and then I will join you all presently."

"When?" she asked.

"In about nine days," I said. "I'm confident my cramp will disappear by then."

She looked at Feltock, at Kest, at Shiballe. Whatever answer she sought from them, she didn't find it.

"You are inconvenient, Trattari. My Lord father has made it clear I am to take my Patents of Lineage and make all speed north to begin preparations for my coronation. I cannot afford any more delays on your account."

"Your Highness—" Shiballe began.

"*Silence.* I've heard your instructions clearly enough: I cannot stay; I cannot take the girl. Very well then. Falcio val Mond, I order you to stay here until you are fit to travel."

"Yes, my Lady."

"Your Highness," Trin said, her expression full of concern, "it is too dangerous. They will have the entire city trying to kill them. Go instead to your father, the Duke; beg him to let you take the girl away. You can save her, give her a home, as your beloved mother the Duchess did for me."

"You forget yourself, Trin," Valiana said without looking at her.

"Ah, yes," Shiballe said. "Consulting with your father would be the wisest course."

I wondered if Trin was really so naive as to believe that the Duke would ever be persuaded by Valiana after he had twisted her request already. More likely he would rub her nose in it.

"Furthermore," Valiana said, "I have developed a special fondness for this girl. I would like to know her better. Should Ganath Kalila be completed by the time your leg is healed, then I instruct you to bring the girl to me."

"Yes, my Lady."

"You still work for me, tatter-cloak. If any of my special friends here in Rijou are inconvenienced by the poor manners of others, you will censure them on my behalf."

We locked eyes. "Of that you can be assured, my Lady."

"Very well then. Feltock, get the men ready and let us be away. I am growing restless to complete my journey."

"Aye, your Highness," Feltock said.

He turned to me briefly. "It was nice knowing you, Trattari. But you're a damned fool."

Kest, Brasti, the girl, and I were out of earshot of Shiballe and his men, who were standing a few feet away.

As the fat man gave instructions to his men, Brasti said quietly, "You can't win at this. There're too many of them—this whole town is a nest of snakes, and each and every one of them will be biting at you for the Duke's favor."

"I'll fear no blade," I said, my voice tight.

"Falcio, they'll kill you, and they'll kill the girl!"

"I'm not running, Brasti. You said it yourself—all we've done is run, and it's got us nowhere."

"How then? Tell me how: even if you do somehow manage to survive the Blood Week, they're never, never going to let you get away with it. What are you going to do then?"

"I'll reach the Rock," I said. I looked at Kest. "You're quiet."

He started pulling something from his pack. "Here," he said, passing me a small package. "It's what I've got left of the hard candy. Maybe it will keep you awake."

"Oh, for the Saints' sake—you think he can do this? Could you do it?"

"No, I don't think so," Kest said, "but I'll wait the full Blood Week and five days more to find out. Falcio, if you haven't returned by then, I'll kill the woman. She won't sit on the throne of Castle Aramor; that I promise you."

He turned and walked toward the carriage. I picked up a small rock and threw it at him, striking him in the back of the head. He spun back around, ready to fight.

"Just wanted to remind you that I do surprise you occasionally," I said calmly.

He didn't smile.

Trin came to me. "Hide," she said, whispering in my ear. "They say this city has a thousand places where people could disappear for weeks, even months. Hide until it's safe and get her out of the city.

Stay away from the Morning of Mercy, whatever the girl says. Her name isn't worth her life."

"I'll do my best," I said.

"Do better," she replied, and kissed me on the cheek before running back to rejoin Valiana.

"What are they doing?" Aline asked, pointing at Shiballe. His two guards appeared to be setting out a chair for him in the street.

"They're going to make sure we don't leave," I said, "not until sunset, when Ganath Kalila begins and the violence starts."

"Then what?" she asked.

"Then we begin," I said.

Brasti was the last to leave. He threw his hands up in the air. "Fine. Good-bye, Falcio. You were a decent companion, if a little pretentious sometimes. I hope you realize I'm going to rob every damned corpse I encounter from now on."

I smiled. "I suppose that's only fair."

He walked away, stopping only once to turn and say, "I'll fire an arrow into the dying of the light in your name, Falcio. That's all I can do for you."

That might be something, anyway.

Having to wait patiently while the sun sets so that three men can kill you is an awkward feeling.

Shiballe had one of his guards bring him a small table for him to set a bottle of wine on while he passed the time. He kept a pistol on his lap and periodically slid his hand across the smooth wooden grip. The girl had tried to stay awake, but exhaustion overtook fear and she was now sleeping on the bench a few feet behind me.

"A few minutes left, Trattari," Shiballe said, sipping his wine. "Are you sure you wouldn't rather rejoin your friends?"

I didn't bother to reply. When you're in a situation like this, every movement, every word, has to be about gaining advantage. I needed to get him and his men on edge, and that meant everything was about timing.

"I wonder, Trattari, what prompts a man to stand there, perfectly still, while Death comes to claim him? Is it that you don't fear Death? Or perhaps that you fear life even more?"

I waited a moment until he stopped expecting an answer and went back to his wine.

"What's your name?" I asked the nearest of the three guards.

"Silence!" Shiballe said, before the guard could speak.

I ignored him. "My name is Falcio," I said.

"You have no name, tatter-cloak!" Shiballe said.

I kept my gaze on the guard. "My name is Falcio val Mond, and I am First Cantor of the Greatcoats. Do you know what that means?" I asked.

The guard didn't speak, but his mouth opened a little and, despite his efforts to stay still, he shook his head.

"It means that no matter what else happens to me, no matter what happens to the girl, and no matter the little toy your fat friend is stroking, the man nearest to me when the light dies goes to whichever hell waits for men who would murder children."

"Stop talking to my men, tatter-cloak!" Shiballe threw his nearly empty wine glass at me.

I congratulated myself on not flinching at all as it hit my right arm and fell to the street, shattering.

Shiballe's men flinched, though.

"My name is Falcio val Mond," I said again.

"Say it again, I seem to forget," Shiballe snarled. "Come on, Trattari, what is your name?"

"You know my name," I said softly, eyes still locked on the man in front of me.

"No, really, I can't remember it. Please do say it again."

"You know my name," I repeated.

The guard in front of me unconsciously mouthed my name. With the slightest of movements he shuffled back a few inches, putting him just slightly behind the second guard, who suddenly looked very uncomfortable. Good. They were scared. They'd be cautious when it started, and caution isn't always a good thing in situations like this one.

"The next man who moves a hair dies," Shiballe said, pointing his pistol at the second man.

"Keep it on me," I said, and Shiballe jerked the pistol back toward me. I smiled just a little, for effect. "What's my name?" I asked.

"I don't know. I don't remember the names of dogs," Shiballe said.

"You know my name."

"I'll kill you right now, dog," he said, but it was largely an idle threat. No one in Rijou would violate the one law of the Blood Week, not even him. On the other hand, the last rays of the sun were just starting to fade out.

"Girl," I said, "get six feet behind me and stay there until it's done."

She got up and immediately started coughing, no doubt from the smoke she'd inhaled inside her home as it burned her mother and brothers to death, but she looked more dazed than scared as she shuffled a few feet behind me.

"What's my name?" I asked the guards again.

"Falcio," one of them muttered, and Shiballe almost used up his pistol on him right there, which would have made things much easier. But I knew I wasn't going to be that lucky.

Shiballe looked over at the soft glow off the edges of the rooftops and smiled. "Another few seconds, tatter-cloak. Any last words?"

I smiled back at him. "Watch out for the arrow."

And then the light winked out, a great bell rang, an arrow fell from the sky, and all hells broke loose.

True to his word, Brasti had fired an arrow in my name when the sun died. I imagine he had stood up on the hill outside the first gate, hundreds of yards from where I now stood, and pulled Intemperance from the locking hook attached to his saddle. Intemperance was a greatbow, nearly six feet long and powerful enough to drive the head of an arrow deep into stone or brick, and more than enough to drive through plate mail. It wasn't suited to any kind of close fighting, but from a distance—well, from a distance it was like dropping thunderbolts from the sky.

Now I've said that Brasti almost never misses, but this was an impossible shot. To get the kind of distance required he'd have had to carefully factor the breeze and distance, and aim very nearly straight up into the sky, with just the tiniest tilt to ensure its giant arc would bring it down into the middle of the street in Rijou. An impossible shot, as I said, and I won't try to turn legend into myth by telling you that he somehow managed to drop the arrow through Shiballe's pistol hand (which would have been awfully nice). But he did get it close enough to give the fat bastard a start so that Shiballe missed what should have been a sure shot. Instead, the ball from his pistol smashed into the ground between me and the nearest of the three guards, and the man very nearly fell into his neighbor as he lost his footing. I launched myself as high and hard as I could, my left elbow aiming for the first guard's face even as my right hand drew a rapier from its sheath. If you're wondering why I moved so quickly and didn't so much as flinch first, the answer is simple: I'd spent the entire time standing there with Shiballe and his men, preparing for the unexpected. You see, it doesn't matter how fast or skilled or clever you think you are, four armed men with their weapons out are always going to beat a single opponent, unless something happens to surprise them. Greatcoats carry a good number of things to surprise an opponent, but they don't work very well if you can't reach into your coat to get them. So if nothing unusual had happened, I'd doubtless have died before I got my first strike in. A small miracle came along, giving me the initiative, and I just needed to act.

The point of my elbow connected squarely with the bridge of the first guard's nose. The other got his blade up in time to block my rapier, but he wasn't my target. I let my point drop right under the guard of his war-sword and flicked it into the face of the third man. People always underestimate the reach of a rapier—trust me, it's longer than it looks.

I heard the girl behind me scream and saw Shiballe reloading, but I ignored it. By the time he'd got that pistol ready I'd either have won or I'd be dead. I will admit that it's a bit distracting to have someone a few feet away from you loading a weapon that would definitely kill you, but I had three other opponents to help keep me focused.

The second man—the one who'd tried to parry me—did a nicely professional job of spinning his block into a downward vertical strike aimed at my left shoulder. Unfortunately for him, I tilted my body sideways and watched it sail down past my nose before stepping on it hard. Then I flicked the tip of my right rapier past the face of the third man again and drew my second rapier with my left hand, getting it out just in time to make an awkward parry against the first man (the one I'd elbowed in the face). He threw the weight of his own sword into a cut at my left side and I took it on the blade. The force of his blow bashed the side of my rapier against me, but it kept me from suffering more than bruised ribs. I pushed the guard of my rapier down hard to knock his weapon off balance.

Shiballe was pushing powder into his pistol when the girl foolishly tried to wrest it from his hands.

"Aline, get away!" I screamed, flicking the tips of both my rapiers up into the faces of my opponents to distract them.

The girl managed to spill Shiballe's powder to the ground, but then he grabbed her wrists and flipped her around, getting his right arm around her neck.

"Trattari!" he shouted. "Drop your weapons, or I'll snap her neck like a twig."

Everyone froze. There wasn't the slightest doubt in my mind that he'd do it, but this is where we get down to the mathematics of the situation. Think of it this way: Shiballe had three men; one, with a broken nose, was bleeding heavily and the other two were getting a little sloppy. Now, let's say he breaks her neck right now: what happens? Well, I almost certainly launch myself at him, drive my sword into his fat belly, and get killed by one of his men. Bad for me, bad for Shiballe—good for Shiballe's men, but that's poor consolation when you've got a sword buried in your stomach. The math doesn't really suit Shiballe here.

Now let's say instead I nobly put down my weapons. The guards kill me, Shiballe kills the girl, finishes his bottle of wine, and goes home happy. The math is good for Shiballe, but very bad for me and for the girl. So that option doesn't work either.

What's really left? Well, let's imagine for a moment that time freezes. Where are we? Shiballe's got the girl so he feels better than if he had nothing and I'm (barely) holding off three guards. No one's dead yet and everything's possible and, strange as it might sound, that's about the best option for everyone.

But of course time hasn't frozen, and something has to happen.

This is where the mathematics really comes into play: you see, while it's true that almost everyone has an interest in nothing changing, Shiballe's position doesn't really change that much whether he has three guards on me or two. I mean, I'm not saying it would be his first choice but he still gets a two-to-one advantage, and he still has the girl. So if something *has* to happen, then one of the guards dying is, mathematically speaking, the best option available to all of us.

That's why I drove the point of the rapier in my left hand into the first man's throat.

Shiballe's arm tightened on the girl's neck. "You're killing her, Trattari," he said.

"Sorry," I said. "Reflex."

"Drop your weapons, dog, and the girl at least will live."

Fat chance. "You kill her and I'll stab you in the face long before either of these incompetents gets a blow on me."

He hesitated. "Then we appear to be at an impasse," he said.

Both his men had their swords ready, but they were waiting for a cue to act.

"Not really," I said. Remember the math? "You see, there are only a few possible outcomes here: one, you kill the girl, I kill you, your men kill me. The second possibility, you don't kill the girl, I kill your men, and then I kill you."

"I think I can see another possible outcome, Trattari," he said. "Another of my men comes down the street, sees what's happening, and kills you."

One of the guards smiled at that prospect.

"Don't get your hopes up," I told him. "This'll be over long before that happens."

The guard tightened his grip on his sword. I looked back at Shiballe. "There is a third alternative."

"Ah, of course, you mean the one where we let you go on your merry way and trust you won't murder me in my sleep?" he asked.

"No, don't be silly. I'm going to kill you one way or another, if not today, then someday in the future. You're a sick bastard and I can't stand the idea of a world that has you in it. No, my solution is much simpler, and actually has a chance of working."

I took a breath. "You order your men to attack me together and you start running as fast as you can. Sure, they'll be sacrificing themselves, but as long as they're trying to stay alive they'll give you the time you need to get away into the alleyways of this shithole you call a city. Chances are I won't get to you before either you're well hidden or someone comes along to kill me and the girl."

I waited for a moment to let him think about it. "It really is the best option, mathematically speaking," I said, to reassure him.

His men were shifting nervously. "I like you, tatter-cloak," Shiballe said cheerfully. "You make good sense. However, if my guards attack you now, it really won't impede my progress that much if I just twist this harlot's daughter's head off first, so I think that's what we'll do."

I sighed. "You really don't understand probability and mathematics, now, do you, Shiballe?"

He screamed for his men to attack, grabbed the girl's head with his free hand, keeping his right arm firmly around her neck, and started to twist.

I threw my right-hand rapier at Shiballe's face, point first. Startled, he ducked, nearly losing his footing. As his men leapt for me, the girl squirmed out of his grasp and—stupidly—ran for the pistol, which was still unloaded. I sidestepped one blade and blocked the other. Shiballe reached for the girl again, but by then I'd kicked the knee out from the guard on my left and Shiballe saw the odds shifting against him. "Fight, you damned fools!" he screamed as he ran for the alleyway on the other side of the street.

The guard whose knee I'd broken did an admirable job of fighting through the pain. He grabbed my left leg, pulling me down to the ground and giving his friend an opening to bring his blade down on me. As I went down on my back I shifted my rapier to my right hand and extended it fully. The tip pierced the attacker's throat and his blade fell from his hand as his knees buckled under him.

That left the girl holding an empty pistol and clicking the trigger futilely, Shiballe long gone into the alleyways of the city, looking for help, and me lying on my back with the first guard still holding my leg and pulling a knife from his belt.

"What's my name?" I asked calmly.

He stopped and looked back at me for a second, maybe trying to figure his chances. After a moment he slid back, dropped the knife, and said, "Idiot should've killed the girl first."

"True," I said, getting my feet under me and standing.

"Are you going to kill me now? I thought you tatter-cloaks didn't do that unless there was no other way?" the guard asked, holding his broken knee.

"No, I'm not going to—"

The point of a rapier stabbed into his right ear. I got my sword up, and only then realized the girl had done it: she had dropped the useless pistol and picked up my fallen rapier and driven it into the side of the man's head.

Calmly as anything, she pulled the blade out, wiped the blood off on the guard's face, and handed the rapier back to me, hilt first.

"We should run now," Aline said.

13

THE BULLY BOYS

My stratagem for keeping the girl alive was simple: find a place to hide and stay there until the week was over. Then she would be free to seek shelter from another noble family, or she could leave the city entirely. Either way, she would be alive, and that was a good enough outcome for me. Find a place to hide, wait until it's over: nothing could be simpler. It was sometime around the third bell of our first night before I realized why it wouldn't work.

Shiballe had assumed that he and his men would be more than sufficient to take out one man and a young girl, and that error in judgment had bought us enough time to make our way from Aline's street, through the merchants' quarter and into the Redbrick District. This had been one of the most affluent parts of the city two centuries ago, but over time the red clay used to make the bricks had begun to wear down, making every building a catastrophe waiting to happen. The richer merchants moved out and the poor moved into the fallen buildings and decaying streets. Those who squatted in the most broken-down buildings were the poorest of all. With broken sewer lines and no running water and with every strong storm promising disaster, it was a terrible place to live—but it would have been a perfect place to hide, if it hadn't been for the magic. Saints, how I hate magic.

It took us less than an hour to find a suitable hiding place. The building had barely any walls standing and was next to a sealed-off alleyway. The top two stories had fallen down completely, and the single remaining floor had one long wall and part of another exposed to the elements. But inside, enough debris had fallen to create a kind of fortress within the husk of the old building. There were good sight lines from inside, and at least two escape routes if necessary. Contrary to my expectations, the girl didn't complain about the standard of accommodation. Instead, she looked around once and then walked in. I made one quick circle around the building to look for possible signs of ownership before I settled down next to her and started rubbing my leg. The wound I'd taken from the constable's crossbow had mostly healed now, but weeks on the road made for a stiff limb. I supposed it would get all the rest it needed now, though we would soon have to find a source of water and at least a little food to survive the week.

"They're coming," Aline said softly.

"They're not." I was confident we hadn't been followed, and I had taken the added precaution of circling back several blocks to make sure before we settled in Redbrick. And if they hadn't followed us, then they couldn't know where we were. And in a city the size of Rijou, the chances of Shiballe's minions happening upon us were very slim indeed.

"I can hear them."

"It's the rats," I said, then realized it might not be helpful to a young girl to remind her of the likely other residents of the building.

"It's not rats. It's people."

I listened for a moment. My hearing isn't exceptional, but it's not that bad either.

"There are lots of people living in Redbrick. Trust me, they want nothing to do with us," I said. Then I heard the slight sound of metal clanging against metal. Metal was, by and large, expensive, and besides, I know the sound a smallshield makes when it's attached at a man's hip and rubs against his sword.

"Shit."

When I peered around the corner I could see them coming: four groups of two, working their way in from separate sides of the building. So much for the escape routes.

I tried to think of a strategy for getting out of this without a fight, but nothing came to mind. It was obvious that they knew their quarry was in the building, and even if I could get by one pair, the girl wasn't fast enough to outrun the others. I didn't see any pistols or bows, just swords and clubs: bully boys; tough, stupid thugs that go from terrorizing other children to killing for money, and sometimes just for fun. I swore under my breath. I could take any one of them—I could take any two of them—but even I can't fight six at once. My plan for an open space that made for easy escape had just turned into a perfect place to snare us. Bully boys weren't known for their tactical brilliance and this bunch were likely far too stupid to figure out a good way to ambush us; they'd needed me for that.

"We should run," Aline said.

"How fast can you run?" I asked.

"Fast enough to get to the alley if we can get past the pair on that side."

"Won't work—the alley's a trap. The one end's blocked off and the sides are narrow. We'll never be able to get by the others once they follow us."

"But they won't be able to get around us, either," she said.

I thought about it for a moment and then marveled that this little girl, still coughing from nearly burning to death and on the run for her life, had worked out for herself that we weren't getting out of this by running. I'd have to fight, and I'd have a lot better chance if they could only come at me one or two abreast.

"All right," I said, pulling a bracer of small throwing knives from inside my coat. There were six of them in all, each one about four inches long and weighted at the tip: not much for distance, but not bad for this situation. "As soon as we break through the pair at the alley exit, run straight for the dead end. From there I want you to stay four paces behind me. Do you understand? *Four paces.*"

Aline looked a little terrified now that she realized we really were going to try and fight our way out of this.

I showed her the bracer. "Each time I say 'knife,' I want you to hand me one of these. You hand them to me with the flat end pointing toward me. Understand?"

As she held out her hand for the knives I heard feet scrape on the ground not far from us. Two of them would be coming to flush us out, so I planned to give them an easy time of it. I gestured to the girl, then pulled one of my rapiers and leapt out from our hiding place.

Exactly as I'd expected, there were two of them, quite close, both tall and stocky, with clubs at the ready. I could see the other pairs all stationed near the exits. I wanted to take the two nearest us out right away, but that would slow us down and was a luxury I couldn't afford. Instead I swung my rapier in a wide arc, as fast as I could, and made them jump back.

"Run!" I shouted, and Aline followed close behind me as we ran straight at the two men waiting by the alleyway exit. These two also held thick clubs—a stupid weapon against a rapier, but then most bully boys don't have money or inclination for a good sword, let alone the training in how to use it properly. But I didn't want these two getting in a blow on the back of my head, so I couldn't just try to scare them and run past. I feinted low at the one on my right. Always feint low when you can with an opponent with a heavy weapon: if he goes for the feint, it takes a lot more energy for him to get the weapon back up than it does to bring it down.

The feint worked, but the man on the left didn't hesitate; he swung his own club at my shoulder. As I ducked under the swing, I stabbed the man on the right in the gut before he had time to get his weapon back up to a guard position. We were all so close together that I couldn't get my blade back into guard myself, so I just pushed against the man's elbow and threw him off balance, then kicked the wounded man back.

"Come on," I said, and we ran through the exit and into the alley. The backs of the two- and three-story buildings all pressed close together made for a dark tunnel, with no visible means of escape—no doors, no windows; people here were more afraid of someone breaking into their houses than they were of needing to get out quickly. We made straight for the dead end.

Six feet before the wall I turned. "Remember, four paces back except when I call for a knife."

"I'm not stupid," she said, taking up her position.

I didn't have time to respond. The uninjured man came through and ran toward us with a yell, club swinging. I let the idiot get within four feet and simply extended my sword as his swing went past my face, missing it by inches. The one thing you don't do when you have a shorter weapon is just run in and swing it at an opponent with a longer pointy weapon. All he has to do is extend his arm and you're done. And he was.

The rest of the bully boys came through more carefully. *Damn.* They all had swords and smallshields and they smiled at each other as they came toward us step by step, knowing that they could make better use of the narrow alley if they held together.

"Knife." I reached back with my left hand, palm up. "Knife!" I said again when I didn't feel anything. The men were about six feet away when I felt the cool metal against my palm.

"I'm sorry!" Aline said breathlessly. "It was stuck in the bracer."

I hadn't oiled the blades or the bracer for weeks; no wonder she had trouble getting it out. I cursed my own laziness as I threw the blade underhand. Some Saint must have favored me for a moment, because it dug deeply into a man's thigh. Greatcoat throwing blades are smaller than usual, but they have a quilled shape to the points that leaves a nasty mark—if you can even get it out.

"Kest, Brasti, hit them with the crossbows!" I shouted, glancing up toward the rooftops as I deflected a straight thrust coming at my face. The man in front of me ignored the ploy, but the one just behind him threw his arms over his head in a pretty vain attempt to protect himself from an attack from the top of the alley wall. When you're fighting a crowd, it's good to shout potentially threatening things like "Crossbows!" or "Fire!" or "Giant Flying Cat!" every once in a while. When people are in the middle of a battle they'll look more often than not, and in this kind of fight, every second is a chance to do some damage and otherwise avoid the inevitable.

I took a chance and slipped my rapier point past the man in front to skewer his more cautious friend in the chest. It's a risky move, for two reasons: First, because your blade is now out of line and the man in front of you has a chance to straighten his point before you can guard against it. I was willing to take that gamble because my opponent wasn't especially fast and he was using a heavier—and thus slower—sword. The second risk is that you should never stab a man in the chest—the gut, the groin, the sides where the soft-tissue organs are, even the face, they're all good targets. But the chest has ribs, and ribs are wonderful things for trapping swords, especially when a man starts to fall backward, and that's exactly what happened to me as I found myself holding my dying opponent's weight on my rapier.

His friend in front saw my predicament and smiled the big, dumb smile of a bully boy who's got you trapped. But the poor man had probably never heard of Falcio's Flying Blades.

You probably haven't either, so it's best if I explain. Early on in my career as a Greatcoat, I had the genius idea of having my rapier blades made with a type of heavy coiled spring in the guard, with a small lever that, if pushed by the thumb, would release the catch and launch the blade into your opponent at a distance. Brilliant, right? Unfortunately, however, as Kest, Brasti, the King, and most especially the King's Armorer, Heimrin, all pointed out, there was never going to be enough force in such a small spring to launch a two-pound rapier blade very far. The result was that when I pointed my very, very expensive rapiers at someone and pressed the lever, the blades just sort of flopped out a few inches and dropped to the ground. So, as it turns out, Falcio's Flying Blades became known as Falcio's Floppy Fumblers. The damned things cost me a fortune though, and they were still perfect weapons if you didn't hit the lever, so I kept them.

Which is why my opponent, standing just a few inches from me and ready to bring his blade down on my head, was very surprised when I pushed the lever with my thumb, pulled my rapier guard back off the blade, and hit him in the face with it. The small studs that adorn the guard make an especially memorable impression, and he fell back unconscious with an expression that indicated he felt the whole thing was really quite unfair.

I dropped the rapier guard and then threw my hand back, palm up, toward Aline. "Knife," I said again as I unsheathed my second rapier with my left hand.

The girl put a throwing blade in my hand more quickly this time, and I threw it hard at the crowd in front of me. There was a pleasant *thunk* as it hit a man in the chest. Throwing knives in the chest are perfectly acceptable, by the way, since you aren't likely to need to pull them back out right away.

"Knife!" I said again, twice more in succession, to give my opponents something to think about. Each time Aline was quick and ready and, by the time I was hurling my sixth and final knife, I was marveling at the fact that I'd never before had this much good luck with throwing knives. Every single one had made contact and taken an opponent out of the fight. Except, of course, for the sixth one.

The remaining two men came straight for me, but by this time I was used to fighting against the alley walls and they had spent too much time with their juices buzzing in their ears while they had to wait for their friends to either win the fight for them or get killed. They were both about the same height, so I used a tight slash across their eyes, missing the first but catching the second. The blinded one fell back and his partner raised his shield arm to protect his face, giving me the perfect opening to stab him through the groin. It wasn't the most elegant finish to the fight, but we were alive and they weren't, so for a brief instant all was right with the world.

I suppose it's worth mentioning that all throughout our fight, the bully boys kept up a steady stream of insults, inducements, threats, and other invective, but none of it was very clever and I feel it would give them too much honor to bother repeating it. They had names, too, and I could describe their physical differences and fighting styles, but I'm not going to. It may be petty, but I don't think these bastards deserve to be remembered.

As the rush of blood started to subside, I looked at the carnage in front of us.

"Can I come closer now?" Aline asked. As she came forward I expected her to be shocked by the sight of the bodies in front of her. Some were unconscious, but most were dead and lying in pools of blood. I was strangely reassured when she hunched over and vomited on the alley floor, but then she stood up, walked over to one of the bodies, pulled out my throwing knife, and started cleaning it using cloth from the man's shirt.

"You don't have to do that," I said as I put a hand on her shoulder.

She flinched, then pushed my hand away. "Someone has to do it. I can't fight, so I may as well do this," she said.

I leaned back on the alley wall and slid down to the ground. I could have slept, right there, right in the middle of an alley strewn with corpses.

When she was done with cleaning the knives and replacing them in the bracer, the girl started to pick over the bodies.

"Leave them be," I said, my voice thick with exhaustion. I forced my uncooperative legs to push me back up so that I could reassemble my rapiers.

"I have no money, and they tried to kill me. The least they can do is pay for our supplies," she said. Brasti would've been proud.

But the men didn't have much money to speak of. Aline showed me a handful of coins and a single silver bit. Their weapons were nothing special compared with what I already carried, so I didn't bother looking any further.

"Can I take this?" Aline asked. She held up one of the dead men's hands to show me a small disk on the palm, a little larger than a caravaner's silver mark. It was made of copper or bronze and attached by thin leather straps looped around his two middle fingers and thumb.

"I don't think it's valuable," I said.

"I know," she said defensively, "but it's interesting and I like how it almost glows a bit when you rub your thumb on it."

I was about to give in, but something started to itch at the back of my neck. I knelt down next to her and examined it more carefully. The disk had very faint markings on it, parallel lines with offshoots and curves, and a bit near the center was shinier than the rest.

"Look," Aline said. She pressed her finger on it and it grew shinier, as if it had just been cleaned in that spot.

I looked at it for a moment and then took her hand and replaced her finger with my own. Nothing happened. The spot near the center was still shinier, but not as much as when Aline touched it. I took my finger off and held her hand above it. The spot looked ever so slightly brighter, and became more so the closer her hand came to it.

"Shit," I said. "Magic. I *hate* magic."

"That's silly," she said. "Why bother making a disk that just gets a bright spot when you touch it? Even the magic symbols look odd—just a bunch of lines."

"It gets brighter when it gets closer to *you*—and those markings aren't magic symbols, they're streets. Look—" I pulled the disk from the dead man's hand and we walked down to the end of the alley. The markings on the disk, barely visible to the eye, changed slightly.

"It's like a map!" Aline said, clearly missing the salient problem.

"It's more than that," I said. "It's a map that leads them straight to you."

Shiballe and the Duke had a mage at their disposal: one powerful enough to create an amulet that could lead their men to us anywhere in the city. It was inscribed on cheap copper—you could make five for a penny. And people ask me why I hate magic.

We made our way farther into the old city. I guessed we had a little time before Shiballe discovered that his bully boys had failed him and sent someone else after us. It was possible that he might send the entire City Guard after us, but Rijou is a bad place to do something like that, what with so many narrow, winding streets and so many other ways in and out of districts. And anyway, most of the Guard are otherwise engaged during the Blood Week, protecting the Duke's favorites and harassing those unfortunates to whom he was less favorably disposed.

Still, the amulet bothered me.

I pulled it out to look at it again. As we'd only found the one, I wasted time on a faint hope that if two were close to each other, they might cancel each other out. Likely nonsense, of course. I'd taken to using it to get a quick overview of the streets and alleyways nearby. Old Town wasn't ideal from a hiding perspective, but since we didn't have much in the way of other options, I was glad of one helpful feature: the buildings were stacked close together. I found a wall with enough protruding beams and bricks on the outside to make it possible to climb.

"Why are we going up? Won't it just make it harder to run?" the girl asked.

"The amulets show where we are, but not how high," I said as we neared the top. "They could be right underneath us and not realize it."

She didn't comment, but I suspected that was more from exhaustion than anything else.

We reached the top of the building. It was a full three stories high, and afforded us what was doubtless a beautiful view of the city at dusk. I could see flames as at least two other noble houses about a mile away went up in smoke: the Duke's friends at work, no doubt.

"Where . . . now?" Aline said weakly, collapsing onto the roof's flat surface. I took a more serious look at her and saw that exhaustion was indeed overtaking her.

"We try to keep to the rooftops when we can. When we can't, we climb down just long enough to find another place to hide."

Two days, I realized: we'd been on the move for two full days and neither of us had slept. The night before, she'd suffered the loss of her family. It was too much. I didn't think she'd make another step.

"Are there any noble houses who might give you protection?" I asked, though I was pretty sure I already knew that answer.

With what looked like a real effort, Aline raised her head. "No. My nanny said we used to be a powerful family, but not anymore."

Supporting the King had never been a way to make friends in Rijou.

"I met your father once," I said. "Lord Tiarren was a good man."

Aline's face was thoughtful, as if I'd said something unusual. "He was always kind to me," she said, "but I do not think he loved me as he did my brothers."

"Why do you say that?"

She paused again, as if looking for the proper words. "He was gentle, and he gave me fine gifts on my birthday. He spoke to me courteously, as he did my mother. But with my older brothers he was always more . . . proud."

"I . . ." Damn. What do you tell a child? That fathers don't always love their daughters as they should? That noble families want strong boys to lead their houses, not girls whose dowries must be paid? "I think if your father could see you right now he would be very proud."

She gave a small smile, but it was a smile for me, not because of me. The exhaustion was overwhelming her.

I knelt down and reached into one of the inner pockets of my coat. I extracted a small package wrapped in silk. "Here," I said.

Aline took the package and unwrapped it, revealing the square of striped candy underneath.

"What is this?"

"We call it the hard candy," I replied.

"Candy?" She looked annoyed.

"Just eat a tiny bit."

She started to take a bite and I grabbed her arm. "Just a small piece," I said. "Just a taste."

The girl looked confused, but she obeyed me and took just a tiny nibble from the corner. Then she made a face, and I thought she was about to spit it out.

I held my finger up. "Just wait."

We sat for a few moments as the sky turned a little darker. Suddenly Aline leapt to her feet, eyes wide, tense as a cat staring down a pack of dogs.

"How do you feel?" I asked.

"Like—like I could run the length of the city, twice over," she replied, looking all around her. "I don't feel tired at all—it's like I just woke up!"

"Try to keep steady and focused," I said. "It takes a while to get used to the hard candy."

"It's all right—I'm fine. We can go now if you like."

"No, now I need to rest for a minute."

She held out the package toward me, but I wrapped her hand around it. "You hang on to it. There isn't much, and I try to avoid using it." When she looked at me quizzically, I added, "It's good for keeping you awake, it's good for running, it's good for staying alive. But it's not especially good for strategic thinking, or for swordwork."

"Then why—?"

"We Magisters have to travel a long way, and sometimes, if we need to get somewhere quickly, we have to keep ourselves going for days—or, just as likely, get away from somewhere before we're caught."

Aline put the silk-wrapped package in her pocket.

"Use it sparingly," I warned. "Too much at once can make your heart explode in your chest."

The girl sat down next to me, though I knew it was hard for her to keep still now. "Why 'hard'?" she asked.

"Hmm?" I said, and only then realized I was starting to nod off. The sky was fully dark. We needed to get moving.

"Why is it the 'hard candy'?"

"Because it's not the same as the soft candy," I said, pulling out a still smaller package from another pocket.

"So if the hard candy is for giving you energy, what's the soft candy for then?" she asked, reaching for it.

I pulled it away. "It's for something else," I said. "It's for something else entirely."

"Falcio?"

I opened my eyes. "Shit. How long was I asleep?"

"Just a couple of minutes," Aline said. "I wanted to let you rest but I think I heard something."

I got to my feet and listened. Nothing. Not for the first time, I wished my hearing was more acute.

"It's there," she said, and then I heard it: soft shoes on stone, climbing to the roof.

"Damn," I said. I pulled out the bracer of knives and handed it to Aline. "Same thing as before," I said. "Stay four paces behind me."

I pulled both my rapiers out. The roof was a wide-open space, and I could use that to advantage.

They came, eight of them, dark as shadows across the roof. Hells, I never should have let myself fall asleep. We should have kept on the move.

"Put your swords down or we'll gut you," came a voice from the north edge of the building. It was strangely pitched: was it a woman?

"I'm fairly sure you'll gut me whether I put my swords down or not," I shouted back. "So I might as well bleed you and your friends first."

"Not if you put those nice blades down, along with any money you've got, and leave our territory," the voice replied.

Territory? Then they weren't Shiballe's men?

"I'm afraid we don't have much in the way of money, and I'm rather in need of these swords of late. How about if we just leave and you can keep your territory?"

I heard Aline gasp, and then made out the sound of someone climbing up the wall right behind us.

"Tell your man he's about to learn secrets only the dead know," I said, keeping my left point up and taking two steps back to the ledge with my right-hand blade ready to sweep. Something whizzed by my right leg and skipped off the ledge. It wasn't an arrow, nor a bolt. Could it have been a sling-stone? I heard a stunned cry from behind me.

"Boxer, y'fool! I told'ja not to try that again. Get the hells back down and keep watch!" the leader shouted past me.

"Can't! My foothold broke! Somebody help me up!" said the scared voice. This one was high-pitched too.

"Look, no point anyone dying who doesn't have to," I called out. "How about you don't shoot at me and I give your little friend a hand up?"

"Call me 'little,' you son of a—"

"Shut it, Boxer!" The leader came a few feet forward, and the others joined him: kids. They were all damned kids no older than Aline. There was a dog with them too, a Sharpney, by the look of him, a big, fast breed that made excellent hunting dogs. I hoped I wouldn't have to kill him.

"You try anything funny and the girl dies first," the leader said. He was about thirteen, and I could make out a shock of straight hair above a dirty face. "And if you get advantage on one of us, Mixer here will tear your throat out." He motioned to the dog.

"Typical," said one of the others, this one clearly a girl. "You always try to hit girls first, Venger."

"Shut it," he said. "No foolin'; you let Boxer up and then y'put down your sword or there's gonna be trouble." The dog let out a low rumble in agreement. "Mixer, stay," he said firmly.

I smiled, put down my left-hand sword, and stepped back. I held my hand over the edge and felt something grab it and tentatively try to pull me over, but I was well grounded and ready for it.

"Try that again and I'll drop you, you little shit-eater," I said in as pleasant a tone as I could muster.

"Boxer! Don't mess around," Venger said angrily.

"A'right," Boxer said.

I hauled him up one-handed—not as hard a task as it might have been if he'd weighed more than air. What I saw when I pulled him in front of me was another scrawny, dirty-faced boy, probably ten years old.

"Y'gonna try and hold me hostage now, bastard?" Boxer said, clearly readying an elbow for my groin.

I pushed him forward and off balance and he fell to his knees a few feet between me and the kids.

"What now?" I asked.

Venger looked me up and down. "You can go, I s'pose, what with Boxer bein' such a fool turd. But you leave the money. And if you value any part of your life you take that coat off and leave it too," he said.

I shook my head. "That won't do, I'm afraid; I need them all. What would you do with a Greatcoat, anyway? It's bigger than you are."

Venger sneered. "Burn it," he said.

It's nice to be so widely loved. "Don't like Greatcoats?"

"Don't like fools that dress up as 'em," he said. "Everyone knows there ain't no Greatcoats no more."

"He is, too," Aline said, stepping out from behind me and leaping to my defense.

"Shut up, girl," Venger said, "you don't know nothin' 'bout it."

That got Venger a slap in the back of the head from one of the girls in his group. "Stop pickin' on girls all the time, Venger," she warned.

"Ow! I'm not. She'd be wrong if she was a boy, too."

"Listen," I said, "my name is Falcio val Mond, First Cantor of the King's Magisters. I'm trying very hard right now to keep this girl alive, and there are a lot of people after me. So you can either take my word that I'm a Greatcoat and get the hells out of our way, or I can take you over my knee and spank you 'til you can't see straight. Now take your pick."

That got a few snickers from his friends, but to his credit, he ignored the jibe and kept to business. "If you're a Greatcoat, then answer me this: how come you let the armies kill the King if you're all supposed to be such tough fighters? How come every one of you betrayed their old Paelis?"

"Because the Greatcoats were ordered to stand down and accept the Covenant. It was an order."

"Yeah? An' who gave 'em the order?"

"I did," I said.

I had been working in the library of Castle Aramor, maps strewn across the long table and two-centuries-old books on warfare in my hands. The Ducal Army would be here within hours and we had only a hundred and forty-four Greatcoats and a small troop of Royal Guardsmen, and the staff and residents of the castle. It wasn't a lot to work with, but I had got a few ideas from the old books. I would have dearly loved weapons for countering sieges right then, but I was ready to make do without.

I heard someone come in and turned to see the King. He was casually dressed, in the gear we wore for practicing swordwork.

"I don't suppose you'd reconsider?" I asked him, still looking at the diagram of the castle on the table for a way to block the South Gate so that I wouldn't have to divert troops there.

"Kings don't get to run, Falcio," he said.

I looked up at him. "Well, if you can't ride fast, you fight hard."

"Not this time. The motto is 'Judge fair, ride fast, fight hard,' remember? 'Fight hard' is the last option. Besides, there's a reason why no King of Tristia has ever been allowed to maintain a private army. The soldiery has always been the Dukes' protection against a tyrant taking absolute power."

"Then what—?"

"You're going to stand the men down, Falcio. I'm *ordering* you to stand the men down."

"But we can fight! I've thought it through and the Magisters are ready. If you'll only go over these plans with me I can show you—"

"Enough. I'm still King, for the next few hours, at any rate."

"But I'm telling you we can fight!"

He started to answer, but a coughing fit overtook him. It was coming on winter and he'd not slept in three days.

"You can fight, Falcio," he said finally, "but you can't win. And even if you could, every one of the Magisters would lose their lives."

"What kind of life will we have when the Dukes take us?" I slammed my fist on one of my maps. "Where are the noble families, damn it? How many trips have you taken, 'courting the lesser nobles'? Where are they now that we need them?"

"It isn't their job to throw their lives away on a war they can't win, Falcio. Saints know what I've asked of them is more than they should have had to give in the first place."

"You're talking in circles again when we should be preparing the Greatcoats!"

The King walked over to me and put a hand on the side of my face. People always seem to do that when they want me to shut up and do something I don't want to do.

"I'm going to tell you what to do now, Falcio. I'm going to give you the new plan. I'm your friend, but I'm your King first. You are going to surrender the castle to the Duke's men, in exchange for safe passage and pardons for the Greatcoats."

He was right; he was my King and my friend and I loved him, but I swear right then I almost hit him. I felt my fingernails pressing into my palms as I clenched my fists. I would have knocked him down, had it not been for the look in his eyes.

"This is how I want it, Falcio, and this is how it will be. The Dukes will agree. They know the Magisters are fierce, and they won't want to pay any more for this adventure than they absolutely have to."

The thought of turning him over to the Dukes was unconscionable. It would mean the destruction of everything the Greatcoats stood for. We had truly believed we could bring law and justice and honor to the world, and now he was taking that from me. I felt sick, betrayed.

"Fine, damn you, *my liege*," I said, pulling away from him. "But don't ask me to give the order. Get Dara or someone else."

The King leaned on the table. "It has to be you, Falcio."

"Why? Why by the Gods? Why would you make *me* be the one to give this order—*this abomination*—to the Greatcoats?"

His voice grew very quiet then as he said, "Because if you don't give the order, no one will follow it."

A few hours later, just before the Ducal Army's vanguard arrived, I gave the Greatcoats the order, and they followed it.

14
THE NEW GREATCOATS

"Reckon he's telling the truth, Venger?" one of the scrawny assemblage asked.

Venger looked at me. "Reckon he is. Reckon he's what he says he is, and he did what he said he did."

I sheathed one sword and picked up the other and sheathed that as well. I took the bracer of knives back from Aline and put it back in my coat. "So we're done?"

"We didn't mean no harm," Venger said. "We thought you was one of those fools goin' 'round calling themselves Greatcoats. Just thought as how we'd put a scare in you, is all."

That gave me a jolt. "Someone's going around pretending to be a Greatcoat? Who would ever do that?"

"I would," came a voice from the far side of the building.

In the blink of an eye my blade was in my hand and Venger's crew were all crouched and ready to fight. The man casually walked over to us. He was young, about eighteen years old, and a little taller than me. He was thin, with sandy hair and an angular face, and he was carrying a rapier much like mine on his left hip. And he was wearing a Greatcoat.

Venger recognized him, and suddenly the tension went out of him and his group. "Aw, Cairn, you dumb pug. Go back and fight your own shadow some more."

Cairn ignored him and walked up to me, disregarding my outstretched sword, and gave me an awkward hug. "Brother!" he said. "When I heard there was another of us in the city, being chased by the Duke's men . . ." He pulled back and looked me up and down. "And one of the first, too! Are you Parrick? I'd heard rumors he was alive and had come through this way."

"Parrick doesn't look a bit like me, and he's nowhere near here. I'm Falcio—"

Cairn gasped, "So it's *true*—!" He dropped to one knee. "First Cantor," he said portentously, "my name is Cairn of the New Greatcoats. My life is at your disposal."

Venger snorted. "Better dispose of it soon, too," he said. "It's likely to smell bad in a few hours."

"Quiet, Venger, or I'll give you a cuff."

"You just try it, Cairn," Venger said. "I've whupped your ass before and I'll do it again."

"That was—that was just luck," Cairn said, adding quickly, "I was still in training."

I interrupted them and put a hand on Cairn's arm. "What is this about 'new' Greatcoats? Who are you talking about?"

Cairn turned back to me. "We've re-formed the Order of the Greatcoats," he said, excitement and pride brimming over in his voice. "Well, really it was Lorenzo who started it. He's *incredible*. I can't wait for you to meet him—meet everybody. This is *amazing*! Falcio val Mond, *First Cantor*!"

"Wait, give me a moment to understand this. You're telling me that a group of you have started your own Greatcoats?"

He nodded.

"But whose laws do you enforce? There's no King."

He hesitated and Venger snorted again. "Tell 'im, Cairn. Tell 'im all about you and your great bunch of heroes!"

"Well, it's—I mean, we're just starting out still . . ."

"Starting out! Ha! You're just a bunch of spoiled pricks—rich kids from rich families tryin' to act all tough and rebellious."

"I don't understand," I said. "If you don't hear cases, then what do you do?"

"We're still forming the Order," Cairn said. "Look, come with me, let me introduce you to Lorenzo and the New Greatcoats. We could *really* use you."

"How many of you are there? I'm trying to keep this girl alive for the rest of the Blood Week—her family's been killed and the Duke's men are after her."

Cairn smiled. "There's almost *thirty* of us—trust me, Falcio, we can help you keep her alive. We're *strong* together—Lorenzo's the greatest swordsman who's ever lived!"

I seriously doubted that, but I needed allies, and I didn't think Venger's child gangsters were going to be much good at keeping us alive.

"You'd be better off stayin' with us," Venger said, as if he could read my thoughts. "I know these streets better'n anyone, and we know ways in and out of every building in Old Town."

It was Cairn's turn to be derisive. "You? Thieves and beggars? You'll probably turn them over to the Duke's men for a shiny coin."

"Say that again," Venger said, a small knife in his hand. "Say it twice more and we'll just see."

"How far to your men?" I asked Cairn.

"Just over a mile, to the other side of Old Town. Come on, we can get there in half an hour!"

I looked at Venger. "Thanks for the offer," I said, "but the men who are after us are brutal, and they won't give quarter or mercy. I know you can handle it, but some of your folk are awfully young."

Venger gave a snort that was almost comical on a boy his age. "Suit y'self," he said, "but I'll tell you straight: I wouldn't trust these fools to guard a dead cat."

Mixer gave a bark, in agreement or hunger, I wasn't sure which.

* * *

I don't know what exactly I was expecting of Cairn's New Greatcoats, but it wasn't what I saw at the stronghold on the far side of Old Town. Inside the wide two-story stone building, small rooms surrounded a single large space in the center. Outside, it was still pitch black; inside, hundreds of candles and a blazing fire in the large central fireplace combined to illuminate the room. A group of musicians were playing reels I'd never heard before, and Cairn's Greatcoats were dancing, their bodies casting undulating shadows against the walls. The result was a primal, almost sexual atmosphere.

"Had you heard anything about this?" I asked Aline. She lived in Rijou, after all.

But she shook her head vigorously. "I remember Mother telling me that the Duke was always sending his men out to find rebel Greatcoats, but I guess I always assumed he meant your people."

I wondered at that. The Covenant specifically forbade any retribution against the Greatcoats. But then again, the Dukes only occasionally played fair, and without exception they played to win.

"Lorenzo!" Cairn shouted excitedly.

The man who turned in response looked like a Saint from an old romance. He was tall, standing at least six and a half feet. His long, golden hair framed a tanned face that would make Brasti look like a decayed crone, and his body made Kest look like an ill-fed orphan. He wore blackened leather pants and a supple mail shirt that I recognized with envy as Ilthen Steel-Ring: hard to make and very, very expensive. The rings blocked both sword and knife, but were light as winter wool. It clung lovingly to his form, showing off his physique to great effect. It was hard not to suspect that might have been intentional. His coat, though . . . His coat was a greatcoat, to be sure; it was certainly well made, and it looked serviceable enough in a fight. But it was not a greatcoat. It wasn't of the Tailor's making. I'd seen every coat she'd ever made, and hers was a cut that couldn't be duplicated by anyone I'd ever encountered. I'd often wondered if the King could have even started the Greatcoats without her.

"Cairn? What in hells are you doing bringing someone here?" Lorenzo said. There was a casual smile on his face but I could hear irritation underneath—irritation, and something more: a sort of mild disdain mixed with tolerance.

"He's one of *us*, Lorenzo," Cairn said, no longer able to contain his excitement. "He's one of the *originals*! It's Falcio, the *First Cantor*!"

Lorenzo eyed me for a moment, clearly unimpressed with what he saw. I had to forgive him that. I was exhausted, road- and battle-weary, my clothes were shabby, and even my greatcoat was torn and patched. He left off his inspection of me for a moment and asked carefully, "Who's the girl?"

"Aline, daughter of Lord Tiarren," I said.

"Saints," Lorenzo said quietly. "I heard what happened." He knelt down, his face now level with hers. "You're safe here now, my Lady. To the hells with Ganath Kalila; the Blood Week won't reach you inside these walls."

Aline gave a proper curtsy and extended her hand. "I am grateful, sir. We are pursued by the Duke's men. If not for this man, I would have died half a dozen times already."

Lorenzo looked up at me. "So it's true then? You really are one of the King's Magisters?"

I nodded.

"The First Cantor?"

I nodded again.

Lorenzo rose to his full height. "Saints," he said, "this is incredible."

He gripped me in a hug and said something that I presumed was "brother" in my ear. For some reason I found the gesture too familiar.

"Brothers! Sisters!" Lorenzo called, his voice carrying above the music, and the musicians stopped almost immediately. Clearly Lorenzo was the man in charge here. All eyes turned to me and I looked around. I guessed there were some forty men and women staring at us, all young, strong, and attractive. I added rich to that list, since the fourth usually accompanies the first three.

"Brothers and sisters, a sign has come to us: a sign from Gods and Saints alike," Lorenzo proclaimed. "This man—this man is Falcio val Mond, First Cantor of the King's Magisters: the man who helped start the Greatcoats has come to us to join our great undertaking!"

At first the cheering was a bit on the unenthusiastic side, as if his audience wasn't quite sure what any of that meant, but it grew steadily until it was a roar in my ear. I felt Aline move closer to me.

"I don't know what this is about," I said quietly to Cairn.

Lorenzo heard me. "It's about you coming here, against all the odds in the world. It's a sign, First Cantor, can't you see? It's the sign we've been waiting for. This is the day we begin the revolution, the day we start the fight for the freedom of our city and our country!"

There was more cheering, and I found myself at a loss. Were these people really planning on bringing the Greatcoats back into the world? How had this started? Was this part of the King's plan? Thoughts swirled around my head, but no conclusion was forthcoming, and all I was left with was an unsettling sense that something wasn't quite right.

"Say something!" someone shouted. A few people laughed, but then others joined in the call until almost everyone was shouting, "Speak! Speak!"

Lorenzo pushed me forward.

Reluctantly, I opened my mouth and started, "I don't know you. I don't know any of you, who you are or what you're about. I'm not here to start some revolution, I'm not here to be a sign, and Saints know I'm not here to lead more good men and women to their deaths."

I paused for a moment, curious about how they would react, but they didn't, so I continued, "The law has been broken—the King's Law. This girl's family has been murdered, and she herself is the target of assassins. Lorenzo spoke true when he told you who I was: my name is Falcio val Mond, and I was First Cantor of the Greatcoats. I've judged in this girl's favor, so it's my job to keep her alive until the end of the Blood Week. That's why I'm here. That's all."

If Lorenzo was disappointed in my speech he didn't show it. He smiled broadly, as if I'd just summoned the ancestors of all good men to battle.

"Did you hear that?" he called out. "The law's been broken, a girl's life hangs in the balance, and a Greatcoat fights to save her. Falcio val Mond's going to save her."

He turned to me and knelt down on one knee. "My Lord Cantor, my name is Lorenzo; my sword is yours; my strength is yours. My life is yours."

Without waiting for a response he rose and turned to the crowd. "Who else stands with Falcio?" he asked.

A deafening roar rose up, my name, shouted over and over. The hells with the amulets; I imagined Shiballe could hear us from the palace.

"I'm grateful," I said quietly to Lorenzo, "but right now we just need—"

He either couldn't hear me through the din or he was ignoring me. "We have begun a great undertaking, my brothers, my sisters—so let's celebrate! Someone get some damned food and drink out here!"

Another roar from the crowd.

Saint Laina-who-whores-for-Gods, I thought, *who are these people?*

I moved through the next few hours as if through a dream—someone else's dream. The hard candy was wearing off and Aline was hungry and weary, so I decided it was better to give her a chance to rest and eat, rather than rely on a mix of herbs and esoteric sugars that would demand payback later on.

"What do you think?" Lorenzo asked me and gestured to his New Greatcoats. The music and dancing had resumed with fervor, and some of the crowd were paired off further down the great hall practicing swordwork.

"They seem very excited," I said, not sure what else to add. They looked to be fair hands with a blade, trained most likely by local fencing masters, as the rich often were. I couldn't fault them for that, and they were certainly eager enough. But something still didn't make sense to me.

"How did all this start?" I asked.

Lorenzo looked at me and smiled, his eyebrow raised. "Ah, now there's a story—but a story for later on. It's time for duels!"

"Duels?"

He rose from his chair and motioned for the musicians to stop. "Brothers, sisters, let's show our Cantor what we can do!"

There were more cheers, and several men and women advanced, pulling swords from their sheaths, waiting for the word from Lorenzo. He pointed to a pair nearby. The woman was strikingly attractive, dark hair framing a sharp but beautiful face, and the look she gave Lorenzo told me they were a couple. The man next to her was close to her height and wiry, and elegant in a dark green shirt beneath his black greatcoat.

"I think Etricia and Mott first, then Sulless and Cole."

There were a few disappointed looks from the others, but everyone parted to make room for the combatants.

"They're fighting with sharps?" I asked. We Greatcoats practiced with blades instead of wooden swords, but we'd had a lot more training than these people had.

"Watch," said Lorenzo.

The man, Mott, launched himself at Etricia, who dodged neatly out of the way and brought the point of her blade in line with Mott's chest. She delivered a thrust I thought for sure would skewer him, but he deflected it with the back of his gloved hand with the sort of calm and precision I normally see from Kest. Then he flipped his hand over and struck back toward her face, far too quickly for her to evade—and yet, she did. It was stunning to watch, almost as if they could read each other's minds and knew each move ahead of time. Then it hit me: they did know each other's moves ahead of time.

I leaned in to Lorenzo and said, "They're not dueling, they're performing. This is all choreographed."

Lorenzo gave me a smile. "Well, yes. We can't really have our Greatcoats injuring each other, can we?"

I was shocked. This was the worst possible way to train fighters: having them work out the choreography together and then performing it. It was as if they thought the speed and sharpened blades somehow made it more real than true fighting with wooden blunts. What were these people thinking?

The fight came to a finish with a delightful flourish of bladework that ended with Etricia standing over Mott in a preposterous pose with the tip of her sword an inch from his eye. The applause was thunderous.

"This is madness," I said to Cairn. "Why don't you train properly?"

"I think it's a bit rude, don't you, to come into our home and criticize our training systems?" Lorenzo said.

"I have suggested—" Cairn began.

"No one asked you to speak, Cairn," Lorenzo said, the warning clear in his voice. Though perhaps not clear enough for Cairn.

"Everyone has a say at a Greatcoats meeting," he said stubbornly. "Why not train the way Falcio suggests? Wooden swords, but *real* fights, *real* training."

Lorenzo sighed and rose from his chair. "All right then," he said, pulling a wickedly long rapier from its sheath. "Let's train, Cairn: straight-ahead combat, you and me."

The crowd moved aside for him, and Cairn looked around nervously. If he was hoping someone would object, he was out of luck.

"But I'm not ready . . . I'm—"

"Leave it," I said. "That's not what I—"

"Come, come, Cairn," Lorenzo said, his eyes locked on his opponent. "A Greatcoat needs to be ready at any time, doesn't he?"

Cairn reluctantly walked toward the center and drew his own sword, a short and obviously cheap weapon. I had the impression that Cairn was not quite so well off as the rest of the people here, and not all that well respected.

"At least use wooden swords," I said. "You're going to damn well kill yourselves like this."

Lorenzo ignored me. He continued to smile as he kept his gaze fixed on Cairn. "You're not afraid, are you, Cairn? Reassure our guest that your honor matters a lot more to you than a scrape here or there."

"Fuck your honor," I said. "Honor's for Knights. Use some sense, boy."

The crowd arrayed themselves in a circle, penning the two men inside.

Cairn looked at me like an animal who has just realized that the door to his cage has been closed behind him. "No, no, he's right. I *want* to be a Greatcoat. I have to be able to fight." He put himself into a rough approximation of a guard position and waited.

Lorenzo signaled to his woman, Etricia, who came over and gave him a wanton kiss on the mouth before smiling wickedly at me. I realized then that this had been a trap, of sorts: Cairn wasn't well respected, he wasn't well liked, and he had embarrassed Lorenzo by bringing me here. They'd all been safe and sound in their make-believe world of Greatcoats and honor and swordplay, but here I was, the ugly truth of the matter. Cairn probably had a lot more idea about what we Greatcoats were really about than the others, and he probably complained a lot more. Now he was going to get a beating.

"Will our guest call the start of the bout?" Lorenzo asked.

"Fine," I said, an idea coming to mind. "When I call the start of the match, you may begin, and you will fight until first blood. Any man goes past first blood shows himself unable to control his blade and forfeits the match." There: see what you can do with that, you pompous cornstalk.

"As you say," Lorenzo said, bowing toward me.

Cairn nodded.

"Fine. Begin," I said.

Lorenzo's blade whipped out and I thought it might be over before it began, but he held the blow before it could connect. A feint, and well executed, for certain—and convincing enough that Cairn had flinched and put his arms up in front of his face, looking to all the world like a child trying to avoid a slap.

The crowd laughed.

"Are you all right?" Lorenzo inquired solicitously, pulling his blade back and leaning forward with an expression of utter concern.

More laughter.

Cairn came back into guard. Lorenzo attacked again, using almost the exact same move. It's not an uncommon trick to make it appear as if you're going to repeat a feint, but this time to follow through with the blow. But in this case, with embarrassment as his aim, Lorenzo simply feinted exactly the same way, and produced exactly the same result. Poor Cairn was humiliated and left off balance.

The audience was stingingly unsympathetic.

At first I was relieved: this would just be a way for Lorenzo to embarrass Cairn and reassert his dominance of the group. But I was mistaken. Lorenzo was an excellent swordsman, and he had all the control he needed to dominate the fight and not draw blood. But as the fight went on, he used that control not to scare Cairn, but to beat him mercilessly with the flat of his blade. No blood was drawn, but Cairn was being badly struck, over and over. When he tried to fight defensively, Lorenzo would sneak past his guard and hit him with the flat. When he tried scoring a touch, Lorenzo punished him with much harder strikes.

To his credit, Cairn kept getting up, taking his punishment—then Lorenzo knocked the tip of Cairn's blade down toward the ground and delivered a vicious strike against his wrist with the flat of his blade. I heard a crack.

"Enough!" I said. "Fighters separate."

Lorenzo stood back for a moment. "First Cantor? I don't understand—I thought you said we fought to first blood?"

I looked out into the crowd. A few looked horrified at what was happening, but more, many, many more, looked gleeful at the show they were getting.

"The boy's had enough," I said.

"I—" Cairn began.

"He can withdraw if he wishes," Lorenzo said soothingly, "but any man or woman who runs from a fight is no Greatcoat and has no business here with us."

I laughed. "Runs from a fight? You *child*. We run from fights all the time—we run from any fight we can get away from. 'Judge fair, ride fast, fight hard'—fighting is *always* our last resort."

It was Lorenzo's turn to sneer. "Well, perhaps that explains why you ran so quickly the last time there was a fight worth winning! Perhaps that's why there's no King and no Greatcoats anymore. Perhaps we"—and here he turned and swept his arms out wide—"perhaps *we* plan on fighting, not running!"

Aline put a hand on my arm. "Let's go, Falcio. I think we should go now."

I shrugged her arm off.

"You're a fool, Lorenzo, and so is anyone here who listens to this tripe. You think you're going to take forty men and women and fight an armored division of Knights? In plate mail? The army that came for the King had a thousand men on horseback. You think you can fight your way out of that?" I felt the sting of irony myself, since I had tried very hard to convince the King to let me do that very thing.

"You know, First Cantor, you look tired. Perhaps you need to rest, and dream sweet dreams of the past, while younger and better men do the fighting for you. Or perhaps"—he turned and smiled wolfishly—"perhaps you'd like to show us all a thing or two about how you used to do it in the old days?"

"Come on, Falcio," Aline said. "This isn't your fight."

But she was wrong: these people were calling themselves Greatcoats. I had devoted my life to this cause, and a hundred and forty-three others had done the same. We had fought and bled and died for this cause. My King had lost his head for this cause.

Lorenzo was right about one thing, though: I was tired. I was tired of Dukes and Knights, and even the common folk, calling us Trattari and tatter-cloaks and worse. I was tired of the memory of what we had tried to do for the world being sullied. More than anything, I was tired of running and hiding. I knew I should just leave with Aline, try and find somewhere else to hide. I could practically hear Brasti shouting in my ear, telling me not to put my anger in front of my reason again. He was right.

But I'd be thrice-damned before I let these fools, these arrogant sons of bitches, put the final death to the memory of the Greatcoats.

I walked toward the center of the hall, checking the crowd. Sometimes these things can turn against you quickly if you misread the situation. You might think you're walking into a duel, but if fifteen men decide they want to join in, you can't just shout "That's not fair" at them and hope they'll back off. But these people didn't care about anything but a good show. They thought Lorenzo was unbeatable, Saint Caveil himself come to teach them the sword. Well, fine. Kest always says that Saints are just little Gods and are probably due for a beating anyway.

When I reached Cairn he looked up in obvious agony. "I'm not done yet," he said. "I can still fight; there's been no first blood."

"He's right, you know," Lorenzo said. "Good for you, Cairn. Let's go again!"

"Get up and go and find a doctor for your wrist," I said.

"I'm not a coward!" he half-cried, half-croaked through the pain.

"Fine," I said. I pulled my rapier out and slashed Cairn's arm. A thin line of bright red appeared and he yelled out.

"Why?" he said through gritted teeth.

"Your honor's satisfied. You didn't withdraw. Now go to the fucking doctor and get your broken wrist seen to or you'll never be able to use a sword anyway."

There was a smattering of giggles around the room.

"Shall we begin, oh mighty teacher?" Lorenzo asked.

I waited until Cairn had pulled himself up and made his way out the door before I said, "I'm going to beat you silly, you stupid, pompous waste of a boy."

I'm not sure what it was about that particular phrase that got to him, but something did. Lorenzo came at me with that long rapier of his with seven damned hells shining out his eyes.

I'd like to be able to tell you that I pulled some very simple but ingenious move and knocked him flat on his back in one blow. I'd like to say that everyone laughed and he was humiliated and skulked off to begin a career as village idiot somewhere. But unfortunately that's not how it happened.

To begin with, Lorenzo really was an outstanding fighter. He was probably as good with a sword as anyone I've met except for Kest. And he was younger than me by more than a decade. He was taller, with a longer reach, and stronger, with a steadier hand. I was tired and injured and had no business trying to teach him a lesson. If this had been a contest of strength or skill, he would have won hands down.

But beat him I did. I beat him black and blue and red.

When he tried to engage my blade, I pulled mine out of line and grabbed the end of his sword with my gloved hand, twisting hard to bend the blade into a small arc and making it difficult for him to pull it away. When he yanked on the sword in frustration, I came with it and smashed my hilt into his shoulder. When he tried using his greater height and strength to strike a heavy blow from above, I performed a dancer's lunge to his right and slapped the side of my blade hard against his knee. When he came at me with finesse, I struck back like a drunken brute. When he attacked in rage I countered with finesse. I used every trick I knew to make an opponent angry and careless, to embarrass a man into making mistakes, to humiliate and to hurt. I didn't want to just beat him. I wanted to break him.

I snapped two of his ribs and the fingers of his right hand. I took the smirk off his face and very nearly went for his entire mouth in the bargain. I beat him because, in the end, I was meaner and more desperate, and because this wasn't a game to me. I said that Lorenzo was outstanding with the blade, and he was. He'd likely never been beaten by anyone, ever. Well, I've been beaten plenty of times and there's something to be said for it: it's how you learn what's truly at stake. The world isn't a romantic stage play; it's not all love or glory. And a sword fight isn't always about skill or strength; sometimes—maybe even most times—it's about who's willing to take a blow just to make sure he delivers a worse one to his opponent.

He lay in a heap on the ground at my feet, looking up at the ceiling as if Saints were coming down from the sky. I think he was in shock as much as he was in pain. I knew I had taken something away from him, something precious. He could have become a legend with the sword one day, maybe even surpassed Kest, but he would have been a monster, too. And I'm in the business of stopping monsters.

"Let's go," I said to Aline. The crowd was as still as stone statues but, when I moved toward the door, they parted for me. All except for Lorenzo's woman, Etricia, who put up her blade and waved it at me.

"Fight me!" she cried.

I looked at her, all wounded pride and love struck. "No."

"Come on, you *coward*! What, you don't think women can fight? Fight me like a man, damn you!"

"Fine," I said, and knocked the point of her sword out of line and then kicked her between the legs as hard as I could. She dropped to the ground next to Lorenzo in visible agony. It was a mean and cheap move, but that day, in that damned city? On that day I was a very mean and cheap man indeed.

"Anyone else?" I asked the crowd.

"Anyone else?" I asked again, louder. My voice was tight, almost shrill. Usually after a fight I'm exhausted; I just want a bath and a bed. But something was different this time. I was angry—if anything, I was more angry than when I'd fought Lorenzo. He was the instigator, but these people had cheered him on. They weren't monsters; they were the people who fed the monster.

"Then take off your coats," I said.

They looked at me as if I were speaking another tongue.

"Take off the coats. Take them off and put them in the fire."

"Falcio, stop," Aline said. "We've got to get out of here."

I ignored her and took a step toward the crowd. "Any man or woman who still has a greatcoat on by the time I reach them will get my sword in their belly. Take the fucking coats off and put them in the fire."

They did, every single one of them. Etricia, still in some discomfort, was helped by another woman to get Lorenzo's coat off. In the end, the large central fire pit could barely contain them, and the flame threatened to go out from the weight of the leather. Gods, but it stank.

"What . . . what do we do now?" a boy barely out of his teens asked.

"Get yourself something else to wear."

No one tried to stop me as I pulled Aline along with me and out the door.

15

THE SOFT CANDY

It was morning in Rijou. Although it was still cold, the light felt harsh enough that wherever it struck it seemed to make the stink rise from the gutters along the pavement.

"That was stupid," Aline said.

I looked down at her for a moment before turning right to head east along the broad street called Pikeman's Way.

"That was stupid."

"Which part?"

"All of it," she said. "But for right now, the stupidest part is that we're walking away in broad daylight and any of them can see where we're going."

"They're fools and cowards," I said. "There's not one of them will come looking for us. We'll keep to the east and make for the Wood-carvers' District. There won't be much happening there during the Blood Week and there are a lot of places to hide."

"It was still stupid," she said, ignoring me.

"How many times are you going to say that?"

She stopped and grabbed me by the sleeve of my coat, trying to turn me around. I decided it was time to clarify who was in charge.

"Look—"

Her face was full of tears.

"Why are you—?"

"Because I'm scared! Can't you see that? Don't you ever get scared?"

I knelt down, trying to talk to her at eye level, but she was too tall for that, so I got up again and leaned down to her—it was remarkably awkward, and it made what I said next sound even more foolish. "I'm scared all the time, Aline. I'm scared right now. But we've got to move on and find a place—"

"You're *not*!" Her voice was half shriek and half growl, and it made me take a step backward. It was early enough that there was no one else about, but I was still worried someone living above the nearby shops might take notice.

"You're not," she said, more quietly. "No one who was afraid would do something as stupid as you did back there. Those people could have helped us."

"Those people weren't—"

She threw her arms up and down in a gesture of frustration and futility. "Those people weren't Greatcoats, but they could have helped us. They could have given us a place to stay, they might have looked out for us, even just given us money or contacts. Something! Anything!"

"I understand that it's hard, but you don't understand everything that's at play here," I started, but she interrupted me.

"No, Falcio val Mond of the Greatcoats, it's you who doesn't understand. You don't understand what it is you're doing." She spoke with all the assurance of a young girl who still thinks life should play out like a storyteller's romance.

But I was tired, and aching from more fights in two days than I'd fought in the last year. "I'm trying to keep you alive, damn it!"

"No," she said, quietly, calmly, "you're trying to get back at them all—Shiballe, the Duke, that woman who calls herself a Princess: everyone who doesn't believe in you and your Greatcoats."

"Don't be ridiculous," I said. "If I was out to hurt them, believe me, I could find lots of ways that would be less work and less dangerous."

"But that would be revenge, wouldn't it? Or assassination? I'm just an excuse for you to fight all these people you hate and beat as many of them as you can before one of them finally kills you and you can die feeling noble and heroic."

"I wish I had the time to stand here and listen to you berate me, little girl, but I'm afraid I have to try and keep you alive now," I said pettishly.

"Then do that! Stop picking fights with everyone you meet and find a way for us to survive this!"

"Fine," I said through gritted teeth. "And how exactly do you think we should go about it?"

"I don't know! I'm thirteen years old. I'm not supposed to *know* how to stay alive while everyone is trying to kill me. You're supposed to be—you're supposed to know how to do that." And with that she started crying uncontrollably.

I reached out to her, but she pushed my hand away and we stood there in silence, her sobs the only sounds punctuating the emptiness of the street.

Finally I said quietly, "I don't know how."

She looked up from her crying and said, "I know."

"I'm sorry. I don't know how we can do it. It's not—I thought it was possible, but this city—it lives on murder and deceit. I don't know how many are after us, or why, but I do know Shiballe can get anyone in this city to do what he wants. This whole place—the people . . . It's practically designed for murder."

"I'm going to die, aren't I?" she said stoically.

I didn't want to say it; it would serve no purpose. Even vain hope is still hope, and some reason to keep moving. But somehow it felt wrong to lie just then. This girl had lost her family, and she would soon lose her life, all for no purpose other than the machinations of men who gave less thought to this than to what wine they drank at dinner. She had the right to choose whether to face or hide from the world as it really was.

"Yes, they're going to find us," I said quietly. "One or more of them is going to catch us. And yes, they're going to kill us."

She looked at the ground, then shook herself and looked back at me, her eyes clear. "I'm ready then," she said.

I shook my head as if to clear it. I wasn't sure what she meant, and I wasn't sure what else to say.

"I want you to do it," she said firmly.

"Do what?"

"Kill me." She saw my reaction and immediately put her hand on my chest before I could turn away. "You have to. You don't know what I know, Falcio. They won't just kill me on the spot. They'll take me and they'll torture me—they'll turn me over to the men who do these things for them. I'm all right—I mean, I can stand to die, but I don't want any more pain. I don't want them to—"

"Aline, you're the daughter of an otherwise unremarkable nobleman who just happened to irritate the Duke by marrying the wrong woman. They're a lot more likely to kill you and torture me," I said softly.

"I don't care," she said stubbornly. "I don't want them to win. If I'm going to die, I want to do it on my terms. I can't run anymore."

I thought about that for a moment. How do you answer when they take the last good thing from your life? It's the same question I've been asking myself all these years, since they killed the King—before that even, in truth: since they killed my wife, my brave Aline. Gods, how in the world had I reached this hopeless place, trying vainly to keep a doomed little girl alive for no better reason than that she shared the same name as my dead wife?

I reached into the inner pocket of my coat and pulled out the tiny package. I handed it to her.

"I don't want any more of the hard candy right now," she said.

"That's not what it is. Open it."

She did. Inside she saw the little square of soft orange and red striped confectionary. "What's this?"

"It's the soft candy," I said.

"You said that before. What's it for?"

"It's for when you can't run anymore. It's for when there's no hope left."

She picked it out of the package carefully with finger and thumb and brought it to her lips.

"There's always hope," the King said, pushing the tiny package back to me. He'd been away on a trip to one of the great cities, "courting the nobles," as he called them, as if it were all a grand joke he told himself for amusement. He wasn't smiling now, though. "You shouldn't have asked the apothecary to concoct this without my permission, Falcio, if for no other reason than that it smells absolutely foul."

"Would you have given permission?" I asked.

He pushed me toward one of the great reading chairs in the library—we spent a great deal of time there during those early days. The King had no experience with war; he had never served in his father's army, nor had he been part of Greggor's administration, nor taken any part in the running of the country. Most of his adult life had been spent imprisoned, with no companionship but the books his mother had stolen for him. Through that mercy she had made him a strong believer in reading, and as a result, we spent hours in the royal library, searching out and reading books on war, on politics, on strategy.

"No, Falcio, I would not have given you permission to create a means for my Greatcoats to commit suicide."

"If one of us is caught, if we know things—"

"What things?" the King asked.

"Things—secret things. Damn it, you know what I mean!"

"And you want to kill yourself before anyone can make you reveal those . . . *things*?"

"Yes."

"Why not just tell them?"

"Why not just—? Are you playing with me, your Majesty?"

The King smiled at me. He had a funny-looking smile for a monarch. Despite being better fed and haler than when I'd first met him, he still had that slightly idiotic-looking smile I remembered from the night in his chamber when I'd gone to kill him.

"Falcio, why in the world would I want to lose one of my Magisters simply to keep a secret that, quite frankly, I'll never know whether they revealed or not?"

"So you want us to just tell them everything when we're captured?"

"Well, I'm sure you can offer a bit of token resistance—a sort of, 'Secrets? What secrets?' type of thing . . . but really, why not? At least that way I'll know that the secret's out. At least that way there's a chance I keep my Magister, who might later escape and bring back vital intelligence."

"Your Majesty, there's something you're not getting here—"

"I'm sure you'll enlighten me," he said dryly.

"If a Greatcoat is near capture, if he's surrounded, he might be more inclined to surrender if he knows there's a chance of saving his skin. No matter how brave or loyal the man, it's a trade he might make."

"Whereas you'd prefer they fight to the death?"

"You said there's always hope. Well, there's always hope if you keep fighting."

The King smiled. "No, Falcio, there isn't. There's just always someone left to kill."

"That's something, then, isn't it?"

The King stood and refilled our wine goblets and we sat in silence for a few minutes, idly glancing at the pages of the open books that weighed down the large oak table.

"You weren't always a Greatcoat, Falcio," he said finally.

"I wasn't always in the Greatcoats, but I was always a Greatcoat in my heart," I corrected him.

He laughed. "Such a romantic! Such an optimist!"

"It saved you from getting a sword in the belly, didn't it?"

"I rather think exhaustion combined with several crossbow bolts had something to do with that as well."

"You think I would've murdered you, then?"

He thought about it for a moment, then said, "No, not once you'd realized I wasn't my father and I was still helpless as an underfed kitten. But if I'd been a little better fed, a little stronger . . ."

"You think so little of me? You think I'd kill someone just because—?"

"You'd kill someone just because they were bigger than you, Falcio, yes. If they were on the wrong side but they were scrawny, you'd find a way to—well, knock them out or some such thing. But if you'd seen me in that room that night, fit and full of health? Yes, I think you'd have killed me and gone off in search of the next closest heir to the throne until you found someone too weak to defend themselves."

I didn't like where this was going, so I picked up the wine goblet and took a drink. It was already empty, so I felt even more the fool.

"Well then, good thing I found you first, isn't it?" I said, putting down the goblet.

The King reached over from his chair and squeezed my shoulder. "A very good thing. A miraculous thing. The best of all things," he said. "The Greatcoats are what's going to make this country better, Falcio. They're my dream. They're my answer. I want them to live."

"Your answer to what?"

"My answer to the fact that a man can be killed for no better reason than it pleases someone above him. My answer to the weakness that fact creates in a country, in a people. My answer to the fact that Avares and the other nations surrounding us will one day decide to come over the mountains—perhaps because they lack food or wealth, perhaps because they want more, perhaps because their clerics tell them that the Gods demand it—perhaps even for no better reason than that they have nothing better to do. Our nation is weakened by a system that breeds a visceral hatred so deep that most people would as soon see the world burn as stay as it is, but lack the will to try and change it."

"And that's your job, is it, being the one at the top of the whole machine?"

"Mine, yes, and yours. And Kest's and Brasti's and all the others, too. First we bring justice, then we bring change."

"Justice is a change," I said.

"No, justice is just the start. It's the thing that will make change possible."

I thought about that for a moment. Then I said, "You forgot women."

"What do you mean?"

"A woman can be killed for no better reason than it pleases someone above her, too."

King Paelis sighed. "It always comes back to that, doesn't it, Falcio? They murdered your wife, and each and every thing you do from that day forth will be because of that, won't it?"

"Is that so wrong a reason? To fight—to die, if need be?"

"If it's your reason then it can't be so very wrong—it's as good a reason for dying as any. It's just not a very good reason for living."

I didn't want to answer. I loved the King, but sometimes he asked more than I was prepared to give. "It'll have to do for now," I said finally. "And if you trust me in anything, trust me that one day a Greatcoat will be in a position where there is no better option than a quick death."

The King pushed the tiny package back toward me. "Fine. You are my First Cantor and, if you really want a way for Magisters to kill themselves, I'll talk to the Royal Apothecary myself."

I relaxed a bit. "Maybe you can ask him to make it smell better, too. Perhaps a strawberry flavor?"

King Paelis slammed his fist on the table, and despite his small stature books went flying. "Don't!" he cried.

I was about to say, "Don't what?" but the fury on his face told me better.

He knew it, too. "Leave it be now, Falcio. You've said your piece and you're getting your way—but don't ever think you have persuaded me. Don't *ever* think this was your reason winning out over my weakness. You've won." He coughed and wiped at his mouth. "Now leave it be. It's been a long trip and I need a rest."

A few weeks later a guard arrived bearing a wooden box. On top of the box was a note that said, *Try not to get them mixed up.* Inside the box were a hundred and forty-four small packages, each containing a square. I opened one, careful not to touch it with my bare skin. It smelled like strawberries, and I couldn't imagine what that meant.

16

THE APOTHECARIES

I had promised myself I would give her the choice, not try to stop her from taking the soft candy. It was a cold, callous calculation born from my own sense of weakness, but if I couldn't keep her safe, and if capture would mean torture and a slower death, then surely it was her right to make her own decision. It's the choice I would have made in her position—and the choice I would have made years ago, looking down at the destroyed body of my dead wife, if someone had given it to me. If I'd held in my hand a tiny package, a berry-flavored sweet that would end my pain instantly, I would have taken it without a thought—and then what? No long journey into and out of madness, no climbing the fetid passageway of Castle Aramor to commit regicide, no discovery of a young, weak, but brilliant King. No Greatcoats. No royal library, no nights poring over ancient texts on swordplay and strategy. No chess with the King or riding into every village and hamlet in the country with Kest and Brasti and the others to bring some small measure of decency and justice to the world. No Greatcoats. *No Greatcoats.*

"Please." The small word shattered the spell.

I looked over and my hand was on Aline's wrist. I'd no recollection of putting it there. My grip was tight and I could see it was hurting her, but I couldn't seem to let go. The look on her face was frightened, desperate, and I could see that she thought I had lied, that I wouldn't let her choose her own death. *It's her death*, I told myself, *not yours*, and my fingers released just enough for her to pull her hand away. She stepped back several paces and rubbed her wrist. She looked hurt and confused.

She stopped backing away and brought the soft candy back toward her mouth.

"Aline!"

The shout had come from behind me, so I pulled my right-hand rapier from its sheath and crouched low into a forward guard. A man and a woman were running toward us, no weapons in hand, nor at their sides that I could see. The man was heavyset but not so muscled as to be a soldier or blacksmith—so someone who worked for a living, worked with his hands but not in hard labor. His clothes told me he wasn't destitute, but his rough beard and dark hair made it clear he wasn't a merchant either. The woman beside him was much the same in clothes and bearing, though slimmer and prettier. I guessed both to be in their middle thirties.

"Aline!" they called again, and I rose up a little. I kept the point at the man's gut.

"Don't hurt her," he said, his voice thick with concern.

"Hurt whom?" I asked.

"Aline, come here," he said, keeping his eyes on me and his right arm protectively in front of his wife.

"Radger?" Aline said from behind me. "Laetha? What are you doing here?"

"We're looking for you, silly girl. We heard what happened and Mattea sent us to find you!"

"Who is Mattea?" I asked, my sword not moving an inch.

Aline tried to push past me, but I barred her with my arm.

"Mattea was my nanny," she said impatiently. "Radger is her son and Laetha is his wife. They're apothecaries—they're my *friends*. Now let me past, Falcio."

"Put up your arms," I told them.

"What foolishness is driving you, man?" Laetha said. "We're here to help Aline to safety. We thought you were one of the Duke's men taking her away."

"All the same, put your arms up and turn around."

"Falcio, stop this."

"In a moment. First, I want them to put their arms up and turn around."

Radger eyed me carefully. "Aline, get ready to run," he said urgently. "If he attacks us, just run and don't look back."

"Hells! You're all fools!" Aline said.

"Everyone shut up," I ordered. "Now, if you're truly friends, you'll do as I say. If you're not, let's get this over with. I haven't killed anyone for several hours and I'm getting a cramp."

The man looked scared; the woman's eyes went from Aline to me and looked furious. But they both complied. They raised their arms as I'd ordered, which pulled their clothes tighter against their bodies, as I had intended: this makes it much easier to see if someone is wearing weapons on their person. As they turned, I looked for bulges in their clothes or places where the cloth was tighter than it should be—signs of things concealed—but there were none. I don't know why people try to pat their opponents down; you're more than likely to miss something that way, and you've made yourself vulnerable by getting in so close, even if you've got a partner with you.

"All right," I said, looking around one last time. As I resheathed my sword, Aline shoved me aside and ran to the couple, who hugged her tightly. Radger said something in her ear, but I couldn't hear what it was.

"Where is Mattea?" Aline asked. "Is she all right?"

"She's fine," Radger said. "Out of her wits searching for you, of course, as is the rest of the damned city, it seems."

"Thank Saint Birgid we found you first," Laetha said. She put an arm around Aline's shoulders. "Is this the man—the tatter-cloak—who took you?"

"You probably don't want to say that again," I said calmly.

"Forgive us, stranger," Radger said. "We don't know your ways. Do you prefer 'Trattari'?" He was either the best actor in the world or he really was clueless, so I decided to let it go.

"I prefer Falcio," I said.

"Falcio, then. I don't mean to offend you, but why did you take Aline?"

"Her family is murdered," I said, "and she's being hunted by the Duke's less-than-courteous lackeys, not to mention every guardsman and bully boy in Rijou. There was no one else to take her."

"You could have brought her to us," Laetha said angrily. She looked down at Aline. "Sweetheart, you could have come to us."

"I didn't want to bring more pain to your house," Aline said. "After Mother had to let Mattea go . . . We didn't have money—the Duke took—"

"Silly girl," Laetha said, embracing her once more. "Do you honestly think Mattea would ever hold that against you? Do you think we would ever turn you away from our door?"

"And how well would you fight off the men trying to capture her?" I asked. "How would you cross blades with the thugs and gangs looking to reap from Shiballe's generous harvest?"

"How well have you been protecting her?" Laetha demanded.

"Not especially well," I admitted.

"Stranger—*Falcio*,"—Radger put a hand on my shoulder, as tentatively as if he were touching a dead eel—"no man can fight off the entire city. It's beyond belief that you've kept her alive until now. But we can help. We can move her from family to family, quiet as a shadow, and keep her from the Duke's men until this damnable

Blood Week is over. Then . . . then she can live with us. We'll care for her, I promise you."

"We can hide you," Laetha said confidently to Aline.

"But Laetha, I don't want you or the others harmed when they realize you've been hiding me," Aline said. "Or worse—"

"Pish!" Laetha said comically, like an old grandmother, and I guessed this was something Mattea the nanny might say. "They'll never know. The common folk of Rijou have been hiding bigger things than you for years, sweetheart."

I strongly doubted that was true; more likely whatever petty smuggling or black marketeering that went on simply wasn't very important to the Duke. But Aline, for some reason, was.

"I don't think it'll be so easy," I said.

"Do you honestly believe she has better odds with you?" Radger asked gently.

The answer was no, of course, but I couldn't bring myself to admit that.

"Falcio," Aline said softly, putting her hand on mine, "I think . . . I think this is worth trying. I don't know what else to do, and I have only one other course available to me."

I realized she'd pressed something into my hand. It was the soft candy. "All right," I said, putting the tiny package back in my pocket. "But I'm coming."

Radger started to protest, but I put my hand up to stop him. "You might still encounter Shiballe's men between here and your home. Once we're there and Aline's settled, I'll take my leave of you and make my way out of the city."

They looked mollified by this, and Radger turned to point the way. "It's half a mile straight down Broadwine Road," he said, "but we'll want to take the alleys, to lessen our chances of running into trouble."

"Lead on," I said. A half-mile journey, and then I would be free of this—free to wriggle my way out of this city like a worm and make my way back to the caravan, to Kest and Brasti. And then what? Help assassinate a childish Princess before she could do more harm? Or fight Kest and lose in a hopeless effort to stop him?

Radger and Laetha's home looked like just about every other apothecary's shop I'd ever seen. One wall was made up of dark wooden glass-fronted cabinets filled with scores of tiny pots and jars. Dried herbs and flowers were suspended from hooks all over the place. A long oak countertop served both for handling money and packaging and mixing formulas. In the back, behind the shop, was one large room with two smaller ones adjoining, and a thick oak door leading to what was most likely the cellar. Behind a curtain hanging in one of the two bedrooms was a hidden door.

"If someone comes in through the front of the shop, we can sneak her out the back here to the alley," Radger said, holding the hanging back.

"They'll be likely to have someone in the alley," I started, but he smiled and pushed open the door. There was a tall wall just to the right of it.

"See that alley wall right there? It looks like a dead end from the street, but actually this segment behind the wall joins up with a notary's office and Heb the carpenter's workshop. They could stand all day in that alley waiting for us and not notice that we'd already left."

I smiled. It was as good as she could hope for.

"Where's Mattea?" Aline said.

It was clear to me that the old woman had been an important and positive force in the girl's life, and the family were more like cousins than servants to her. That was good.

"She's still out looking for you," Laetha said. "Here, let's get both of you something to eat. You look as though you haven't had anything in ages."

Laetha motioned for us to take a seat at the large table in the center of the main room. The wooden chairs were hard, but it felt like sinking into a cloud for me. I was exhausted, but sleep was miles away yet. I had to make sure the girl was safe; then I would take that back alley route and make for the rooftops as fast as possible. I would go through the most crowded parts of the city on my way to the outer wall, and then . . . Well, then I'd just have to figure out how to haul my exhausted body up a twenty-foot stone surface. Maybe the trees . . . I'd noticed people had stopped trimming the trees near the outer wall. Foolish, that. Makes it easier for people to sneak in and out. If not, maybe one of the broken sections . . . maybe . . .

"Falcio, food!" Aline said, lifting me out of my somnolence.

"How long . . . ?" I asked wearily.

"Almost an hour. I thought it best to let you sleep. You looked comfortable, like you might not try to kill the next person that comes through the door. For a moment I didn't recognize you."

"Funny."

"Enough talking, you two," Laetha said. "Eat."

I'd expected to see simple fare in front of me but this was hardly Cheapside food. There were roasted potatoes and greens, fresh bread, and the dark-reddish butter they favored in Rijou. There was gravy and salt for dipping. Finally, Laetha brought in an entire roast duck. I could smell the fat dripping from the bird and, tired though I was, I very nearly grabbed the whole thing with my hand.

"Saints, man," Radger said with a laugh. "You look like you're going to pass out in Laetha's lovely roast dinner! Here, drink this." He picked up a glass from the sideboard and poured a clear but yellowish liquid into it.

I took the glass from him as he watched me expectantly. I hesitated.

Laetha noticed, and put down the knife she was using to carve the duck. "Oh, for the love of my ancestors!" She picked up another glass from the sideboard and filled it from the same flask. She took a drink. "See? Not dead. It's just lemon juice with zinroot—it helps you stay awake."

I let my breath out and drank gratefully. "To your health, then," I said.

"All right, enough foolishness now," Laetha said firmly. "Let's eat."

As she heaped food onto our plates I realized the zinroot was indeed waking me up. Saints, but my arms were stiff—in fact, all of me was stiff, really. I wasn't relishing the thought of what the next few hours would bring once I left the apothecaries' home.

"Will Mattea be back soon?" Aline asked between mouthfuls.

"Oh, I imagine she'll be a few more hours," Laetha answered.

I barely paid attention to the conversation, so enamored of the roast duck on my plate was I. "The food is *wonderful*," I said, and Aline nodded, grinning, bits of duck dribbling from her mouth. Hardly the portrait of a young noblewoman, I thought, and far away from the despairing creature who had been moments from taking her own life.

Saint Caveil, what value does my blade have if it brings so little good to the world?

"Well, I'm just glad we found you," Laetha said. "We'd had no luck at all, and then *poof*, there you were, right on the—"

"Laetha," Radger interrupted, "let's not make them relive the experience. It was grand luck that brought us together, and with a little more we'll be able to take good care of our Aline here."

"I've learned not to believe too much in luck," I said, and speared a potato, only to drop my fork on the table. "Sorry."

The meal wasn't making the stiffness in my joints go away. Not one bit. I looked over at Radger and his wife.

"Where's Mattea again?"

"As we said, out looking for Aline with some of the others."

Laetha started picking up the now empty plates. We had practically obliterated the bountiful meal, and in less time than you could butter a bread roll.

"And yet you haven't gone out to let any of your friends know that you've found us."

"Well, they're—they're all out. There's no one to tell yet. No one expected to find you so soon."

"But find us you did," I said.

"Grand luck, bountiful luck of the Saints," Radger said piously.

Aline was looking back and forth between us, not sure what this was all about.

"This is certainly the finest meal I've had in an age," I said, placing both hands on the table. They wanted to shake, but they didn't: they were stiff and achy and not responding much at all. Everyone else looked fine, including Laetha, who took her seat once again to the right of me. Aline was to my left and Radger sat across the table.

"Well, I'm just glad you're well fed," she said, smiling. Nervous. Still nervous.

She knows, but isn't sure how far gone I am.

"Well fed, ready for bed, soon to be dead," I sang with a laugh.

Aline giggled at the old children's rhyme, but the others did not.

"One problem, though," I said with a smile.

"What—?" Laetha began.

"Now I need dessert!"

They laughed with me, but looked a bit confused. "We didn't have time to prepare . . . I suppose I could toss some sugar cakes and jam together," Laetha said.

"Falcio, don't be rude."

I shook my head. "No need, I always bring my own. Aline, dear, could you do a tired, old, worn-out, and beat-up man a favor? Reach into my pocket and pass me one of my sweets, won't you?"

She looked at me, clearly confused.

"Come now, I'm all settled and comfortable here; I just want one of my candies. The hard one."

She rose, and for a brief instant I saw Radger start to reach for her, but then he stopped, catching my eye. I smiled back at him. I could barely move, so I had to do my best to make him think I was still functional. I suppose this is as good a time as any to mention that my very worst night terrors involve being paralyzed.

Aline reached awkwardly into the inside pocket of my coat and pulled out one of the tiny packages. "No dear, the *hard* candy. The soft candy tastes too much like strawberries and it won't settle with the duck."

She reached into the other pocket. Her hand was shaking now, but she was trying to mask it, either because she understood what was happening or because she thought I was losing my mind.

"There now," I said. "That's the one."

Without further instruction she unwrapped it and popped it into my mouth and I tasted the harsh, almost metallic flavor of the hard candy. A sniff of the stuff will wake you up from a deep sleep. A small bite will let you go for two days and nights on the move without sleep. The amount I swallowed at that moment could prevent a paralytic from stopping my heart—if it didn't make it burst. I made the sounds I imagined one might make when tasting the tits of Saint Laina-who-whores-for-Gods.

"You certainly seem enamored of your confectionary," Laetha said drily.

"I am indeed, mistress. I am indeed. I would offer you some, but that was the very last piece. Perhaps you'd like to try some of the other candy I have with me? It's soft, and tastes of summer strawberries."

"Thank you, no," she said. "As you say, strawberries go ill with duck."

Aline sat in her chair, inching closer to me each time she fidgeted, looking back and forth between us all and clearly terrified. Radger looked at me from across the table with eyes that betrayed nothing, simply waiting.

Well, fine: I was waiting too. But I still couldn't move my arms.

"Where did you say the old woman was again?" I asked.

"We've told you three times now, she's out with the others, searching for Aline." Laetha's voice held only irritation, but her shoulders betrayed fear. Radger rose and headed to one of the cabinets in the corner.

"Right, right—forgive me. And how did you find us again?" I asked.

"We told you, it was luck. Just luck."

"Of course. What's wrong with me?"

"Falcio . . . ," Aline said.

"And that drink you gave me—delicious! What was it again? Zinroot?"

"Yes." Laetha looked over at her husband, unsure of what to do.

"It was the glass," Radger said casually. In his hand he held a thick iron rod, a bit under two feet in length. Each end was wrapped in tanned leather. This was a weapon for disabling a man, perhaps crippling him, but not killing him. "In case you've been wondering, the poison was in the glass already, not in the drink."

"Ah. The glass," I said as the paralytic began to assert itself on my limbs and organs. "I should've realized."

"Few would," Radger said. "It's how we sometimes get children to take their medicine when they're being obstinate: put it on the rim of the glass and fill it with plain water, then drink some yourself from a clean glass to make them feel safe."

"Radger! What are you doing?" Aline asked.

"Shush, girl. You come with me now," Laetha said, rising from the table.

Aline jumped from her seat and came behind me. She took the bracer of knives from the inside of my coat and pulled one free, holding it out in front of her.

"Don't be foolish, child," Laetha shouted.

Radger took a step forward and Aline threw the knife at him. She missed him by a city block, but the knife did give a satisfying *thunk* as it stuck into the wall. She quickly pulled another one out before Laetha could grab her arm and swung it in an arc in front of us.

"Where is Mattea?" Aline demanded.

"Let's all settle down now, my sweetheart," Radger said.

"Where is she? You can't tell me she would do this to me—you *can't*!" With her left hand she started shaking my shoulders, trying to get me to move, but I held, stiff as stone.

"Aline," Radger said, taking another step toward us, "it's time for you to be grown up now. There's enough limerot in that man's blood to stop a pack of dogs in their tracks. So just you go with Laetha and leave me to do what I've got to do. I've got no call to hurt you, but I will if you don't stop misbehaving now."

"Damn you!" Aline screamed, waving the knife as Radger took another half step toward us and as Laetha started reaching out, looking for an opportunity to catch Aline's wrist. "Damn you all! You were supposed to be my *friends*!" She started reaching back inside my pocket for something and it took me a second to realize she was reaching for the soft candy again.

"No," I said to her, "that won't be necessary. Leave be and step back a few paces, Aline."

The girl paused a moment and then complied, but she kept the knife in hand.

Radger and Laetha looked relieved. "See now, you listen to your man there," Radger said. "He knows when it's done. No need to make a fuss."

"In case you're wondering later on," I said, "it was the candy."

"The what?"

"The candy. You're an apothecary," I said. "Haven't you heard stories of the King's hard candy?"

"That's—that's a myth," Radger said. "No one's ever been able to make that recipe."

"Fool," I said. "You stupid. Fucking. Fool. Did you think you were the first person to ever come up with the idea of poisoning a Greatcoat? Did you really think that the King, with all his money and all his apothecaries, the finest in the country, and all his books from the most ancient libraries in the country—did you really think he never thought we'd have to deal with a fucking *poisoner*? Did you really think we wouldn't have a way to deal with that?"

"You're bluffing," he said. "You're trying to buy yourself time, hoping your stupid little candy will work, but it takes longer than this, doesn't it?"

"Take a step forward," I said. "Just one more step, and find out."

Radger hesitated.

"Come on! I'm right here—I'm sitting down! My sword's in its sheath. On the best day of my life do you think I could get up, draw my blade, and stab you before you can take one step and thrash me across the head with that iron bar? So what are you waiting for?"

He looked at Laetha for a moment, then back at me, and with a roar he stepped forward and swung the iron bar.

In my own defense, I did actually manage to push the chair back, get up, and draw my sword faster than I would've thought possible, but the hard candy moves through the body from the inside out. The first thing to work, thankfully, are the internal organs, then the chest, shoulders, and thighs. The hands and fingers are the last to come out of the paralysis, which in this case meant my aim was off and the blade went to the side, and the result was that instead of smashing my brains in, Radger hit the side of my ribs with less impact.

He pushed me hard, and I fell back onto my chair, the rapier dropping from my hand, and he pulled back for a final swing, only then noticing the small knife buried into his side.

"Aline?" he said, disbelievingly.

She had snuck in under his blow when I'd stood up and jammed the blade into his side. A big man like that, he could've shrugged it off for long enough to finish the job on me. But if you've never been stabbed before, it's damned painful, and shock takes you quickly.

Radger stumbled back a few feet. Laetha raced to his side. I leaned over and picked up my sword before pulling myself to my feet.

"Now," I said, "why don't you give me the amulet?"

"What?" Aline said.

I held my sword point very close to Radger's bleeding wound. Laetha reached into a pocket in her skirts and pulled it out. She tossed it onto the table and Aline ran over and picked it up.

"It's exactly like the other one," she said. Then she reached over and felt in the left pocket of my coat.

"It's not there," I said. "It must've fallen out in the fight with Lorenzo. That's why we 'suddenly' appeared for you, wasn't it, Radger?"

He nodded grimly, biting back pain. "They gave us all these copper things," he said, "but nothing was happening and we just wandered around, looking through the district. But then all of a sudden there it was, a light on the surface and the lines of the streets."

"They must not work if we've got one on our person or too close to us," I explained to Aline. "If we hadn't lost it, they never would have—"

Shit. If I hadn't been such a damned fool and picked a fight that could have waited, then I wouldn't have lost the damned thing.

"They just gave you one?" I asked.

He shook his head. "They gave each of us one."

"Each of you . . . ," Aline whispered.

"You don't understand, you stupid girl," Laetha screamed. "They came to all of us! Everyone who ever knew you or your damned family: 'Find them and be rich, fail and be dead.' That's the choice we were given."

She looked pleadingly at the girl, and then at me. "What else could we have done?"

"But Mattea—she wouldn't . . . ," she whispered. "I *know* she wouldn't. Where is she? Tell me where she is!"

Laetha looked furious, but her glance flickered for a moment.

Aline ran to the cellar door. "*You* . . . What did you do to her? Mattea! *Mattea!*" Aline screamed as she ran to the door and pried it open. I heard her thumping down the stairs into the darkness.

Radger slumped to the ground and Laetha knelt beside him, crying and staunching his wound with the edge of her long skirt.

I wanted to sit back down myself, but it was best to stay on my feet, stay moving. The combination of the paralytic they'd slipped me along with the hard candy was a dangerous mixture for the heart, and the more I moved about, the quicker both would get out of my system.

Radger looked up at me and I could see the guilt breaking through. He wanted someone to tell him it was all right, that anyone would have done the same—or at least to scream at him, to beat him to within an inch of his life.

I chose to do neither. For once in my life I didn't feel vengeful. I just felt tired. Damn this loathsome city.

A moment later I heard Aline's footsteps, and another's, climbing the stairs from the cellar. She emerged with an old woman. Gray, tightly curled hair framed a face that might've been a map of the world, if the world had been made up only of mountains and valleys. Her hands were still bound and her mouth gagged. Aline ran and pulled the knife out of the wall where she'd thrown it earlier and made quick work of both ropes and gag.

The old woman coughed and cleared her throat, and straightened as much as she could. She was still bent over and wizened, but I could see strength in those old bones, and there was iron in her eyes. She opened her mouth and gave a sneer that promised foul language and a brutal temperament—and that's when I finally recognized her.

"Tailor!"

She looked me up and down—not my face, mind you, nor my hands or feet. Just my coat.

"I see you've done your level best to ruin my greatcoat, Falcio val Mond."

I felt unnaturally self-conscious. "I—"

"Shut it. I've got more important things to deal with right now."

The Tailor turned to Radger and Laetha. "Well now, children. What unwise things have you been up to while you had me roped in the cellar?"

Neither replied, and she kicked Radger, who groaned.

"You have *children*?" I was incredulous.

"Bah. Certainly not Radger and Laetha. No, I paid these two fools for a place to stay and a story people would believe."

She kicked Laetha, hard. "But it turns out they were even stupider than I'd believed, eh, Laetha? Thought you'd tie up an old woman and make some easy money?"

"And 'Mattea'?" I asked.

She smiled her evil smile again. "Would've thought you'd've picked up on that, Falcio. It's an old Pertine word, after all."

Mattea. *Thread.*

"So you make your living as a nanny to noble houses, spreading stories of the Greatcoats?"

"Does more good than livin' out in the pissing rain huntin' for scraps, don't it?"

Aline suddenly gripped the Tailor around the waste and started sobbing.

The Tailor returned the child's furious embrace. "Oh, my sweet," she said. "Oh, my sweetest of girls. I'm sorry if my little lie hurt you any. You keep callin' me Mattea if you like. And I promise, there are only nine hundred and ninety-nine more lies that I told you—but never, never, never would I have thought my foolishness could bring you into such peril. Never, *never*."

". . . Not your fault," Aline said between sobs.

The Tailor sighed. "No dearie, I suppose you're right. Not my fault, but my responsibility, yes. My responsibility now." She squeezed the girl tight one more time before gently pushing her arms aside.

"You have to go," she said to me, rising. "Radger and Laetha didn't lie entirely: near everyone on these streets is lookin' for you and the reward you mean to 'em."

She reached over to the table and took the amulet and put it around Aline's neck.

"Filthy magic," she said, "but cheap too, thanks to the laziness of men. Easy enough for a master mage to make, but they don't work too well together. Keep this on and the others won't work, at least 'til they think of something else."

She turned back to me. "Fly now, Falcio val Mond, you great damned fool. You've made a good mess of things now."

"How is this my fault, exactly?" I asked. I felt like she was scolding me.

"Rijou and the Blood Week: so how many d'you think you can trust for a hundred miles in any direction?" she asked.

"No one," I said. "Not one soul."

She gave a mean smile. "*Soul?* Some ass-kissing God must've made you an optimist, boy."

The Tailor kissed Aline on the top of the head one final time. "Now, get yourselves out of here. Find a place to hide until the Blood Week ends." The Tailor turned to me, and all the fires of every hell were in her gaze. "It's on you now, Falcio. Get her to the Teyar Rijou.

When you reach the Rock, make sure her name is called. You owe him that."

I didn't see how I owed Lord Tiarren any more than I had already given in trying to keep his daughter alive, but I wasn't about to challenge whatever it was that was driving the Tailor.

"What about them?" I asked, pointing at Radger and Laetha in the corner.

"Them? You don't need to worry about them."

"What about—what about the Duke's men?" Laetha asked, tears streaming down her face.

"Ah, now, sweet little Laetha, you don't have to worry even a little bit about those nasty big men. Not one little bit." She took the knife from Aline's hand and weighed its balance. "Nice little knife this. Think I'll keep it, if it's a'right with you."

I nodded—what else could I do?—and she pointed us toward the back door before turning her attention to her "son" and "daughter-in-law." "Now go, like I said. What comes next is not right for her tender eyes nor your foolish conscience."

We left the Tailor to her responsibility.

I took Aline's hand and pulled her out through the hidden door in the bedroom into the back alley. It was only later that I realized that, when she had given me the hard candy from my coat, she'd also pocketed the soft candy for herself.

17
THE DASHINI

A few hours later we were in another small alley and had very nearly made it to the outer wall when the two Dashini found us. Dashi'nahiri Tahazu, to give them their full title, is actually a phrase that means "The hunt once started ends only with blood." They are difficult to find, expensive beyond the value of any man's life, and have a bad reputation for occasionally killing their employers after the target is eliminated. They are the most secretive order of assassins in the civilized world, though it's hard to call any world civilized if it can produce murderers of this caliber.

The Dashini wear dark blue silk from head to toe, covering them completely. The fabric is as ingenious, in its own way, as the leather used to make our greatcoats. A man wearing Dashini garb can see out with near-perfect clarity, but his opponents can't see anything, not even the color of his eyes, which works out well for all concerned since the true identity of a Dashini hunter is never revealed—not even to the other members of his order. They enter the temple at Zhina as babes, sacrificed to—well, whichever God you sacrifice your newborn child to, I suppose. A dark-blue-clad monk wraps the child in its first silken swaddling clothes, and that's it; the child's face will never be seen for the rest of its life. They always fight in pairs, but even their Azu—their partner—knows neither their name nor their face.

Over the years the child learns how to move without being seen or heard, to make poisons from whatever plants, fish, or animals exist where they are sent, to play mind tricks on their enemies, and, of course, to be able to defeat any opponent. And in case you're wondering, yes, that includes Greatcoats. A great many Greatcoats, in fact.

The King spent several years trying to devise a way for us to beat them, but it was a bit difficult to test his theories, and the solution he finally settled on wasn't entirely reassuring. On the other hand, at that precise moment it was all I had.

"Girl . . . ," I started, reaching each hand across my chest and into the inner folds of my coat.

"I know, I know," she said, slipping a few feet behind me.

"We come for the girl, not her coat," one of them—or maybe it was both of them (the fabric covering their faces makes it hard to tell)—whispered at me. "Trust your fear and turn your back."

"*Viszu na dazi*," I said. It was just about the only phrase I knew in their language. It means "No one saw," and it refers to the fact that the Dashini don't leave witnesses.

They moved like snakes, dancing sinuously with their long stiletto blades flicking out like tongues. We had never figured out how, but somehow those thin, light blades could pierce through our greatcoats more easily than a regular sword could.

"Better one chance in a thousand than no chance at all," they whispered, and, almost imperceptibly, they started to move apart, positioning themselves to get on either side of me. I backed up a step and drew my rapiers. The girl was smart enough to step back as well, keeping the distance behind me.

"Could we get started with that shit-breath you call a poison?" I called. "We're sort of on the run, and I'm feeling a bit exposed out here."

Their faces, of course, revealed nothing other than the usual expanse of dark blue cloth, but I fancied they probably got at least a tiny surprise from that. You see, the Dashini, good as they are, have absolutely no notion of a fair fight. That's why, although they'll always finish you off with the point of their stiletto blades, they don't take chances, and, above all, they don't let pride get in the way of a good murder. So before the fighting starts, they like to get in a little close, do their little dance, and then blow a thin, almost mist-like purple powder into your face. They call it the "fear-tongue," and it does pretty much what you'd expect: makes you terrified and disoriented, and does something to your throat that prevents you from talking. It pretty much guarantees you're going to end up with a long, thin piece of metal buried deep inside your eye, which is how they like to wrap things up.

The way they moved, undulating back and forth while leaning backward, made it easy to miss that they were bridging the distance between you. They probably could have spat the poison into my face from that distance, but the Dashini don't get cocky; they don't rush. They make murder the way a master baker makes bread, knowing that timing is everything. So they slipped back and forth to gain those few extra inches they needed to know they'd hit me with the fear-tongue and paralyze me with nausea and dread.

A wiser man than I once asked a question, though: if the fear tongue is so powerful, why doesn't it affect the Dashini? After all, they hold the stuff in their mouths, so they must inhale a lot more of it than their target does. The answer is fairly simple, really: they build up a resistance to it. It turns out that the first time you get hit with it (which is usually the only time, since you don't survive your first encounter with the Dashini) the effects are extremely powerful. The second time, you're still terrified and disoriented, but you don't tend to get the constricted throat. And the third time the disorientation goes away and all that's left is the fear. That never really gets any better, but who can't handle a little terror? Fear-tongue is incredibly expensive to buy, and it's no easy trick to find, but fortunately for us we had a King with all kinds of money and contacts who was of the opinion that it might look bad if his Magisters pissed their pants falling over themselves and crying in vain for their mothers whenever a Dashini assassin hove into sight. So, at great expense to the country, every Greatcoat in the order was lucky enough to experience enough fear-tongue so that, if they did just happen to get attacked by Dashini assassins, they wouldn't piss their pants before they died. Money well spent, your Majesty.

So when they blew the sparkly purple dust straight into my face, I took in a nice deep breath and let a pair of throwing knives fly from my hands toward their chests. Their long stilettos flicked out and beat away the knives. It was a neat trick that I doubt I could have pulled off—Kest, maybe, but not me. I would have liked them to have said something complimentary about my little surprise, but they don't really talk when they don't need to. However, it threw their weaving dance off just a hair, and that was all the satisfaction I could expect at this point.

They did, however, do me the honor of finally attacking me. Their blades were perfectly synchronized, so I used the parry we call "the dismissal," so-called because it looks a bit like you're making a tiny, disdainful gesture to send someone away. In reality, it's a double-circular parry that works well against long, straight blades. The maneuver threw their points out of line, but they had plenty of tricks of their own and I couldn't count on guessing the counter for each one, not with two of them coming at me at the same time.

We circled some more, and as the dust of the alley started stirring up I could feel the edges of that drug-induced terror start to reach up to my chest from my stomach. I did my best to ignore it. I needed to focus on the King's big idea.

"It's nice seeing you again, Toller," I said to no one in particular.

The Dashini said nothing but flicked out their blades again. This time they intentionally went just slightly out of time, which meant that trying another double-dismissal would fail, as the timing on at least one of my parries would be off. I focused instead on blocking the one on my right and doing a counterclockwise half slip with my left foot. The blade missed me and the assassin's attempt to draw a cut on his return draw didn't even scratch my coat. Their points are sharp as hells, but the blades themselves won't cut through our leather, not with that weak a blow.

"You know, your timing is still off, Toller," I said conversationally.

I kicked hard against the ground in front of me and as the dust went up like a cloud I double-lunged straight at the one on my right, all the while keeping my left blade guarding against a thrust from the other side. My attack failed, of course, as the Dashini skipped backward out of range. The assassin tried to get a thrust into my arm over my blade, but a small lift of the wrist let the point clang against my guard.

"Almost got your friend there, Toller. Are you ready to quit playing and help me end him?"

"You wish to be asleep," they whispered, and I almost did. Fucking Dashini mind tricks. Don't know how they work, but you just have to deal with it.

"You know how we beat you?" I asked the one on the right. "It's kind of a funny story."

"You wish to be silent," they whispered again, but this one was much easier to ignore.

"No, really, it's a great story. You see, a few years ago, the King had this idea—to be frank, it's something you people should have figured out long ago. You see, the thing about all that secrecy? You know, never showing your face to one another, never knowing each other's names? Those lovely face masks that disguise your voices so well that you wouldn't know if it was your own mother behind the thing? Well, the King, clever fellow that he was, realized that if, let's say, we caught a pair of Dashini and killed them, and if—and do follow along with me here—if we just replaced them with two of our men . . . well then, it would be awfully easy for them to blend in, wouldn't it?"

They tried a rain of thrusts, but I flicked my points straight up and out and used my greater range to keep them back.

"Now, what do you suppose we might do with two of our own inside the temple?" I shook my head and said, "No, no, we wouldn't waste our time on some heroic attack that would just get our fellows killed while you all found a new hole to hide in. That would be a real waste, wouldn't it? So what if, instead, we had our two fellows split up and set them to spy on the temple? That way, if—and I know this sounds far-fetched, but just go along with this for now—if, say, the bastard monks at the temple took on a contract to kill Greatcoats, then one of our fellows could make sure he was one of the Azu sent on the mission. And then—well, why don't you show him, Toller?" I asked.

For a second, just a split second, they froze in their dance and looked at each other with an instant's distrust. Then they looked down at the blades of my rapiers stuck, point ends first, just below their chests. I've heard stories that the Dashini can slow the flow of their own blood—that they can survive a wound that would kill a normal man. So I pulled the blades out and stabbed them a few more times each, just to be sure. I'm not sure if that countered their preternatural resistance to injury or if their dignity finally demanded they do something—anything—to stop getting stabbed over and over, but they finally slid down to the ground.

I resisted the urge to fall down on my ass and sit there for a while and instead took a small cloth from my coat (I didn't want to risk some other contact poison on their dark garb) and carefully pulled their silken masks from their faces.

"Well, that makes sense," I said out loud. "Turns out they have some very exotic and, I expect, individualized tattoos on their faces. I suppose that *would* make them hard to impersonate. I wonder if they all have them. Seems like a lot of work, considering most of them are killed by their own teachers before they can be given their first mission."

The girl came up behind me and put one hand on my arm. She stood looking down at them but still staying well out of reach. "You mean, you didn't get any men inside their temple?"

"Hmm? Of course not—I mean, the King tried to send spies a few times, but they all turned up dead. They took some rather creative liberties with the return of the bodies. As for capturing two trained Dashini assassins and getting them to talk? Ridiculous idea."

"But you made them believe . . . The King's idea?"

"Yes," I said, "the King figured that people who spend their entire lives learning the art of murder and never being around books, people, conversation, or even the occasional dirty limerick are probably prone to a little paranoia now and then."

She looked up at me like I was an idiot.

I was feeling a little giddy. I'd just defeated two Dashini assassins. *Let's see Kest do* that. I smiled back at Aline and let out a big, long breath. Her eyes went wide and she did something strange: she turned away and started running as fast as she could. That was when something hit me hard in the back of the head and I lost consciousness.

I awoke a few times between where we were captured and arriving at the Duke's palace. My hands and feet were tied to a sturdy wooden pole and I was swinging from side to side. The man in front of me was tall and broad-backed; the one behind must have been a bit shorter, because my head seemed to hang lower than the rest of me.

"He's awake," I heard the man behind me grunt.

"Hit 'im again, then," replied the one in front.

"No, not yet." The new voice was male, but lighter, the accent higher class and somehow familiar. Suddenly a face came into view: long golden-blond hair hung down and almost touched my nose. The face was handsome, and not nearly bruised enough for my liking.

"Lorenzo."

He smiled. "Imagine us meeting again, First Cantor."

"Lorenzo, your face looks remarkably healed for such a short time."

"Magic—expensive. And can you believe this? It does nothing at all for the pain—it hurts just as much as when you finished putting your boots to me, Falcio."

"Yes, I meant to apologize about that. I'm sorry, Lorenzo, really sorry."

I looked to my right, trying to catch a glimpse of where we were. From the thick press of people we had to be on one of the main streets—probably Kestrel Way, the road that ended at the Ducal Palace.

Lorenzo grabbed my face with a strong hand—his left, I noticed. I'd done some fairly nasty things to his right.

"I'm not sure I can accept your apology, Falcio. Not until I'm absolutely sure of your sincerity."

I tried to shrug, but my limbs were numb so I'm not sure it produced much effect.

"Where's the girl, Lorenzo?" I asked.

"We've taken her on ahead," he replied. "We want to get started on her as quickly as possible."

I sighed. Aline had kept the soft candy, so she would certainly be dead by now. At least she had got to pick the time herself. I wondered how they'd caught up with us, but then a different question came to mind.

"*We*," I said.

"Hmm?"

"You said, 'We want to get started.' I assume you mean the Duke. How do your so-called New Greatcoats feel about the fact that a light slap is all it takes to make you abandon your high and mighty principles and go running to the Duke?"

Lorenzo looked at me with a quizzical expression on his face. "Are you serious?" he asked, genuinely. Then he gave a short bark of laughter. "Really? You don't know?" More laughter. "Saints, Falcio! You didn't know? And yet you beat me blue and bloody—for what? Because I offended your sense of the grand dignity of the Greatcoats?"

"Ah. Well, that makes more sense now, doesn't it."

He sounded highly amused. "Falcio, you may be a fool, and you're certainly going to die a gruesome death, but you've got style."

"So these New Greatcoats of yours—?"

"Useful, potentially. I suppose in one sense you were right, though—they do lack a great deal of dignity. But that was the whole point: bring back the people's beloved Greatcoats, but with more tractable—more *noble*—dispositions."

"You mean, make sure they're stupid, vain, and largely useless?"

He smiled. "Not an entirely unfair characterization, I suppose. But yes, give people something that looks like a Greatcoat and talks like a Greatcoat, but who can judge a case in a way that produces a more satisfactory and predictable outcome."

"And when people start to realize they can't trust them?"

"Then they'll turn away from the Greatcoats and the result will be just as good."

I thought about that for a few moments. "I must apologize again then, Lorenzo."

"For what?"

"Next time I beat you down I'm going to have to make sure you never get up again." The swinging was starting to make me nauseous. "Hey up there," I said to the man in front, "keep it steady or there'll be no tip for you when we get to the palace."

"Ha! See, that's the Falcio I've learned to admire in such a short time. You've got a sense of humor, of style."

The swinging stopped. "Ah, but see, we've arrived at the palace. It was nice seeing you again, Falcio val Mond. I regret that we are unlikely to ever meet again." Then Lorenzo pinched my nose with the fingers of his right hand and put his left over my mouth until I passed out.

18
THE DUCHESS

My first day or so of torture turned out to be the best sleep I'd had in years. I'd been going for days without rest, and I'd been in half a dozen fights that I'd barely survived. I had dozens of bruises and shallow wounds all over my body, none of which had had time to heal, and of course I'd been poisoned with a deadly paralytic that was only offset by a slightly less deadly overdose of the hard candy.

But worse than all these other things was the complete realization that I had failed. I'd failed as badly as any man in the history of the world had done, and no action or intent of mine could change that. Aline was dead, I was soon to die, and even if Kest made himself a murderer to stop Valiana from taking the throne, I suspected that the Dukes would have their way in the end. The long line of failures that made up the story of my life started with my failure to save my wife, Aline, and continued with my failure to save my King, to maintain the Greatcoats, and now I had failed to protect a simple young girl whom I tried to save for no better reason than that she had the same name as my wife. There was nothing left but torture and death, and I felt free. I doubt you'll hear it said by clerics, but the truth is that those who truly and completely fail are those who sleep the deepest and softest of all.

Eventually, though, I did awaken, to find myself in a cell only a few feet longer than my own height, with my wrists held in manacles hanging from a wooden structure that looked something like a gallows. I supposed they could have attached the chain at a more unfortunate location on my body, so I counted myself lucky.

It took a moment to realize there was a man in the room with me, sitting on a wooden stool.

"Oh, hello," I said.

The man looked up. He was a big one, for sure, thick at the shoulders and at the waist. He wore the customary red leather mask of a torturer.

"Did I miss breakfast?" I asked.

Torture in Rijou is administered using a mixture of beating and poisons, a variety of ointments and creams that produce every degree of pain, from blinding agony all the way up to a simple itch that won't go away. The itch is the worst in many ways; they rub it on a bit of bare flesh and leave you in your cell with no chains or manacles, and then they wait for you to start tearing the skin from your own bones. The substance they use to produce the itching isn't a contact poison, so the feeling spreads over all the body, so that there is literally not an inch of you that doesn't itch. It's quite common that the first thing to go is your eyes.

But they didn't start with that. I guessed they might want to soften me up first, which is why I wasn't surprised when he began pummeling me in the face, stomach, and back, asking questions all the while. His accent was so thick, I could barely understand him, but he kept repeating one question, as if by rote.

"She wants to know, are there any others?" A blow to the stomach.

"She wants to know, are there any others?" Another blow, this time to the ribs on my right side.

"Any other what?" I asked.

Another strike, this time to the face. "She wants to know, are there any others?"

Our relationship went on like that for some time.

Sometimes he stopped for a while, but only so he could lavish my skin with creams that burned like spilled lighting oil across my chest.

Then he would begin again with the beatings.

I didn't try to hold my tongue—that's a big mistake. Expressing pain is part of how the body releases it. He wanted me to talk, so talk I did: I told him how I felt. I told him where it hurt. I told him all about myself. I grunted and I moaned and I wept for mercy, and in those moments when he stopped, when I could get myself to speak again, I did what a Greatcoat is supposed to do when we're captured. I recited the King's Laws.

"The First Law is that men are free," I sang softly. "For without the freedom to choose, men cannot serve their heart, and without heart they cannot serve their Gods, their Saints, or their King."

"What is the Greatcoats' most powerful weapon?" King Paelis asked us. He was standing on a low dais in the courtyard as all one hundred and forty-four Greatcoats stood at attention. It was the first day of spring and, for the very first time, the full power of the Greatcoats would go out to the cities, villages, and hamlets of the country, to hear cases and administer the King's Justice. We had trained; we had prepared; we were ready. But the King—never one to leave well enough alone—still felt the need to impart one more lesson before we left.

"The sword is the greatest weapon," someone shouted.

The King shook his head. "There will always be someone better with a sword."

"Well, maybe Kest's sword, then," someone else said. There was laughter.

"Secrecy," another offered.

Again the King disagreed. "We are at our best when people know who we are and what we bring."

"Speed!"

"Strength of will!"

It went on like that for a few moments, and the King looked down at me as if expecting me to speak, so I said, "Our greatcoats. It is our greatcoats that shield us from danger. Their surface protects us from the swords of our opponents. Their lightness makes us move faster than an armored Knight. Their warmth protects us from the freezing cold. Their pockets hold the things we need to survive. Our greatcoats are our best weapon."

There were murmurs of agreement from the others.

But the King shook his head. "Ah, Falcio, even you . . . No, your greatcoat is still just a thing. It can be taken from you."

"Never!" someone shouted.

The King put his hands up for silence, then stepped forward to the very front of the dais. "Your greatest weapon is your judgment," he said simply. "Everything else can be taken from you; everything else could be provided by someone else. There are many men and women with swords; anyone can fight or run or kill. But only you, my Magisters, only you bring the power of your judgment to the people. It is your knowledge of the laws—not just the words, but the meaning behind them. That's why we sing the laws, so they will be remembered! You sing the verdict so the men and women will carry it in their minds and in their hearts, long after you have left their villages. Your ability is to render judgment, not just as punishment, but as a solution to the fracturing in the heart of the people that occurs when the laws are broken. It is your judgment that sets you apart. My Greatcoats, in your dark hours—and there will be many, make no mistake—in your dark hours, turn first to your judgment, to your voice, and sing the words."

Turn first to your judgment, to your voice, and sing the words. And as my torturer battered me with his fists, that's just what I did.

My efforts to convince my torturer of the error of his ways had not produced much in the way of results, though I was gratified the morning when I awoke to the sound of him humming the melody of the King's Law of Free Travel. He must have been embarrassed that I'd noticed, because he gave me a particularly bad beating that morning.

By my fourth day in the cell I was not far from ended. Despite the healing salves they periodically smeared on my body to keep me from expiring in peace, there really wasn't much left of me. Since I could barely lift a finger, never mind devise an escape, they had even released me from the chains.

It is at times such as these that we Pertines believe an angel will come to hear your last words.

"And here sits Paelis's great hope," a voice said. It didn't sound much like an angel. I opened my eyes.

What I saw was a woman in her middle years. Her form was slim but well shaped, and she wore a gown of dark red, with matching jewels—rubies—hanging from her ears and around her neck. She had striking gray hair, well fashioned above a lined and unsmiling face. She wasn't beautiful—she had probably never been beautiful—but in the sharp edges of her features and the coolness in her eyes there was still something seductive, something that suggested she knew what you wanted, what you needed—something that would sway commoner or nobleman alike to her will.

Then I saw the rings on her fingers: seven of them, large and gaudy and shaped like wheels. Despite my weakness, I lunged forward to kill her.

My torturer, whom I called Ugh since that's what came out of my mouth when he struck me, grabbed me with one hand and held me, though he needn't have bothered. My attempted attack was more than my body could handle and if he'd let me go I would have dropped to the floor myself. Instead, he punched me in the face and threw me back against the wall.

"Ugh," I said.

"My, my. An execution with no trial? I thought you Greatcoats were supposed to be above such things," said Duchess Patriana.

"You killed Tremondi, you bitch." I coughed something up that I hoped wasn't a tooth before adding, "Did you do it yourself? Or did someone do it for you? I swear if it was your daughter I'll put the blade in her myself."

She looked down at me with a calm expression. “You are uncouth,” she said, “and common, and unimportant.”

“Perhaps you should take your leave, in that case. I was just about to instruct Ugh here on the finer points of landholder contracts and farming rights.”

She smiled. “Ah yes, your King’s Laws. So just, so honorable—to master them is to master the sunshine, or the light of the moon. Even to utter them out loud will rouse the soul of the peasantry and free the land from the oppressive nobility!”

“Something like that,” I said.

“One wonders why Paelis never saved himself the trouble. If he had taught his wonderful laws to the Dukes, he could thereby have freed us of our own ignorance.”

I smiled. “For the same reason we don’t try to teach cats to count. They’re either too fucking stupid or they just don’t care.”

Ugh lifted me off the ground and punched me again.

I coughed, and tasted blood on my tongue. “Right you are, Ugh. It’s time to get back to it . . . Much to talk about . . . Anything else . . . I can help you with, your Ladyship?”

Patriana leaned in close and inspected my face with the languid attentiveness of a healer examining a rather unimportant patient. “Some of them work for me now, you realize?” she said quietly.

“Some of whom, your Ladyship?”

“The Trattari. Your fellow Greatcoats—half of them work for me. The other half are bandits these days.”

I snorted. It hurt.

“Laugh if you want, First Cantor, but it’s a fact: your noble Greatcoats make their living ravaging the countryside. There have been robberies, Falcio, and murders. And rapes. And all of these committed by your men.”

“Liar,” I said, despite my intent to keep silent.

She shook her head. “Innocence might be a virtue, Falcio, but willful ignorance is not. It’s been five years since you were disbanded. Did you really think they’d all stay loyal to a dead King?”

“My Lady, there are no traitors in the Greatcoats. Not one.” I let the lie slip from my lips like a trickle of blood.

Patriana laughed. "Traitors? You poor, deluded fool. The Greatcoats serve the state! The King has been dead for five years and the Dukes are the lawful rulers of this country. The men working for us aren't traitors, Falcio—*you* are."

When you're being tortured, the most important skill is to ignore what you hear. The pain is horrible, but what breaks you is what they say. That's why you have to live with the pain but block out the words.

"Well then, your Ladyship, you seem to have everything you need. If you don't mind, I'll take my leave of you now." I let my head slump down and closed my eyes.

Ugh punched me in the face.

The Duchess arranged her gown carefully and sat down on the wooden stool. She crossed one ankle over the other.

"Are there others?" she asked.

"Ah, yes, that. Ugh's been asking me the same thing for some time."

"And apparently you have failed to answer. So let me ask you again: are there others? Your attempt to escape the city failed and there's little reason to prolong your agony. So answer the question: where are the others? Do any still live?"

The truth was, I honestly didn't know. Other than Kest and Brasti, I hadn't seen another Greatcoat in years. I'd tried to convince myself that Parrick, Nile, Dara, and some of the others would have survived, that we would all find each other again one day, but the truth was, the only land we would likely ever share together was the land of the dead.

"Lots," I said. "Hundreds. And I swear the numbers grow by the day."

"Answer me!" she screamed, rising from her stool and slapping me across the face. The force of the blow surprised me.

She went on: "I've spent my entire life in an endeavor that will reshape this country—that will make it strong in the eyes of Saints and Gods—and I will *not* have my plans shattered because one of Paelis's little bastards runs off and rouses the peasants or the damnable Lords Caravaner."

"I thought you said most of us either worked for you or had turned to banditry. Perhaps you give us more credit than you'd like to admit," I said, a little confused by her overestimation of the Greatcoats' persuasiveness.

"I give you no credit at all, fool. Now, if you value your sanity or your soul, answer the question: *Where are the others?*"

Something about the way she asked the question—the fear, the anger, the deep and utter need to know—something about this strange sincerity coming from the mouth of the woman who, more than any other single person alive, was responsible for destroying my world, compelled me to answer truthfully, "I don't know. I really don't know."

She reached down and dug her nails into the sides of my face. "You filthy, stupid *boy*. You *dog*. You think you've been tortured? You think you've known pain? The things they do here are nothing compared to what *I* can do to you. I'll have them slice your skin open and bring starving children in to suckle the blood from your wounds while you watch. I'll put an ointment on your cock that makes it hard, and have them use you to rape old women to death. I make *monsters*, Falcio val Mond, and I can make a monster out of you. I know more ways to torture a man than this dog with his poisons and beatings can ever imagine."

"Shh," I said. "You'll hurt Ugh's feelings if you keep talking that way."

She let my head drop. "Bring him," she ordered Ugh. "And have someone bring the girl, if there's anything left of her."

The girl?

19

THE FEY HORSE

When I regained consciousness, my hands were bound at the wrists, but it didn't bother me much. Dazed as I was, Ugh had to half-carry me through the passageways of the Duke's dungeon. The walls were the same hard stone that formed the base of the palace and the promenade out front. Here truly was the Rock of Rijou: an inescapable prison for the Dukes to use to entertain themselves with the suffering of others.

I was crying, not for any reason I could put into words, but because as much as the mind may grow to disdain the body, the body will always mourn the desecration of the spirit. Ugh was singing softly as we walked, and I wondered if he knew he was humming the King's Law Against Unjust Punishments. If not, it was ironic, and if he did, that was something I couldn't really understand.

"We say good-bye soon, I think," he said in his thick accent that I still couldn't place. Perhaps he was from somewhere in the far north?

"Good-bye?"

We reached the end of a long passageway that ended in a set of narrow stairs going up. There was a door at the top with bars revealing fading afternoon light.

"I take you through this door, then to stable. She commands. When horse is done, nothing left to bring back."

"Horse?"

"Shush now," he said. He threw me over his shoulder and started up the stairs. "Talk gets me trouble with Lady. But you interesting man. Funny songs. No music for me usually. Maybe not such a bad man as they say. Makes me want to say good-bye."

At the top of the stairs he pounded hard on the door, six times. A guard on the other side looked through the bars and then pulled a key from his neck and opened it up. "Destination?" the guard asked.

Ugh set me back down on my own feet, still holding me up, but more roughly now someone was watching. "Stable. Lady give him to horse."

"Orders?"

"Orders are in my fucking fist, like always. You want to see them closer?"

The guard stepped out of the way and let us pass.

"Guards are like fucking dumb animals here," he said to no one in particular as we proceeded along the open courtyard, then, "Maybe you like to run, eh?"

"Sure," I replied. "Just need a bit of a head start."

"They say you Greatcoats fucking tough guys in the day. Tricky, eh? Maybe you have trick to use on me, too?"

I looked at him. "I've used up all my tricks, I'm afraid."

Ugh pushed me forward. "Is not important. Guards from here to palace gates. You not get ten paces before they pull you down." He turned me and looked me in the eye. "So no trouble, yes? No point, yes? No making trouble for me, yes?"

"Let's go see the horse," I said.

He grunted, turned me back around, and pushed me onward.

It was a short distance to the stable—I'd imagined he was talking about the palace stables, but this was different. We entered through the wide doors into a single large building that stank like sixteen different hells. Inside was almost completely empty, except for a cage made of iron bars in the center. Next to the cage was a chair, where the Duchess Patriana sat sipping something from a small cup. Inside the cage was a monster.

The beast was massive, almost twice the size of a Knight's charger. The head was huge, and stood almost an arm's length above even a tall man. Its coat was tattered, almost skinned, and every inch of its body was covered in welts and scars. Its ears were flat against its head and its eyes were black as coal. When it opened its mouth, I saw that its teeth had been filed to points. The sound that came from its mouth was closer to a growl than any sound I had ever heard a horse make.

Patriana motioned for Ugh to bring me forward. When we got within a few feet of the cage he let me go, but I started to fall and only his sudden grip on the back of my neck saved me from having my head ripped off by the creature inside the cage. Its eyes were burning with fury at being denied its prey.

"Saints," I said. "What is it?"

Patriana smiled. "This? This is one of my pet projects, if you'll pardon the humor."

Inside, the cage was filthy. It had likely never been cleaned, so the horse's waste just piled up until it dripped through the bars. Hanging from the ceiling of the cage were the torn corpses of some kind of creature, although it was hard to make sense of their shapes, stripped of skin and sinew as they were.

"You need a different hobby," I said conversationally.

She smiled again. "You don't recognize it? I would have thought a romantic like you might recognize one from the storybooks. After all, they are a sort of namesake for your kind, aren't they?"

My stomach fell and my heart came up into my throat. "It can't be—"

"Oh, trust me, it is. And very expensive it is to find them, I can assure you."

"A Fey Horse . . . you did this to a *Fey Horse*?"

"Come now, don't be modest. Didn't they also used to be called Greathorses? I would've thought you'd feel a connection."

I'd heard of Greathorses, of course, or Fey Horses as they were more commonly known. But they didn't look anything like this. Fey Horses were noble and wild. The few herds rumored to exist were the subject of children's fantasies, mine maybe even more than most. The dream of finding a Fey Horse, of riding a beast that ran faster than anything else in the world, that could run for days, that could face down a pride of mountain cats or any other beast . . . The Fey were to horses what Saints are to men—but better than that, for Saints can be capricious, even evil. The Fey Horses in the storybooks were noble protectors. But not this . . .

"Yes," Patriana said, reading my expression perfectly, "this really is one of the Fey. She is the last of her herd, in fact."

I remembered the old stories, some that Bal Armidor had told at the inn near my childhood home and others from books in the royal library. Paelis and I used to joke about how much faster the Greatcoats could travel if we only had Greathorses to match. "Four days' ride to Warrelton, I think, Falcio, or two if by Greathorse," he used to say. There was one book, a favorite of both the King's and mine, about a boy who learned the language of the Fey Horses and rode them to battle against the Knights holding his mother captive. "*Dan'ha vath fallatu*," the boy would say in their special language. "I am of your herd."

"What happened to the rest?" I asked, my eyes still locked on the frenzied creature held inside the cage.

She sighed. "Failed experiments, I'm afraid. Can you imagine, twenty of the beasts and only one comes even close to my desires? No, I must be honest with myself, this was not a very good investment."

"But *why*? Why in the name of every God and Saint would you take something so beautiful and—?"

"And what? And *ruin* it? What use is a Greathorse running around in the plains, Falcio? What *purpose* does it serve? The beasts exist to serve, just as the peasants do, just as you do. What use is a beast that doesn't pull a plow, or provide food, or carry a Knight to war?"

"Twenty," I said, my throat numb. "Twenty Greathorses and you destroyed them all . . ."

"I trained them, after a fashion, but it wouldn't take. I burned them. I cut off pieces of their flesh. I fed them poison, beat them bloody, had them strangled with ropes, pulled out their eyes. *Nothing* would turn them to my purpose."

"What possible purpose could you mean for them with such practices?"

She looked genuinely surprised. "Why, to make them into warhorses, of course. Imagine a division of Knights riding into battle on these brutes: they'd be unstoppable. Do you know you can fire arrows into these things and their hide is so thick they won't die? They'd just keep going, and oftentimes as not the arrow will eventually fall out and the damned thing will recover completely from its wounds. Truthfully, killing them was so much work that I still wonder whether it was worth the bother."

"What are those things strung from the ceiling?" I asked, horrified.

"Ah, you've noticed. Well, that's what finally did the trick. This one's a female, you see. So what we did was, we impregnated her with the fluids of another horse. They're able to crossbreed, probably how such small numbers have been able to maintain their herds. When she gives birth, which is just about the only time the damned thing is weak enough for my men to get in there, we take the foal and we torture it to death. After the fourth or fifth one, the beast finally found its rightful purpose, which is to kill, of course. It's a bit of a shame that it took so long to figure out, and of course there are still a few problems to solve, such as making it obey commands and not just tear anything it finds to pieces. But that just needs a bit more time, that's all."

She said the words as casually as you might tell your neighbor about the weather. I looked around the stable, at the other guards by the doors, at Ugh. How could any man not pull his sword from its sheath and run her through? How could any man endure this?

"You're not going to get emotional on me, are you?" Patriana asked, noticing the tears on my face. "After all, we're not done here yet."

"Why have you shown me this?" I asked. "Why not just leave me in my cell, or kill me?"

"Because," she said soothingly, "I am a teacher at heart. I want you to *learn*. I want you to *understand*."

"By every God and Saint, understand *what*? That you're a monster?"

"No, Falcio: understand that I am *right*."

"You're insane."

She shook her head. "Can you really be so blind? Are you really no smarter than the beast in the cage? Look at her! That's you, don't you understand?"

She stood up and came to face me. I felt Ugh's hand clutching behind my neck, reminding me that I had no power here.

"Your precious King Paelis was no different. He had a need for weapons, and so he chose you. He selected you like he selected the others, conditioned you for the purpose he'd devised, and then used you to attack his enemies."

"You compare building a judiciary to protect people's rights with making a monster that can do nothing but rend and tear and kill?"

"Yes!" she said. "Yes. It's exactly the same. People have no rights, Falcio, save those granted them by their rightful Lords, their rightful *owners*. Paelis was no different from any of his fellow nobles, though he certainly liked to pretend he was. So he enjoyed watching peasants pretend to be happy? How is that any different from the Duke who has a different purpose for them? In the end, Paelis had power and he used it to create the world he wanted. But he went too far, Falcio. The monarchy have always understood that within our individual realms we have supreme power, but he wanted to change that. He was the one who broke the natural laws of this land, Falcio. He was the tyrant!"

My head dropped and my eyes stared at the ground as I said, "He wanted people to be free, that's all. He wanted—"

"He wanted to be loved," she said softly in my ear. "That's all it was. The idle desires of a weak and feeble mind never meant to hold a crown. It was an accident that took the life of his brother, Dergot, the rightful heir. If that stupid bitch Yesa hadn't set him on a window ledge he'd still be alive. Greggor could hardly have done worse than his first wife, but in Yesa he came very close."

"Why are you telling me this, Duchess? You're cold and you're malicious, but you aren't vain. If I'm so irrelevant, then why am I here? Why was it so important to show me that you'd corrupted a Fey Horse?"

She took my chin in my hand. "Because, my dear boy, I wanted to prove to you that it could be done. You'd never have believed me if I'd just told you, would you? This will make my next experiment that much easier."

"What is your next experiment?" I asked wearily.

She smiled and kissed me warmly on the cheek. "You are, Falcio val Mond."

Despite myself, I almost laughed. "Me?"

"Don't hold yourself too cheaply, Falcio. You're almost valuable to me now. You see, I honestly believe you hate me more than any other man alive today."

"On that one point we may agree, your Ladyship."

"And so I have much to learn from you, Falcio val Mond. In the process of turning you, of changing you from Greatcoat to my own loving creature, I will learn much about how to train my people, how to make them more useful to me. That's what I do, Falcio: I make things useful."

"You make monsters," I said.

"If you want to call it that. But make no mistake, I do it very well."

"Not so well with your own daughter, though. She may be foolish, but she has none of your vile spirit moving her."

Patriana laughed. "My *daughter*? Oh, my daughter is much more dangerous than I am. I dare say she is my finest accomplishment!"

I thought about that. Was she lying? I'd put my life on it that Valiana wasn't evil. Were Kest and Brasti even now dead at her hand? How could the Heart's Trial not show something like that? Was it rigged? Was all this just a ruse?

"Enough now," Patriana said. "Let's begin your training, shall we?"

She walked back and sat down on the chair.

"You've been unwilling thus far to tell me where the others I seek are hiding, Falcio, and since the girl clearly doesn't know—" She motioned to one of the guards, who opened a door and pulled Aline out. She was bloodied, and her clothes were in rags. A gag was tied around her mouth and her eyes were wide. The guard brought her toward us and dropped her on the ground in front of me. I felt Ugh let go of my neck and I dropped to my knees in front of her.

"Why?" I asked. "Why didn't you take the soft candy? Why did you let them—?"

"Enough now, Falcio. It's time to get started."

At the guard's signal, the others around the room brought a number of long poles with them. One of the poles was shorter and made of metal, and the end had been cunningly worked into the shape of a simple key, which the guard shoved into the lock. As he twisted it, the other guards used the poles to keep the beast from getting out. Finally, one of the guards attached the end of his pole to a cord, and attached the other end to a collar around Aline's neck.

"What are you doing?" I shouted, but they ignored me. "Stop!" I snapped my head forward and managed to pull free from Ugh's grip, but another guard pushed me to the ground just outside the bars of the cage. Before, the horse had tried to attack me when I was that close; this time its eyes were wide and it was obviously seeking a way to escape through the gradually opening door to the cage.

As soon as the gap was wide enough, they pushed Aline inside and snapped the door closed again.

"Watch what it does now, Falcio. See how it first terrorizes the prey before killing it, as if it wants every other living creature to experience the fear and suffering it witnessed in its own foals' eyes."

"Damn you!" I screamed. "Damn you, woman—get her out of there! Get her out and I will do whatever you want—do you understand? You won't have to do anything to me, I'll do your bidding—just *get her out of there*!"

Aline was huddled in the corner as the Fey Horse towered above her, teeth bared and a sickening growling sound coming from its mouth. Its hooves struck the ground.

"Now, Falcio, that's not quite how this works." The Duchess turned to me. "What I find the most fascinating, and I hope you will as well, is that all of this hate and anger you feel will actually help speed things along. Isn't that odd? Watching this girl get torn apart, followed by the other entertainments I have planned for you, will actually make you more malleable, not less. It turns out that the human mind has limits to what it can deal with, and once you break those limits . . . How can I put this? It's like returning a statue to its original marble: you can chip away at it and make it into whatever you want, as if the original form had never existed."

The horse was getting closer to her now, and nipping its teeth near her face, her hair. The anger coming from it was almost palpable: rage at every*thing* and every*one*. Aline's mouth was gagged, but I don't think she even tried to scream, so filled with terror was she.

"For the sake of the Gods, there must be some human decency inside you—"

I heard Aline now, her screams muffled, but obviously terrified. She was bleeding from her left shoulder.

"See how it starts with little bites? That's what we do with the foals. It takes an age to finish the job. You'd almost think the creature was intelligent."

Seeing the look on my face she said, "You know, in retrospect it seems hardly fair to call this beast a failed experiment. It does have its uses."

I pushed myself up and threw myself at the bars. "*Dan'ha vath fallatu!*" I shouted at the horse. "*Dan'ha vath fallatu!*"

The Duchess looked confused. "What on earth is that? Danna-vath? Is that some kind of—? Oh my—" She put a hand up to her mouth and started laughing. "That may just be the sweetest thing I've ever heard!" She turned to one of the guards. "You know, I think he's quoting fairy tales at the beast!"

The guard didn't reply, but he grinned at me.

"Fey!" I screamed into the bars. "You are Fey! You are of the unbound, you cannot be controlled, you cannot be chained. *Dan'ha vath fallatu!* I am of your herd! The girl is of your herd! *Dan'ha vath fallatu!*"

I was crying and screaming through the bars like a madman. I reached toward the beast—it was too far away, of course, and if anything it was likely to tear my arm off. But it ignored me and took another bite, at the girl's face this time.

She screamed again. Her cheek was bloody.

"They cannot chain you!" I screamed. "They cannot bind you! The Fey are free! The Fey protect the herd! *Dan'ha vath fallatu!* She is of the herd! You must protect the herd—"

The beast wasn't moving away from her; if anything, it was getting wilder, more enraged. It stamped its great hooves, less than a foot from her body; then it reared and stamped again, this time an inch away from her.

"*Dan'ha vath fallatu*," I cried again. "I am Falcio val Mond. I guard the herd, as you do. I am broken, as you are. *Dan'ha vath fallatu*: we are of the same herd. *Dan'ha vath fallatu.* The girl is of the same herd. Protect the herd. You cannot be bound. You cannot be controlled. *Dan'ha vath fallatu.* You must protect the girl: she is like you, like me—"

My eyes were bleeding tears and the world was a blur. I couldn't tell if the girl was dead or if the beast was about to rip off my own head through the bars. I just kept talking to it, begging, pleading, saying anything that came into my head, through the sounds of hooves smashing against the ground. The growling from its throat shifted between snarling and neighing and pounded at the inside of my heart. Somewhere in the background I could hear the guards shifting restlessly and the Duchess shouting at them, and through it all I just kept repeating, "*Dan'ha vath fallatu*," over and over again.

Something struck me on the head and I fell back and cleared the tears from my eyes. I saw the horse smashing its head against the bars over and over, trying to break free, and I looked into the corner and saw Aline on the ground, unmoving. I thought she might be dead; then I saw the guards trying to use their poles to push back the horse so they could remove her from the cage. Her chest was moving up and down very rapidly. The horse bit at the poles and smashed its hooves against the side of the cage, and the guards would go no closer, even with the Duchess shouting at them. The horse was screaming, shoving hard against the cage with its whole body, and the iron bars were beginning to look as if they might buckle.

Ugh, still standing behind me, picked me up. The Duchess brought her face close to mine. She was smiling. "You marvelous, marvelous boy," she said, patting me on the cheek. "How wonderful—I've never seen anything like it! I do believe you've managed to reach through to something deep inside that monster's brain—and do you know what that means?"

"It means all your vile tortures have failed, Duchess."

"Oh, don't be silly," she said, and kissed me once again on the cheek before whispering in my ear, "It means I can reach it too."

She stepped back to watch again as the horse threw itself against the bars of the cage. "Take him back to his cell," she said to my guard.

"What about the horse? What about the girl?" asked one of the other guards, who was holding the broken end of a pole.

"Leave it," Patriana replied. "Either the horse will knock itself out against the bars, or it will tire of trying to escape and go back to killing the girl. Either way works. I've other things to think about here.

"*Dan'ha vath fallatu,*" she said to me. "How utterly delightful!"

Ugh threw me over his shoulder and carted me back to my cell. This time, he said not a word nor made a sound the entire way back.

20

THE TORTURER'S CONSCIENCE

I awoke to a strange noise. My head was full of fog and I was back hanging from my wrists on the strange wooden gibbet that occupied much of the space in the small room. It took a moment to recognize that the sound I was hearing was someone crying.

I opened my eyes. It was dark in the room, apart from a small candle glowing near the door. I guessed it must be past midnight, though there was no way to be sure. I looked around for the source of the sound, thinking that perhaps I had been awakened by my own weeping, but it wasn't me. In the corner, sitting on his stool, was Ugh, my torturer. In his hand was a knife, one of those he used to flay the flesh from those unfortunates who fell foul of the Duke's ire. Ugh was weeping softly, sniffling periodically and wiping his nose against his forearm. Then he'd take the knife and make a small cut against his arm and watch the line of blood appear where the knife had been.

"What are you doing?" The croak of my voice made me realize I'd screamed myself hoarse by the Fey Horse's cage. In my head I heard Brasti saying he hadn't thought that was possible, and I gave a small, weak laugh.

"No laugh," Ugh said, still looking down at his knife.

"I wasn't laughing at you. I was . . . well, never mind. What are you doing?"

"Horse choose," he said, almost in a grunt. "You make it so horse choose."

"I don't understand," I said.

"Horse not killing girl. You say things to horse, and horse choose. It choose not to kill girl." His voice was so thick with pain and confusion that for a moment I wanted to tell him it was all right. But it wasn't all right.

"Fucking horse," he said, and cut his arm again.

I didn't know what to say, how to make him feel better—or if I even wanted him to feel better.

"Fucking horse," he repeated, and looked up at me with tears in his eyes. "You talk to fucking horse. You say it should not be killing girl. The horse . . . fucking hells, the things they do to that horse—the things she make *us* do to that horse . . . and you talk and horse stops killing. I—"

He sobbed again and put another cut across his arm, harder and deeper this time. "I do what I am told. I do what Duke says. I do what bitch Duchess says. But I am *man*!" He stood up from his stool and it fell behind him and rolled toward the wall. "I am fucking man!" he shouted as he brought the knife to my face.

"You are a man," I said softly.

"I am man," he repeated. "Fucking horse, poor fucking horse, is mind gone. Is no more mind, no more heart. She take away—she take away, but horse . . . Fucking horse. Fucking horse listen and stop. Not kill girl. Fucking horse listen and then not kill girl. We tortured . . . we killed . . ."

He sobbed again and pulled away from me. "I am man, but fucking horse is better than me. Crazy fucking thing with no mind, no heart. *Is better than me!*" He screamed out the last sentence over and over for a while, smashing his fists against the walls, cutting himself, cursing himself. It was horribly like watching the Fey Horse trying to smash out of its cage.

Finally he dropped the knife. He pulled the key from his shirt pocket and came close to me. The thick smell of alcohol bled out from his mouth, and the misery bled from his eyes.

"You tell me," he said, half-threatening, half-pleading. "You tell me how I can be . . . how I can be like horse, not like me. How I can be as good as horse. You tell me, and I let you go. I let you go. I get you out. Only, you tell me first."

I thought he was lying, but then I noticed a bundle on the ground near where the stool had rolled. It was my greatcoat and my rapiers.

"You tell me. You—"

"Shh," I said. "I'll tell you."

"Tell me, tell me now," he said, turning his face away from me, as if he wanted this secret knowledge to be transmitted straight into his ears and into his heart.

I took a hard, painful breath through my mouth. "The First Law is that men are free," I sang softly. "For without the freedom to choose, men cannot serve their heart . . ."

"First Law is freedom," Ugh sang awkwardly as he hauled me through the passageway. "First Law is freedom. Man has heart, must be free. Must choose. No God, no King take away heart; take away freedom."

It was an awkward revision to the King's First Law, but no worse than many versions I'd heard.

"Where go?" he asked as we reached the bottom of the stairway.

I looked upward. "The girl—is she still there?"

He nodded. "Horse not let anyone near. Almost break cage."

Saints, but the girl must be out of her wits with fear.

"Take me there, then. To the stable."

Ugh shook his head. "No, is wrong idea. I take you there, guards will see, shout for other guards."

"I'll get the girl and take her with me."

He shook his head again. "No, you still stupid. Know many things—laws, horses. Not palace. Too many guards that way. I take you other way: cooks' entrance. Cooks not care. I give them money; I tell them I kill them if talk. We get you out."

It was my turn to shake my head. "The girl. I have to get the girl."

"Then how you get out from stable to palace gate? How you open gate?"

"I suppose I'll need a fast horse."

He looked at me for a moment as if I had lost my mind. Then he laughed. "All right. All right, man of laws, I take you to stable. But then I go. I don't think horse like me."

"Perhaps he doesn't know you well enough yet."

The humor was lost on Ugh, who just said, "Shut up now. I must take you past first guard."

He threw me over his shoulder again and pressed up the stairway and knocked six times on the heavy door again.

"What in hells are you doing here?" the guard asked as he opened the door and let us through.

"She," he said as if that explained everything. When the guard didn't move, he said, "He go back to horse. Go in cage. Not come out."

"I don't have any orders to that effect," the guard said cautiously.

Without another word Ugh punched him hard in the face and the guard fell back and hit his head against the opposite wall. He slid down, unconscious.

"Told you: orders in my fucking fist. Now you see up close." Ugh put me back down and we walked along the right side of the courtyard back to the stable. When we reached the edge he said, "Good-bye now. We say good-bye. No guards in stable at night. Just man who check courtyard, come every hour and look inside. I go back and out cooks' way. Never come back. You go, die with girl and horse. You free. You choose."

"Thank you," I said.

He shook his head. "I told you I would kill you when you arrive. Now you go kill yourself. This no different."

"It's different to me," I said.

He nodded at that, then turned and headed back for the other side of the courtyard.

I entered the stable and saw the beast in the cage in the center of the building. It was still stamping and fuming, but it wasn't throwing itself against the bars anymore. I crept toward it silently, aware that, despite Ugh's reassurances, other guards might come by, if for no other reason than to see if the girl was dead yet.

The horse made that sound between growling and neighing that I found so unsettling.

"Falcio?" Aline whispered.

"It's me," I whispered back. "Are you all right?"

She nodded, the movement barely showing in the shadowy light of the stable. "The bites were shallow," she said, "but she won't let me move. She growls at me when I try to get up."

"I understand," I said.

I reached through the bars toward the horse's mane. "Hey there, girl," I said softly.

The horse bit me and reared her hooves, striking them against the bars.

The pain brought me back to my senses. "*Dan'ha vath fallatu*," I said. "I am of your herd, damn you. Don't bite me anymore."

The horse made that growling noise again.

"She's angry," Aline said.

"I know she's angry!"

"She's angry—but she understands, I think. When I talk to her, she seems to understand. If I say I won't stand up, then she leaves me. If I say I want to move, she gets mad again. I think she understands, Falcio—but she's very angry."

I sighed. "I'm angry too," I said. "They took my King. They killed my King and they killed my friends and they killed my wife. Do you understand, you great fucking beast? They took my wife from me. My *wife*—she was everything. She was of my herd, you fucking brute. *Dan'ha vath fallatu.* You're angry? Look at the girl. She's angry too," I said, pointing to Aline. "They took her family as well, her herd." The horse nearly took my hand off, but I pulled it back in time. "All right. No more pointing for now."

I walked over to the wall where the metal pole with the key was hanging and pulled it off.

"They killed your herd," I said to the Fey Horse. "They killed all of our herds. Now we have a choice. *Dan'ha vath fallatu.* We can be one herd and fight together, or we can die alone."

I put the key into the slot in the cage. The horse started stamping and smashing at the bars again.

"It's time to choose," I said over the racket. "I'm going to open this door. You can attack me and I'll be dead, and the girl will be too when they come for her. Or you can just run off, and they'll kill us and eventually find and kill you too. Or you can carry us. None of us can get out of here alive alone, but if you carry us, we can charge the gate and we might—we just might get through alive and into the city."

The horse slowed her efforts, but she gave no other sign that she was understanding my words. I'm not sure what signs I was hoping for.

"Open the cage, Falcio, quick! I hear them coming," Aline said.

"Show me you're going to help us," I said to the horse. "*Dan'ha vath fallatu.* Show us we are one herd."

I could hear shouts. Someone had seen me and there would be guards soon. Hopefully not too many, but I was so weak it would take only one or two at this point. But I still wouldn't move. But then, slowly, ever so slowly, I saw the horse start to move, almost as if the great beast was shrinking. But she wasn't; she was just kneeling on the ground. I turned the key in the lock and swung the door open.

"Get on," I told Aline.

She looked at me as if I was crazy.

"Either she's going to help or it won't matter one way or the other. Get on." I picked her up and placed her on the back of the horse. She didn't kill the girl, so I took that as a good sign and awkwardly climbed on the beast's back myself, just as the first pair of guards came through the doors.

I leaned low on the creature's back. "*Dan'ha vath fallatu*," I said, patting the side of her neck. Then I brought my mouth close to her ear and said the only other word I remembered from the storybooks. "*K'hey*," I whispered. "*K'hey, k'hey, k'hey.*" Fly. Fly. *Fly*.

As the guards reached the entrance to the cage, their swords drawn, I felt the Fey Horse's muscles bunch beneath us, and the thunder of an angry God exploded from the cage as she slammed through the door and into the guards, leaving them dead on the ground as we bolted away from the stable and into the night sky.

21
GENTLE SORROWS

It was like trying to hang on to an earthquake. I was jostled up and off the creature's back, and only her own twisting movements managed to keep me from falling to the ground. It was worse for Aline.

"Put your arms through the loops of my coat," I shouted as we raced past the entrance of the courtyard, leaving another guard dead beneath the beast's hooves.

The Fey Horse was utterly merciless with the guards, as if she remembered every cut, every beating, every slight. She probably did.

"Out!" I screamed in her ears. "We have to get out! You can't kill every guard in the palace!"

I suspected she understood my meaning if not my words, for she very nearly threw me off then and there.

"Fine! You can kill them all—you can kill everybody, but the girl will be killed by their swords," I screamed. "Protect the girl! *Protect the foal!*"

I don't know if the horse heard me over the shouting guards, but she did finally break for the far gate. The doors were twelve feet high and made of bars just as strong as those of her cage. I had to hope that the lock on the door was a weak point.

"Hang on!" I said to Aline, and knelt low on the horse's neck as she bolted forward. For a moment I feared she'd run headlong into the gate, but at the last instant she reared on her hind legs and let the momentum carry her as she smashed her hooves into the metal bars of the gate. I saw them bend and sway even as the lock exploded, and just like that we were out. I heard more shouting behind us, and felt the crossbow bolts fly by our ears. At least two landed in the horse's haunches but if they hurt her, she showed no sign; she just kept running down the main street. I thanked the Saints that it was late and few people were out to be trampled underneath the beast's hooves.

We must have traveled at least a mile outside the palace before the horse let me rein her in. Without bridle or stirrups I had to use the meager strength left in my legs to try and guide her.

"Where are we going?" Aline asked as we finally slowed to a walk.

I slipped down from the horse's back and tried to stretch my legs, but I had to lean against her haunch to keep from falling. "I just need to get my bearings," I replied. "Then we'll make for one of the smaller city gates and hope we can make our way out through sheer force."

"No," Aline said.

"What do you mean, no?"

"It's the last night of Ganath Kalila," she said. "Tomorrow at the Teyar Rijou the noble houses will be recognized once again. We'll go to the Rock; I can stand for my name."

"Are you crazy? They'll kill you—they'll definitely kill me."

"The day after the Blood Week is the Morning of Mercy. No one can be harmed and no one can be arrested, not unless they attack another first."

I sighed and looked up at the night sky. "Tell me how this ends," I asked wearily. "Tell me what happens after that."

"I can get sanctuary from one of the other noble families—I can even leave the city. But I'll keep my blood rights, Falcio."

"Your blood rights? And what value does that have when the Duke wants you dead?"

"It's all I have! It's all I have left of my mother . . . of my father . . ."

"I'm sorry," I said. "I never met Lord Tiarren, but I'm sure he was—"

"Oh, shut up," she cried. "You don't understand *anything*."

I relented, and we kept walking. Could the girl be right? Was it really as simple as all that? Even with the Duchess here, could the ritual of Ganath Kalila itself really protect Aline?

The streets were deserted. The last night of the Blood Week was the time to stay indoors, although by this point most of the fights had been fought, most of the murders committed. It's hard to express how much I hated this place.

"Hello," a female voice said, leaning forward from a street bench in the shadows.

Aline screamed, my rapier came into my hand, and the horse leapt toward her, her hooves ready to strike out.

The woman didn't run; she stood slowly and reached out to the horse's face as if she had no fear of the beast at all.

"*Dan'ha neta vath fallatu*," she said softly. "I am not of your herd, Mother. But I am no enemy either."

"Who are you?" I demanded, my rapier still pointing at her body.

The woman was beautiful. She was dressed in a white gown that covered her body, shoulders, and arms—a gauzy material that shimmered in the moonlight. Her head was partially covered by a kind of hood made from the same cloth, and dark hair spilled out to frame a face that was smooth and soft and smiling gently. It was a face that a man would never forget, and yet it was her voice that made me recognize her.

"You're real," I said. "You came to talk to me in my prison cell. You were at the Duke's ball."

The memory made me tighten my grip on my rapier. "Who are you, and whom do you serve?"

"I am the friend in the dark hour," she said. "I am the breeze against the burning sun. I am the water, freely given, and the wine, lovingly shared. I am the rest after the battle, and the healing after the wound. I am the friend in the dark hour," she repeated, "and I am here for you, Falcio val Mond."

"A sister," I said. "A sister of the Merciful Light."

"A what?" Aline asked dubiously.

The Order of Merciful Light was a very specialized clerical order. The nuns were reputed to have remarkable healing and precognitive powers to go along with their . . . other charms.

"She's a prostitute," I said.

The woman laughed. "I am that, I suppose," she said, without ire or shame.

"What do you want?" Aline asked.

"To fulfill my oath, to honor the will of my God and the commandments of my Saint."

"Saint Laina-who-whores-for-Gods is one of my favorites, sister," I said calmly. "But the timing is suspicious."

She walked to me and casually pushed the blade of my sword aside before reaching out to touch my face. "You've been hurt, Falcio. You have many reasons to question the kindness of strangers. But I am no enemy. My name is Ethalia, and I am here for you, to hide you from your enemies, to heal you from your wounds, to salve your heart." She looked into my eyes. "But you remain suspicious. You are a man of laws, a man of evidence, of proof, and so I shall give you three proofs. Will that suffice?"

"It depends on how convincing they are," I replied.

"I will show you, Falcio, with magic, with memory, and though I wish it weren't needful, with heartache."

"Falcio, I don't trust her," Aline said.

Ethalia smiled at the girl. "Your father would tell you differently, little one. Shall I speak his name aloud?"

Aline froze at that.

"As you wish. But time is passing, and the darkness which cloaks us will not last, and so let my first proof be this." She walked over to the horse and reached up to place her hands on either side of her face. I thought the beast would take her head off, but instead she dropped her muzzle down to Ethalia, who kissed the Fey Horse on the spot between her eyes.

"Thank you, Mother," she said. "You will see your children again, in the far fields that stretch past the long night, but not now, and not for many years yet. There is much to do."

"How did you—?" I was stunned.

"How did you get her to save the girl?" Ethalia asked back. "How did you get a Fey Horse to let you ride upon her back? She let you because she knows your heart, as she knows the girl's, and as she knows mine."

Ethalia returned to me. "The second proof is this," she said. Then she knelt before me and held both hands up as if in prayer, opening them, then closing them. It was an ancient and formal way of expressing gratitude.

"I don't understand; why are you—?" I started.

"Expressing thanks? Because you saved my life, Falcio val Mond, and my second proof is to give you a reason you can understand for my assistance."

"Lady, I've never met you. I doubt I'd forget the face."

She smiled and rose. "I was younger the last time you saw me in the light."

"How old are you now?" Aline asked.

"I've watched twenty-three summers pass. But when Falcio saved me, I was just thirteen, no older than you are now."

I tried to remember back. It was true that I'd been in Rijou ten years ago, on the King's business. It was the jeweler's dispute; I'd come to hear a case against his landlord. The King had wanted to begin seeing justice done even in Rijou, which had never seen any but that which resulted from the Duke's fickle commandments.

"Ah," she said, "look how your mind wanders along its narrow paths. You think so much of your King and his laws that you don't even remember the little mercies you give along the way. Like a girl, being held against her will by a man in the street . . ."

"The whore!" I said stupidly. "I mean, the girl . . . You were the girl. I remember, out on the street corner—"

She smiled patiently. "Yes, and a man who had given me money for my services wanted more and I refused."

"He offered you more money," I said, remembering the coins on the ground as he slapped her across the face.

"But the money we take is to help those we serve take value in our gifts, not as a price you would pay to buy pigs at a market."

"I'm sure they'd be happy to get them for free," Aline commented.

"Hush child," Ethalia said. "Let him remember."

"There's not much to remember," I said. "I remember the man; I remember telling him to stop. He wouldn't, so I dealt with him. He went home bruised but alive, and I left. It's no different than what any city guard or half-decent shopkeeper would have done. I was on my way out of the city, having failed utterly to save the jeweler whose case I had come to hear."

She shook her head and looked disappointed in me. "Three city guards walked past, as it happened," she said. "And many shopkeepers saw, and Lords, and Ladies. And no one stopped. No one but you. Can you not take some measure of happiness knowing you saved my life? Even a whore's life, as you put it?"

"Forgive me, Lady, I meant no offense."

"I take none, but instead apologize as I give you the third proof."

She put her hands on my chest and leaned forward. For a moment I thought she might be about to kiss me, and I wasn't sure how I felt about that, when her mouth turned and she whispered softly and sadly in my ear, "I know you love me, and I know you would fight for me, but not here, not now. I will do this thing and I will pay the price for both of us and I will not scratch or claw or scream and he will leave us and go with his filthy men and his filthy King and you and I will grow old together and laugh at the day these silly birds came to rest in our fields."

I pushed her away. "No!"

She kept her eyes on mine. "I am sorry, so sorry, for her loss."

I grabbed her roughly by the shoulders. "How—? How can you know that? How could you possibly know what she'd said to me? Tell me!"

"Because I am Ethalia," she said. "I am a sister of the Merciful Light, and it is my *geas* to help you. And because nothing else would convince you, Falcio val Mond of Pertine. Because you demand pain before you will accept mercy."

Ethalia turned from me and began walking down one of the side streets.

"Falcio?" Aline asked. "Falcio, what are we going to do?"

"We go with her," I said, putting a hand on the horse's mane, knowing she would come, and began following Ethalia down the path.

22

ONE NIGHT OF MERCY

It's hard for me to describe that night—to describe what Ethalia did, and what she took from me. She had unleashed a pain inside me that was so deep it made the torture of the last several days feel like when a child touches a hot stove by mistake: the pain is hot, but it passes quickly. But this . . .

When we arrived at the temple, which I reminded myself was as good as a brothel, I was taken up to Ethalia's private room. Aline had insisted on staying with the horse and they had been given a place behind the temple with enough space for the horse to feed and a bed for the girl to sleep in. Ethalia promised me that we could not be found here and, lacking the will to do anything else, I chose to trust her.

She told me to lie back in her bed. "I need a bath," I warned.

"I will bathe you," she replied, motioning me to remove my coat. What was left of my clothes were torn and caked in blood, dirt, and things fouler-smelling than those. With a small pair of scissors she began cutting my shirt off of me.

"Stop," I said.

She pointed to a neat pile of clothing on a table near the door. "Those are for you," she said. "These rags no longer fit you, and the memories they carry are no sweeter than the smells they emit."

I started to laugh, but she didn't join me. Instead she kept cutting away at the fabric of my clothing, carefully moving her scissors along the seams until she'd removed my shirt and pants, and even my boots fell apart at her ministrations.

She bade me lie back in her bed, naked and filthy, and went into the small room attached to her bedroom. When she returned she was carrying a basin and cloth. She set it down next to me on the bed. From another table she took a jar.

"I am sorry," she said. "I know they used oils and ointments to bring pain, but I promise that these bring only healing."

She began gently cleaning the wounds and washing the caked-on filth from my chest, my face, my legs, and every part of me. It was a slow and painstaking process, and as gentle as she was, it still hurt like the devil. The skin underneath the dirt and dried blood was sensitive, and in some places the wounds were infected, and all of these she tended to without comment. The ointment stung at first, but then provided blissful relief. When she was done I felt no pain, and I found the sensation almost unrecognizable.

"It is not yet time for sleep," she said, as my eyes started to close.

I reopened them and looked at her. She had removed most but not all of the layers of thin gauzy fabric from her body and those that remained clung to her and, in the soft light of the moon coming through the window, revealed her body to me.

"No," I said.

"You are afraid," she said, without malice or hurt.

"I . . ." I realized I was afraid—but not of what she might think. What I was afraid of horrified me, and I was too ashamed to say it aloud.

She pushed me fully onto my back and gently straddled my hips. "You are afraid of the thing inside you," she said, letting the softness of her skin whisper to me. "You are afraid of the thing you found inside you that day that they took her from you."

I tensed, and started to shift her off of me by trying to turn, but she pushed me back down. "You think you will harm me, Falcio. You think that if you let go, even for a moment, that the rage will come out of you and you will hurt me with your fists, with your violence."

"Ethalia . . . don't," I said.

"I do not fear you, Falcio val Mond. I know what is inside you. You have carried it for too long. It saved your life, and the lives of others, when you lacked the strength and the skill to defend yourself, but now you must let it go. You are strong now, you are powerful now, and it isn't right to carry such a dark vessel in your heart. We must work it from its moorings, Falcio, and send it away."

She moved her hips, ever so slightly, but the sensation felt like energy passing through every part of my body, removing my resistance, letting loose the chains I hadn't admitted to myself were even there.

"Please," I said, "please stop."

She leaned forward and took my left arm, then reached behind the headboard. I felt her wrap something around my wrist. I tried to pull away, but I was caught tight. I started to move my other arm, but she had already shackled it.

"Stop," I repeated.

"I am not afraid, Falcio. I do not believe the violence inside your body is greater than the compassion in your mind, even when you are hurt and angry."

She arose and went to the foot of the bed, producing another strap, this one attached to the floor. "But I cannot make you believe me, for you hate yourself too much to believe in your own truth. So I will bind you, and you can let out whatever rage is inside your heart and know that you won't hurt me."

She looked at me as if she was waiting for an answer, but I couldn't speak. I felt nothing but shame at that moment, and no words would come out.

As if that were answer in itself, she returned to the bed and straddled me once more.

That part of me that always tries to be clever managed to break through. "This is likely to be—"

Ethalia put a finger on my lips. Then she began moving her hips again, slowly, gently. I made no movements in return, and we stayed like that for such a long time, I believe I fell asleep for minutes at a time. But somehow I found myself inside her, and still she just moved gently, back and forth. At times I thought I might start saying things, terrible things, but the soft movement of her hips seemed to quiet my voice. Other times I felt I was beginning to cry, but there too I was pulled back by the flow of her hips, and the feeling of her hands on my chest. How long we stayed like this I do not know; I remember only that the first probing of daylight pushed its way through the window before I spoke. My voice was so soft she had to ask me to repeat myself. Or maybe she didn't. Maybe she just wanted to make sure I heard myself say it.

"The straps," I said. "Take off the straps."

That morning was as unlike the days that had preceded it as anything you can imagine. I awoke again and the pain was gone from my wounds. Even more striking, the pain was gone from inside me. I'd like to say it stayed that way forever, but I knew there would be more pain to come. But not yet, not just yet.

I heard the soft sound of singing and I looked over to see Ethalia standing near the far window, pouring something hot into a cup, then putting food onto a plate. She wore a simple summer dress this morning, blue and white, and looked completely unlike the ethereal mystery who had greeted me the night before. I found this version much more beautiful.

"It is time to eat," she said, putting two plates and the drinks on a dark wooden board and bringing it over to the bed. She balanced it on a small table before sitting down beside me.

I drank from the cup. It turned out to be a mild herbal tea with hints of honey in it.

The food was simple, bread with jam and a wedge of cheese. I was about to say something clever about wanting an entire roast chicken when she shook her head. "What they've fed you, what they've done to you: it will not be well served with heavy foods. You must eat lightly, and carefully, for a little while at least."

I nodded my agreement, but in truth I felt better than I had in such a long time that I had trouble finding the right words. I rubbed my hand across my jaw and was surprised to find no beard there. Somehow she had shaved my face while I slept.

"Thank you," I said simply.

She smiled back at me. "Well done," she replied, as if I'd said something wildly ingenious.

We ate the rest of the meal in silence. But after we were done I felt compelled to speak.

"The girl, where—?"

"Running up the stairs as we speak, I suspect," Ethalia answered.

And right then there was an insistent pounding at the door and a voice calling, "Falcio—Falcio! Are you in there? They said I wasn't to disturb you but I don't believe them. Falcio! Are you hurt?"

Ethalia rose and unlatched the door. "He's here, child. No need for concern or to break your hand on my door."

Aline ignored her and raced to the bed. I managed to quickly get the sheets around me, having only just then remembered that I was naked.

"Falcio! Are you all right?"

"I'm well," I answered. "How are you?"

"I'm fine. Monster's fine too."

"Monster?"

"The horse, silly. Are you sure you're all right? You look dopey to me."

"I promise I'm fine."

"Good," she said more seriously. "We need to go soon, Falcio. The ceremony will begin in a couple of hours and we need to get there before the names are called."

I was still unsure of the wisdom of this plan.

"Go and wait downstairs, child," Ethalia said. "There is food there, and Falcio and I have some things to discuss yet."

"What kinds of things? Payment?" Aline said wickedly as she strolled out the door and back down the stairs.

Ethalia closed the door and latched it again before coming back to sit on the bed. "The child is not entirely wrong," she said.

It wasn't my place to question their ways, and Saints knew she had done more for me than I could ever pay for. But still it hurt. "I don't have much money, but what I have is yours. What I do not have, I will find and bring to you, when I can. Name your price, Ethalia, and no matter its cost I will always be grateful."

She leaned down and kissed me on the forehead. "Such wise and gracious words. It's a wonder you aren't a poet."

I shrugged, trying to think of something witty to say. Nothing came.

"You have asked, and so I will name my payment, dearest."

I wondered if she called all those she helped "dearest" in the morning. I hoped not.

"My fee is this: there is an island off the Western Coast in the south, not far from Baern. It is a beautiful place, off the trade routes, untouched by conflict. There are plenty of fish, game birds, plants, and berries to be found. The water from the streams is clear and clean, and the sunlight in the morning floats down through the trees by the beach like soft rain upon the sand."

"I don't understand," I said. "You want me to—what? Get you this island?"

She smiled. "Yes. I want this island. It is mine by right, the inheritance left me by my mother and father before I joined the Order."

"Then what—? I'm sorry, Ethalia, I don't understand what you're asking of me. If you already own the island . . ."

She leaned down and kissed me on the lips. "I want *you*," she said. "I want you to come with me. We will leave this place and take the southern trade route to the coast, where we will buy a small boat to take us to the island, and back to the mainland when we need a change of scenery."

"But, you're a sister, of the Order . . ."

She smiled. "This has been the first part of my life, Falcio, and I honor it now by knowing when to leave it for the next. It was my destiny to await you here, to heal you and set you free. And now I have, and now I must go."

"And you want me to come with you? But Ethalia, you barely know me."

"Silly man. I know you very well. But I agree that you do not know as much about me. Do you believe me when I say you would like me once you did? That you would love me?"

"I . . . I have no trouble believing that. I just—"

She looked at me with gentle eyes. "You have trouble believing we are destined to be together? Don't you think it at all possible that you are meant to be happy, that I am meant to be happy, and that our happiness can be found together?"

"I don't know. Yesterday I would never have believed . . . But today . . . I just don't know."

She rose and put her hands on my chest and kissed me again. "Then I will have to know for both of us, for a little while at least." She kissed me again and we stayed like that for a long time, until I gently pushed her away.

"I can't," I said quietly, more to myself than her.

Ethalia took my hands. "We can bring Aline with us. There is no hope for her here, none out there either. Her father was a fool to think his crazy plan would ever bear anything but bitter fruit."

"My friends, the Greatcoats . . . You don't understand . . . My King gave me a command, and I must see it through."

"And what?" she asked. "Find the King's Charoites? You've nearly died how many times for your King?"

"One less than he did for me," I said, more coldly than I had intended.

"Falcio, listen to me. I have shown you that I know whereof I speak. There is nothing out there for you but pain, and hurt, and death. You have fought long and hard and the Gods, wherever they are, are grateful. They have guided me to you, and I am no small reward."

"I don't want to be given a woman by the Gods like some copper goblet at a festival," I said pettishly.

"And that is how you see me? As a thing you would rather earn than be given? As a *whore*?"

"I didn't say—"

"I am a whore, Falcio, and proud of it. I whored myself to find out where you were kept when the news came of your capture; I whored myself to a sad, broken guard to find you mercy, and I whored myself again last night."

"The guard . . . the torturer. That was you?"

Of course it made sense. She had used her charms to win over the guard; that's how she managed to visit me in the prison. That's what had turned him.

"I thought . . . I thought it was my words, what I'd said to him . . . I would never have asked you to . . ."

"Foolish man. Of course your words helped change his heart, but so did my touch. Your wisdom opened his mind, and my body opened his heart. Sometimes that is the way of the world, and it is nothing I will be ashamed of, even if you insist on it for me."

"I'm sorry," I said. "For all of it."

"And again you cannot believe you are worthy of love," she said, turning away.

"I—" I reached out for her but she took a step away.

"I cannot forsake the girl," I said. "Even if I give up on Kest and Brasti, on the King's command, on all of it. The girl is determined to wait until the end of Ganath Kalila to preserve her family's name and I cannot let her go alone."

"Say 'will not,' Falcio, for you sound like a child when you pretend you have no say in the matter."

"I will not forsake her, Ethalia."

She turned back to me and there were tears in her eyes. "Then you are just as broken as you were before, for you still believe you do not deserve love. You still believe you must fight and fight and fight until you are dead and only then, in that moment of release, will you set yourself free and reach for me. You are still wounded,

Falcio, and thus owe me no payment. Go to your doom, and leave me to mine."

And just like that, it was over. She sat on the chair by the window and cried softly while I put on the clothes she had set out for me on the table. I put on my greatcoat last, and never had it felt so heavy on my shoulders.

I spoke one last time, knowing it was foolish, but not able to stop myself. Ethalia was right, and so were Kest and Brasti. When we stood at the Rock of Rijou for the end of the Blood Week, the Duke would simply break his oath and send his soldiers to kill us then and there. I had come here not to win, but to die trying.

Still . . .

"When it's done," I said, and knelt at her side. "When the girl is safe, I will come back here, or wherever you are. If I do, will you have me then? Will you believe that I want happiness, that I want love?"

She turned and smiled sadly, one last time: a parting gift.

"If you come back, I will be here. If you come back, I will say yes." It was the way she said it, her voice full of such resignation and sorrow, that left me convinced that I would never see her again.

23

NO MAN BREAKS THE ROCK

The ritual that ends the Blood Week takes place at the Teyar Rijou—the locals call it simply the Rock of Rijou. The site of the city's original founding, it sits in front of the Ducal Palace. Imagine a large, nearly flat rock, almost as large as a city block, surrounded by lush grass and a profusion of brightly colored, sweet-scented flowers. Now imagine all that beauty and serenity surrounded by the most corrupt city in the world.

The crowd was massive, mostly because the Duke had made it clear that every citizen of Rijou was required to appear at the Rock on the Day of Dedication. Originally, this had been the city's annual festival to remember and celebrate the battles fought by their ancestors to hold Rijou. When the Duke brought Ganath Kalila with him from the East, he simply timed his Blood Week to end on what had been the Day of Dedication, now renamed the Morning of Mercy: the time when he would grant mercy to every citizen as part of their promise to fight for Rijou if and when required.

Aline and I were hidden amongst the crowds, listening to the Duke. His speech was well written, and long on the themes of *duty* and *honor*—although he had an interesting way of conflating the two so that by the end of the speech duty and honor appeared to mean basically the same thing. They boiled down to: follow the laws and obey those of more noble blood.

The Duke stood on a broad dais, flanked by Shiballe on his right and his son, the boy I'd seen helping Bal Armidor, on his left. Dozens of guardsmen stood around the dais, keeping watch on the crowd. We stayed at the far end, as far away from the Ducal party as possible.

"And now, my good citizens of Rijou," the Duke intoned, "the City Sage will speak the names of the noble families, that you might better know your duty to those of high blood."

The City Sage was an old man who looked half-blind and more than half-senile to me. It was his job to recite the name of each noble house in turn; the more noble your blood in the eyes of the Gods, the further up the roster your name came and the later your name would be spoken.

"Speak the names," the Duke instructed the Sage. "Speak the names, and let all here know that the City Sage speaks for the Gods and his word is beyond question."

"Calabrian," the Sage said in a wheezy voice, barely waiting for the Duke to finish.

A man in blue robes held up his fist. "Irobel Calabrian stands in Rijou!" he called out.

There was a smattering of applause.

"Oldeth," the Sage said.

Now a woman standing with her children raised her fist. "Mallia Oldeth stands in Rijou!" she shouted.

More applause.

It went on like this for some time as they proceeded from minor nobility to higher stock. I asked myself how accurate the City Sage's spell could be; did the Gods really recognize one man's blood over another? Did they have a preference—and if so, what was it based on? I had no idea; in my experience they liked to see all kinds of it, and shed in quantity more than quality.

"Humber," the Sage said.

Richel Humber: another noble, another declaration, another cheer.

I wondered how entertaining this was for the lower classes of the city—but these nobles were their landlords, their patrons, their customers, so it probably helped to keep track of who was alive and who was dead, which house had risen in prominence and which had fallen on hard times.

"Barret," the Sage called.

"Yerren."

"Quistellios."

"Zierry."

And on it went, every noble house being listed, but still the name Tiarren had not been called.

"We had better go," I said, taking Aline's arm. "This isn't going to work."

She pulled away from me. "He hasn't finished yet!"

"Look," I said, pointing to the dais, where the Duke was preparing himself to speak. "The Sage has said all the names he's going to. The Duke's obviously last, since—just as obviously—he's got the most noble blood."

"Jillard," the Sage called out, his voice no different than when he had called any other name before it.

"Andreas Jillard stands in Rijou!" the Duke shouted with practiced ease. He held his fist up high to the cheering from the crowd. As it began to die down he kept his fist there and pumped it again until the cheering resumed. He did this three more times before stopping.

"And now," he said, "I call the—"

"Aline," said a wheezy voice.

Everyone looked to see who had spoken, but it was the City Sage, his eyes focused on nothing in particular, looking for all the world as if he'd said nothing important, unaware that every eye was upon him.

"What?" demanded the Duke.

Shiballe went over and shook the City Sage's arm, saying something that looked unpleasant into his ear, but the old man ignored him.

"Aline," he said again, as if nothing had happened.

There was dead silence as the Duke scanned the crowd. Even I was confused. The City Sage was calling her by her first name—why?

"Aline, daughter of Lady Tiarren, stands in Rijou!" Aline shouted.

Confused noises erupted from the crowd, and the Duke motioned for silence.

"Aline, daughter of Lady Tiarren, stands in Rijou." She said it again, and it sounded as if she'd been practicing this one sentence her whole life.

For my part, I still didn't understand what was going on. Why had the Sage called her—and why call her last? And why call her by her first name, not her house name?

"Silence!" the Duke screamed when the noise grew again. "Who dares violate the sacred ritual of Ganath Kalila?" he demanded, looking around, trying to spot Aline, who was still hidden by the crowds. "Who brings shame upon the Morning of Mercy?"

"Seems like 'twas your own Sage!" someone in the crowd shouted.

As laughter rippled through the people, the Duke cried, "Who said that? Who spoke?" and turned to Shiballe. "Find the man who talks back to his Duke. Find him and kill him."

The crowd was silent again. So, time for me to speak up then. I sighed, then shouted, "Pardon me, your Lordship, but my understanding is that no one is ever killed on the Morning of Mercy—hence the name."

"Take that man," Shiballe shouted to the guards. "He is a criminal—an escaped convict, guilty of treason!"

The guards looked helpless as they tried to figure out how to get through the entire crowd to us.

"The girl is false," the Duke cried. "She is—the Sage has made an error—"

"The Sage cannot make an error," I shouted back. "He is speaking on behalf of the Gods, remember?"

"The girl is *false*," he repeated. "Her *blood* is false. Her house does not exist. Even if it did, the Tiarrens were petty nobles, barely worthy of notice—so how could her name be called after that of—after that of more noble houses?"

Some of the other "petty nobles" in the audience looked offended, but everyone kept silent.

"'Let all here know that the City Sage speaks for the Gods and his word is beyond question,'" I repeated. "Those are your very words, your Lordship."

"I—"

Shiballe whispered into his ear, and I heard him mutter, "Yes—yes, you're right. I can."

The Duke looked around at his people and cried, "Men and women of Rijou!" He had a warm smile on his face. "Rejoice! Rejoice, for as Ganath Kalila has made our city strong in the past, now shall it make us stronger in the future. I hereby declare, as is my right as Duke and Lord Ruler of the City of Rijou, that Ganath Kalila is extended. *Today* is the final day of the Blood Week. Let it stand as a reminder that we must always be vigilant, we must always be strong against our enemies. And tomorrow we shall come together again for a . . . for a festival. A *feast*! The Feast of Mercy! There will be food for all and—"

"A high price," I shouted. "A high price for a nice meal."

The Duke looked down at me from his dais all the way across the promenade. "And what does the Trattari have to say?" he said, the scorn dripping from his voice. "A tatter-cloaked traitor, even to the tyrant he served: a traitor to the entire land. What wisdom do you have to say to the people of Rijou? Shall you tell us about your murderous King's false laws?"

"I have no wisdom," I said. "None at all. And certainly Rijou is the last place I would come to recite the King's Laws."

There was a rumble of agreement to that. The Greatcoats had never been popular in Rijou, for the people had always seen themselves as a separate city-state and heartily disliked being subject to the rule of a man hundreds of miles away.

"But if you'll forgive me, I do know something of the laws of Rijou itself."

The Duke laughed. "You would tell us our own laws, Trattari? A man will pay a high price for listening to your lies—a high price indeed for any man here today who acts upon your words." This last he directed straight at the silent crowd.

"It is a high price to remember your laws," I said, speaking to the assembled audience. "His Lordship is quite correct. But that same price was paid by your own ancestors, by the men and women who built this city, who fought for it, died for it, bled into the very stone beneath your feet. Their blood seeped into the Teyar Rijou for hundreds of years as they fought off attackers from the north, from the south, the east and the west, so that today you might stand on it, that your children and grandchildren might stand on it, and feel something stronger than rock beneath their feet. People of Rijou, your blood—your *courage*—is the alloy that makes this place strong, that binds you to the Rock. For that is what you are: *you* are the true Rock of Rijou. You have turned back every enemy for a thousand years and more because, even when you were lawless, there was always one law that held. *Your* law."

I drew a breath and then said the words: "No man breaks the Rock."

A muffled cheer broke out somewhere, and I thought I heard a few old-timers muttering the phrase back at me: "No man breaks the Rock."

"No man breaks the Rock," I repeated. "But look into your neighbor's eyes and tell me what you see. Do you see the Rock there?"

I didn't wait for a response but shook my head sadly. "No, you see *fear*. Fear has taken hold of this city, and it has been wearing it away, not just in your time, but in your mother's time, in your father's time. Look into the eyes of your children and you will see the fear there, too, taking root. And what will become of their children, your grandchildren? Fear has struck the Rock, and year after year it strikes again, like rushing water, wearing it away. Look beneath your feet. Do you see how fear begins to erode the Rock? How many more years of Ganath Kalila before the Rock is worn away? How many more Blood Weeks before the Rock is no longer in your hearts?

"No man breaks the Rock," I said.

"No man breaks the Rock!" I heard a woman yell. "No man breaks the Rock!"

I saw the Duke whisper into Shiballe's ear and the little man stepped down from the dais and spoke to one of the guards, who took one of his fellows and began pushing through the crowd to where that call had come from.

"And look," I shouted, "here comes fear once again, worming its way through the cracks in the Rock. Watch: they are pushing through you to take that woman—and for what? For treason? For murder? For theft? No, they come to take her for speaking the first law of Rijou. Will they take her from you? And if so, will others fear to speak the words upon which your city is built? And if that fear carries to your children, will they live their whole lives without speaking it? And if they never speak it, will your grandchildren grow to adulthood never knowing the words? Do you even remember the words? Do you even remember your own first law?"

"No man breaks the Rock," an old man shouted from deep inside the crowd. "Take me! Come take me away, damn your black hearts! You can break my old bones. You can break my neck. But no man breaks the Rock!"

"No man breaks the Rock!" came the cheer. "No man breaks the Rock!"

"No man breaks the Rock," I agreed, holding up my hands for quiet. "The Duke is your lawful ruler," I said. "I am a Magister, and I have no say over who rules you, or whom you *allow* to rule you. The Khunds to the east claimed to rule you, didn't they? What happened to them?"

"They met the Rock!" came a shout from somewhere to my right.

"And the Lords of Orison: they came south with their armies and said Rijou was theirs too, didn't they? What happened to those armies, I wonder?"

"They met the Rock!"

"And the barbarians from Avares, to the west? They have skirmished along your borders many times, have they not? And one day they will come again and throw their hordes against this city: rank upon rank of fighting men armed with swords and clubs and spears. Do not fool yourselves: the men of Avares fear neither death nor mutilation. Their bloodthirsty warriors are bred on battle and bathed in the blood of their enemies and they will come back one day soon, of that you can be sure. And what then, when they do?"

"THEY WILL MEET THE ROCK!"

I could see Shiballe speaking to more of the guards, issuing orders to the captains. There looked to be some hesitation there.

"They will meet the Rock," I agreed, once the noise had died down. "But only if the Rock is still here."

The crowd didn't look happy at that suggestion, but I continued, "Your Duke—your *lawful* ruler—has brought you Ganath Kalila. It is a tradition from the East, not from here."

There was some angry murmuring; a great many people remembered when there was no Blood Week.

"He says it makes you strong. I ask you, when you sit hiding in your homes as assassins openly wander the streets, do you feel strong?"

Silence.

"When you hear your neighbors being pulled from their beds and slaughtered in the night, do you feel strong?"

More silence, but the anger was palpable now.

"This girl," I said, taking Aline's hand and raising it, "this girl's family was taken from her, each and every one of them, and slain—not in battle, for that is not the way of Ganath Kalila. Instead, men came—men dressed in black, wearing no family crest. They boarded up the family's home—*before the Blood Week had even begun.* The guards didn't stop them. The Duke didn't stop them. *You* didn't stop them." I choked for a moment before saying, "*I* didn't stop them.

"And now they are dead, and this girl is alone in this world. And despite that—despite *all* that, she is standing here now, fulfilling the

Duke's law—fulfilling *your* law. She could have fled, but she would not. Instead, she stands here upon the Rock of Rijou."

I pointed to the Duke. "Your Lord says he can make the laws as he sees fit, and so Ganath Kalila will see one more sunrise, one more sunset. And why should you complain? For he adds just one more day to the Blood Week—*just one more day.* I will tell you this: I have traveled the length and breadth of this land a dozen times over, and in every part of the country, in every town and village and hamlet, and even here in Rijou, *a week is seven days.* And yet already Ganath Kalila—*the Blood Week*—lasts nine days! And so now it will be ten—and next year? And the year after that? The Duke says Ganath Kalila makes you strong. Think how strong you'll be when every day of the year is Ganath Kalila!"

A dozen of the Duke's men were pushing and shoving their way through the mass of men and women between us. The crowd was densely packed, but while their progress was slow, it was steady. We were running out of time. I looked down at Aline for a moment before turning back to the crowd. "This young girl is a small thing, no bigger than your own children. She weighs barely as much as a mug of ale on a dry day. And so I must ask you, will the Rock take her weight? Or will it break under the pressure of your fears?"

"No man breaks the Rock," a woman said. She was big and broad-shouldered, and she stepped toward us before kneeling in front of Aline. "I will guard the girl's life if she stays, and I will guard her name if she leaves. I will pay the red price."

"I will pay the price too," said a man, more a boy really, barely taller than Aline herself. "No man breaks the Rock," he said as he knelt.

"No man breaks the Rock," another voice said. I couldn't see who spoke this time, but soon I could hear the phrase repeated over and over as men and women knelt upon the ground. When the sounds stopped there was a wide circle in front of us, and behind that almost every member of the crowd was on one knee.

I heard clapping: the Duke. He stood on the opposite side of us, some hundred feet away, flanked by Shiballe and his guards, and fifty bowmen were arrayed in front of him, arrows nocked and aiming at the crowd.

"Such pretty words," he said. "How masterful, Trattari, that you can make treason sound so noble."

A man stood up and said angrily, "The first law of Rijou ain't treason!" An arrow appeared in his neck and he dropped to the ground.

"Treason is what I say it is," the Duke replied calmly. "And any man or woman who speaks again is a traitor and subject to execution. Ganath Kalila will hold today, and forever. The girl is a criminal and she will be taken and dealt with, and her name and bloodline extinguished, as will all those with traitor's blood in their veins.

"Well?" he said finally, into the silence. "Well, Trattari, is that all you have to offer them? Words? You'll not get much from that. A dead man cannot feed his family. Where will they be when you run away, tatter-cloak? Where are your fellow Magisters to come and enforce your interpretation of the law once you leave? Come on now, 'Greatcoat,' you have heard the evidence! Now tell us your verdict!"

The crowd was looking at me and all at once the fear was back.

"My verdict is this," I said firmly. "Ganath Kalila is unlawful. It violates the laws of this land—and more, it violates the laws of this *city*. My verdict is that henceforth there shall be no Blood Week in Rijou.

"But the Duke is right," I said. "I will leave here—alive or dead, I will leave here today. So I cannot be here to preserve the decision. There is no army of Greatcoats coming to protect the verdict. There is only you. There is only the Rock."

One by one I pulled the plain black buttons from my coat and popped off the soft leathery caps to reveal the solid gold disks beneath, each stamped with the symbol of the King's Magisters. Within a few moments I was holding enough money in my hand to feed each of twelve families for a year.

"I need a jury," I said, "twelve men or women who will see to it that the verdict holds. Twelve people who must face what comes after I leave, who will see to it that no man forgets what was said here. Twelve who may well die in the attempt." Then I threw the golden coins onto the ground in front of me and waited as they clattered and rolled.

No one reached for them.

Silence filled the Rock of Rijou as nobles, soldiers, and commoners waited to see what would happen next. Aline squeezed my hand for reassurance, but I couldn't bring myself to look at her face. I had failed her. I had brought death to this little girl and to myself, because I was obsessed with the belief that my King had some ingenious plan—that he'd had it all along—and that the quest he'd given me all those years ago had some meaning.

"Find the Charoites," he'd said, as if jewels could change the world any more than words could. And now Aline would die, for no better reason than that she'd wanted to hear her family's name called out, to preserve her rights of inheritance—as if those had any value in this hellhole. In the end, the City Sage hadn't even given her that. He'd spoken her name, but not that of her family.

The Duke smiled at me from his distance. He would smile until the last coin stopped spinning, until he could see the resigned despair on my face, and until someone in the crowd, realizing they had pushed their ruler as far as they dared, decided they would do better to curry his favor by killing us.

The City Sage sat next to the Duke, looking as if he'd fallen asleep. *The old fool couldn't even remember to give Aline's family name.* That realization brought back the memory of the wreckage of Aline's home, now the unconsecrated tomb of the Tiarren family; dead and gone now, their names never to be spoken in Rijou again. Almost every pair of eyes in the crowd was locked on to the spinning coins on the ground, but a few stared at me. Did any of them know Lady Tiarren and her children? Did they blame me for what would come next? How many deaths had I faced only to bring this thirteen-year-old girl to meet her end at the Rock of Rijou, gambling her fate on the hope that, somehow, the people of the most corrupt city in the world would stand up and risk their own lives for hers. I turned to

Aline and she gave me a brave little smile, crooked on the left side, like the hint of a secret about to be told. *That smile.* I wanted to hold her, to say, *you are precious to me*, even though I didn't know why; I had no right and no cause. I wanted to tell her that all would be well, that I would protect her no matter what happened, but I couldn't. Her life lay in the shining metal pieces and the hands that would either take them up or watch them fall. Aline and I turned together to look at the coins, spinning slower and slower on the ground, coming to the inevitable conclusion.

No one reached for the coins.

So I listened.

24
THE JURYMEN

"Yer don't look none too comfortable there, Mister Magister," the lady blacksmith had said, years ago in Uttarr during one of my first missions as a King's Greatcoat.

She was quite right. The stocks in the town square had been passably well built from the local greenwood trees, making a sturdy if not very accommodating structure.

It was my second day in the stocks. In my first attempt to resolve the dispute, I had gone to speak to the local Lord, to plead for his intervention. One of his own clerks had challenged a farmer's son to a duel after the boy had tried to protect his sister's maidenhood. Though dueling was legal—even if it did involve a grown man with military experience fighting a boy barely seventeen—forcing that boy to fight without the benefit of a weapon was not.

The man had renewed his interest in the woman, and now it was her elderly father who stood in the way.

"Yer know what yer problem is, then, eh?" the blacksmith asked.

I craned my head up to look at her. "I don't listen?"

"Yer don't listen. Words came out yer damned mouth, but none got in yer damned ears."

She had warned me when I'd first come to town. I had verified the information in the poorly written complaint brought to us by a minstrel who had come through town and seen the initial events take place.

"Yer didn't listen when I told yer to leave well enough alone. Yer didn't listen when I told yer the boy was already long dead. Yer didn't listen when I told yer no one else wanted to die."

"And the girl?" I asked.

"Yer think she's not goin' to end up in some nobleman's bed afore this is done?"

The Lord had refused to take action against the man, so I'd done it myself. I challenged him to a duel and beat him bloody, and when he'd tried to sneak up on me from behind after the duel had ended, I taught him the first rule of the sword and put my point through his belly and killed him.

"Yer talked and yer talked and yer talked," the blacksmith went on.

The blacksmith had warned me that the Lord himself would have me put in the stocks before hanging me the next week, during their monthly trials.

"Yer talked about the laws, and the King and rights. Imagine: rights fer people like us?"

When the men had come for me, I'd given a pretty speech to the people of the town, all about the laws that were meant to protect them, that *belonged* to them, and that sometimes they themselves would need to fight for themselves. And when I was done, I did as the King had instructed us and asked for twelve men and women of the town to take up the role of juror, to safeguard the verdict after I was gone and ensure no harm came to the boy's family. No one had come forward to take up the gold coins. Two days later they still sat on the ground in front of the stocks where I was now held.

"Ma'am, if I might be honest, I'm not clear how this is my fault. I administered the law, I fought to protect the girl and her father, and yet I am the one in the stocks."

"Aye, that's true enough. But there's no one in this town wants t'trade places with yer."

"And what exactly should I have done differently?" I asked.

She knelt in front of me, her knee almost touching one of the gold coins.

"Yer should have listened," she said. "You spoke the words—they were fine words—but when no one jumped up and said, 'Aye, sir, take me! I'm yer man!' yer just looked at us like we were dogs or children. And then yer leaped on the Lord's men all alone like a fool."

I tried to shrug. "I thought if I could get the jump on them I might be able to get out before they caught me."

"Next time, just run," she said.

Then she pulled something out of her bag, a hammer and some other tool that looked like a narrow chisel. She set it on the edge of the lock holding the stocks and with one powerful blow she broke the lock. She put the tools back in her bag and then reached down and picked up one of the gold coins.

"Don't look like all that much," she said before rising.

I pulled myself out of the stocks and rubbed life back into my aching shoulders.

"Yer best head on now. Yer horse is tied up around back the barn there. Get on out and I'll take it from here."

"They'll come after you," I said.

"I'll beat me stupid husband into service; he'll help. And there's another few around here I can get to back me up if it comes to it."

"I don't understand," I said finally.

"What's to understand? Yer spoke the words. I listened."

I listened, and the wait was as awful as you can imagine. A huge crowd of people, and a dais on the far side with the Duke and his young son, and his men all around him, ready to come for us. And small gold coins were spinning idly on the ground, slowing to their ultimate conclusion.

Then suddenly there was a flash of legs and fur and a dog raced out, a Sharpney, fast as a racehorse, and picked up one of the shiny coins in its mouth as if it were a rat.

An arrow hit the ground where the dog had been.

"Mixer!" a boy called out as he ran out from the crowd. It was Venger, the little tyrant I'd met days earlier. The boy ran right into the empty space and grabbed one of the coins. As he left the circle and vanished back into the crowd, making a rude gesture at me, then at the Duke, another pair of arrows fell into the circle, breaking against the hard stone.

"Any man or woman who picks up one of those filthy coins will take an arrow!" the Duke roared. "Now go back to your homes or I swear I'll make every one of you pay the red price!"

Then the woman, the big one who had been the first to promise protection for Aline, ran in and took one of the coins and disappeared back into the crowd. Another figure ran in, this one with one arm splinted and bound tight to his chest: Cairn, the poor fool who'd wanted to be one of Lorenzo's Greatcoats. Then another came forward, and another, each racing inside the circle to grab a coin and then run back into hiding.

But one woman wasn't so lucky: three arrows pierced her body and she fell to the ground, the coin still clutched in her hand.

People were murmuring. I could see anger on their faces, defiance. More than one looked ready to jump into that circle and pick up one of the coins and swear themselves jurymen, but now the archers were firing in sequence, every few seconds. *Thop, thop*, went the sounds of arrows breaking against the stone. But they wouldn't break against flesh.

I heard a shout, and saw a disturbance in the crowd as someone pushed their way through, like a narrow little wave, between the Duke and us.

"Tommer! Stop, Tommer!" the Duke was shouting, and when I looked at the dais, I saw that his son was no longer there. Suddenly, the boy was right at the edge of the circle. Half a dozen arrows hit the ground in front of him and I marveled that he hadn't been hit.

"Stop, you damned fools—that's my *son*," the Duke raged.

The boy walked calmly into the center of the circle and looked carefully at the few coins left before bending down and picking one up. He held it between thumb and forefinger and lifted it before the crowd. "No man breaks the Rock," he shouted in the shrill, high-pitched voice of an angry youth.

The crowd went wild. They lifted the boy up on their shoulders, cheering wildly. Men and women milled around and through us, and suddenly we were barely noticeable.

The Duke's son had picked up a Greatcoat's coin. The Duke's son had said the words.

Now I could make out eleven men and women who had picked up my coins, and a happily barking Sharpney dog. Cheers of "The Rock! The Rock!" chorused around the Rock, the sound echoing against the hard stone. Everything else was ignored—the Duke, Shiballe, Aline, myself, the guards . . . We all ceased to exist in the minds of the crowd.

I was struck dumb by the sight. "She was right," I muttered to myself.

"Who was right?" Aline asked.

"A woman—a blacksmith. She told me I needed to listen."

Aline grinned, as if that was the very same advice she'd planned on giving me. "You do talk a little too much, Falcio," she said.

"Talk is just about all he ever does, but once in a while it's enough." I turned and saw a shabbily dressed gray-haired old woman with lines on her face and steel in her eyes. The Tailor was holding a heavy travel sack in one hand. "But the time for talk has passed and now is the time for the two of you to get out of this thrice-damned place."

"Mattea!" Aline screamed in delight and hugged the Tailor fiercely.

"Yes, child, seems I'm not done taking care of you yet." The old woman looked me in the eye. There was a hint of softness there I hadn't seen before. "You must go now, child," she said, looking fondly down at Aline.

"Why? Why can't I stay here? I wouldn't burden you, Mattea—"

The Tailor said gently, "That's not your purpose, child, nor is mine to keep you like my own, though I'd very much love to do that.

You've done what had to be done: you've survived the Blood Week, and now your name and your blood are acknowledged. No man will be able to deny you your name, sweet Aline."

"I don't understand," I said. "Why—?"

Mattea cut me off. "Yes, Falcio: you've made it quite clear you don't understand. So instead, you'll do what I say. Your pretty words were fine and now the people are in an uproar, wanting something better than what they've had with that miserable bastard the Duke. But that will die down soon enough and Shiballe will once again set his games in play to master the city. So go now: take the girl and get out of Rijou as fast as you can. Go and find those other great fools before they do something stupid and make a mess of all my plans."

Then she gave a wry smile. "I don't suppose that giant beast hidden in that burned-out shop back there belongs to you?" she asked.

"That's Monster!" Aline said.

"It damned well is," Mattea replied.

"Don't say that—Monster is a *good* horse," Aline insisted. "She's a Greathorse."

"She nearly took a man's head off when he poked it inside. Does a proper horse do that?"

"Well, does a proper horse do this, then?" Aline put her hand to her mouth and shouted at the top of her lungs, "*Dan'ha vath fallatu! Dan'ha vath fallatu!*"

There was too much noise from the riotous crowd. "She can't hear you, Aline," I started. "We'll go and get—"

I heard a crack like thunder and down the far way I saw the burned-out doors explode outward, and there it was: the fires of every hell charging toward us. The few people nearby parted like a desperate wave before the thundering onslaught and within seconds she was here.

"Saints," the Tailor said, "that's no horse I've ever seen. But thank whatever angry God who made it that she serves you, child."

Mattea kissed Aline on the forehead and I lifted the girl onto Monster's back, then pulled myself up behind her—no easy task on a beast that tall. Then I leaned down and extended my hand to Mattea. "Come with us. We can keep you safe."

The Tailor laughed. "Aye, but who'll keep you safe if I'm pulled away from my task?" Then she handed me the travel sack. "I've served this girl since before you met her, and I will serve her after you've gone."

I did not quite understand, but I accepted the truth evident in her face. She began to turn away, but something in my expression made her pause and she looked at me. "You really don't know what you've done here today, do you?" she asked.

I smiled. "I took something from the Dukes," I said. "Something small, perhaps insignificant to them, but I took it nonetheless. They wanted the girl dead, and despite everything Jillard and Shiballe had at their fingertips in this Gods-damned city, I've kept her alive. It won't end their corruption or their conspiracies, but at least I've reminded them that they can still be opposed."

The Tailor's expression was aghast. "Gods, Falcio—is it possible that you really believe that's all this was about?"

"That's all it's ever been about—but for today at least, it's enough." Then I leaned down to Monster's ear. "*K'hey*," I said, feeling those great muscles bunch. Her hooves shook the earth beneath my legs as I cried, "*K'hey, k'hey, k'hey—*"

25
THE ARCHERY LESSON

Every once in a while I manage to convince myself that there's no such thing as magic, that it's just charlatans' trickery. But those next few days as we raced northward along the Spear, I was reminded that at least some magic must be real.

My evidence was not the massive beast carrying us faster than any horse I'd ever ridden, for if one horse can be large, then surely another can be even larger. Nor was it even the City Sage and his calling of the names, for that might have been simply the product of senility. No, my proof that magic existed was that somehow Shiballe was managing to send men after us, and that they were *ahead* of us, a hundred miles after leaving Rijou.

The men could not have come from the city, for their horses were nowhere near as fast as Monster, and I refused to believe that Shiballe had placed guards on every road out of Rijou in case we actually managed to escape. No, somehow his mages were communicating with agents in the towns nearby, obviously promising huge rewards for our capture.

Monster could ride at full speed without stopping, but we couldn't. The effects of the Blood Week were taking hold once again.

Ethalia's ministrations had gone a long way toward healing my body, but I was utterly exhausted, deep in every fiber of my body, and I couldn't ride without having to stop every few hours. And even if I had been able, Aline couldn't. And so our journey north turned into a deadly game of cat and mouse.

When we did have to fight, Monster was deadly. The rage that defined her was not diminishing with her freedom, although she remained fiercely protective of Aline and only rarely tried to bite my head off. But anything else that got in our way was doomed: the Fey Horse just charged it down, her hooves and teeth deadlier weapons than my rapiers.

The attacks lessened as we put more distance between us and the city, but the very last one nearly ended in disaster. Four of them came at us from the sides, swords drawn. They'd obviously been waiting in the undergrowth lining the road, and they timed their attack perfectly, for Aline and I had been riding for hours and were near asleep in the saddle—if we'd had a saddle, that was.

Monster wanted to fight, but I kept urging her forward, and though she growled in frustration, she kept going straight. As we came over the rise, we saw a man standing in the middle of the road a hundred paces ahead of us, an arrow nocked and aimed at us. Monster roared a challenge and raced even faster, preparing to run the man down, but just a few paces later I recognized him and screamed, "Jump! Monster, *jump*!" in her ear. Squeezing my thighs as hard as I could, I pulled back on her mane—I'd pay for that later, I was sure of it—but at the last instant the man calmly crouched down and Monster jumped over the top of him. I turned to see Brasti fire arrow after arrow into our pursuers, and by the time he was done two of the men had fallen from their horses and the other two were slumped over in their saddles.

All of them were dead, of course. Show-off.

Aline convinced Monster to stop and I jogged back to where Brasti was retrieving his arrows and searching the men.

"Stop, Brasti," I said.

"Look, Falcio, these men are mine. You had nothing to do with it, so—"

"They were trying to kill me," I reminded him.

"Well, you had nothing useful to do with it, anyway. So whatever they have is mine to do with as I choose, and if you don't like it you can take it up with the local Greatcoat."

I couldn't help myself: the fact that he was so irate over my interference overcame me and I hugged him like a fool. "Ah, Brasti, Brasti," I said, laughing hopelessly.

"Uh . . . there, there, now. There, there, Falcio. It's all right . . ." He patted me on the back awkwardly and this sent me into another spasm of laughter.

"What in the name of Saint Birgid's frigid cunt is that?" he exclaimed. He must've only now taken in the size of the Greathorse as Aline walked back toward us, Monster in tow and following along as peaceful as could be.

"That's Monster," Aline said, "and I don't think you're allowed to say 'cunt.'" She walked past us and looked at the men lying dead on the ground.

"How did you do that?" she asked Brasti excitedly. "There were four of them and just one of you—you beat them so quickly!"

"I'm an archer, little girl," Brasti said, casually checking his nails. "It's like being a swordsman, only faster." He looked at me and added, "Come on, Falcio. I've been scouting the roads behind us in case you didn't die. The others will be wondering what's taking me so long and I don't want to miss supper."

"What's—?"

"Happened? Nothing, really. Kest wanted to kill Valiana a few times, but he kept reminding himself that he swore an oath not to do so. I tried to reassure him that you were almost certainly dead, but for some strange reason he seems convinced that you're unkillable. Trin wasn't. Feltock caught her trying to steal a horse and ride back to Rijou to help you. Not sure what she hoped to accomplish. Valiana was furious with her but then gradually became ridden with guilt, which I find almost as annoying as when she's being an arrogant bitch."

"Brasti!" said Aline.

"Right; sorry. Anyway," he went on, "Feltock's in a bit of a strop, and that's getting worse the further north we go. The rest of the men have softened up, but they do pick up on the captain's moods. Frankly, the only person I can stand is Trin—at least she's got a happy disposition." He looked at Aline. "Of course, there's a bit more than that to tell—bandit attacks and deeds of derring-do and such. I don't mind telling you I've been quite the hero while you were gone. And that's not even counting this last bit of saving you and the girl. Ten men attacking on the road, spears at the ready, you screaming for mercy—"

"Four men," Aline said. "Don't lie: it was four men."

Brasti looked down at her. "Little girl, you really don't know anything about how to tell a story, do you? Well, don't worry, Falcio, I'll tell you all about my adventures after supper."

He looked at me appraisingly. "What about you? Anything interesting happen?"

Over the next week we settled back into the life of the caravan, but it took me a long time to feel strong again. The monotony of the road and the lack of immediate danger carved out an emptiness in my thoughts that would have been welcome, were it not filled with a constant replay of my last moments with Ethalia. She had offered me happiness and instead I'd chosen—what? I couldn't call it honor. Traitors can't lay claim to honor. I couldn't even blame it on the King's final stupid request. I still had no clue where his Charoites might be, nor what I would do with them if I found them. Were they magical? Even if they were, I didn't put a lot of faith in magic. It was always something other people used against me, not something I could ever wield as a tool myself. If the Charoites were precious, where could we ever sell them if we found them? And what were we supposed to do with the money—finance a revolution? Rally the people around . . . who? *Us?* My experiences in Rijou had emphasized how fractured a people we were. The crowd had supported me, but only because I had appealed to their sense of being unique, of being better than the rest of the country, and really, that made me no better than the Duke himself, except that he had overreached. If I ever tried to rally them to the cause of the Greatcoats, I had no doubt I would find myself with less support than if I tried to bring back the Blood Week.

So I spent my time on the road recuperating. Ethalia had healed my wounds in ways I couldn't begin to understand, and yet, with her absence and my guilt over leaving her, I felt as if the effects of her ministrations were fading too fast; as if my own inability to take pleasure in my short time with her was nullifying her treatment. I think she would have been sad if she had known that.

I felt even worse that I couldn't bring myself to talk about her to Kest and Brasti. A gulf was growing between us. Kest was still maintaining that he would put a sword in Valiana before she took one step inside Castle Aramor, and I was equally determined he would not. Brasti tried to make a joke of it by offering to put an arrow in the back of whichever one of us brought it up next, thereby solving the dilemma. We laughed at that, and pretended these arguments could be put aside for a while, but it felt to me as if every day our friendship was fading a little more. I sometimes wondered why Kest and Brasti even stayed with the caravan, except that there was only the long, straight road now, and nowhere else to go.

Valiana was the only one who behaved as if she were truly happy about our return. She took to Aline immediately, as if the child were a new pet, showering her with attention and making her ride in the carriage with her.

Aline herself became very changeable, her mood veering from giddy young girl to sullen, angry young woman, from happy to sad to very quiet. She spent no time with me at all and for a while I thought she blamed me for our capture, despite everything else I'd done. But she stayed away from Monster too, though the great beast had saved her life. I felt an odd kinship with the Fey Horse. She wouldn't stay near the other horses, much to their relief, and we often ended up keeping a distant vigil on the girl together.

"You make an odd pair of guards," Trin said, eyeing Monster carefully as she brought me some hard bread and a piece of harder cheese. Monster and I were at the back of the caravan, so perhaps that's the reason why I noticed several of the other men with better fare in hand.

"Thank you," I said as she was leaving.

She turned back to me. *Does she think I'm mocking her?*

"I mean, for trying to help us," I said. "Brasti told me that you tried to take a horse back to Rijou."

"I was merely . . . It was nothing. A foolish impulse, quickly forgotten."

"Would you like to walk with us for a while?" I asked.

"If it would please you."

We stayed quiet at first, watching the long stretch of the Spear laid out in front of us, the mass of close-growing trees and shrubs somehow making everything feel too closed in. I felt awkward, almost as if I were being unfaithful to Ethalia, despite the fact that I was unlikely to ever see her again.

"You're different," Trin said after a while.

"Oh? How so?"

She looked at me, her eyes examining every part of my face. "You've lost something. There was something there before, in the folds of your eyes and the furrow of your brow. It seems lessened."

"You sound disappointed."

Trin looked as if she had just realized she'd given some kind of insult. "No . . . it's just that you've proven to be different from what I had expected when we first met."

I thought back to the day at the market in Solat. "What precisely were you expecting then?"

"Whatever it was, I can't be faulted for underestimating you. Who could imagine men like you really existed?" She smiled at me, her eyes locking on mine.

If I were younger and less cynical, or if I were Brasti, I would think that smile a sign of adoration.

"I have to get back," she said. "The Princess will wonder where I am."

As Trin walked away, Monster's eyes seemed to follow her. So did mine. "Do you suppose that a beautiful woman half my age—and for no particular reason—is falling in love with me?" I asked.

Monster snorted.

"Yeah," I said. "I didn't think so either."

Was she simply playing the odds—looking for protection from whoever could give it to her? What else did I have that she could want? Perhaps it was simply a game for her—but from what I'd seen, she wasn't really the type to play such childish games.

Kest came and joined us. "Am I interrupting something?" he said, noticing the expression on my face.

"Just calculating the odds," I said.

Kest raised an eyebrow. "Of a fight?"

"Possibly. I don't know yet."

"Is this about Aline?"

"No," I said. "Though I suppose that is another problem waiting to be solved."

Aline's situation was bound to become complicated. She was still a noblewoman, though it was unclear what that meant, given that she no longer had property or retainers. I wasn't even clear on what her title was now. The City Sage hadn't called it out; I supposed that meant Tiarren had been simply a Lord and not anything higher. Valiana was acting enthralled with the girl for now, but when we got to Hervor things would begin to change, and soon the child would be discarded. Would her enemies still pursue her? If so, how was I supposed to protect her? "I don't think she wants anything to do with me," I said aloud.

"She's young," Kest said. "I think she just wants to be a normal girl for a while."

"She wants to be away from broken things," I replied.

"In her heart she understands. In her heart, she might even love you and the horse. She knows you saved her life. But in her head she's still reliving everything they did to her. It will take time."

I patted Monster's rough, scarred hide absently. She let me ride her more often these days, but I preferred to walk now that my leg had finally healed from the crossbow wound.

"The King lied to me," I said, absently.

Kest looked at me. "How so?"

"The soft candy—the girl ate it. When they took her, when she realized we were caught? She ate it, and yet she lived to endure the horrors they inflicted on her. I think she blames me for that too."

"Perhaps it just went off—it's been years since they made it—"

"The hard candy still works," I pointed out. "The King never wanted it made in the first place. He lied to me."

"I doubt it was the only time. Let it be, Falcio. The King did as he thought best, just as you did. The girl is alive, after all, and she will heal, as children do—but it will be in her own time."

Aline might have nothing but disdain for me, and a slight wariness about Kest, but she had taken an immediate liking to Brasti.

"Show me again! Show me again!" I heard her squeal.

I could see Brasti's broad smile. He loved to show off to a receptive audience. "Fine then, what this time?"

Aline put a hand up to shield her eyes from the sun and pointed. "Over there, on that tree—do you see it?"

He leaned forward on his horse. "What? I don't see it."

"The apple, silly," she said.

Brasti peered at the crooked tree that half-encroached on the road far off in the distance. The rest of us watched them while we ate our bread and cheese and rested the horses.

"There's no apple there," he said after a dramatic pause. "Why, it couldn't be bigger than a pea—a little red pea."

Aline giggled. "It's an apple, *any*one can see that."

"Well, even if it is—and mind, I'm not yet convinced it isn't a tiny red pea—it's *much* too far." He rolled his right shoulder back and shook his hair out of his face. "What manner of man, what manner of great, *great* man, we must ask, would have the strength, the skill, the iron-forged courage, to attempt a target like that?"

Kest looked at him out of the corner of his eye. "Courage? You think the apple is going to try and bite you?"

Aline giggled.

"Quiet, swordsman," Brasti said haughtily. "This is real man's work." He rolled his right shoulder a second time and nocked an arrow. At first he sighted down the arrow and pulled back hard on the bowstring; then he lifted his point up and away to the left.

"You're aiming the wrong way," Aline said, concern in her voice, but Brasti ignored her and let the arrow fly.

At first I thought he might have overshot, but there was a light wind and as the arrow began arcing back down it veered a little to the right and took the apple clean off the tree.

Aline clapped excitedly. "You did it, Brasti!"

Brasti was checking his fingernails as he said, "Truly, what manner of man must do such great and terrible things?"

"One who's too lazy to pick the apple off the tree himself?" I offered.

Aline ignored me studiously and focused her attention on Brasti. "But how did it work? You aimed too far to the left."

"Wind," he said. "You have to factor in the wind."

"But the wind isn't very strong at all."

"Look at the small branches on that tree over there. You see how they're swaying? This part of the road is protected by that ridge, but up ahead there, the trees are in the open."

She looked at him with awe. "Can you—?"

"What, hit something else? Uncle Brasti needs to save a few arrows for miscreants, sweetheart."

"No, I don't mean—well, what I'm wondering is . . ." She swallowed hard and with hope shining out of her eyes asked, "Can you maybe teach me to shoot like that?"

Brasti looked down at her and then over at me. I shrugged. It wasn't my decision.

"All right," Brasti said, "but you learn my way, not yours. Agreed?"

Aline nodded very solemnly. "Agreed."

"You're going to need a bow."

The girl thought about it for a second. “I don’t have a bow,” she said, “and I don’t have any money.”

Brasti crossed his arms and looked around at us, then said, “I suppose if I’m to be your archery master then I should give you the bow my master gave me when I became his student.”

“Really?” she asked, her voice full of awe.

He walked over to the rear wagon several feet away and rummaged around in the back. When he returned, he held out his hands as if he were holding something incredibly precious. There was nothing there.

“Here you are,” he said. “Your first bow.”

It looked like the joke had gone too far, for the girl looked as if she might start crying.

“Oi, now, no need to be cruel,” Kurg said, waving his big bear arms toward her. “You come here, little girl. I’ll make you a nice wooden sword to play with.”

I could tell that Aline didn’t want to learn to play with wooden swords, but she started to turn toward the man anyway.

“Is that your decision then?” Brasti asked.

“What?”

“Have you decided that you no longer wish to learn the way of the arrow?”

“You know that’s not true,” she said. “Why are you being mean? Why are you all so mean?”

Valiana called from the carriage, “Come in here with me, Aline, and leave the silly men to their toys and games.”

Aline started to go, but Brasti stopped her. “Last chance,” he said without a trace of humor in his voice.

“You know I want to,” she said miserably.

“Say it,” Brasti demanded. He still held his arms out in front of him as if a bow rested on them.

“I want to learn the way of the arrow.”

“Say it again.”

“I want to learn the way of the arrow.”

Brasti knelt on one knee in front of her. “Then take this bow,” he said.

She hesitated.

"Take it."

Gingerly she reached forward and pretended to lift the bow from his outstretched arms.

"Now swear, Aline: swear that you will follow my lessons, always aim true, and above all, treat this bow as if it were the last you will ever own."

She looked confused but she stammered out, "I swear it."

Brasti rose. "Good. Go and put the bow away for now and then come back. You won't need it for your first lesson."

Aline ran off to one of the wagons and did a very good job of pretending to place the bow carefully amongst the supplies.

Kest looked at Brasti. "I must confess, I've never studied archery," he began.

"Well, it's a bit too sophisticated an art for your kind, Kest."

"Perhaps—but I admit to being confused as to the purpose of an imaginary bow."

"If you can aim and shoot with perfect form with an imaginary bow, you can do it with a real one."

"So this really is how you learned to shoot?"

"My master did the very same thing to me when I was about her age. An archer needs to trust his form, not the feel of the bow. The archer is the true weapon; the bow is just a long piece of wood."

A couple of the men snorted at that, but it was hard to question Brasti's words when he never seemed to miss.

Aline returned and looked up at Brasti. "Could you teach me about the wind?" she asked. "How can you tell how much it's pushing?"

"Well, you use your eyes first, of course, but then you have to close them so that you can use your ears."

"Your ears?"

"Close your eyes," he said.

She did and so did I, and then I felt a little foolish.

"Now listen. What do you hear?"

"I hear you, and I hear the men moving around."

"Good. What else?"

"One of the horses is snorting, and I think something is creaking—his bridle, maybe."

"Keep going," Brasti said. "Deeper."

"I hear the wind picking up the leaves."

"That's right. You're doing very well. Now try to listen *past* it. Try to listen to the sound of the wind coming up again. What does that sound like?"

"It sounds like—it sounds like a cat, stepping on leaves."

"That's right, like a cat, it's—oh shit!"

I opened my eyes and saw Brasti jumping on top of the forward wagon and pulling out his bow and arrows. The real ones.

"What is it?" Feltock asked.

"Cats stepping on leaves," he said. "At this distance the only thing that sounds like cats stepping on leaves is a group of men trying to move quietly."

Feltock didn't hesitate. "Arm up—now, damn it! Get the horses back, get the wagons circled, carriage in the center. Protect the Lady."

As the men jumped to obey, Feltock asked, "Can you tell me how many?"

Brasti shook his head. "I can't be sure, except it's a lot more than us."

It didn't take long to find out, for as soon as the brigands realized that we were pulling out weapons they began to rush toward us. I could see movement in the forest on either side of us.

"Damned trees," Feltock swore. "Can't see a damned thing—and we're sitting ducks out in the open road like this."

The men were forming up, using the cover of the wagons to prepare for a charge, if the right moment came. Brasti was looking for targets, sighting along his bow.

I saw Aline rushing to the wagon where she had put her own "bow" and shouted, "Aline! Go to the Lady Valiana and stay there!"

I had to turn because a flurry of arrows hit the ground in front of me.

"Do you have any more pistols?" I asked Feltock.

"They're shit," he said. "They have to make a dozen of the damned things to get one that shoots straight. Besides, they're single-shot; they take too damned long to reload."

Brasti let fly an arrow and I followed its path into the forest, where it hit a man in the shoulder.

"I wouldn't do that," called out a voice from the trees.

"Yeah? Why is that?" Feltock called out.

Arrows rained down, lodging in the dirt in front of our feet. There must have been thirty of them.

"Damn, Feltock—why didn't you bring more men on this journey if it's this bad up here?"

"Her Ladyship's orders: ten men, counting me, and no more."

"Why would Valiana do that when she knew she would be in danger?"

Feltock looked me in the eye. "It wasn't her—it was her mother, the Duchess. She gave the orders."

Kest and I exchanged glances; he looked as confused as I was—maybe even more so, in fact, because he was still planning on killing Valiana.

The brigand leader shouted out again: "Leave the wagons and be on your way. There's no need for bloodshed here."

An arrow flew out of the forest and lodged itself in Blondie's shoulder.

"Except for him. That's for my man you took in the shoulder. Fair's fair, after all."

"We can't leave the wagons," I called out. "The road ahead is too long and too dangerous. We'll starve."

"Better you than us," the leader answered. "Every man has the right to eat and to take a measure of comfort."

"Says who?" Feltock muttered.

The brigand leader had good ears. "Says King's Law, my salty old friend. You can look it up yourself if you can find someone to teach you how to read."

"Well, isn't he well spoken for a bandit?" Feltock said to me.

Well spoken indeed, and right on King's Law. Interesting.

"Negotiation," I called back. "Every man or woman has the right to negotiation before blood."

There was a pause.

"Very well," the leader said. "We'll come out, twelve of us for twelve of you, but mark that I have more than enough archers here to put you down if you try anything, and we'll have our weapons at the ready."

"Marked and fair," I said.

They came out of the forest: rough men, mostly, with ragged clothes and beaten iron swords or wooden spears for weapons, followed last by their leader. He carried a longsword that shone when the sun hit it: no rust on that weapon. On his head he wore a brown broad-brimmed hat, weather-beaten and worn. On his back he wore a Magister's greatcoat.

"Damn hells," Brasti said.

Feltock looked at me through narrowed eyes. He had told me as much, that some Trattari had taken on brigand ways.

"He can't be a Magister. He's just killed one and taken his coat."

"No," Kest said, "I recognize him now. That's Cunien from Orison. He was a cantor."

I marked him too now. Cunien became a cantor not long after I did. As a cantor, he settled matters of law when another Magister had failed. To be a cantor, you had to be ready to go back and deliver the justice denied when another Magister had been killed or captured.

"Well now, isn't this a fine reunion," Cunien said. He ambled over to us and surveyed our company. His eyes fell on Valiana in the carriage. "You're a pretty one, aren't you? Can I have a kiss?" Then he noticed Trin next to her. "Oh, my. Two for the price of one—how delightful!"

"Don't," I said. "No one's been seriously hurt here yet."

"Why should that matter to him?" Valiana said, leaving the carriage and striding toward us, Trin behind her.

"My Lady—" Feltock began.

"Why would he care? He's a Trattari—this is what they do, isn't it?" She turned on me and slapped me hard in the face. "That's for all your high words and self-righteousness about what's wrong with everyone else. You and yours are no better than anyone else—worse, even, because you look down on your betters."

Cunien smoothed down his mustaches and smiled at Valiana. "Will this take long? I don't mean to rush you, but I'd like to get a look in those wagons soon."

"I am the daughter of the Duchess of Hervor," she said, "and I'll die before I let you take anything from me, tatter-cloak!"

Cunien's voice was deadly cold. "That you will, girl, if you call me that again. But as much entertainment as you're providing here, I'm afraid we've reached the end of our negotiations. When I saw you from the trees I was curious to see if you were really Greatcoats, or just some soldiers who had killed Magisters. But now I see you're neither of those things. You're just trained dogs working for the Duchess of Hervor: the bitch who had our King murdered. You've sunk low, First Cantor."

"Look who's talking," Brasti said.

"When there's no law and no King, all you have left is a bit of food, the occasional woman, and whatever small justice you can mete out in this world."

He signaled to his men and they started to pull back toward the trees, leaving room for their archers. This was bad. He didn't trust us, and I couldn't speak to him with so many onlookers. I needed to know what he was doing out here with these brigands. I needed to know if any Greatcoats remained true.

"Duel," I said quickly.

Cunien turned to look at me and smiled. "Duel? I don't think so, Falcio. We'll just take the wagons—feel free to fight, though. Knowing I've taken out a few of the Duchess's men will keep me warm tonight."

"You have no choice," I said. "It's the King's Law."

"For matters of personal dispute, yes, but I don't think killing you is going to make any difference to the Duchess, so I'll have to settle for the wagons."

I smiled at him and spoke loudly and clearly. "You're absolutely right, Cunien. You have more men than us, and you'll get your wagons. Of course, we'll take out a few of your men. Brasti is the best bowman here by far, and we have a pistol. And Kest and I will take out a few before we go down. But what price is that compared to you having to fight a duel with me? You win, you get the wagons without a fight; I win, you let us go. But really, why take a chance on being beaten when I'm sure your men are more than willing to die to protect your pride."

Cunien glared at me. "Gods, Falcio, you always were a talker, weren't you?"

"I think, if you give it a chance, you'll find my blade speaks more eloquently than my tongue."

He raised his longsword. "Very well, then. I always did want to see if I could beat the man who supposedly bested Kest in a fight."

I let my rapier out of its scabbard and stepped into first guard. "I am at your disposal," I said.

Cunien didn't adopt a guard position but walked casually around me, forcing me to change my position.

"I have to be honest with you, Falcio," he said softly, almost soothingly. "I used to look up to you—but now all I see is a man who is a little too old and a little too soft for this kind of work. I don't think you have the fire in your belly anymore."

"Hey, Cunien," Brasti called out. "I don't suppose you have an ax, do you?"

"What?"

"Never mind."

Cunien aimed his point low and walked straight toward me, spinning his sword up and around in a ribbon-cut at the last second. The blade came at my neck but I lunged forward on the diagonal to my left and let it pass by without parrying it. I tried an inside thrust to his sword arm, but he brought his weapon back with a hard downward parry that almost knocked my rapier out of my hand.

Fine, then: he wanted to get the pleasantries out of the way.

I let the point drop down and continued its motion into a windmill, bringing the blade down on his head. His sword snaked up on a slant and caught the cut, coming back down at my own head.

I lifted my rapier up with the blade parallel to the earth and we locked blades. He grabbed my sword wrist so that I wouldn't be able to free my blade and I did the same to him and we struggled against each other for a moment.

"This is pleasant enough," Cunien said, "but if you don't mind, I'd like to get on with it."

I lifted my left heel to kick his knee out, which forced him to step back and loosen his grip on my wrist. We separated again, and that allowed us to get the real conversation started.

He came at me with a harlot's foible, a straight-on thrust that turns at the last instant to avoid the parry and returns to strike the same target. I wasn't sure if he was serious about it so I let it through and stepped by to avoid the point. He did it again and so I circled my sword counter to his, which allowed me to envelop his blade for a moment and push it out of line. I struck side-bladed toward his chest, which would have given him a nasty cut and pushed him off balance if he had let it through. The side-blade attack was a question, which he answered by ducking and slapping the blade up with the back of his gloved hand. So the answer was no, then.

I tried again with a feint-cut to his left thigh, pulling back the point just before his downward parry to let his blade pass before I thrust in. The move is called the snake's tongue, and he looked genuinely surprised by it. He responded with a half turn, followed by several swift cuts aimed at my arms and legs, all of which I beat back easily.

And the conversation continued.

We went on like this for some time, and then I saw him leave a small opening on his right leg and I knew it was time to end this. I came in high toward his head and let him beat my blade aside with his longsword before making a hard horizontal cut at my neck. At the last instant I swung onto my back leg and dropped down into a low crouch and speared his exposed calf. He gave a yell and dropped his sword, which hit me on the top of the head. I almost stabbed him again for that, but I suppose fair's fair.

"Yield. It's decided," I said, pulling the point of my blade out of his calf.

Cunien fell down on the ground and I saw his men tense up.

"Stand down," he shouted. "Stand down. Fair's fair, and this has been decided."

His men, shabby and poor as they were, obeyed as quickly as any soldiers would have.

I sheathed my rapier and reached an arm down to help him up.

"Damn, man," he said. "That hurts worse than I remember."

"You opened the target, not me. Besides, who drops his sword on another man's head? I mean, truly, what kind of grace is that?"

Cunien smiled. "I couldn't let you get away without a scrape." He turned and waved to Valiana. "Another day perhaps, my Lady! Don't let Falcio seduce you with that fair tongue of his. If you must sleep with one of them, settle on Brasti. He has more experience." He turned to his men and led them back into the forest.

"I always liked him," Brasti said. "Good head on his shoulders."

Feltock let out a sigh of relief and so did his men. They began moving the horses and packing up the wagons. Everyone kept their weapons out, though.

Aline was still standing there, looking at the forest, into which the brigands had vanished.

"It's all right, girl," Kest said. "They won't come back."

"It's not that," she replied.

"What is it, then?" I asked.

"Well, at first I was scared—I thought you might be killed and we would lose the wagons."

I chuckled. "Glad to hear you were so concerned for my safety."

She ignored the comment.

"But then the fight seemed to change—it didn't look quite right to me."

"What do you mean?" Brasti asked her.

"I mean, it almost didn't look like a fight at all. It was more like a conversation, like the blades were talking to each other."

Kest, Brasti, and I didn't look at each other for a long moment.

"And what do you think they said?" Kest asked carefully.

She frowned. "It was hard to tell. At first it was like Falcio was asking questions and the brigand seemed to be saying no, and then they started going back and forth and it was too fast for me to follow."

Brasti smiled and rumpled her hair. "Now there's the mind of a silly girl at work," he said. "Let's leave all this foolishness with swords aside and I'll show you how to hold that bow of yours properly."

She giggled for a second. "You can't hold an imaginary bow properly or improperly. It's just in your head."

The way she switched from fearful to angry to childish so quickly worried me. What she had been through had been enough to drive a grown man or woman frantic with terror, let alone a child, and I had no idea what this behavior meant—or what we could do about it.

She and Brasti wandered back to the horses and Kest and I followed.

"So," he said, speaking low, "what did Cunien have to say?"

26

THE PRINCESS AND THE PAUPER

"Cunien's looking for the King's Charoites too," I said as Kest and I walked our horses behind the caravan. "He knew we weren't supposed to be in this region. At first he genuinely believed we might have turned Duke's Men."

"How many of us are left?" Kest asked.

"He didn't know. He says he saw Quillata working a ship when he was in Cheveran."

"Quillata? In Cheveran? Doesn't she hate water?"

"I'm not sure if he meant her or not, now that I think about it. It was one of the original twelve, and a woman—so he might have meant Dara. You know it's not a very precise language."

"So has he found any signs of the jewels?"

I sighed. "No. He's been moving steadily north and found himself in a bit of a jam when he was taken by that band of brigands."

"So now he leads them?"

"He convinced them he could provide them with a better living than his predecessor," I said.

"How did he manage that?"

"He killed his predecessor."

Kest's eyes narrowed, but I put up a hand. "He swears the man was a butcher and it was a fair fight. Anyway," I said, and stopped to pull Monster away from what was left of the bush she'd taken a fancy to. She gave me one of those strange growls of hers to remind me that we had a truce, not a relationship. "Anyway, Cunien's band has grown solidly since he's been able to keep them better fed and less wounded."

"He has the makings of a small army there," Kest mused.

"Forty men, well trained and armed. But he's moving them further north as he searches for word of the Charoites. Since we don't know what they look like, they could be anywhere, and knowing King Paelis, they're as likely to be in a small village as a great city."

"Has he managed to find out if there are more than one of these Charoites?"

"No, but I suspect there is. Paelis liked to spread his bets, didn't he?"

Kest looked at the twilight sky. "Falcio, how are we supposed to find these things? Five years now, we've been living on rumors and gossip and hope. What are the chances, *really*, that we'll ever find anything?"

"I don't know," I admitted, "but we'd better do it before the Dukes finally solidify their hold on the throne. This 'Council of Regents' isn't going to serve them half as well as a genuine Queen in their pocket. With Tremondi dead, and the possibility of the Greatcoats becoming wardens of the trade routes with him, there's really nothing stopping them."

"Then why not kill Valiana and at least slow them down?" Kest asked. I admired him for using her name when he was talking about murder.

"Has it occurred to you that she is not actually the best choice?" I asked.

"What do you mean?"

"Well, if you had plotted for almost eighteen years to take over the kingdom with a puppet Princess as the sovereign, wouldn't you—I don't know—train her a little better?"

"She's reasonably petty and vain—what qualifications does she lack in your mind?"

I thought about that for a moment. "Cruelty," I said finally. "I mean, wouldn't you have expected someone a little more calculating?"

"I don't know, but I think you're reaching here."

"Describe her mother," I told Kest.

"The Duchess of Hervor?" And when I nodded, he went on, marking each property on his fingers, "Cold, calculating, but also brilliant—and bold, too. She's a tyrant's tyrant."

"I can certainly attest to all of that," I said. "So why hasn't she trained her daughter better? Valiana is arrogant and demanding, but she's not heartless. And what about the girl, Aline? When the Duke of Rijou finds out his puppet Princess is harboring someone he has personally marked for death, he's not likely to be thrilled, is he? He signed Valiana's Patents of Lineage at Rijou, so she can present herself before the Council of Regents, but that doesn't mean he can't hurt her in the meantime—there are any number of ways he can manipulate his fellow Dukes against her."

"This is politics, Falcio," Kest said impatiently, "politics and philosophy and strategy. You sound like the King when you talk like this, and that makes me nervous."

"You don't think it matters if the Dukes take the throne forever?"

"Of course I do. That's why I'm going to wait for the right time and then kill Valiana. I waited for you, Falcio—I waited even longer than I'd promised. You wanted to go off and try to save a little girl in the hope that somehow you'd find the answer to stopping the Dukes' conspiracy? Well, you didn't. The girl's alive and that's all well and good, but it doesn't change anything that I can see, so I'm going to do what you won't do and kill Valiana. And if I can get her bitch mother in the process, I'm going to do that too. And if you had a brain left in your head you'd be with me on this. You'd be the one—"

"Don't start with that again, Kest," I said. "I'm tired and I'm sore and a man dropped a longsword on my head back there. Give it some time."

I couldn't believe I was even considering his plan. Had we really fallen this far?

"Brasti's with me on this, Falcio," Kest said quietly. "He hasn't wanted to say it, but he is."

"So that's all the great minds of the Greatcoats heard from."

Kest sighed and said, "Where did we all go, Falcio?"

"What do you mean?"

"I mean, how is it that we all split apart so fast? Quillata, Dara, Nile, Jakin, Old Tobb . . . There were a hundred and forty-four of us, and yet in five years we've encountered no more than two or three of the others."

"I think that's how the King wanted it," I said. "He wanted to make sure we weren't together, because that would make us too dangerous to the Dukes, and sooner or later they'd send an army after us."

Kest smiled. "They'd have to, wouldn't they? A hundred and forty-four Greatcoats riding across the land on horseback, swords drawn and coattails flying in the wind as we scream war songs for damned justice in the world—that would be a sight to see, wouldn't it?"

I couldn't speak. It would indeed have been a sight—it was the sight I had believed we would see when the Dukes sent their armies to Castle Aramor: the entire Greatcoats force, arrayed against an army fifty times our size, but with not one tenth of our skill or passion. It would indeed have been a sight to see.

But I had given the order to stand down, and instead we had shuffled past like stooped old folks begging for food. One of the Dukes' generals gave us our pardons while his men dragged the King off to the top of that same tower where his father had kept him locked up all those years.

Kest's hand on my shoulder shook me from my thoughts. He pointed to Feltock, who was riding back toward us. We had fallen quite a way behind the caravan, but the captain had insisted we make sure we weren't followed.

"We're not far from Orison now," Feltock announced. "An escort from Perault, Duke of Orison, has arrived to take us into the city."

"That's good," I said, yawning. "I wouldn't suffer from a decent bed tonight."

"No, that's *bad*," the captain said. "We never asked for an escort from Orison, and we never planned on going into the city."

"Kill me now," I told Kest as I mounted Monster and urged her to a trot.

"I suspect that's precisely what they have in mind," he replied.

There were forty of them, all in armor and all on horseback. I counted eight with crossbows and shortswords at their sides and the rest were armed with war-swords and lances. They were arrayed in four rows, and between the third and forth was an elaborate carriage led by four horses and carrying the banner of Orison.

A man stepped out of the carriage. He was slightly taller than me and well groomed, with short dark hair and a well-trimmed beard in the military style. He wore a dark blue jerkin and matching pants with high black boots; a short cloak was slung around his shoulders. The rapier at his side marked him as a duelist and the crest on his right breast revealed him to be Perault, Duke of Orison.

"Valiana, sweet cousin," he said advancing to our party. "I understood that you would be coming to visit me in Orison. Why have you chosen to spurn my company without so much as sending a messenger to inform me?"

Valiana curtsied. "Forgive me, your Grace. I—my servant Trin must have forgotten to send word. She can be absentminded sometimes."

Duke Perault smiled. "Really? I've always found her exceptionally diligent."

"Your Grace? I hadn't realized you had met . . ."

Perault peered over at Aline, who was peeking out from Valiana's carriage. "And who is this sweet child? Come, dear, let me have a look at you."

"The girl is ill, my Lord," Valiana said. "I wouldn't want you to catch something from her."

The Duke gave a look of genuine concern. "Oh my, what might I catch?"

"Fire," Brasti muttered behind me, "if past is any prediction."

"Shut your mouth," Feltock told him.

"Regardless, my Lord," Valiana went on, "I am bound straight for my mother's home in Hervor and cannot delay my return with a trip to Orison, as delightful as that would no doubt be."

The Duke smiled again. "It would no doubt be very delightful for me, cousin."

Something wasn't right. Perault was far too confident, pushing his luck with the woman who was soon to be his Queen.

Feltock turned to me. "Think you can do to one of these armored buggers what you did to my axman back at the market? Get through those plates?"

"Maybe," I said.

"Think you can do it forty times, nice and fast?"

"Probably not."

He sighed. "That's what I thought."

Valiana was raising her voice now. "I am the sovereign daughter of Patriana, Duchess of Hervor, and you might as well find out now as later that I am also the daughter of Jillard, Duke of Rijou. I am the Princess Royal, and soon to take the throne. You will not impede my journey home, *your Grace*."

The Duke had started laughing halfway through her speech and was still laughing now. "You are a foolish little girl, neither Princess nor Queen, nor in truth even a Duchess, and the only thing you are going to be put upon is my knee, so that I may give your bottom a good slap, which will be fine preparation for the other activities I have planned."

Perault's voice was beyond arrogant, almost theatrical—as if he were performing for an audience. *Someone has betrayed Valiana.* I looked around, at Feltock, at his men, even at Kest for a moment, and then—

Trin. Trin wasn't here. She'd stayed in the carriage. I looked toward the carriage and saw her sitting inside, the sun's light shining in. She was smiling. But why? If she'd betrayed Valiana, did she expect protection? A reward? Once Perault had what he wanted, why should he honor any agreement he'd made with a servant?

"How dare you speak to me this way?" Valiana said. "When my mother hears of this she will—"

"Applaud," a voice said. It wasn't very loud, but it was clear as cold water and the sound froze my soul. I had hoped never again to hear this voice. It was brilliant and bold, and everything I hated in this world was carried in its tone.

Patriana, Duchess of Hervor, stepped carefully out of the Duke's carriage.

It was all I could do to hang on to Monster, whose angry jaw opened so wide you could count all the sharpened teeth in her mouth.

"If you attack now, we'll all die. The *girl* will die," I whispered fiercely in her ear.

"Ah," Patriana said, unperturbed, "I see you've brought my other property with you as well. Nicely done, Falcio. I told you that you'd make a wonderful servant. I am glad you seek to prove me right."

I looked at Kest and I looked at Brasti, and I knew that what I saw on their faces mirrored what was on mine.

"Mother?" Valiana asked, her own voice weak and uneven.

"I must thank you, girl. You've played your part as well as I could have hoped. But now the dream is over, and I shall require the scrolls that Duke Jillard gave you."

"But these are *mine*—they confirm my lineage and rights of royal blood!"

Duke Perault was laughing again. "She still doesn't understand, Patriana. She thinks she's the Princess Valiana. What a little treasure!"

Oh hells. Suddenly I was back in Rijou, in that cell, and Patriana was laughing and bragging about her expertise in creating the creatures she needed. When I told her she had failed to make a monster out of her daughter she'd said, *"My daughter? Oh, my daughter is much more dangerous than I am. I dare say she is my finest accomplishment!"*

"Ah," said the Duchess. "Well then, perhaps I should ease everyone's confusion. Come out now, my dear."

From inside the carriage, Trin emerged—but it wasn't our Trin, at least not the woman I had thought of as Trin. She shook her hair back and stepped forward, her chin high and looking down on all of us. Gone was the uncertain, tentative, pretty girl; this woman was all pride and arrogance, her eyes shining viciously in the light. There was something familiar in those eyes, and when they locked on mine it was as if the veil made from that damned blue dust she had blown in our eyes was suddenly lifted.

"It's—" Brasti began, his eyes wide.

Kest's mouth barely moved as he said, "The assassin—the one who killed Tremondi and framed us for it."

Trin smiled at me. *She wants this—she wants us to know. The game is about to end.*

Valiana—or the woman I had known as Valiana—was barely coherent as she said, "But . . . this is *Trin*, my servant, Mother, she's my *lady-in-waiting*. She's always been my lady-in-waiting, almost since—"

"Almost since you were born," the Duchess finished. "And she was faithful, was she not? Attending you in all ways, coming to your lessons with you, helping you study, learning the ways of the court—and yet always your servant. Imagine how that must have been for her, knowing she was my true-born daughter, to bow and scrape and giggle at your follies."

The evil in the Duchess's voice was palpable. It had a rhythm, and it pounded in my head and my heart and I swear she was looking right at me when she said, "Imagine the discipline and calculation that would instill in a girl, to live as a servant all those years."

The girl with the hard eyes smiled. "We must find you a more suitable name now, my secret sweetheart, and more suitable clothes, and more suitable hair, and most of all, more suitable duties."

"How could you do this?" Valiana cried.

"I won't tell you it was easy," the Duchess said, "but it was necessary. That fool Jillard would never have granted recognition of your rights if he had thought you were anything but the stupid little doll that you are. I couldn't take the chance that he might see the potential in my true work—or worse, decide to kill my daughter, rather than let her take the throne. So I brought you up to be pretty and gullible, and my dear Duke, seeing a puppet whose strings he could easily pull, has given his sworn recognition of Valiana as the daughter of Hervor and Jillard, and soon to be Queen on the throne."

Valiana gave a terrified sob and ran to the Duchess, holding the packet of credentials in her hands as if they were made of gold. "This isn't right—it's not true! *I'm* your true-born daughter, I swear—I *swear*!"

Patriana, Duchess of Hervor, who had no doubt comforted and coddled the girl many times over the past eighteen years, slapped her so hard she fell backward and hit the ground. Then, with infinite calm and a kind of grace, she reached down and plucked the packet held between the girl's hands.

"You are, in fact, nothing more than the refuse one of my men pulled out of the cunt of a peasant whose only redeeming feature was that she happened to look a little like me."

Valiana was crumpled on the ground and crying uncontrollably, her face in the dirt.

"Now, now, don't be so sad, dear. Most peasants live miserable, short lives. You had eighteen years as the daughter of a Duchess, living in splendor and believing you were a Princess. It's the dream of every silly girl, and you got to live it. For a while. But now it's time to come to Orison, where Perault can put you to some use. Perhaps for his men, perhaps for his dogs."

She signaled to Feltock. "Put her on top of one of the wagons and gag her if she screams."

"No!" Aline screamed and ran out from behind one of the wagons to stand between Valiana and the Duke's men.

Brasti ran behind her and put a hand on her shoulder. "Easy now, girl," he said.

Aline's eyes were full of tears and she was blinking furiously. She held her left arm straight out in front of her and the other was bent by her ear and tensing as if holding an invisible bowstring. "You don't touch her," she yelled.

Duke Perault laughed and took a step toward us. “My goodness, what a delightful girl! Are you the little darling who has caused so much trouble for my dear Patriana? That was very naughty, girl. We’ll have to devise some very special punishments for you. Very special indeed.”

“Stay back! I will not warn you again,” she shouted, tears streaming down her cheeks.

Perault laughed and signaled to one of his men. The man had his sword drawn and an evil grin on his face as he began walking toward her, taking little steps and then hopping, as if playing a game, and laughing as the girl’s terror magnified.

She pulled her arm back even further.

“Aw, no, not a deadly ’maginary bow!” he said, pawing theatrically at an invisible arrow lodged in his chest. Then he smiled again and took another step forward.

Aline gave a little cry and flung her right hand back, as if she’d fired an arrow.

“Stupid—that’s not—” the man said, suddenly looking down at the arrow sticking out of his gut.

Brasti’s hand was right back on Aline’s shoulder where it had been a moment ago.

“That’s it, girl,” he said softly to her. “Pick your target, wait for it, and don’t let go until you know you’ve got it.”

Duke Perault’s mouth took an ugly shape.

“Any man reaches for this girl, he will be dead before he blinks,” Brasti said, his voice resonating across the field. “If you have ever wanted to bet on a sure thing in this life, now’s the time.”

“What is your name, dead man?” Perault asked, his voice bringing a chill in the air to counter Brasti’s fire.

Brasti looked him straight in the eye, his right hand still relaxed on Aline’s shoulder as his left held his bow.

“My name is Brasti Goodbow,” he said. Then he glanced briefly back at Kest and me and said slowly, “And I am the King’s Arrow.”

Kest took a step forward beside him. “My name is Kest of Luth,” he said, “son of Murrow the Swordsmith.”

He drew his sword from its sheath. "And I am the King's Blade."

Each of us had a name like that, given to us by the King himself. Dara was "the King's Fury," Nile was "the King's Arm," and I . . .

I had always hated the name I was given because I hadn't deserved it. It was the King who made the Greatcoats, the King who had given us everything. I had only failed us all in our hours of greatest need.

"It's all right," Kest said to me, then more softly, "He'd want you to say it."

"Say it, damn you," Brasti spat. "If not now, when?"

I took a deep breath and stepped forward. "I am Falcio val Mond of Pertine," I said. "And I am the King's Heart."

I heard a sob from Aline as she looked back at me. Then one of Perault's men pulled his sword and she aimed her imaginary bow once again.

"Enough of this," Duchess Patriana spat, safe in her carriage. "No more posturing, Perault; no games. Take them all."

Feltock stepped forward to us and turned to Brasti, Kest, and me, his back to the Duke and his men. "Well, boys, I won't say it's been pleasant, but you've been all right to fight with. Now it's time," he murmured.

"Time for what?" Brasti asked.

"When the moment strikes, you take Valiana and the girl and travel east, as far and as fast as you can. Ten days' ride from here is the village of Gaziah. There's a monastery there, and an old monk, his name's Hajan. He keeps an old woman there. She will take the girls and hide them until they can be moved further east to the Desert Kingdoms. They can join a Sun Sisterhood there—it's not a great life, but it's as good as we can hope for."

"You knew this would happen," I said.

"I never knew what the old sow was planning but I could always tell she didn't love Valiana, not the way a mother ought."

"But you work for the Duchess," Brasti pointed out.

"Aye, I do. And a soldier follows orders. She told me to keep the girl safe, and that's the order I am going to follow."

"And your men?"

"Most are loyal to me. The rest—well, let's just say I don't begrudge you spiking that axman in the face like you did."

Something important occurred to me just then. "You *wanted* us," I said. "I was going to walk away, but you taunted me, and when I came back she goaded me into fighting those men."

Feltock clamped his lips together, but there was a gleam in his eye.

"There were plenty of men for hire in that market but you wanted us—why?"

"I wanted Trattari," he said. "There's no man alive the Duchess can't buy if she wants to, and more than half the time she doesn't even have to do that to get them going her way. But I reckoned if any man hated the Duchess enough not to get bought then it had to be Trattari, seeing as what she did to your King and all."

He was your King too, I wanted to say, but I let it slide.

"Feltock!" the Duchess's voice rang out.

"You don't owe me nothing, nor the girl either, for that matter, but soldier to soldier, I'm begging you, ride fast, ride hard, and don't look back."

"What about you?" I asked.

"Reckon me and the boys are going to die right about now. But we're Gods-damned well going to take some of them with us. We'll give you time to get away."

I looked over at the men. Blondie was slowly pulling a sword out of one of the wagons. He caught my eye and nodded. He looked scared, but he looked solid, and I guess that's what brave looks like, so I nodded back.

I looked at Valiana on the ground and Aline standing next to the carriage. "All right, Captain. We'll move on your signal."

Feltock smiled, a big toothy grin like a man who's just thought of a dirty joke. "My signal, eh? All right, here's my signal, then!" And with that he turned, drew his sword, and shouted at the heavens, "Come on, you great filthy whore! I've licked your bony ass long enough and now I'm gonna fuck you and your damn Duke until you start pissing pirates out of your privates!"

His men gave a roar and I saw Kurg and one of the other men pull crossbows from the wagons and fire at the Duke's men. I saw Perault staring in disbelief, and horses neighing and rearing in the chaos as Feltock's men threw something heavy and round into their midst that promptly exploded into fire and dust.

"Go!" I said to Kest, and he raced for Aline, grabbed her up with one arm, and threw her over the saddle before mounting himself. Brasti jumped on his own horse and nocked an arrow. He took a shot at the Duke, who was running back to the carriage, but the arrow hit him in the leg.

"The girl!" I shouted at him. "Take out the girl!"

But it was too late: four armored men stood around Trin, their shields protecting her and the Duchess.

I leapt onto Monster and kicked her hard toward Valiana, who had risen from the ground but was looking around in confusion.

"Your hand, girl! Give me your hand!" I cried, but she didn't hear me.

One of the Duke's soldiers tried to slice at Monster's exposed neck. I parried the cut but he pulled back and aimed for me. I saw the shaft of an arrow appear in the slit of his helm—an almost impossible shot—and I thanked Saint Merhan-who-rides-the-arrow for Brasti's miraculous aim. The man fell down—and then I saw it.

Two of the four men guarding the Duchess and her daughter had stepped out of formation, and I had an opening: with one good thrust I could kill the daughter and, if I was lucky, I might get the Duchess too, before the other soldiers got me in the back. I wanted it—and Monster wanted it too, I could tell: two broken creatures running headlong for the cliff.

I had a brief vision of seeing my King again, standing with the Saints, as I pulled my arm into line for the thrust; then I felt something on my left hand. Valiana was trying to get up behind me onto

Monster. I turned back, but the soldiers had re-formed and all I saw in front of me were shields.

I gave Valiana my arm and pulled her up, and then Brasti, Kest, and I raced like damn black death for the rising eastern sky. I felt sick at leaving behind Feltock, Blondie, and the others to die, but this wasn't the first time in my life that I had followed an order like that.

27
THE TAILOR OF PHAN

We rode through the morning skies and the evening sunsets, past the boundary markers for Orison and all the way into the yellow fields of the Duchy of Pulnam. I had to force Monster to stop often enough to keep the horses from running themselves to death, but though we rode for as long and as fast as we could, we never made it to the village of Gaziah or the monastery. The only way to pass Pulnam and get to the beginnings of the Eastern Desert was through the Arch: a fifty-foot gully with massive sheer walls on either side, formed by the wind and sand that blew west from the desert itself.

We stopped to rest in a small village a few miles west of the Arch. Valiana and Aline weren't trained for hard riding and they were saddle-sore and exhausted. And then there was the matter of their lives being shattered . . .

When Brasti went to scout ahead, he saw the army arrayed there, waiting for us.

"I don't think their scouts saw me," he said, "but they were already starting to march this way. There's no way forward, and with the Duke's men and who knows how many reinforcements from Orison after us, there's no way back."

"Where are we now?" I asked.

"The village is called Phan," he said. "There's not much here. I asked a boy down the road and he said there're just a few merchants here, along with the butcher, the smithy, and a tailor's shop, if I heard him right."

"Hide, ride, or fight?" Kest asked.

"Can't ride, can't fight," Brasti said.

I didn't have an answer. Something was bothering me.

"Then we hide," said Kest. "Can we make do in one of the forests?"

"Look around," Brasti said. "It's mostly fields in Pulnam until you get to the Arch, and the forests they do have are too small. That army looks to have a good five hundred men. They won't have much trouble smoking us out."

Aline started crying and Valiana, who hadn't spoken since Orison, put her arms around her.

"Then where?" Kest asked.

"I suppose we could try to hide here, but I don't imagine the locals will lie for us when the Duke's men arrive."

"How far behind us are they, do you suppose?" I asked.

Brasti took a deep breath. "Honestly? I don't think they're very far. They had better mounts and more of them, and we've had to stop far too often to outdistance them by much. The damn wagons could have caught up to us by now."

"Doesn't it seem like an awful lot of work?" I asked.

"They want the girl dead," Brasti said.

"They want the scrolls proving Valiana's lineage, and they already have those."

"No, they don't," Valiana said, looking up from where she and Aline were huddled. "Feltock made me take them out when we left Rijou. He told me to keep my traveling papers in the packet instead."

She reached into a pocket in her blouse and pulled out a pair of scrolls marked with Ducal seals.

"Well, isn't he a cunning old fox?" Brasti said, admiration in his voice.

Kest looked at me. "It does give us something to bargain with."

Bargain with the most powerful and canny woman in the world, in front of the army she was commanding? And then what? She kills us, and what's the difference? Better to just burn the damn papers and see what chaos that brings.

I was tired and sore and more confused than I'd ever been. I walked over to Valiana, who was still hugging Aline.

"I'm out of ideas and out of hope," I said. "Just tell me what you want me to do, Valiana, and I'll do it as best I can."

"I'm not Valiana," she said. "I'm no one and nothing—or if I am something, it's just what you said in Rijou: a foolish girl who dreamt of sitting on a Queen's throne without ever thinking about what she would do when she got there."

I felt a hand on my arm and looked down into Aline's eyes. She sniffed and then said, "We hide, Falcio. We hide, and then we ride, and then we fight."

I started to pull my arm away but she hung on to it. "I don't think we can win, Aline," I said softly.

She took a deep breath and stood up a bit straighter. "I know that, but what they're doing isn't right. It isn't *fair*. And maybe if we fight a little, we can make it a bit more fair. The world should be a more fair place, don't you think?"

Then I put my hand on her cheek and she gave me a little smile, just for an instant, but I swear with every Saint at my back that in that moment my heart broke and my mind followed, and great wracking sobs filled the air as a thousand hurts arose in my body that I hadn't felt in so long, from my first bruise to the arrow I took in the leg, and every wound I had forgotten on the long walk to Castle Aramor, where I went to kill a King; the sight of my wife's wasted body on the tavern floor and the sight of the burned mansion in Rijou; the knowledge that I had failed my King to the knowledge that I was about to fail this little girl—all of it came out of me until every wound, every memory, every sorrow was voiced. The tears bled from my eyes until I thought there was nothing left—but there was one thing there. Nothing grand, no great plan or hope.

Just a small thing.

"Brasti," I said softly.

He came over and knelt beside me.

"What can I do?" he asked gently.

"Did you tell me that there was a tailor's shop in this village?"

It was a small village, so it shouldn't have taken as long as it did to find the little house on the outskirts, but finally we did find it. We stood outside a tiny tailor's shop, supported on two sides by crooked trees.

"I don't get it," Brasti said. "What good is a tailor going to be?"

Kest answered for me. "Have you ever in your entire life heard of a tailor's shop in a village this size? It doesn't make any sense."

"Then what do you—? No—you don't think . . . ?"

A cackling voice broke the silence. "Well now, ain't you just about the sorriest-looking pack of half-dead rabbits I've ever seen?"

Though it had been only a few weeks since I'd last seen her, I found the sight of the Tailor strange to behold. She was her usual disheveled and disreputable-looking self, and yet there was something changed in her bearing.

"Mattea!" Aline shouted, and ran two steps toward the Tailor. Then she stopped abruptly, as if she too could tell there was something different about the old woman.

"Come on then, girl," the Tailor said, one eyebrow raised. "I don't have all day."

Aline tentatively took a half step backward and curtsied.

"Hah," the Tailor shouted. "Did you see that? She curtsied at me like I'm some fine, high-born lady!"

The Tailor came over, took Aline by the shoulders, and looked her straight in the eyes. "Nobody bows before a Tailor, do you hear me, girl? *Nobody.* The Tailor's much too important for bows and curtsies and pleases and thank-thees and all your other fine claptrap."

"Yes, ma'am," Aline said.

"And we don't take to no 'ma'ams' either." Then her gaze softened. "Ah, child, there's no need for this shyness now, is there? I'm still your old nanny Mattea underneath it all, aren't I?"

"You're scaring her," Brasti said.

The Tailor rose and her mouth twitched, but then she sighed. "Aye, I am at that. I suppose the time for pretend is past." The old woman turned. "Come, sit down here at the table, all of you. I'll give you food and drink. We have a little time, though not much."

She ushered us into the shop and motioned for us to take seats around her large sewing table.

"How—?" I asked, my mind struggling to put together how we could all be meeting here, at this place. "How is it possible that you're here? Right *here*? In a village we had no reason to ever come to?"

The Tailor brought out a plate of cheese and bread and favored me with that twisted smile of hers. "You had every reason to be here, boy. You followed the strands of your life and they led you here, from Paelis's foolish quest to Tremondi's death and through that bitch Patriana's machinations: all of it pulled you here, and a good Tailor knows where every thread leads."

Then she grabbed the collar of Kest's coat roughly. "And what in the name of every hells-bound Saint have you been doing with my coats?" she demanded. "Take those damned things off and get in here."

"There's a small army down the road," I said, "and another one coming up behind us."

"Quiet, boy. I know where they are, just as I know where you are, where you've been, and where you're going. I know where every thread in the coat travels and I'm too old to listen to you tell me your tales at your slow, sorry pace. Now, give me your coats. They ain't much use to you in the state you've got 'em."

We took off our greatcoats and handed them over to her and she began examining them, talking all the while. "Cheveran, eh, Falcio? Damn piss-rain there, full of Gods knows what mixing with the mill fumes. Burn holes into your clothes if you're not careful, but not these coats, not my pretty ones."

She turned over my coat and then picked up Brasti's and gave it a sniff. "Damn, boy, can't you take off your clothes before you rut?"

The Tailor didn't give him time to answer but instead went back to looking at every patch, every stain, every thread of our greatcoats, muttering as she went.

"Well, that's it, then," she said at last.

"Can you mend them?" I asked. I realized I had been hoping as she scrutinized them that she might actually repair a few of the frayed edges of my coat.

She froze then, just for a second; then she looked at me and her face was scrunched up and I thought she was going to sneeze or spasm, but she just burst out laughing. "Can I mend them? Can I *mend* them? Saints alive and dead, Falcio, may all the Gods who never were bless your name and send me a thousand more like you."

She dropped the coats on the table and clapped her hands together. "Here he is, the most completely buggered man in the whole world, with an army on one side of him and an army on t'other, with no way to run, nowhere to hide, no chance at fighting, and no idea what he's fighting for. The fate of the entire world is resting square on his shoulders and there's not a savior in sight—and the first thing he asks me is if I can mend his holes in his greatcoat, thank-you-please!"

The others were laughing too, but I didn't find it nearly as funny.

She kept chuckling and snorting and clapping her hands together. Finally she said, "Ah, if for no other reason than this, Falcio val Mond of Pertine, you have the gratitude of a Tailor."

I wondered if perhaps that came with an army attached to it, but I thought better of asking. Instead, I asked, "Can you tell us anything about the other Magisters? Have you seen any of them? Has anyone found the King's Charoites?"

"Aye, all of 'em, and aye, one of 'em," she said. "But I won't tell you more, and I won't mend your coat, but I will give you this."

She went to a cupboard at the back of the shop and brought out a large bundle tied with reeds. She dropped the bundle on the table and pulled the reeds apart and, even after all those years and the hells we'd been through, the sight still took my breath away.

There were greatcoats there on the table, new and perfect, and each one bearing the crests that Brasti's, Kest's, and mine had borne.

"How is this *possible*?" Kest asked. "How could you know we would come here? Tailor, why did you come to this village?"

"I told you," she said. "A Tailor must know where every thread starts and where every thread ends up."

Kest and Brasti picked up their coats, and then I took mine, the last in the pile. Only it wasn't; there was something underneath. Another greatcoat, a little smaller than ours, made of the same dark brown leather. The inlay on the right breast panel was rich purple: it was a bird, rising from the ashes.

"You can't be serious—you can't think that—Aline? A *Greatcoat*?"

Aline came forward and examined the coat. She ran her palm along the smooth surface of the leather, then reluctantly pulled it back before shaking her head. "It's not for me," she said, and then she pointed at Valiana. "It's for her."

Valiana stood from her chair and her eyes flitted from the coat to me, and back again. "But I don't—I mean—I don't know what this means."

"What's your name, girl?" the Tailor asked.

"I've been called Valiana of Hervor," she said, sounding doubtful.

"No, that ain't your name. And you know that now, right?"

She nodded, slowly.

"You hate the Duchess, and that's fair, but I'll tell you this: if the old hag hadn't taken care of your real mamma while you were in the womb, she never would have carried you to term. She was a poor woman, your ma, and not a healthy one at that."

"I was never meant to live," Valiana whispered.

"That's right. You weren't meant to live then, and you ain't meant to live now."

"What—?" I began.

"Now you just shut your fool mouth, Falcio." She waved me aside. "Truth be told, girl, you ain't got no place in this world. I know the weave of things, and you ain't meant for nothing but the blade of a

Knight's sword across your belly. But the world needs a few good shocks now and then, so let's make the best of it."

She held out the coat to Valiana. "Now, you're goin' to need a new name, and you're goin' to have to pick it for yourself. In this world people don't have to make themselves up; they have parents who tell them what their name is, what they believe, what they are—but you don't have that, so you're goin' to have to find it all out yourself. But for a start, you've got this." The Tailor held open the coat and Valiana slipped her arms in. It fit her as if she'd been born into it.

"But I can't be one of—I'm not qualified or trained or . . ."

"Says who?" the Tailor asked. "You've studied the laws, King's and Dukes' alike, haven't you?"

"I had to, to prepare for—"

"And I'll bet Hervor had you take sword lessons just to make sure her little vixen could be there with you to learn how to stick the pointy end in someone's back."

"Yes, but I was never all that good at it."

The Tailor chuckled. "Well, neither are these three, and they do all right on occasion. Don't worry, girl. Being a Greatcoat isn't just about judgin' and ridin' and swingin' a sword, no matter what these fools tell you."

She straightened the lapel of Valiana's greatcoat. "But that's for later. For now, you've got to take the oath."

"What oath?" Valiana asked.

"Well now, if it was just as easy as someone telling you what to say, then it wouldn't be much of an oath, would it?"

Valiana looked around at us. "I don't understand—do you want me to swear fealty to the Greatcoats? Or the King's memory? Or some Saint?"

"Is that what you believe in? What you want to die for? 'Cause, make no mistake, girl, the end of this road is a shallow, dirty ditch with your corpse in it."

Valiana looked into the Tailor's eyes for a moment, then looked away. "No," she said softly, "I don't . . . disbelieve in those things, but then, I don't know what it means to believe in anything, really.

My life was always about me, and so was everyone else's life around me, too. I don't even know what I *should* care about. I never made a promise to anyone else, except—"

She looked at Aline, who was sitting down on a stool, looking at her hands.

"—you," she said. "I promised you I'd protect you, didn't I?"

Aline nodded and sniffed a little.

Valiana looked to the Tailor. "Is that—?"

The Tailor put a hand on her face and then gave her a light, almost affectionate slap. "No one can tell you but yourself. That's what being free means—not the right to do whatever you want, but the right to take a stand and say what you'll die for."

Valiana stood motionless for a moment and then knelt before Aline and took her hand. "Listen, I don't know what any of this means. I don't know who I am or how long I have to live. I thought I was the most important girl in the world and now it turns out I'm worth nothing, not even the coat on my back. I'm not innocent—I know that now. Just being ignorant doesn't mean I'm free of guilt. But you are. You didn't do anything wrong, and now people are coming to—well, they're coming to do bad things. And you didn't do anything wrong. You should have the right to live and figure out who you want to be. I'm not strong, and I don't know how to use a sword, not really anyway. But I think—I think I can be brave, or I can try, at least. I think that if someone tries to kill you I could . . . I don't know, put myself in front of you. I don't know how well I can fight, or run, or judge, but when the blade comes, I swear on whatever they want me to swear on, I'll stop it, with my body if nothing else."

I wanted to speak, but I couldn't. There was a heaviness in the room as we all stood there and listened to Valiana's quiet tears.

I don't know how long we waited like that before Valiana looked around to the Tailor, who nodded at her, just once.

"Tailor—how—?" I choked on the words before I could get them out.

"Shush," she replied, her eyes still on the girls.

After a moment Aline took Valiana's right hand and placed it against her cheek. Somehow I knew she was going to do that . . . I knew because—

"No," the Tailor said to me, "not yet. You're not ready to understand." Then she made the tiniest gesture with her hand, like someone pulling a needle through cloth, and the question was gone.

"Is that all right?" Valiana asked. "Is that an oath? Did I say it right?"

The Tailor looked at me now. "Well, Falcio, do you reckon she said it right?"

"It's my oath," I said. "It's the same oath I made to the King. And you said it just right."

"So is that it, then?" Kest asked quietly. "Are coats and oaths the only things we have left?" A look passed between him and the Tailor and she walked up and took his hand.

"You know the answer already, don't you, boy?" she asked, tapping a finger on his forehead.

Kest nodded.

"And you know who's comin', don't you?" she asked, more gently this time.

"I do."

"So you've been trainin' and practicin', and now you reckon yourself the best in the world, don't you?"

"I have. I am."

"And you know it ain't enough, right?"

I thought I saw the hint of a tear in his eye when I heard him say, "I know."

She patted him on the arm. "I'll say this for you: you've tried hard and you've learned a lot. But you have too much here"—she tapped him on the forehead—"and too much here"—she patted his arms—"and not enough here." She put the tip of her finger on his chest. "And now your time is comin' and you ain't ready."

"How long?" Kest asked.

"How long is the thread in my hand?" she asked.

"I don't know," he replied.

The Tailor said, "Tonight. It's going to be tonight."

"I don't understand," I said to her. "I don't understand any of it anymore."

"You ain't supposed to," she said irritably. "Damned Magisters: you always want to know what to do or where to hide or who to kill. This ain't that anymore. There ain't much time left, and what there is ain't for judgin' or ridin' or fightin'. It's for livin', for as long as you have left."

She walked stiffly over to the door and opened it. She clucked at Monster, waiting outside, and the Fey Horse opened her mouth and growled.

The Tailor ignored the warning and put her hands on the side of the scarred creature's face. "You'll come with me now, Horse. I've got a job for you. You can't help them right now, much as you might want to. We're sisters, you and I," she said absently, "old and broken and scarred and angry. They've taken it all away from us."

She turned back to the rest of us. "They've taken it all," she said. "They've taken every last good thing in the world."

Then she swung the door wide. "Now go and show them your answer."

28
THE SAINT OF SWORDS

Whatever I expected to find when we reached the roadway, it wasn't Patriana, Duchess of Hervor, with a single armed guard at her side. She was sitting on a stump, as elegantly as one could, and reading a book. Her guard was armored head to toe, but he was only one man and that didn't present much of a threat for us. So naturally I assumed we were completely surrounded.

"We are quite alone," the Duchess said as we approached. "You needn't fear an arrow in the back just yet."

"Well, that's a relief," Brasti said, pulling an arrow from his quiver. "Hang on, boys, I'm just going to go kill the old cow and I'll be right back."

The Duchess smiled politely at him. "Ah, if it were only that simple."

I gestured at the two horses tied to the tree near the stump. "You traveled light," I said.

"Alas, but the wagons would not have been able to keep quite the pace we needed to reach you. But traveling light is pleasant enough in the right company."

"I take it you wanted to get here before Duke Jillard did?" I asked.

"Yes. I do thank you so much for stealing the little girl out of Rijou. Apparently the Duke is quite determined to kill her, and I can't really have him getting hold of the five of you. He managed to field an army of his more loyal soldiers and bring it up the Eastern Passage and through the Arch, and in a short while they'll make their way down this road. I don't plan on being here when they arrive."

She looked the five of us over. "But my, haven't you been busy, getting all nice and cleaned up for our visit. And you, my sweet child," she said, looking at Valiana, "don't you look all grown up in that lovely coat."

"I'm bored," Brasti said. "Is there any way I could possibly just kill you now and then we could go and—I don't know—play games with your head?"

"I don't think you would have much fun tossing my head around like a ball, Trattari. Trust me, I've tried it more than once and even a traitor's head just gets soggy after a while."

I wondered, not for the first time, that the world could bear the weight of so many foul people.

"Besides," she added, "you'll find patience is a worthwhile companion. I've been patient nearly twenty years now, and I suspect the sensation of completing my task will be made even more satisfying by the delay."

"All right, now even I'm bored. What is it you want?" I asked.

"Negotiation," she said.

"What?"

"No need to be coy. You have the Patents of Lineage and I need them. I don't want Jillard to get them back, and I'm willing to negotiate."

"All right," I said. "Safe passage for the five of us and a barrel full of gold onions."

The Duchess thought for a moment, then said, "No, I'm afraid that won't do. Though the gold onions would be feasible, I suppose, if you'd care to settle for those. But I'm afraid I really do need most of you to be dead as soon as possible."

"I imagine you can understand why that doesn't work very well for us," I pointed out.

"I'm not being cruel," she said earnestly. "The girls must die because none of my plans really work out very well with them alive. The archer insulted Duke Perault, and so he must die. And of course Kest here, 'the King's Blade,' well now, he's spoken for."

Patriana smiled pleasantly. "But *you* can come back with me, Falcio, you and that delightful horse. Wherever is she? We've got a great deal to talk about, you and I."

"Brasti, put an arrow in the guard's face. Kest, knock her head off—see if you can get it to thunk on that tree over there," I ordered.

"Duel," Patriana snapped.

"What?"

"I claim the right of duel to resolve this matter. King's Law gives it to me."

Brasti was sighting the guard down the line of his arrow. "Lady, you can claim the right of boiled fish for all I care, but I'm done playing with you."

Brasti let the arrow fly. I have seen him shoot a thousand times and I have never seen him miss the target, not at this distance.

"It's all right," Kest told him quietly. "You didn't miss."

The guard was still standing, and he didn't appear to have moved. But I noticed that his sword was in his hand now and there, on the ground in front of his feet, lay the arrow, cut perfectly in half.

"We all dream of meeting the Saints when we die, don't we?" the Duchess of Hervor said. "Well, now you have, and now you will."

The guard removed his helm. He had short red hair and piercing eyes and his face was red, the color of spilled blood. The air glowed red around him. At the sight of him our horses reared and then let out terrified screams as they raced from the clearing.

"Gods and Saints," Brasti whispered.

"We prefer it if you don't summon us in vain," said Caveil-whose-blade-cuts-water, the bloody-faced Saint of Swords. "Sometimes it even makes us angry."

"It's not possible," I said. "Saints don't . . ."

My mind raced, trying to understand what was happening. Was this a ruse? Was this just a scary man with a painted-red face? But the arrow—

"Oh, it's not as difficult as you might think," the Duchess began. "If you try hard enough and you're willing to make sacrifices, you can work out an amicable arrangement with anyone, really."

She rose and said, "This is my negotiating position: you can duel my champion, lose, and then I'll take the scrolls and your lives, or you can try and run, Saint Caveil will kill you, and then I'll have the scrolls and your lives anyway."

"What's the difference?" I asked, still staring at a Saint walking the Earth.

"My way you get to die doing something grand and honorable. I know how much that means to you, Falcio."

The Saint removed his armor, a piece at a time, revealing a powerful, lean frame underneath. He wore a black jerkin that covered his torso; where his skin was revealed it was as blood red as his face. Despite all that, his appearance didn't impress me all that much more than a hundred other opponents who were equally muscled and tattooed. But somehow you could sense the power in him. A Saint: the ultimate expression of an ideal, in this case, the mastery of the sword.

Well, I thought, *if I have to die, at least there is a pretty damn good chance someone will write a song about it.* Except that he was going to kill all of us regardless, and then there wouldn't be anyone to tell the story. Unless, of course, the Duchess would oblige.

"All right," I said, pulling my rapier from its scabbard.

The Saint laughed. "You? Don't be silly. You don't even hold that thing properly."

He turned to Kest. "You. You're the one I've come for." Then he looked Kest in the eye. "You've always known it, haven't you?"

"I have," Kest said simply.

"And you know how this is going to end, don't you?"

"I do."

Caveil smiled. "It's not good to put yourself above a Saint, child."

Kest shrugged. "A Saint is really only a little God, after all."

The Saint kept smiling. "I like that coat, though," he said. "May I have yours after you're dead?"

"Marked. I have one request in return," Kest said.

"That sounds reasonable, if pointless."

"Let my friends go first. If I lose, you'll have no trouble catching them, and if I win, they deserve a head start in case the Duke's men arrive."

"Unacceptable," the Duchess said. "Your friends stay here. This won't take more than a few seconds."

The Saint kept his eyes on Kest, but he spoke to the Duchess. "Keep silent, woman. Your braying offends me."

"You are marked," she began.

"I am marked," he said, "to kill this man. But I have not come here to destroy with a single stroke. You will have your vengeance, but I will have my sport. Fear not, I grow bored easily, and I am sure this one will suit me for only a few seconds. You can hold the scrolls 'til then, if it pleases you."

The Duchess grabbed the scrolls from Valiana and inspected the seals.

Kest turned to me. "Go. Take the others. The hells with what the Tailor said. Run fast and run hard."

There was no point in arguing: one of us or five of us, we didn't have a chance against the Saint of Swords. But if we could run and catch the Fey Horse, I might be able to get Valiana and Aline on it; they'd have a chance to flee the Duke of Jillard's army, if the Duchess had spoken true and the Duke of Orison's men weren't behind us.

"Get ready," I told the others. "We go for the trees and into the fields." I doubted she was stupid enough to believe me, but I didn't feel like really telling her where we were going.

I turned back to Kest to say good-bye. He was my oldest friend and he was about to die to give me one last, hopeless chance.

"Kest?" I said.

He was staring at Saint Caveil, who stood smiling at us, his feet shoulder-width apart and his sword resting casually in one hand.

"Can't . . . see," Kest said, squinting his eyes.

"What's wrong?" I asked. Had Caveil done something to his eyes? Do Saints cheat?

"Falcio, I can't see . . . I can't see him moving his sword . . ." Kest's eyes were blinking furiously and he was breathing strangely.

I looked back at the Saint. He hadn't moved.

"Kest, what are you talking about? He's not moving."

"Listen," Kest said. "Just listen."

I did, and at first I thought I was just hearing the wind from the east, but then I found a rhythm to the gentle whooshing, an almost-melody of subtle vibrations: the sound a fine sword makes when it cuts the air.

I looked back at bloody-faced Saint Caveil, who didn't appear to be moving at all but was cutting the air with his sword so quickly my eyes couldn't see it.

"I can almost . . . almost make it out," Kest mumbled. "A blur . . . yes, there it is, no, wait . . . almost . . ."

I didn't know what I could do for Kest. "Go," I shouted to Brasti and the others.

Kest grabbed me by the shoulders and looked me in the eyes. He looked crazed. "Falcio, I need you to do something for me."

"Anything," I said.

"You beat me—that one time at the castle, you beat me. Tell me how you did it. Maybe I can . . . maybe there's something I haven't tried, something I haven't seen, or some technique—"

My heart fell. I could have lain down on the ground and simply let the Saint kill me, or the Duke's army run right over me, or been taken by any of a hundred other deaths that awaited me. For my whole life Kest had been like the mountains or the oceans or the sky: he feared nothing and was angered by nothing. Everything was simply interesting to him—and now he was going crazy.

I put my hands on his shoulders and whispered into his ear, and I told him how I had beaten him that day at Castle Aramor. And when I was done, I kissed him on the forehead and said good-bye.

He gave me a little smile for a second and said, "Well now, I don't think that's going to work here, is it? But I suppose anything's worth trying once."

And with that he turned and gave a war cry, which I had never heard him do, and his sword flashed under the sun as he walked toward the Saint of Swords, and I turned and ran as fast as my legs would take me.

When the Ducal armies arrived at King Paelis's castle, they brought five hundred horse, a thousand foot, two hundred archers, and a host of siege engines, enough men to fight a war that could rage for weeks. When they reached the front gates, they met Pimar, the King's valet.

Pimar was a good boy, eleven years old and eager to please, and when the vanguard reached the gate, he opened it for them and asked if anyone wished some refreshment to clear their throats from the dusty ride. In his left hand he held out the King's crest, and in his right he held a treaty signed by the King and the First Cantor of the Traveling Magisters.

According to Pimar, the generals spent some time reading the document and then turned to Pimar and asked that tea and biscuits be set out for them. And they asked to see me.

When your enemy is offering complete surrender and the only alternative is black damned war that will surely take a fierce toll of your men, it's easy to be generous.

"Full pardons for every Magister? Nothing else?"

"Nothing else," I said calmly.

"No tricks now, boy," the general said to me. "You'll find there are worse things than a quick death by the sword if you're lying."

"On my honor, sir, I swear to you that the castle will be yours, the Magisters will be disbanded, and the King will await your pleasure in the throne room."

"Good, good." The general pressed the treaty down on the table to sign it. One of his fellows snorted, and caught my attention. He was an older man with coarse gray hair and a thick mustache. His coat looked strange to me for a moment, but then I realized it was just the oily blue flower pattern on the right breast.

"I have seen seven wars in my lifetime," he started. "Wars against barbarians from Avares, against the East, and even wars against other Dukes. I have seen cowardice; yes, I have, many times. But there are cowards and then there are *cowards*, and boy, a man who lets his Lord rot for a pardon on a scrap of paper is a coward unlike any I have ever seen."

"Is there some service I can perform for the general?" I asked.

He snorted again. "Yes, boy, you can tell me what Duchy grew such a coward as you, so that I might go there and correct their Duke."

"Why, General," I said, "I hail from Pertine, where cowards grow like wildflowers on the side of the hilltop."

"I should kill you for your impertinence, dog," he bellowed.

"Yes, General," I replied, "it was impertinent. But I'm afraid that, under the circumstances, you'll have to pardon me."

"Enough," the lead general said, passing the paper to his next-in-line. "The decision is made. We accept the treaty. We'll move our vanguard into the castle at once."

I bowed and stood to one side as they passed. The general from Pertine shot me a look of pure venom, but there was nothing he could do but swallow the shit that had been served him. So we had that in common, anyway.

Hours later I was still outside the castle, waiting for word. A messenger summoned me and I was brought once again before the lead general.

"The usurper's asked a favor," he said.

"The what?"

"The King, boy, the King. He's asked a favor and I'm inclined to grant it, given the circumstances."

"What is the favor, General?"

"He's asked to see you."

For a moment my mind raced and I tried to devise some kind of plan—an escape, some kind of poison for his guards, anything.

The general chuckled. "Boy, sometimes life feeds you bitter fruit, doesn't it?"

"Yes, General, it does."

"Well, don't go getting any ideas. Two of my men are going to escort you up to the tower where Paelis is being held. You'll see him, talk to him, sing to him for all I care, but when the guards come to get you, you'll come back down quietly and exit the castle with your fellows."

"And then what?" I asked.

"And then we execute the King and move on."

"I'm sorry, General," I said, "but I vow to you that you will not."

He looked me square in the eyes and chuckled. "I would almost wish you luck, boy, but I'm afraid there is no luck at all in this world for you."

I caught up to Brasti, Valiana, and Aline along the sloping landscape of fields that filled the Duchy of Pulnam. Valiana was doing her best, but Aline was only thirteen and her legs simply couldn't keep up. I scooped her up and carried her on my shoulders for a way, but we had all been pushed to exhaustion since Orison and we couldn't go on any farther. When we reached the top of a slope, we all slumped to the ground and rested.

"How long do you think we have?" Valiana asked.

"I don't know," I said. "I doubt the fight could have lasted that long, but who knows how fast a Saint walks?"

"Pretty fast," Brasti said, looking down the slope. I rose and followed the line of his arm. About half a mile away we could see a figure walking toward us. I couldn't make out the details at this distance, but I could see the faint red aura he carried with him.

Brasti has better eyesight than me. He squinted down the path. "I can see the red-faced bastard," he said.

I took another look and now I could just make out the blood-red color of his face. And then I saw he was wearing Kest's greatcoat. I drew my rapier and started down the hill.

"Falcio!" Brasti called.

"Take Valiana and Aline and go. I'll hold him off for as long as I can."

"Falcio, come back, *please*!"

"Go!" I shouted.

They kept calling, but I ignored them. Saint or no Saint, if nothing else worked I could throw my body in his path and hope he tripped over it. A dusty haze was rising with the afternoon heat and it began settling into my nostrils and mouth, making me cough. I found a solid place to stand in the middle of the path and closed my eyes. If I couldn't see him swing his sword anyway, I might as well swing blind and hope I got lucky. I don't know if Luck is a God or not, but if he is then I'd sure like to make a better deal with him one of these days.

I heard the Saint's footsteps as he approached, but I kept my eyes closed and prepared the fastest cut I could. When I felt the heat from his body I let it fly. I might as well have been aiming for myself. I heard the blow sail by him and dropped the point of my blade to await the inevitable.

"Now I ask you," said a hoarse voice, "what kind of man fights with his eyes closed?"

My eyes opened wide and I saw him there. His face was indeed the color of blood—mostly because it bled from a dozen shallow cuts.

"Kest!" I shouted. "*Kest!* How is it possible—how could you *possibly* have beaten Saint Caveil-whose-blade-cuts-water?"

"I told you," Kest said, coughing, "he was a Saint—really just a little God, as these things go."

And then he collapsed into my arms.

I heard screams as Brasti, Valiana, and Aline raced down toward us. They wrapped themselves around Kest, who was fighting for breath.

"Who knew it took so little effort to make women fawn over you," he said at last.

"Little effort," Brasti breathed. "Gods, man, you've killed a Saint! Do you know what that makes you?"

"Blasphemous?"

"No, man, you killed Caveil—he was the Saint of Swords. That means you're the new Saint of Swords. I have a Saint for a friend!"

"Trust me, Brasti, all of your friends have to be Saints."

"Something is horribly wrong," I said to Kest.

"What?"

"You're telling jokes."

"Life is funny," he said.

"Why?"

"You remember what you told me before you left? About how you beat me?"

"Yes, but—"

"Believe it or not—and I don't think you really have any choice in the matter—I think it may have worked."

I started laughing, but Brasti interrupted, asking, "What about the Duchess?"

"She fled. I'm afraid I was a little too busy to deal with her."

"Leave him be a moment," Valiana said. "He needs to rest. We have a little time."

He shook his head. "No—I'm afraid there's a reason why I was moving so fast."

"Why? What is it?"

"Oh shit," Brasti said as we saw the dust rise in the distance as the Duke of Jillard's army marched up the slope toward us.

"One more try for a brave death, eh, friends?" Kest said. Then he lay down and stretched out on the ground as the rest of us watched them come.

29
THE WAR SONG

I wish I could say that my King met his death fearlessly, with a smile on his face and a joke on his lips. But when the guard let me into the tower chamber, I found Paclis huddled in the corner, shivering and weeping and coughing.

"I didn't think it would be here," he said at last. "I thought . . . a trial or a public execution, some chance to speak—but it's to be in here, tonight, in the dark."

He looked as small and weak as he had the day ten years ago when I'd come to Castle Aramor with a blade in hand ready to murder a King. I couldn't find any words to reply.

"No," he said, composing himself. "No, I'll be all right. I didn't think I'd get to speak to you again, but their general is a reasonable man and he said he'd grant a request if it wasn't unreasonable. It hadn't even occurred to me that he might offer and so I couldn't think of anything except that it would be good to talk to you again, Falcio."

He looked around the room for a moment. "Gods. I had finally convinced myself that I wouldn't end up back in this room. Can you imagine that? A decade of freedom and just as soon as you take it for granted—"

"We would have rather died, you know. You took that away from us," I said at last. He was my King and my friend, but I couldn't help saying it. His last act had been to strip us of everything that mattered.

He took my hand and kissed it. An odd gesture for a King. "I know you would have," he said, "but I couldn't allow that. My time is over, Falcio, but the Greatcoats are my gift to the world. The one truly important accomplishment of my lifetime."

"But it's over now," I said. "We are disbanded for all time."

"No," he said. "Remember King Ugrid? He tried to disband the Greatcoats, and for a hundred years his order stood. But we brought them back, Falcio, you and I: we brought them back to the world. And you can do it again."

"How?" I asked.

"I haven't been idle, Falcio, and I haven't told you everything I've been doing. Years ago I began hiding my Charoites throughout the realm. You have to find them now. You and Kest and Brasti."

"My King, you told me this before, and I'll do my best to look for them, but can you not tell me anything more?"

"Only that they are priceless beyond measure, and even just one of them can bring down the Dukes."

"But how will we even know if we've found one?" I asked.

"If we're both very lucky, you won't know—that's the only way the jewels will be safe until the time is right. Look for them, but do not expect to find them. Do you understand?"

"No," I said, irritation overcoming sadness, "of course I don't understand. No one could, because it doesn't make any sense."

"Hush then, for a moment, and listen," he said. "There is one more thing you're going to do for me."

He told me what he wanted me to do and I agreed and then we sat and he talked and I listened but I don't remember what he said. After an hour or so we heard the guard coming up the staircase and I drew the four-inch blade concealed in one of the pockets of my greatcoat and I jammed it straight into the King's heart.

And so I kept my vow to the general that he would not kill my King.

It didn't take long for the Duke of Jillard's army to overtake us. There wasn't any point in trying to run any farther.

"You've led us on a merry chase, Valiana," the Duke said.

Shiballe, by his side, grinned.

"That's not her name, actually," Brasti said.

The Duke ignored him. "But imagine my surprise to learn from Shiballe that you are not, in fact, Duchess Patriana's and my daughter at all but the progeny of some peasant woman. Ah, well, perhaps you're still my daughter. I bedded many a maid in Hervor during my bachelor days."

"You don't need her," I said. "You can let her go."

The Duke frowned at me. "Now why would I want to do that? I have her, and soon I'll have the scrolls back and, since they bear Duchess Patriana's seal as well as mine, I may as well take the girl and make her a Queen after all. I'm sure that she will be pliable to my wishes after the proper training for a year or two."

He looked down at Aline. "The little one has to die, though. She has unfortunate qualities I wish to see extinguished from the world."

"Why?" I asked. "Why is it so important to kill off the Tiarren line?"

The Duke smiled. "Tatter-cloak, I couldn't care less for the Tiarren line. Lord Tiarren was a buffoon and his Lady was only interesting to me insofar as her previous entanglements were concerned."

"You can't do this," I said, though I had nothing whatsoever to back up my statement.

"Why not? I seem to have an army behind me."

"We have a Saint," Brasti said, pointing at Kest.

"Your Saint seems to be unconscious," the Duke replied.

"My Lord, there's someone coming up the path," Shiballe said.

The Duke looked around, and so did we. A stooped figure was making its way gradually up the hill.

"Oh, hells, not her again," Brasti said.

"Who?" I asked.

"You know who," she bellowed from halfway up the slope.

Several of the Duke's men ran down and grabbed her. They dragged her to the Duke and dropped her at his feet.

"Bless you, boys," the Tailor said to the soldiers. "I honestly didn't think I'd make it up that hill."

"What are you doing here, old woman? Do you not value your life?" Shiballe demanded.

"Not especially," she said, "since no one else appears to. But to answer yer Lordship's question, I came to deliver you a message and these here a gift."

"You have time for the message but not the gift, I'm afraid," the Duke said. He motioned to one of the soldiers, who brought his lance into line with the Tailor's belly.

"My Lord," Shiballe said, "I know who this woman is now. I've heard rumors about her, about her influence on the Greatcoats. She may have information as to their whereabouts. Give me leave to break the information from her."

"No need fer that, tubby," the Tailor said. "I'll tell yer exactly what y'want to know—what you've wanted to know for a long time."

"And what's that?" the Duke asked, almost amused.

"Where the Greatcoats are," she said casually, brushing more dirt from her sleeve.

"Well then? Where are they?"

"Ah," she said, wagging a finger at him. "That'll cost ye. Not much, mind; a very reasonable fee and one I'm sure ye'll be willing to pay."

"My Lord, give the woman to me. I'll—"

"What do you want?" the Duke asked.

"It's jest a wee small thing," the Tailor said. "It's jest that the Covenant you fine Dukes and the King agreed to, it's always irked me. You can't kill me; I can't kill you . . . so if you could just break it fer me, I'd be much appreciative."

The Duke threw his head back and laughed. "The Covenant? Woman, don't you think the Covenant's been broken for some time now? What do you think I plan to do once you reveal the locations of the Greatcoats to me? Oh, old woman, have no fear. The Covenant is well and truly broken."

"Grand," she said, then, "See?" She turned to Shiballe. "Now, was that so hard?"

Shiballe's eyes were shifting furiously as he tried to understand what was happening. "Tell us then, you stupid old cow. Tell us where the Greatcoats are, if you truly know."

The Tailor looked up at the Duke and then smiled. "They're here," she said.

Then she screamed a single word at the sky, so loud and so clear that I swear the trees themselves would carry the sound imprinted in their bark for all time.

The word was "*Paelis*."

30
THE ANSWER

At first the reverberation of her voice was the only sound, but then thunder roared from below us and a cloud of dust rose from the slope.

"Horses," Brasti said.

"How many?" I asked.

He shook his head. "No way to tell. There's too much—"

"A hundred," Kest said, pushing himself up off the ground. "Possibly a hundred and two."

Brasti gave the new Saint of Swords an annoyed look. "You can't possibly know that—"

"Shut up," I said.

For a moment all I saw was Monster, her hooves pounding the earth as she raced ahead of a cloud of dust. And then they came through the cloud and the sight I had once dreamed of seeing appeared before me: a hundred Greatcoats on horseback, swords drawn and war cries on their lips.

"I told you," the Tailor said to me, an evil grin on her face, "I know where every thread is and I know where every thread's going."

"But how—?"

"The Dukes were so busy trying to find and kill all the Greatcoats—they knew every name and face—and, while they searched for ways to kill all of you, I found myself some new ones, trained by me and trained right. It's taken time to assemble them, though, I'll give you that. That damn fool, Paelis. He had the makings of a great army and what did he do? He scattered them to the four winds. But I've made my own Greatcoats, and now we're going to do this my way."

The Duke had five times as many men as we did, but few were on horseback and the rest were not exactly what you'd call a battle-ready army. They were conscripted house guards and he'd dragged them up the Eastern Passage to deal with the Duchess of Hervor. When they saw that first charge of the Magisters, they very nearly scattered then and there.

"Kill her," Shiballe shouted. "Kill all of them!"

But my rapier was already in my hand and Kest, Brasti, and I knocked the lances away from the Tailor and surrounded her, protecting her from anyone else who might try to fulfill Shiballe's order.

The captains were screaming at their men to get into formation and, as they did, Shiballe urged the Duke to get to the back lines.

"I showed you!" the Tailor was cackling behind us. "I showed all of you!"

I looked around and caught a glimpse of her face. It was terrifying to look at, half-joyous and half-enraged, and she was tearing her clothes off and shouting at the sky, "You took him away from me! You took every last good thing away from me!

"This!" she screamed. "*This* is my answer! *This is my answer!*" And now she was whirling around, naked and dancing like a madwoman, as the battle began to rage around us.

"He was my boy," she screamed, crying insanely, "my own little boy! You took him from me!"

"Saints, what's wrong with her?" Brasti asked.

Something was forming in my mind: a thought, a memory, pieces of things I'd seen and wondered about in passing, starting to come into focus.

"I think . . . ," I started. Was it really possible? "I think she might be his mother," I said as all the sadness in the world unleashed itself inside me. "I think she might be the King's mother."

"But how?" Brasti stared at her. "Greggor would never . . . I mean, *look* at her."

Kest interrupted, "Yes, look at her: her face—it wasn't always like this. Someone . . . perhaps someone beat her, mutilated her—"

"He sent me away," she shouted in response, as dust and horses and death raged around us.

"When the baby was born, when he didn't like the signs, he beat me and he locked me away—but I took it, I took it because I still got to see my baby, even when he grew and Greggor called him weak and locked him up too and finally sent me away. Even when he married that stupid cow and had another child, I took it, because I am a woman and it was a man's world. It was *his* world."

She shook her fists in the air. "But there had to be an answer for such things, and so I brought him books and I told him stories. I made him *think*."

"The Greatcoats," Kest said, awed. "It was her, all along: she taught the King, shaped his thinking."

"I started all of it," she cackled, standing naked and wrinkled and proud in the sunlight. "There had to be an answer for what he did, so I made you. I gave the world a great King and I gave it justice."

Then suddenly she started crying, like a small child discovering the body of a dead bird for the first time. "But then they took him away from me. He wanted nothing but to do right in the world and they took my boy. So there must be an answer," she growled. "When they take the last good thing from your life, there must be an answer."

"Go!" she said, grabbing me by the collar of my coat, her eyes so wide and wild that I could see the bright red of the skin that encircled them. "Go, and give them my answer!"

As Kest and Brasti grabbed horses from fallen men and mounted up, Monster came up to me and nudged me with her great head. I needed no other invitation and leapt onto her back.

"Come, you Dukes, you fools of men," the Tailor shouted. "Come witness a woman's answer—"

My mind was reeling from the knowledge of what she had done, but Kest pulled at me. "Let's go," he said. "I'm ready to give my answer now too."

We rode into the heart of the battle. I was exhausted, and I longed to see the faces of those comrades I'd been missing all these years—Dara, Winnow, Parrick, and the others—where were they? But these men and women on horseback, they were Greatcoats too: skilled and fearless. I felt excitement building inside me and I brandished my sword as we plunged into the Duke's army, breaking their lines. We fought like hunting birds, swooping in and out and taking lives with each attack.

Kest and Brasti and I sang: we sang the war song of the Greatcoats. We sang of justice and mercy, and we sang of blood and violence too. We sang until our voices were hoarse and blood and dust mixed into the ground, wedded forever into the landscape of violence.

The battle lasted only an hour, but it felt much longer before the Duke's men gave up their arms and knelt before us on the ground.

"Is it possible?" Brasti asked absently to Kest and me as we stood together.

"That we won? It certainly looks so," Kest replied.

"No," he said, "look around. I see dead men everywhere. There are soldiers and Knights littering the ground. I see a few Greatcoats sporting injuries, but I see none of us dead."

I looked around, sure that he was wrong, that I would see at least one Greatcoat on the ground.

"Gods," Brasti said at last. "What an army we would have been."

"Ye were never meant to be an army, fool," the Tailor said.

Brasti looked at her. "I see you've found your clothes again. Thank you for that, at least."

She grinned at him. "Didn't like the sight of a real woman, eh? Ah well, no mind. Sometimes we all have to go a little crazy, don't we, Falcio?"

I thought about that for a moment. "And sometimes we have to return to sanity."

"Aye, that's true enough," she said. "Now, leave the rest of the playing for them others. Go and deal with the Duchess. This is all for naught if she gets away with those Patents of Lineage and comes back in force with that damned daughter of hers."

"How will I find her?" I asked, grabbing Monster's reins.

"She's gone west," the Tailor said. "She has a horse, but she's still an old woman like me and she'll need to rest. You saw the caves past those hills when you came here from Orison? Go there—that's the only place out of the open. And with her patron Saint dead, I don't think she has long."

Someone pulled at my sleeve. "Take me," Aline said, "and then the Duchess will want to find us."

"Why?" I asked.

The Tailor slapped me. "Stop askin' such fool questions fer once in yer useless life." Then she looked down at the girl and smiled. "You're a good girl," she said, patting her on the cheek. "Go now, Falcio, and do what has to be done."

"Was this your plan all along?" I asked, as I lifted Aline onto Monster's back. "Did you set Tremondi up to get killed, too?"

"I did what I had to do, Falcio. The Dukes would have never let the Lords Caravaner reassemble the Greatcoats—but it kept them distracted, and while it did I brought the Greatcoats back together."

"Plans within plans and conspiracies to foil other conspiracies. What makes you any different from Patriana?" I asked.

She gave a snort and wiped her nose on the sleeve of her dirty coat. "I never killed her son," she said, and then turned and walked away.

It didn't take us long to reach the caves. There were several openings into the mountain, but not many passages tall enough for a man or woman to make them a good place to hide. Patriana hadn't bothered to cover her tracks.

"You brought the girl." The Duchess's voice echoed in the caves.

“I brought something else, too,” I said, drawing my rapier.

“So did I,” she said, appearing around a corner. I could see where she'd been hiding then: a small alcove, formed naturally in the rock. There was a brazier, its fire illuminating the cave walls, and I could see the scrolls on the ground next to her. She held a crossbow trained at my chest.

“You can leave the girl and go,” she said, “or you can kill her yourself, if you think that's more merciful, but either way she dies now.”

I started to say something, but the Duchess was a rude opponent and fired the bolt straight at me. I've always made fun of Kest for thinking a sword could block a crossbow bolt, but every once in a long, long while, a man gets a piece of luck. In my case it was the guard of my rapier that I managed to bring up to my belly just in time to block the bolt. The force dented the steel cup around the guard and it jabbed deep into my right hand, but it wouldn't stop me from killing her.

“If you think I'm going to stand here and let you reload that thing, then I'm afraid you've confused me for someone much more civilized,” I said.

The Duchess dropped the crossbow to the ground. “Very well,” she said, “enough of these games. We are done. Go, and take the brat with you.”

I almost laughed. “You can't be serious,” I said. “This is the best part—the part where I take your head off.”

“You want the scrolls? Take them. Destroy them any way you see fit. I am old and I am tired, and the things I fought for will never come to pass in my lifetime. So go and live and rut and do all the things men do with their futile lives.”

She warmed her hands over the brazier. “You wish to kill me?” she asked. “Then do so. Come on, show the girl how decisions of power and policy are really made.”

I looked at her in wonder. “Listening to your clever remarks and profound declarations, I can't help but wonder: what's it like, to be truly insane?” I asked.

She laughed. "You are a boy," she said. "A boy past his prime, I'll grant you, but a boy nonetheless."

I coughed. I wasn't getting much out of this conversation, considering I was the one holding the sword.

"Consider: with these scrolls you could take Valiana and shape the world to your liking. Imagine a thousand Greatcoats, a hundred thousand, all of them bringing whatever justice you choose across the land."

"I really don't think you understand how this works," I said. "I'm going to destroy those scrolls, and Jillard won't sign them again, not knowing Trin is the one you'd see put on the throne. He knows you set her up to rule in your interests, not his. With the Patents of Lineage destroyed, your conspiracy goes with them. I'm going to let the rest of the world solve who should rule it."

She looked at me through narrowed eyes, then started laughing. "You don't—Gods, Falcio, if you didn't know about . . . then why have you gone to such trouble to—? No, I'll leave that for you to discover. I'll say this for you, Falcio val Mond, you are indeed the most valorous man I've ever met, and only about the third stupidest."

She picked up the scrolls in her right hand and held them over the flame. "Here, then. Let us burn them together. A tribute to the dreams of an old woman."

She let the scrolls fall, and only then did I see the powder in her left hand. "Aline, run!" I screamed, and the girl fled just as the Duchess dropped the powder onto the flames. There was an explosion, and for an instant the old woman and I were covered in deep-red smoke. Just as quickly, it was gone.

Aline was at the mouth of the cave, past where the cloud of smoke had spread. "Run!" I yelled to her. "Go and get Kest or Brasti."

Then I turned back to the Duchess, but she was already dead. I coughed a bit, from the dust and smoke in my lungs, and realized I was too.

* * *

I did think it kind of odd that in my entire life I had never been poisoned before Rijou, and since then I'd been poisoned three times. In the past I'd been beaten, yes, tortured, yes, and had cuts, bruises, wounds from arrows and bolts, and countless encounters with the pointy end of someone else's blade, but never poison.

Now I couldn't get away from the stuff.

I was lying back against the wall of the cave as the feeling began to fade from my toes and fingers. I could feel the numbness traveling ever so slowly up my arms and legs, and I wondered what would happen when it reached my heart.

The lack of feeling was strangely pleasant. I hadn't realized how many pains I had accumulated in my limbs over the past few weeks—Saints, over the past many years.

I wondered why all this had happened. The Duchess and her conspiracy—that I understood, as much as one can ever understand madness, hunger for power, and avarice combined, but much of the rest was still a confusing haze to me. I suppose that's the way it goes. Poets and minstrels see the whole picture, but people like me live their whole lives inside one or two cleverly worded lines and never know what they really mean.

I heard Aline returning with Kest and Brasti. Valiana was with them too.

"Gods, what's happened to him? Falcio, where are you hurt?" Brasti asked.

"Almost nowhere, now," I said, smiling.

He knelt down beside me, and I suppose whatever the Duchess used must do something to the color of your face because Brasti asked, "Poison?"

I nodded. Or I think I did. I couldn't tell anymore. I felt light-headed.

Valiana moved to the other side of me and Brasti grabbed her arm. "What do we do—? What can we do for him?"

Sad eyes looked into mine for a moment before she said, "I don't know. I believe it's *neatha*. My mother—the Duchess, I mean—she used it on her enemies sometimes. No one ever survived. It is very quick, but it's not painful."

With some of the last feeling in my face I felt something wet hit my cheek. Brasti had tears in his eyes.

"Gods, man, don't you start now," I said softly. "We're going to get a terrible reputation if we just keep traveling across the countryside crying all the time."

"Falcio?"

"Hello, my nameless friend. Have you thought of something to call yourself yet?"

"I am so sorry . . ."

"Don't," I said, my tongue thick in my mouth. "Nothing to be sorry for. Just be something now. Be something that counts."

She looked at me for a moment, shy and unsure. "Is there a feminine version of 'Falcio' in Pertine?" she asked.

"I think 'Falcio' is feminine enough," Brasti said reflexively, unable to hold back the impulse to joke, and making me hopeful for him again.

"No," I croaked. "But I like 'Valiana.' It's a good name."

"It's not mine," she said.

"Then take it. Make it yours."

She looked down at me, tears in her eyes.

"I know what this poison does," Valiana said. "And I know I'm not that important, so I won't take up much time—"

"Stop it," I said. "Be important. If . . . If I give you a name, will you take it?"

She wiped the tears from her eyes. "I will take anything you give me, for it will be more than I have now, and more mine than anything I have been given before."

I took a moment to gather my breath. I wanted to say this properly. "You don't have to be the victim of someone else's story. You can be a Greatcoat. You can be . . ." I was reaching for the word when suddenly I understood the one thing I'd been looking for all these years. The one thing I could never find. The one thing even the King couldn't give me.

"You can be my answer, Valiana val Mond," I said softly. Something warm slipped down my cheeks and I guessed they were my own tears this time.

She put a hand on my chest and said to me, "My name is Valiana val Mond of the Greatcoats. And I am Falcio val Mond's daughter, and his answer to the world."

Then she was gone, and Brasti came and kissed me on the forehead and I had something very clever to say about that but I'm pretty sure nothing came out.

I felt as if I were floating up from the bottom of a lake, my eyes half seeing the world of the water and half the world of the sky. I could see a hilltop not unlike my homeland, but this one was green and rich and blessedly free of those damned blue flowers. There was a figure standing there, and I could see him clear as could be: it was my King, and he was saying something to me but I couldn't make it out.

I could see the girl, Aline, kneeling over me in this world, and though I couldn't see as well there as I could in the clear world, I could hear her crying.

I tried as hard as I could and I managed to say, "Smile for me. Just once." She probably thought I wanted her to feel better, but the truth was that I really did need to see that damned smile again.

And she did.

And suddenly I understood it—all of it. The attack on her family, the King's mysterious *jewels*, the Tailor's cryptic words, and most of all, her name.

So maybe those of us who live our whole lives in just those few lines do get to know what it all means, after all.

I saw my King again but I still couldn't quite hear him. He had someone with him, and I think he was trying to introduce me. The figure came into focus—it was *her*. She looked like a different person to me, perhaps because my memories of her had drifted over the years. Paelis had sworn he would bring her back to me one day, my beautiful, sweet wife, Aline, and he had fulfilled his vow. My King had named his daughter after her, and now she looked at me with a very annoyed expression. I wondered if the dead knew when we spoke to them, and if the rather unfortunate things I had said about her during my hallucinations on the road to kill the

King might have reached her. If so, I would have some explaining to do.

The clear world began to pull me away entirely, but I struggled against it. *Damn it*, I thought, *I've done enough for Saints and Gods and you're going to give me this moment.*

"Kest," I croaked, and I saw him kneel next to me. His face was still covered in blood, and those cuts didn't look good at all.

"Falcio," he said softly.

"You look terrible," I said. I knew somewhere a God or Saint was wondering why they had given me a few more minutes if I was just going to be rude, but I didn't care. "The girl," I whispered. "It's her, the King's jewel. His *Charoite*."

"I know. Brasti figured it out, if you can believe that." Then he smiled. "Can you imagine? The King's grand plan to save the world after he was gone was to go out and bed a few noblewomen so that we could find his offspring and put them in power." I felt Kest's hand on my shoulder. "She doesn't know, Falcio. She still thinks she's the daughter of Lord Tiarren. The Tailor is talking to her now."

"She's going to be Queen," I tried to say, but the words were barely a whisper now. "And you . . ."

"I know," he said, "now comes the hard part. But with a hundred Greatcoats at our backs, I like our chances."

I tried shaking my head. *Not me*, I tried to say. *I've done my duty. I've solved the King's damned riddle and fought his damned battles. I'm going away now to see him again, to listen to his crazy dreams and his bad jokes, to sit under shady trees with my wife.*

"Said your good-byes, have you?"

The voice was old and mean and full of hard-packed sand. My vision blurred in and out and back again and finally settled on the ugly face of the Tailor.

Please don't let her face be the last thing I remember of this world.

She laughed. "Ah, Falcio, ever the sense of humor."

Through the dull softness of the poison I felt a hard, callused hand grip my jaw and shake me. "All done?" she asked. "Said all your good-byes?"

I tried to tell her that I had, that I was ready now.

"I can hear you just fine, Falcio."

Good. Then let me go. And can I suggest you do something about your breath?

She ignored the jibe—or maybe she had lied about being able to hear me. "Ready to make the sacrifice now, Falcio?" she asked.

I already did. I did everything he asked of me.

I slipped under the water again—or was it out of the water? I felt my King's hand on my shoulder, my wife's fingertips touching my cheek. The air was scented, pine and baked bread. *I want to wake up to this, now.*

"Get the girl over here." The harsh voice of the Tailor broke through the sounds of leaves rustling and running streams. "Kest, give me your sword."

"Why?" he asked.

"Just you shut up and do as you're told. Saint or not, I can still put a beating on you better'n you deserve."

The hand on my jaw shook me again. Foul breath filled my senses and dragged me back into the world. "Do you want to know how the *neatha* works, Falcio?" the Tailor asked.

No. Why would I care?

She shook me again, and my vision returned for a second. The Tailor's face was close to mine. In her hand she held Kest's sword. Aline stood behind her.

"It's a powdered form of the soft candy, Falcio—just what you forced Paelis to have his apothecaries make. It works by tricking your body into letting go of itself. That's why it doesn't hurt. The poison's not killing you—it's just letting you die. It takes away will and need and the stubborn anger of relentless life. Ironic, isn't it?"

Not especially. Her mention of the King made me seek him out again, but she shook my jaw a third time. "No, no, Falcio. You haven't answered my question. Are you ready to make the sacrifice?"

Yes! Yes, you foul old bitch. I've sacrificed everything. *I fought for his laws and I fought for his daughter. I've fought and fought and fought until all that's left of me is a blade in my hand and anger in my heart. I've made the sacrifice. Now let me go!*

"Ah, you fool. *Dying* isn't sacrifice. Haven't you figured that out yet? All those years of trying to get yourself killed in battle? That ain't sacrifice, boy. That's self-loathing. It's gleeful suicide. It's *vanity*."

I felt her hand release my jaw and saw her stand up. She pushed Aline in front of me and took the sword in both her hands, pulling it back in line with the girl's neck. "Now this? *This* is sacrifice!"

Aline's trusting eyes held mine as the blade began its arc toward her neck.

No—! Kest! The old woman's lost her mind—she's crazy with grief, and no one but me can see it . . . she's going to—

Pain exploded in every fiber of my body. Blurred vision sharpened into a narrow tunnel in front of me, though I could see nothing but red. The world was all blood and dust and agony was everywhere, radiating first and foremost from my left hand. My ears were filled with the sounds of my own uncontrollable coughing and tears came streaming from my eyes. I forced them shut. It was as if all my senses were trying to expel all traces of peace and gentleness from me.

"Falcio?" Was that Kest's voice?

I tried to will away the clarity that was coming back to me. *No—let me go. Let me go back.*

"Falcio, you need to open your eyes now. You need to let go of the sword."

Unwillingly, unbearably, my eyes opened. I was on my knees, and Aline was still there in front of me. She hadn't moved. A sword was held in midair, its blade an inch from her neck, held in place by my bleeding hand, its weight making it cut even deeper into my flesh. The Tailor had already let go of it and only my grip was keeping it from clattering to the cave floor.

Kest took the sword in one hand and gently pulled my fingers apart with the other. His eyes were soft and sad for me. Someone wrapped my hand in cloth. If I'd had the strength, I would have ripped it off. I had tasted peace, and love. And reward. I had been at the edge of the warm lands, near those I longed most to see again, and instead, here I was, back in this foul world with all its corruption and putrefaction, its broken hopes and desperate need.

The Tailor shoved Kest aside and grabbed me by the back of the head. Her fingers entangled themselves in my hair and pulled back hard, forcing my gaze up to the ceiling of the cave. She leaned in so that her face filled my vision. "This, Falcio: *this* is sacrifice. This is the price you pay for your valor." She kissed me on the lips. It was perhaps the most disgusting sensation of my entire life, but it did take my mind off the pain in my hand.

Then she smiled her crooked smile at me. "Now get off your ass and let's get to work."

I stayed that way, on my knees, for a few minutes more. I knew I should move, get up, deal with whatever was coming next, but I couldn't. I had tasted joy and release and an ending to all the pain and rage that had filled my life. Since the day I'd found my wife's broken body in that tavern, I had taken refuge in madness. Now the madness was gone, taken from me, and only the pain remained. I cursed the Tailor for what she had done. I cursed the King for breaking his promise to reunite me with my wife. And I cursed her too, for having been so damnably brave on that day. *You and I will grow old together and laugh at the day these silly birds came to rest in our fields.* She had been wrong and stupid and she had left me alone in this place that was so full of festering rot that I could no longer even see the edges of the decay around me.

Hands gripped me by the arms and lifted me up. I knew it was Kest and Brasti, for no one else would have dared. I lacked even the desire to resist, and so I let them carry me out of the cave, my arms slung around their shoulders like a drunk. My eyes were closed, but I felt the warmth of the early morning sun on my face and so I opened them, hoping the harsh light would blind me, at least for a little while.

"Hells, Falcio," Brasti said, his voice soft. "There aren't words to say how sorry I am."

Out of reflex I opened my mouth to speak, but there was nothing to say.

"Leave it," Kest said.

"No," Brasti said. "No. This has to be said. We have to acknowledge what's happened here." He let go of me and I found my feet. Kest tried to steady me, but I pushed him away.

Brasti turned to me and put his hands on my shoulders and shook his head. "Gods and Saints, Falcio. I'm so sorry. I'm so, so very sorry. I can't imagine what you've just experienced."

"Brasti, let him be," Kest said.

"Falcio, I have to know. What was it like? How bad was it?"

My eyes found his. I couldn't believe anyone could ask me such a thing.

Brasti gave my shoulders a small shake. "I need to know, Falcio," he said, the sympathy in his expression suddenly replaced by a manic grin. "What's it like having to kiss that hideous old woman?"

For a moment it felt as if everything around me stopped completely. Even the wind held its breath. Until that instant I had never truly understood despair, though I had lived with it my whole life. I thought despair was something you fought and died fighting—something you had to clothe yourself in madness and rage to protect against. But then, against all logic and decency, Brasti had decided, in that impossible moment, to turn all the pain in the world into a joke. *You and I will grow old together and laugh at the day these silly birds came to rest in our fields,* she had said to me. Hollow words, and yet their very emptiness left a hole that demanded to be filled. The sound that broke through my lips was harsh and awkward, like a man who'd forgotten how to speak, but it set Brasti off and he started laughing like a fool.

"Gods, Falcio, she kissed you so hard your jaw doesn't even work right anymore."

Then I heard what was quite possibly the most ridiculous sound I'd ever heard: Kest was giggling. "It's not funny," he said, trying to stop.

"Of course it isn't, you stupid Saint," Brasti said. "There's nothing funny about those mottled lips, that foul breath reaching deep inside a man. Tell me, Falcio, could you actually feel your balls shrivel up when you tasted her tongue?"

"Stop it," Kest said, still chortling so hard he looked as if he could barely keep upright.

"I really need to know," Brasti said, plaintively. "If you get to be the Saint of Swords, I should at least be able to be the Saint of Lovers. I imagine that, since you have to be able to defeat anyone in battle, I'll have to be able to defeat them in bed—and what better preparation could there be than bedding the Tailor? Come on, Falcio, put in a word for me, help me become the Saint I've always been meant to be!"

Kest stumbled back and fell down on the ground. "Enough," he said, "I can't take it anymore!"

"Hah!" Brasti said. "I've defeated the great Saint of Swords!" He started hopping back and forth, his fists in the air in mock imitation of the unarmed combat lessons Kest used to teach. "Come on, Kest, how long did you last as a Saint? Half a day?"

In the distance behind him I saw a small figure standing alone. I left Kest and Brasti and walked toward her. She had her arms crossed. "Why didn't you tell me who my father was?" she asked. Her voice was thick with anger and hurt.

"I didn't know," I said. "I only realized it when I was . . . when the poison was in me."

"And Trin? The Tailor says she's still out there somewhere."

"I—"

Patriana's laughter back in Rijou still haunted me: *"My daughter is much more dangerous than I am."*

"No, I guess I didn't realize who she was, either."

"Well then, you're a very stupid person, aren't you." It wasn't a question.

"I am just starting to discover that, yes." Then I looked down at her, as if for the very first time. She was a pretty girl, I thought, though her sharp features would likely prevent her from ever possessing the legendary beauty of storybook Princesses. My King's long nose and wide mouth had seen to that. So many of his little quirks were written in her expression and, despite everything that had happened, I found myself smiling. How could I not have seen it before?

"What?" Aline said, kicking me.

I laughed. "Your face."

"What about my face?"

I knelt down and hugged her. "It delights me."

Her arms suddenly gripped tight around me and great sobs filled the air, but whether they were hers or mine, I could not tell.

"I never even knew him," she said, "so why do I miss him?"

I wanted to tell her that I had known King Paelis better than my own self. I wanted to tell her that he was a man of humor, of dirty jokes and wicked smiles—that he had known darkness and despair, and emerged determined to light candles for everyone else. He read every book he had ever chanced to find, and from them he drew a thousand ideas. He had spent his life putting them in motion, but he never forgot his friends or his compassion. I wanted to tell her how she had got the name Aline.

But not now; not yet.

"Well, first of all," I said, "he was a terrible swordsman and a lousy cook."

I felt her cheek rub against mine as she started giggling uncontrollably, and that's how we stayed for a few minutes more, while wild hopefulness surrounded us and spread like rainwater over the hard surface of the world.

ACKNOWLEDGMENTS

In lieu of acknowledgments, here's a seven-step plan to get published:

First, marry a librarian. My wife, Christina, knows more about books and readers than I ever will. She inspires me with her brilliance, her beauty, and her limited patience for my whining.

Second, you need one of your best friends to be a better writer than you are. Eric Torin has read this story almost as many times as I have and every time has guided me in making it better.

Third, you need alpha readers. John de Castell, Terry Lanthier, Jessica Leigh Clark-Bojin, and Dennis Boulter were all kind enough to read this book long before it was worth reading.

Fourth, well, when you get to step four, you'll know exactly what you have to do. It's the hard part. It helps when you work with uniquely creative people like those at Vancouver Film School.

Fifth, once the book is getting close, you need people who can read your work and tell you what's missing. Kathryn Zeller, Kim Tough, and Samarth Chandola all provided great insight into those last few miles of writing.

Sixth, you need an agent who is savvy and supportive and who smiles when you talk about your ridiculous ideas and expectations.

Heather Adams of the HMA Literary Agency is my publishing guardian angel. I would never have met her if not for Christina (see step one: marry a librarian).

Finally, you need a publisher and editor willing to get to know your story better than you do. The remarkable Jo Fletcher and Adrienne Kerr work with authors I idolize and yet they spend just as much time on my writing. Jo also once helped foil a bomb plot. Seriously.

Sebastien de Castell
Vancouver, 2013

Author photograph © Pink Monkey Studios

SEBASTIEN DE CASTELL had just finished a degree in archaeology when he started work on his first dig. Four hours later he realized how much he hated archaeology and left to pursue a very focused career as a musician, ombudsman, interaction designer, fight choreographer, teacher, project manager, actor, and product strategist. His only defense against the charge of unbridled dilettantism is that he genuinely likes doing these things and that, in one way or another, each of these fields plays a role in his writing. He sternly resists the accusation of being a Renaissance man in the hopes that more people will label him that way. Sebastien lives in Vancouver, Canada, with his lovely wife and two belligerent cats.